CUSTARD, CULVERTS AND CAKE

Academics on Life in *The Archers*

CUSTARD, CULVERTS AND CAKE

Academics on Life in *The Archers*

Edited by

CARA COURAGE
Independent Researcher

NICOLA HEADLAM
University of Oxford, UK

United Kingdom — North America — Japan
India — Malaysia — China

Emerald Publishing Limited
Howard House, Wagon Lane, Bingley BD16 1WA, UK

First edition 2017

British Library Cataloguing in Publication Data
A catalogue record for this book is available from the British
Library

ISBN: 978-1-78743-286-4 (Print)
ISBN: 978-1-78743-285-7 (Online)
ISBN: 978-1-78743-440-0 (Epub)

ISOQAR certified
Management System,
awarded to Emerald
for adherence to
Environmental
standard
ISO 14001:2004.

Certificate Number 1985
ISO 14001

INVESTOR IN PEOPLE

CONTENTS

SECTION TWO

EDUCATING AMBRIDGE

SECTION THREE

THE GEOGRAPHY OF AMBRIDGE

SECTION FOUR

POWER RELATIONSHIPS

SECTION FIVE

AMBRIDGE ONLINE

SECTION SIX

THE HELEN AND ROB STORY

LIST OF FIGURES

LIST OF TABLES

CHAPTER SYNOPSES

SECTION ONE: GENTEEL COUNTRY HOBBIES?

Chapter One: 'My Parsnips Are Bigger Than Your Parsnips: The Negative Aspects of Competing at Flower and Produce Shows', Rachel Daniels and Annie Maddison Warren. It ought to be obvious how Bert Fry comes to this subject, having devoted a lifetime to the various feuds and intrigues of the 'Flower and Produce'. He will be disgruntled to hear that this was the only paper which was passed unanimously by our listener peer review panel and academics and was awarded a prize at the conference of two parsnips for this clean sweep.

Chapter Two: '"Big Telephoto Lens, Small Ticklist": Birdwatching, Class and Gender in Ambridge', Joanna Dobson, commenting on the gender dynamics of birdwatching, with a reply from Jennifer Aldridge who somehow manages to get in a mention of Phoebe being at Oxford.

Chapter Three: 'The Ambridge Paradox: Cake Consumption and Metabolic Health in a Defined Rural Population', Christine Michael. This chapter was awarded the prize — of a tin of shop-bought custard — for the most Ambridge paper of *Academic Archers 2017*. The often culinary-slighted Christine Barford has been given the right to reply concerning the campaign of intimate terrorism deployed by her closest friends regarding her bake-off credentials.

SECTION TWO: EDUCATING AMBRIDGE

Chapter Four: 'Ambridge as Metaphor: Sharing the Mission and Values of a 21st-Century Library', Madeleine Lefebvre, talking of the place and absence of a mobile library in Ambridge.

Chapter Five: 'We Don't Need No Education? The Absence of Primary Education in *The Archers*', Dr Grant Bage and Jane Turner. Nic Grundy, mum-of-four and one of the silent characters at the time of writing, finds her voice in response, giving her view before rushing to meet the school bus.

Chapter Six: 'Educating Freddie Pargetter: or, Will He Pass His Maths GCSE?', Ruth Heilbronn and Rosalind Janssen, bringing a UCL Institute of Education analysis to ask whether Freddie Pargetter is an underachiever and if so is this attributable to his bereavement aged twelve. State-education advocate, Jill Archer, responds.

Chapter Seven: 'Phoebe Goes to Oxford', Felicity Macdonald-Smith, turning our focus from early years to elite higher education, and Jennifer Aldridge, whose pride in and hope for self-reflected glory from Phoebe led to fairly Olympic-standard boasting.

SECTION THREE: THE GEOGRAPHY OF AMBRIDGE

Chapters Eight and Nine: These two chapters concern complementary analyses of the Ambridge Flood.

First, 'Get Me Out of Here! Assessing Ambridge's Flood Resilience', Angela Connelly sets up a review from the very disgruntled Stefan, who may or may not have more to say in the future.

Second, 'After the Flood: How Can Ambridge Residents Develop Resilience to Future Flooding?', Fiona Gleed, turning our attention from developing resilience to future flooding, offers an action plan for another casualty of the flood, Charlie Thomas.

Chapter Ten: 'Locating Ambridge: Public Broadcasting, Region and Identity, an Everyday Story of Worcestershire Folk?', Tom Nicholls considers the midlands location of Ambridge, to which loyal Ambridge resident Clarrie Grundy will add her thoughts.

SECTION FOUR: POWER RELATIONSHIPS

Chapters Eleven and Twelve: Both have a visual element as authors seek to present information about the relationships that underpin the village.

First, Louise Gillies and Helen M. Burrows, 'A Case Study in the Use of Genograms to Assess Family Dysfunction and Social Class: To the Manor Born versus Shameless'. Their analysis somewhat vindicates the much maligned Horrobins and we hear from the most incorrigible of them, Clive Horrobin in response.

Second, 'Kinship Networks in Ambridge', Nicola Headlam warms to this theme and presents *The Headlam Hypothesis*, *The Archers* are dead, long live the network. Hazel Woolley responds.

Chapter Thirteen: Revd Dr Jonathan Hustler, 'God in Ambridge: *The Archers* as Rural Theology' and a response from Alan Franks.

Chapter Fourteen: Jessica Meyer tries to locate the Ambridge war memorial and approaches *The Archers* as *lieu de memoire* of the Great War in Britain. Jim Lloyd, whose interests are more classical than modern, replies.

SECTION FIVE: AMBRIDGE ONLINE

Chapter Fifteen: 'An Everyday Story of Country Folk' Online? The Marginalisation of the Internet and Social Media in *The Archers*', Professor Lizzie Coles-Kemp and Professor Debi Ashenden argue that for the younger characters particularly this has been a gap.

Chapter Sixteen: 'The Importance of Social Media in Modern Borsetshire Life: Domestic and Commercial', Olivia Vandyk, presenting her social media marketing perspective to the villagers. Josh Archer, who appears to making a path for himself combining eBay with Grindr, replies.

Chapter Seventeen: 'Being @borsetpolice: Autoethnographic Reflections on Archers Fan Fiction on Twitter', Jerome Turner, proposing an (auto)ethnographic understanding of *Archers* fan fiction on Twitter, a pursuit that results in him being interviewed at Felpersham police station.

SECTION SIX: THE HELEN AND ROB STORY

Chapters Eighteen to Twenty-four: We turn our attention to the most serious storyline of recent times the controlling relationship between Helen Archer and Rob Titchener which culminated in the violent stabbing of April 2016 and the ensuing courtroom drama where Helen was acquitted.

Chapter Eighteen: The conference keynote from Professor Jennifer Brown, 'Understanding the Antecedents of the

Domestic Violence Perpetrator Using *The Archers* Coercive Controlling Behaviour Storyline as a Case Study', which sets the criminological and social context for the storyline.

Chapter Nineteen: 'Bag of the Devil: The Disablement of Rob Titchener', Katherine Runswick-Cole and Rebecca Wood, arguing that by stigmatising Rob the storyline could have been clearer in educating about stoma, but that this opportunity was lost. *Bag of the devil...* both won the award of Best Title at *Academic Archers 2017* — and was awarded the prize of a bottle of cider — and the attention of Rob Titchener, who has written his retort to the chapter.

Chapter Twenty: Amber Medland, 'Culinary Coercion: Nurturing Traditional Gender Roles in Ambridge', on all things food, identity and domestic labour in the village, and which is reviewed by the domestic goddess herself, Jennifer Aldridge.

Chapter Twenty-one: 'The Case of Helen and Rob: An Evaluation of the New Coercive Control Offence and Its Portrayal in *The Archers*', Elizabeth R. A. Campion, taking the legal line on coercive control.

Chapter Twenty-two: Anna-Marie O'Connor takes a forensic science approach to the crime scene as in *Forensic* 'Blood Pattern Analysis in Blossom Hill Cottage'. Reviewed by the first officer on the scene, PC Harrison Burns.

Chapter Twenty-three: 'Soundtrack to a Stabbing: What Rob's Choice of Music over Dinner Tells Us about Why He Ended Up Spilling the Custard', Emily Baker and Freya Jarman, on what Rob's choice of music over dinner tells us about why he ended up spilling the custard, reviewed by Alan Franks. Winner of a bottle of bubbly at conference for audience participation (a group *dum tee dum* for the Dum Tee Dum podcast opener).

Chapter Twenty-four: Caroline M. Taylor tells us of 'Helen's Diet Behind Bars: Nutrition for Pregnant and Breastfeeding Women in Prison'.

INTRODUCTION

THE ARCHERS ANALYSED: ACADEMIC PERSPECTIVES ON LIFE IN BORSETSHIRE

This book builds upon our slightly grand attempts to develop a 'new academic community' (Courage, Headlam, & Matthews, 2016) quite deliberately connecting subject-specific knowledge from a cohort of academics, researchers, and professionals present at the 2nd *The Archers* in Fact and Fiction: Academic Analyses of Life in Rural Borsetshire conference, with the wealth of material available through 18,000 episodes of the world's longest running soap opera (or docudrama as Archers Anarchists and Dum Tee Dum podcast fans would have it).

We announced our intention for Academic Archers to be 'a fine-detailed, open, cross disciplinary space' in our first book (*ibid*.) and have described elsewhere our maturation from 'idle tweets' through to now combining social media curation, events management, media and PR (see Academic Archers website and press work) as well as holding down day-jobs. This volume is the latest output of our experimental *modus vivendi*. In everything we do we have invested significant hope in the cognitive surplus afforded by the wisdom of the crowd or the hive mind of the wider *Archers* firmament. By our calculations on the day, the collective listening time of the audience at the second Academic Archers conference amounted to half a million minutes. There are many hubs of *Archers* lore and obscure trivia lurking in the message boards.

This introductory chapter seeks to flesh out some of the elements of our thinking in developing Academic Archers since our founding in 2015. As previously, each academic chapter contribution is 'peer reviewed' in the voice of an *Archers* character/real person of Ambridge (depending on your disposition). Uniquely within this volume the Helen and Rob storyline represents almost a book within the book – the conference and this book coming at a time when we are in the wake of this substantive storyline. We sincerely hope that the varied contributions of these wonderful (all-female researched and written) chapters in this section can go some way to offer catharsis for those still deeply affected by what was a very traumatic, brave and controversial storyline for the programme.

BUILDING ACADEMIC ARCHERS

From an ethos perspective Academic Archers has been influenced by the political decentring of knowledge production — that being to form and take knowledge outside of the academic academy and its predominantly white, male, and elder constituency — specifically from within feminist scholarship, critical disability studies (Runswick-Cole, 2017) as well as cultural studies and sociology (Thomas, 2017). We intuitively feel that a focus on the processes and practices of relational and meaningful social research should continue to be wholeheartedly embraced by the higher education academy. However, there is a risk that rather than a carnival and celebration of different bodies of knowledge, the 'impact agenda' that universities have to place front and centre of research to secure State funding, can mean such social research becomes co-opted and as calculable as other reforms to research practice as incorporated into the neo-liberal university. Academic Archers is a means to, through *The Archers* lens, develop and present a cross section of scholars and listeners and to explore more subtle ways of being together differently. This is a move to make knowledge production and dissemination horizontal rather than vertical and a mode of investigation that is 'a rite of communion between thinking and acting human beings, the researcher and the researched' (Fals Borda, 1997, p. 108).

When convening the conference, for this modus operandi to have any meaning at all, non-specialists needed to have positions of power and authority within the paper selection processes. Further, we needed to ensure the quality of contributions and from a wide spectrum, within and without the academy. We began the second cycle for the Academic Archers year with a conventional call for papers but backed up by a novel and slightly terrifying blended peer reviewing process whereby eighteen Academic Archers Research Fellows subjected all submitted paper abstracts to their scrutiny. These peer reviewers were found through an open call within our social media community and offered free conference places and training and support in exchange for their efforts. The reviewers cohort had a range of backgrounds and were not selected because of prior familiarity with academic peer reviewing processes. We developed a peer review protocol, based on the work conducted by the British Medical Journal (BMJ) on peer review of articles by patients (BMJ, in Headlam, Academic Archers website) and waited to see what happened. We are very keen to further interrogate the role of 'non-academics' within circuits of knowledge production, and will discuss some of the state of the conversation on these matters in this chapter. The outcome of this process was a day and a half of a programme with the same thematic areas as we present in this volume, and a delegation of 120 at the second conference superbly co-organised with Professor Carenza Lewis at the University of Lincoln, her superlative PA, Julie Barclay, and her brilliant staff team. We had the broadening of the audience in our minds as we set out into brave new worlds of online streaming all content, and of building on the social media links we had made on Facebook and Twitter.

In this process, as in all things we self-consciously blur the boundaries between subject and object, expert and non-expert, and fact and fiction in a way that some people struggle to 'get'. This is part of the pleasure for us, we firmly believe in the interface between popular culture and serious academic research, in the political and epistemological possibilities opened up by probing the interplay between the real and the imagined communities and further, in closing the feedback loops between 'who knows?' 'who listens?' and 'who gets to say?' The answers ought not to be simple or settled if one takes seriously the privileging of alternate forms of knowledge and experience.

ACCIDENTAL 'ACA-FANS' AND THE 'FANDOM' IN CO-PRODUCTION OF KNOWLEDGE

Having felt our way towards a form of practice which felt right as regards how we engaged with the wider *Archers* community it made sense to check our own lived experience. We approach *Archers* scholarship in this vein and have continued to explore our activities within a wider frame of a co-produced ethics of Action Research, but also one which is alive to the aesthetics and affect in simultaneously being in and building a community of this nature and our enthusiastic participation in the online worlds of the fandom we, these mediated selves, suggest as an ethics of encounter.

In case this sounds overly intellectualised or grand for what may also be seen as 'p*ssing about on Twitter rather than doing any real work' it is striking how far technology has accelerated the possibilities for activities of this nature threading around the everyday. As relative social media digital natives, we were comfortable in moving between these performed selves of online and offline worlds, but it is immediately obvious that the colossal wealth of user-generated content, on Twitter, Facebook, in fan podcasts, blogs, and fanfiction was actively creating 'boundary objects' for investigation. A boundary object is any object that is part of multiple social worlds and facilitates communication between them; it has a different identity in each social world that it inhabits. As a result a boundary object must be simultaneously concrete and abstract, simultaneously fluid and well defined (Star & Griesemer, 1989, p. 393).

The broadcast 'canon' itself is a boundary object for the wider listening community. The listeners then in their acts of interpretation merge 'common identities' across all the many *Archers* online communities (see Thomas, 2009, 2014, 2016; Turner, this volume) for example the policing of behaviour and swift acculturation to different online fan groups. One thing that we were absolutely clear about from the beginning was that we were not lurking anonymously round the edges of the online communities with our notebooks. Waves of fan studies and scholars of popular culture have engaged with subcultures, fan bases and fandoms with more and less respect. We have always seen Academic Archers as an example of aca-fandom. We understand this to mean referring both to the study of popular culture with academics in the position of fans themselves and to the study of the associated fan subcultures. In this, we are hopefully navigating

some of the edges of proper fandom studies featuring academics translating fan culture into academic currency. This
way of working, we feel may run the risk of extractive relationships. It is most striking when reading the literature on
fans that there is an 'othering' or 'weirding' by the author of
the fans going on — the fans are treated as something separate to the 'norm' and in this process, shamed. Certainly
long-established fan groups such as Trekkies or Buffy fans
are scathing about the roles of anthropologists who focus on
fan-fiction, geek cults and conventions. Whilst an academic
study of fandom can work to variously celebrate, validate or
rehabilitate fan practices:

> '... a pervasive sense of shame permeates both fan
> spaces and academic approaches to the subject.
> There is shame about being a fan at all shame over
> the extremity of some fans, shame over certain fan
> practices over having those practices revealed to the
> rest of the world...there is also shame about studying
> something as "frivolous" as fandom - or worse yet,
> taking frivolous pleasure ourselves "sitting too
> close" instead of remaining suitably detached obser-
> vers' (Zubernis & Larsen, 2012, p. 213).

The key here is that in 'sitting too close' to our radios we
expose ourselves to ridicule (see Courage, 2017). In Courage,
Headlam, and Matthews (2016), we wrote about our different
relationships with the programme. I have been reminded of the
steps required for 'becoming' from the classic article by Becker
(1953). Becker argues that there are distinct phases in the
acculturation of any supposedly pleasurable behaviour — with
getting high as the example he uses in the article — and it is
worth reflecting that until two years ago I had never had a

conversation with anyone outside my immediate family about *The Archers*.

FAN STUDIES

The first wave of fan studies followed De Certeau's (1984) definition of powerful producers and disempowered consumers, as befitted a mass and broadcast-only mediascape. Second and third wave fan studies continued to focus on class and subversion (subcultures). Theorists are now more interested in the roles of fans in identity work and in the social and cultural performance of identity and in the distribution of power/knowledge prioritizing the emotional aspects of 'fanning'. This later work on the emotional affect is most productive in terms of our engagement with both *The Archers* and *The Archers* fandom.

The point, of course, is to seek to work in a way that disturbs some of the false oppositions and binaries that have governed scholarly life by being different together to some purpose, and it is in this territory that Cristofari and Guitton (2016) have developed their theories of the ways in which both subject positions, of academic and of fan, may be nearer to continuums than divisions.

In seeking differentiated points of entry between distance/proximity, professional/amateur, rational/emotional, orthodox/unorthodox, analytic/appropriative and fundamentally between the individual/community, Academic Archers hopes to unsettle some of the power dynamics that govern the mobilisation of knowledge. It may be that calibrating these continuums differently may serve to radicalise the production of useful and useable knowledge.

Another emotive and emotional feature of the fan clans surrounding *The Archers* is that many fans seem to have quite deep-seated antipathies towards some (or all) of the characters in the show (Courage, 2017). This is quite brilliantly explained using the example of queering *Star Trek*. Trekkies get so exercised about the lack of gay characters on the bridge of the Starship Enterprise that they vent against the show itself, creating hostility between fans and the show's creators (or 'showrunner fans' as some fan communities have it.) The intensity and depth of engagement from fans are a very temperamental resource indeed. *The Archers* fandom has sat at an angle to the show's creators as long as they have had the means to express this. As we wrote in the first book (Courage, Headlam, & Matthews, 2016), there has been a curious but intense elision between *The Archers* and social media.

In order to examine how the interactions between the show and the fan communities has been changing it is worth exploring the controversy surrounding the unilateral closing of *The Archers* message board site, Mustardland. This story has a number of unique features — explained by Thomas (in Courage, Headlam, & Matthews, 2016) — but the dimension of the power of the BBC in framing and shaping how *The Archers* is received has appeared to change drastically in the very recent past.

Early engagement with social media shows the patrician attitudes of 'Auntie Beeb' in coming to terms with the power of message boards in shaping the ways in which the programme is received. Auntie Beeb, is in this case more or less personified by then-*Archers* editor, Vanessa Whitburn, whose twenty-two-year tenure had begun in pre-social media days. Speaking to *Feedback* on Radio 4 about her retirement in 2013, she described a vexatious relationship with fans, and that she had been subject to 'cyber-bullying' online. It is clear that the relationship between formal channels and the wider fandom were on precarious ground around this time as the BBC closed Mustardland. Reported here in The Telegraph:

In two weeks' time, the site (bbc.co.uk/dna/mbarch-
ers), or "Mustard Land" as it is known to fans
because of its yellow background, will be no more.
The official reason is dwindling numbers: the BBC
claims that, out of five million listeners who tune in
to The Archers, *just 1,000 regularly post on the*
forum, so it can no longer justify the cost. Listeners,
however, claim otherwise. They say the BBC is try-
ing to censor them, in particular their candid
comments..."How to get rid of the pesky, wrong
sort of listener!" ranted one angry fan on the site,
who felt that message board users were seen by the
BBC as "too critical, too old and too much trouble".
(Sarah Rainey, The Telegraph, 13 February 2013)

It is fair to say that — as Facebook group mediators and
as @AcademicArchers on Twitter — the 'candid' and 'proper
criticism' can shade over into quite personal invective at
times. The robustness of this criticism may have come as a
shock to Vanessa Whitburn. There is a very particular role
for the BBC in this space. Fandoms in the US are linked with
the market imperatives of their creators and can function as a
form of marketing and PR, albeit highly reflexively. The justification of 'only' 1000 active posters on Mustardland within
the click and attention economy could have been seen as a
vital resource for the BBC at this time.

The ensuing five years has seen huge shifts in this relationship, and a flowering of smaller, more fleet of foot forms of
commentary, on social media, and through *The Ambridge
Observer* and *Dum Tee Dum* podcast for example. The new
regime of Editor Huw Kennair-Jones appears to be much
more enthusiastic about engaging with the fandom on social
media. Kennair-Jones crowd-sourced questions for an outing

on Broadcasting House on Radio 4 and we will enthusiastically watch how this relationship develops.

ACTS OF CREATION AND INTERPRETATION: ALL WE HAVE IS AN ABILITY TO STRUCTURE INFORMATION

Something that has tickled us from the beginning has been the ingenuity of many of the parody accounts on Twitter, the cartoons and gifs and memes and tropes which circulate in mega-quick time in direct response to the broadcast of *The Archers*. This instant response, coupled with often a snort of laughter or a smile of recognition, is the main way in which the community of *Archers* listeners develops. More recently the show itself has been more active in participating in the fun and a relevant, funny post can get widely retweeted by the official BBC *The Archers* Twitter account before the end of an episode even. Rather than viewing academic practice as some lofty thing, we approach academic endeavour as just an example of us being able to bring the thing that we can do to this party. Not adept as cartoonists, we can offer solely our subject knowledge and the learnt ability to structure knowledge in the way that renders it visible to other scholars and the wider *Archers* culture.

Table 1 from Cristofari and Guitton (2016) shows how far these various categories are linked through the currencies of 'involvement' and 'structure of knowledge'. This is salient as it places our endeavours as Academic Archers firmly within the acts of creation and interpretation that we admire so much in the wider fandom. This table connects specific skills, fan spaces, practices and modes of participation.

It is our hope that in participating and helping to curate *Archers* content that Academic Archers moves from an extractive or consumptive mode and toward a productive

Table 1. Currencies of 'Involvement' and 'Structure of Knowledge' of Fandom (Cristofari & Guitton, 2016).

Skill	Fan Space	Fan Practices	Participation
Technical	Public spaces	Info gathering	Consumptive
Analytic	Semi-public (fans only)	Forums, discussion, blogging	Productive
Interpretive	Private, fans only	Creation of fan works	Productive

and engaged academic community. We hope that you enjoy the book, and that we can continue the conversation online on Facebook (Academic Archers), on Twitter (@AcademicArchers) and via our website (www.academicarchers.net).

Dr Nicola Headlam
Dr Cara Courage
Editors

REFERENCES

Academic Archers, Facebook. Retrieved from https://www.facebook.com/groups/AcademicArchers/?ref=bookmarks

Academic Archers, Twitter. Retrieved from https://twitter.com/academicarchers?lang=en

Academic Archers, website. Retrieved from http://academicarchers.net

Courage, C. (2017). My BDSM relationship with The Archers. *The Odditorium*, February 2016. Retrieved from:

http://oddpodcast.com/portfolio/bdsm-relationship-archers-cara-courage/

Courage, C., Headlam, N., & Mathews, P. (2016). *The archers in fact and fiction, academic analyses of rural Borsetshire*. Oxford: Peter Lang.

Cristofari, C., & Guitton, M. J. (2016). Aca-fans and fan communities: An operative framework. *Journal of Consumer Culture*, p. 3.

Rainey, S. (2013). Archers controversy: How online message boards are giving silver surfers a bad name. *The Telegraph* (online), Retrieved from: http://www.telegraph.co.uk/technology/social-media/9867839/Archers-controversy-how-online-message-boards-are-giving-silver-surfers-a-bad-name.html. Accessed on February 13, 2013.

Reeve, D. K., & Aggleton, J. P. (1998). On the specificity of expert knowledge about a soap opera: An everyday story of farming folk. *Applied Cognitive Psychology*, *12*, 35–42.

Roach, C. M. (2014). "Going Native": Aca-Fandom and deep participant observation. *Popular Romance Studies Mosaic: A Journal for the Interdisciplinary Study of Literature*, *47*(2), 33–49.

Star, S. L., & Griesemer, J. R. (1989). Institutional ecology, 'Translations,' and boundary objects: Amateurs and Professionals in Berkeley's Museum of Vertebrate Zoology, 1907 – 1939. *Social Studies of Science*, *19*, 387–420.

Zubernis, L., & Larsen, K. (2012). *Fandom at the crossroads, celebration, shame and fan/producer relationships*. Newcastle, UK: Cambridge Scholar Press.

SECTION ONE

—

GENTEEL COUNTRY HOBBIES?

CHAPTER ONE

MY PARSNIPS ARE BIGGER THAN YOUR PARSNIPS: THE NEGATIVE ASPECTS OF COMPETING AT FLOWER AND PRODUCE SHOWS

Rachel Daniels and
Annie Maddison Warren

ABSTRACT

The Ambridge Flower and Produce Show is the source of frequent scandals. For example, the misunderstanding that resulted in Chutneygate in 2016 caused feelings to run high. However, there is also evidence of deliberate cheating. Toye (2009) records three confirmed instances between 1975 and 2008, two planned and one opportunist, along with a number of unproved allegations. According to Michaels and Miethe (1989, p. 883), 'cheating is a general class of deviance that occurs in a variety of contexts', whilst DeAndrea, Carpenter, Shulman, and Levine (2009) believe that it is now commonplace throughout society. Houser, Vetter, and Winter (2012, p. 1654) argue that 'the perception of being treated unfairly by another person significantly increases an individual's propensity to cheat'. Taken at face value, Flower and Produce Shows are charming, community-based events showcasing personal endeavour for little in the way of reward. However, both the Ambridge experience and the literature suggest that the competitive nature of the event aligned with the potential for perceived unfair treatment by the judges may mean that the likelihood of cheating is high. Given this, how representative is the Ambridge Flower and Produce Show of a real-life Flower and Produce Show? This chapter examines the emotions and behaviours that these shows engender by reviewing scholarly thinking on competition, competitive behaviour and cheating, and then comparing critical incidents at the fictional Ambridge show with evidence derived from interviews with the committee and contestants of the annual Flower and Produce Show in a small market town in Wiltshire.

Keywords: Flower and Produce Shows; competition; competitive behaviour; cheating

FLOWER AND PRODUCE SHOWS: FACT VERSUS FICTION

Over the years, the Ambridge Flower and Produce Show has been the source of misunderstandings, impropriety and scandal. For example, there was uproar in 2016 over

Chutneygate when Jill Archer's chutney was confused with Carol Tregorran's and she was wrongly awarded Best in Show. Toye (2009) records a number of unproved allegations of impropriety and three confirmed instances of deliberate cheating between 1975 and 2008. The idea of using the Flower and Produce Show as a dramatic device is intriguing. On the face of it, it is a charming, community-based event, showcasing personal achievement for little reward. Yet, the drive to succeed causes characters in *The Archers* to break the bounds of acceptable behaviour. Can this fiction possibly be representative of a real-life Flower and Produce Show? To answer this question, this chapter reviews scholarly thinking on competition and competitive behaviour, then identifies critical incidents at the fictional Ambridge show before seeking similar examples at an annual Flower and Produce Show held in a small market town in Wiltshire.

WHY DO PEOPLE COMPETE?

The academic literature was reviewed to find out why people compete and why competition encourages both positive and negative behaviour, potentially tipping over into cheating. Gilpatric (2011) argues that competition is often valued for its own sake, positively motivating a desirable activity. Earlier work by Harackiewicz, Barron, Carter, Lehto, and Elliot (1997) categorised this positive motivation as an inner drive to succeed, which affects behaviour, actions, thoughts and beliefs. Some people have higher standards than the societal norms and a stronger implicit need to achieve their goals (Garcia, Tor, & Schiff, 2013). Inevitably, their inner drive and associated achievement goals affect the way they perform a given task, not only demonstrating competence but also driven to improve their performance (Harackiewicz et al.,

1997). Competition is clearly valued for its own sake, encouraging personal endeavour in order to succeed.

The sense of personal achievement is often more important to the driven competitor than any rewards on offer and, whilst they enjoy victory, they also view defeat positively, determining how to improve themselves through a process known as social comparison (Garcia et al., 2013). This theory states that individuals are motivated to improve their performance by the need to minimise any discrepancies between their achievement and that of others (Garcia et al., 2013). In a competition, individuals are ranked relative to the other competitors and being awarded first, second or third is a clear acknowledgement of one person's higher capability and, therefore, higher status in relation to others (Schurr & Ritov, 2016).

As already discussed, the behaviour that results from competition is not always positive. Competing often leads 'good people to act in bad ways' (Shields & Bredemeier, 2009, p. 10). It can cause undesirable, even prohibited, behaviour (Kosiewicz, 2011). More specifically, it sharpens the incentive to cheat (Gilpatric, 2011). Cheating is defined as 'an attempt to gain unfair advantage by violating the shared interpretation of the basic rules (the ethos) of the parties engaged without being caught and held responsible for it' (Loland, 2002, p. 96). However, deciding what is and what is not a violation of the rules is not as simple as it may seem. As Kosiewicz (2011, p. 40) notes, competition should not be viewed as 'a strict adherence to the rules … but the optimal use of their content in order to achieve success'. In other words, it is considered acceptable to have the wit and ability to stretch the rules, often to their furthest point, in order to achieve success. If they are stretched beyond their perceived limits, then they are considered to be broken and breaking the rules is viewed as cheating, unless it is considered to be

'unintentional or unknowing' (Green, 2003, p. 140). Chutneygate is, therefore, a case of mishap rather than cheating
as, in Jill Archer's own words, 'I didn't do it on purpose;
I wasn't trying to cheat.'

Michaels and Miethe (1989, p. 883) see cheating as 'a
general class of deviance that occurs in a variety of contexts',
whilst DeAndrea, Carpenter, Shulman, and Levine (2009)
describe it as being commonplace throughout society. Early
thinking linked cheating to the lure of financial rewards
(Pike, 1980) but, more recently, Houser, Vetter, and Winter
(2012, p. 1654) have argued that 'the perception of being
treated unfairly by another person' is sufficient to significantly increase the 'propensity to cheat', whilst John,
Loewenstein, and Rick (2014, p. 101) have found 'mounting
evidence that psychological factors also matter and that
dishonesty is not simply the result of economic cost/benefit
analysis'. Interestingly, work by Schurr and Ritov (2016)
suggests that a competition winner is more likely to be dishonest than a competition loser due to their need to maintain
a positive self-concept. In this case, the act of cheating must
not violate their perception of themselves as fundamentally
honest and this may lead to them failing to notice the unethical implications of what they are doing, a condition known
as ethical blindness (Schurr & Ritov, 2016).

Overall, three key themes within the literature explain
why people compete: the inner drive to succeed, achievement
goals and social comparison. It is acceptable to stretch
the rules in order to succeed, but cheating is unacceptable.
Competitive behaviour, however, may change from positive
to negative as a result of seeking a reward (not necessarily
financial), of responding to unfair treatment or trying to
maintain a positive self-perception. The literature examines
the effect of competition on behaviour in a number of contexts, such as sport, school and the workplace. There has

been no examination to date of Flower and Produce Shows. Therefore, in order to determine whether the same factors are at play, examples of unethical behaviour at the fictional Ambridge Flower and Produce Show were identified and categorised before evidence of similar incidents was sought at a real-life Flower and Produce Show.

THE FICTION: THE AMBRIDGE FLOWER AND PRODUCE SHOW

The Ambridge Flower and Produce Show is one of the most recurring themes of *The Archers*, held most years in mid-September (Dillon, 2011). There have been a series of incidents, categorised here according to an increasingly negative continuum ranging from 'strategic planning', 'mishap', 'questionable judging' and 'disqualification' to 'cheating'. Cheating is further classified as being 'suspected', 'inadvertent', 'opportunistic' or 'pre-meditated'.

Possibly the most benign form of competitive behaviour relating to the Ambridge Flower and Produce Show is strategic planning, whereby potential contestants prepare their campaign 12 months or more in advance to increase their chances of winning. Pru Forrest campaigned strategically in 1995 to become overall winner, neglecting to feed her husband, Tom, in the process. Poor Tom became the subject of village gossip, even suffering snide jaunts at the pub. Chutneygate, the chutney mix-up discussed above, is an example of a mishap, simply an unlucky accident. Questionable judging was apparent in 1994 when young Will Grundy won the best onion category, which was judged by Henri Touvier, the French mayor of twinned village, Meyruelle. Tom Forrest claimed that this 'butcher' did not know what he was talking about. Examples of disqualification include Clarrie Grundy's greengages in 1986 and Lynda Snell's photographs in 2008, whilst in 2010, Jim Lloyd's onions were disqualified following illicit use of twine, despite the fact that Bert Fry (the winner) may well have done the same thing.

Turning to cheating, there are two examples of suspected cheating. In 1977, Laura Archer suspected that Doris Archer's prize-winning jar of lemon curd was one that she herself had given her. In 1982, Walter Gabriel accused Pru Forrest of using Women's Institute products in the homemade jam category. Any concrete evidence of these suspicions would, of course, have turned both into instances of pre-meditated cheating. There are two examples of inadvertent cheating, possibly due to poor understanding of the rules, and both providing further examples of disqualification. In 1978, organising committee member and winner of the overall prize, Jean Harvey, was disqualified for using a pro-fessional gardener. In 2012, Jack 'Jazzer' McCreary's surprise entry in the men-only bread-making class was disqualified after it transpired that he had used a bread maker.

Opportunistic cheating may have occurred in 2007 when Ambridge Village Hall was evacuated during the Show due to a burst water pipe. Bert Fry was convinced that Derek Fletcher had taken advantage of the situation to swap the labels on the runner beans. Firmly believing that Bert's beans were the best, Phil Archer swapped them back to ensure that the best man won. Another clear example of pre-meditated cheating was Sabina Thwaite, who entered one of Jill Archer's fruitcakes as her own in 2008. The admirable Jill decided to let her win. Interestingly, these two incidents, the most probable examples of cheating and deserving of dis-qualification, if not worse, were actually covered up by those bastions of rectitude, Phil and Jill Archer, perhaps employing ethical blindness to maintain their self-esteem.

Overall, the evidence from the Ambridge Flower and Produce Show confirms a competitive spirit spilling into an array of negative behaviour, although it is the lack of adherence to the rules that causes the most issues. However, as noted above, this is not considered to be cheating. Given these conclusions, the next stage of the research was to determine whether this fiction is representative of fact.

THE FACT: A FLOWER AND PRODUCE SHOW IN WILTSHIRE

To identify incidents at a real Flower and Produce Show, in-depth interviews were held with six long-term participants, with one interviewee answering on behalf of two children, who were also veteran competitors. As this was an exploratory investigation, intent on obtaining qualitative data in order to understand attitudes and behaviour, there was deemed to be no requirement to obtain a statistically representative sample.

The interviews began by asking competitors why they compete at these shows, seeking evidence of the three key themes identified in the literature: the inner drive to succeed, achievement goals and relative ranking. All of the competitors demonstrated their inner drive to succeed:

> *I want to do the best I can — that's more fun. And for my own benefit. It's satisfying to know that I've done something good.*

One interviewee explained how the inner drive manifested itself in relation to vegetable growing:

> *I improved my soil, I planted slightly differently ... we moved house and the first thing*

*I did was to dig up half the garden ... You end up
planting things in just the right way and then you
can get a bit more competitive for the show.*

This also shows that achievement goals are being set in order to improve ranking year on year, so confirming the second key theme.

Evidence was also obtained of contestants seeking recognition for their time and effort. One noted that:

*In the gardening world, I've already achieved a
lot ... I'm not too bothered about entering now
because I've had the first, second and third, the com-
mendation, so that drive for me isn't there anymore.
When I didn't get anything, I had the drive then.*

On the face of it, this contradicts Schurr and Ritov's (2016) assertion that a competition winner is more likely to be competitive. However, it was evident that this contestant had not lost their inner drive to succeed and was still setting achievement goals despite their winning run:

*I have grown a broccoli that's famous. I have grown
a pumpkin that was famous — it was four stone!
(Sigh) I've not grown an onion that's famous. I want
to set a challenge. I want to grow an onion that's on
the radio!*

Contradicting the spirit of this statement, size is not as highly valued in vegetable categories as consistency and presentation, although one of the judges revealed that large vegetables are always appreciated:

*... a cabbage so big it couldn't even go on the bench!
We had to bring up a chair for it! A cabbage that
had its own chair!*

It was clear that, for some, the inner drive to succeed and the resulting achievement goals are about self-improvement as much as winning. Inevitably, this affects the amount of effort that they put into their entries:

> *Improving every year, the show has helped me to do that.*

> *It's a lot of work. And as it's gone on, it's snow-balled really. I've put more and more effort into it.*

Similarly, there was clear evidence that the third theme, relative ranking, also drives competitive behaviour. People like to be ranked higher than other people, but particularly if they know the other people:

> *I think about specific people that I am competing against. These are all my friends from Church.*

A theme strongly evident in the interviews was the need for external validation, which relates to the notion of a positive self-concept, as identified by Schurr and Ritov (2016). To some, it felt almost pointless producing vegetables, cakes and crafts without them being judged and rated:

> *If there wasn't a show, then I wouldn't be showing them and I wouldn't have other people looking at them so it wouldn't really matter.*

> *People want to be appreciated for what they've done, for what they've grown and for what they've cooked.*

It became evident that the need for external validation is about more than being ranked to show relative position. Validation goes deeper, recognising or affirming an individual's perception of their own value, almost confirming their very existence:

> *It's a self-defining thing — here I am, this is me,*
> *I can do this.*

It is both poignant and telling that a couple of contestants related this to parental validation. One regretted that his father's abilities and, therefore, his worth had never been recognised:

> *My dad was a good grower of veg but he didn't*
> *have anyone recognise that.*

For another, it was the lack of parental recognition that drove the need to obtain an objective, external validation of personal worth:

> *There is something in the confirmation of*
> *ability ... mum always said I was a disaster in the*
> *kitchen.*

Overall, the interviews confirmed a high level of competitive behaviour, influenced by the inner drive to succeed, achievement goals and relative ranking, as well as the need for external validation. However, above all of these, the key reason for competing was feeling part of the community and showing support for communal events. There was a strong desire to ensure the future of the show and to preserve the related skills. Some of the interviewees reflected on the increasing importance of such events in today's society, where it can feel that the old forms and traditions of community are disintegrating.

RULES ... AND UNWRITTEN RULES

A key theme to emerge from the interviews that was not so apparent in the literature was the existence of unwritten rules, described here as 'the etiquette'. There was a clearly perceived difference between the rules that appear in the competition information and the unwritten etiquette. These are the codes that entrants are expected to observe but that can only be learned by observing successful entries. This etiquette is handed down from the bigger Royal Horticultural Society (RHS) shows but is not included in the written rules for this smaller, local show. The committee members explained that they tried to avoid too many prescriptive rules, fearing that it might deter people from participating. However, one of the judges admitted that this causes issues:

> *Sometimes people come back to us and complain, usually because the rules are ambiguous. We should be clear.*

Despite this, the judges employ the RHS principles when rating the entries:

> *There are ways of presenting your produce. It comes down from the RHS Shows. For example, standing your shallot on a cardboard cylinder.*

Lack of knowledge about the etiquette often leads to failure the first time a category is entered:

> *There is nothing on the sheet that says your shortbread must be traditional and presented in a traditional way. I thought I had got it wrong ... I put the shortbread in a pretty tin but everybody else's was the classic round of shortbread on a plate. And mine just looked wrong. They weren't what the judges were expecting. And I didn't get anything.*

It is only through trial and error that competitors learn what is really expected of them:

> *I wasn't confident (the first time). I became confident when I knew what the judges looked for and I knew I had good items to display.*

> *It took a bit of practice and looking at others to work out what they were after. They're not looking at one thing.*

> *I did Google what judges look for. If you know what they want you to do, then you can please them.*

One of the judges argued that working out the elements of a winning entry is part of the challenge, making it clear that the etiquette plays a major part in both success and failure. Given this, the interviewees were next asked how they felt about both failing and succeeding in order to identify whether this led to any negative attitudes and, potentially, resulted in negative behaviour, as demonstrated at the Ambridge Flower and Produce Show.

TRUTH IS STRANGER THAN FICTION …

Failing to be placed in the Show was an evident knock to personal pride but on a relatively small scale:

> *I just felt a bit embarrassed. At that point, I thought that I did badly because what I took in was quite small compared to the others.*

> *I used ferns … arranged them in a basket and, by the time we got back, they had completely wilted.*

(My husband) was nudging me, saying how embar-
rassing is that — pretend it's not yours!

However, it was evident that the experience of failing
did not deter people from entering future shows but rather
encouraged them to learn about the etiquette and to improve
their performance. Everyone enjoyed success but, interestingly, only if the category was properly competed. Being
the only person to enter and, therefore, winning by default
does not fulfil the need for relative ranking or give sufficient
external validation:

My first win, only two people entered. I didn't want
to tell people that only two people entered. I beat
one other person — it's a bit of a hollow
victory ... but I still got the certificate!

Turning to the categories of incidents and evidence of
competitive behaviour, there were examples of strategic planning that included setting aside the best produce throughout
the year and working out how to amass sufficient points to
become the overall winner:

You make the preserves throughout the year, squir-
rel a jar away and you don't have to think, just get it
out. I have a deliberate strategy. I eye up the marma-
lade, thinking is that good enough, is it going to
beat X, Y and Z?

[My son] had seconds for his bughouse, photograph
of a garden creature, and drawing of a treasure map
and no place for his decorated biscuit — yet he won
overall because he had entered every class!

Turning to the more negative categories of incident, a
mishap occurred in one of the children's categories when

a vegetable queen (it was Jubilee year) was mysteriously damaged. Her crown had been removed and set to one side before the judging took place. This could have been a simple mishap but cheating was suspected and, if confirmed, would have been an example of opportunistic cheating. In certain circumstances, mishaps can be turned to advantage with some creative thinking:

> *When my friend's jam didn't set, he put a label on it saying 'French Set Preserve' to make it seem like it was meant to be like that! And he got placed!*

This might be considered to be questionable judging but, interestingly, all of the issues with the judges came from the children's categories. One judge explained that they try to give a prize to all of the children who enter in order to encourage them to compete again. Inevitably, this is seen as unfair by those parents whose children have put in more effort and, as a result, produced better work. One example concerned an edible necklace made of sweets. It was awarded only second place, condemned as 'not healthy' (a point that was not specified in the rules). The irony is that it was the only entry that was totally edible and, therefore, fully met the written rules.

Evidence of suspected cheating also came from the children's categories. For example, the high standard of a winning Lego model of a kingfisher gave rise to the suspicion of significant parental input. Indeed, the level of assistance that may or may not have been received from parents was one of the biggest causes of suspicion in the children's categories, raising questions about how far 'helicopter parents' will go to ensure the success of their offspring.

The charge of inadvertent cheating resulting from failure to observe the etiquette was demonstrated by the use of cake

mix and a possibly unorthodox approach to the growing
of onions:

> *It doesn't say you can't use a packet (but) you're not*
> *going to win, that's for sure.*
>
> *When it comes to growing onions, I have suspected.*
> *There is a guy that regularly enters and the three*
> *onions he enters are so massive that they haven't*
> *been grown from seed and they haven't been grown*
> *from a normal set ... this is bigger ... I would imag-*
> *ine that he's planting an already grown*
> *onion ... they don't look right ... but he's clearly*
> *done that in his garden, he hasn't gone to a shop.*

Despite the suspicion, the onion-growing example was not
condemned:

> *I don't think it's cheating ... I just think that the set*
> *he uses is a fully grown onion ... It's in the spirit*
> *of growing big so I guess I kind of like it ... I wish*
> *I'd done it ....*

This demonstrates that there is a clearly perceived distinction between the acceptable manipulation of the rules, which
is part of the competition, and actual cheating:

> *People will always stretch the rules. But that's not*
> *cheating.*

However, the dividing line is different for each individual:

> *Everybody's got a different point at which they*
> *think playing the system becomes cheating.*

The literature noted that the self-perception of being
fundamentally honest must not be violated, often resulting in
ethical blindness, a failure to notice the unethical implications

of the act being undertaken. Similarly, stretching the rules is clearly considered to be acceptable where an ethical justification can be brought into play. For example, faced with low entries in the scone category and the desire to provide a good show for local people, a mother and daughter rushed home to bake more scones. They entered half each and one took first prize and the other third:

> *If I'd gone out and bought them from a shop,*
> ***THAT*** *would have been cheating!*

Not surprisingly, the interviewees were loath to identify examples of either opportunistic or pre-meditated cheating, particularly relating to their own actions. However, a tale from the longest runner bean category provided the most compelling example:

> *Someone brought two in, which they'd cut and laid*
> *on the plate as if it was a single bean, just placed*
> *together. It didn't win. It seems so unbelievably daft.*
> *I'd call that cheating.*

Interestingly, and unlike the fiction, it became apparent that no one had ever been disqualified, even when blatantly not adhering to the rules, as in the runner bean incident. In true British spirit, '*it's just mentioned quietly.*' Whilst entries are often disqualified at county shows, the local judges were motivated by their aim of not discouraging participation. Subconsciously, they might also recognise the potential unfairness of the etiquette to the uninitiated.

CONCLUSION

This study was inspired by the frequent scandal that occurs at the Ambridge Flower and Produce Show, asking whether it is representative of real life. The interviews revealed that the depiction is not simply a convenient plot device but an accurate account of the significant competitive behaviour generated by a Flower and Produce Show, despite its inconsequential rewards. It is evident that competition is valued for its own sake as people demonstrate their inner drive to succeed and the need to meet their achievement goals, as identified in the literature. Relative ranking is critical, providing validation, but enhanced if competing against friends and diminished if there is a lack of competition. Overall, it is the external validation of achievement that competitors seek, the reinforcement of a positive self-concept.

Examples of strategic planning and mishap, along with suspected, inadvertent and, possibly, opportunistic cheating are found in both fiction and fact, with suspicions of cheating being particularly rife in relation to the real-life children's categories, something not yet seen in *The Archers*. For obvious reasons, examples of pre-meditated cheating are difficult to identify in real life and are, therefore, more evident in the fictional depiction. However, the commitment to these competitions and the competitive behaviour that they generate is such that the motivation to cheat in reality cannot be discounted, as evidenced by the tale of the longest runner bean.

The local show confirms the theory that competition is not about a strict adherence to the rules but rather using them to their optimum. The importance of etiquette and the unwritten rules was clearly identified, with individuals each employing their own moral code to determine the breaking point of these rules. In the face of potential rule breaking, the need to maintain a positive self-perception is critical, although there may be a failure to notice the unethical implications, so-called ethical blindness. Related to this, unintentional or unknowing rule breaking is not considered to be cheating.

The only clear area of disparity between fiction and fact was the number of disqualifications at the Ambridge Flower and Produce Show. Whilst the Ambridge judges are stern, the real judges at this local show are comfortable with tacitly ignoring even the most blatant cheating to ensure a happy event that encourages everyone to take part. This leads to the most critical finding of this chapter and the most important and universal driver for anyone entering a Flower and Produce Show. This is its importance as a community event, eliciting not only the desire to contribute, but also to preserve and maintain it for others in the future. Therefore, the clear link between the fiction of Ambridge and the fact of real-life is this sense of community and tradition, something that has always been at the heart of *The Archers*.

ACKNOWLEDGEMENTS

We would like to thank our six interviewees for their time and sharing their experiences — both good and bad — of the Flower and Produce Show. We wish you many more victories.

REFERENCES

DeAndrea, D., Carpenter, C., Shulman, H., & Levine, T. (2009). The relationship between cheating behavior and sensation-seeking. *Personality and Individual Differences*, 47(8), 944–947. doi:10.1016/j.paid.2009.07.021

Dillon, R. (2011). *The Archers: An unofficial companion*. Chichester: Summersdale.

Garcia, S. M., Tor, A., & Schiff, T. M. (2013). The psychology of competition: A social comparison perspective. Scholarly Works. Paper 941. doi:10.1177/1745691613504114

Gilpatric, S. M. (2011). Cheating in contests. *Economic Inquiry*, *49*, 1042–1053. doi:10.1111/j.1465-7295.2010.00244.x

Green, S. P. (2003). Cheating. *Law and Philosophy*, *23*, 137–185.

Harackiewicz, J., Barron, K., Carter, S., Lehto, A., & Elliot, A. (1997). Predictors and consequences of achievement goals in the college classroom: Maintaining interest and making the grade. *Journal of Personality and Social Psychology*, *73*, 1284–1295. doi:10.1037/0022-3514.73.6.1284

Houser, D., Vetter, S., & Winter, J. (2012). Fairness and cheating. *European Economic Review*, *56*(8), 1645–1655. doi:10.1016/j.euroecorev.2012.08.001

John, L. K., Loewenstein, G., & Rick, S. I. (2014). Cheating more for less: Upward social comparisons motivate the poorly compensated to cheat. *Organizational Behaviour and Human Decision Processes*, *123*, 101–109. doi:10.2139/ssrn.2208139

Kosiewicz, J. (2011). Foul play in sport as a phenomenon inconsistent with the rules, yet acceptable and desirable. *Physical culture and sport. Studies and Research*, *52*, 33–43. doi:10.2478/v10141-011-0012-x

Loland, S. (2002). *Fair play in sport: a moral norm system*. London: Routledge.

Michaels, J. W., & Miethe, T. D. (1989). Applying theories of deviance to academic cheating. *Social Science Quarterly*, *70*(4), 870–885.

Pike, D. (1980). *How inflation brings out the criminal urge.* U.S. News & World Report, September 8, p. 56.

Schurr, A., & Ritov, I. (2016). Winning a competition predicts dishonest behavior. *Proceedings of the National Academy of Sciences of the United States of America, 113*(7), 1754–1759. doi:10.1073/pnas.1515102113

Shields, D. L., & Bredemeier, B. L. (2009). *True competition: A guide to pursuing excellence in sport and society.* Champaign, IL: Human Kinetics.

Toye, J. (2009). *The Archers miscellany.* London: BBC Books.

PEER REVIEW, BY BERT FRY, BROOKFIELD BUNGALOW, AMBRIDGE, BORSETSHIRE

BERT'S ODE TO THE FLOWER AND PRODUCE SHOW

I think these clever ladies
Have hit the nail right on the head,
As there's a lot of suspect behaviour
In the chutney, jam and bread.

There is nothing more unsettling
Than a judge who doesn't know
The difference of a packet mix
From one made of proper dough.

I've seen some awful things occur
So someone can win First,
But there's something about a runner bean
That just brings out the worst ...

Now I can appreciate the etiquette –
All the rules not actually stated –

My Freda had a lot of those
And none could be abated!
My Freda loved the Ambridge Show
Her joy did never fizzle;
The only thing she ever feared
Was Jill Archer's lemon drizzle!

There's one last thing on which I must
Insist till my last night,
There was NOTHING wrong with that there twine –
Jim just hadn't tied it right!

CHAPTER TWO

'BIG TELEPHOTO LENS, SMALL TICKLIST': BIRDWATCHING, CLASS AND GENDER IN AMBRIDGE

Joanna Dobson

ABSTRACT

This chapter explores the role that birdwatching plays in The Archers. *It demonstrates some significant similarities between the way that birdwatching is portrayed in present-day Ambridge, and the way it was presented in both fictional and non-fictional literature of the 1940s. These similarities suggest that birdwatching in Ambridge is an activity that tends to perpetuate traditional class and gender divisions. Particularly in terms of gender, this is a surprising discovery, given the many strong female characters in the show, and suggests that cultural assumptions about gender and birdwatching run deep in*

UK society today. The chapter warns that a failure to recognise these assumptions not only hampers the progress of women who aspire to be taken seriously as ornithologists, but also risks reinforcing dualistic thinking about humans and nature at a time when the environmental crisis makes it more important than ever to recognise the ecological interconnectedness of human and nonhuman worlds. However, the recent development of Kirsty Miller's storyline, in which she is rediscovering her earlier love of the natural world, not only offers hope of a shift away from this traditional bias but also opens a space for a more nuanced examination of the importance of birds in human–nature relations.

Keywords: Animal studies; *The Archers*; birdwatching; ecocriticism; ecofeminism; natureculture

Birdwatching in Ambridge is one of those topics like lambing or visits to Underwood's: it's seldom a significant part of any plotline but it's important for creating an overall impression of everyday country life. As such, it provides a context in which characters can interact and develop, and these interactions can reveal much about their attitudes to one another and also about the unwritten assumptions that underlie their birdwatching practice. The most prominent birdwatchers in the village are Jim Lloyd and Robert Snell, and the title of this chapter references one of Jim's many put-downs of Robert's ornithological abilities. Recently, Kirsty Miller has also rediscovered her love of the more-than-human world and her birdwatching skills have resurfaced after a long period in abeyance. A comparison of the different ways in which these characters approach birds and birdwatching provides important insights into the way that human—nature relations are communicated through *The Archers*.

Birdwatching is phenomenally popular in Britain. The Royal Society for the Protection of Birds has more than one million members, making it the largest nature conservation charity in the country. The beginnings of this enthusiasm can be traced back to the 1930s, when interest in natural history in general and birdwatching in particular grew at an unprecedented rate. Hundreds of new field guides and natural history books were published, and an important landmark was the founding of the British Trust for Ornithology (BTO) in 1933. The BTO stressed the importance of enabling amateur birdwatchers to make a contribution to national research: the idea was to have a network of enthusiastic people whose observations would be incorporated into a central knowledge base. The trust was careful to stress the egalitarian nature of the project: special training was not necessary; participants should simply be people of good behaviour, interested in birds but not necessarily knowledgeable about them, and capable of recording their observations in plain language (Macdonald, 2002, p. 60).

Toogood links what he calls the 'new ornithology' (2011, p. 348) with the work of the social research organisation Mass Observation, which was formed in 1937 as 'a scientific study of human social behaviour, beginning at home' (Toogood, 2011, p. 349) and with the similar objective of recruiting a network of ordinary people to keep detailed records of regular observational practice. For him, they both represent 'a new openness of opportunity and a degree of change to doing observation, in particular the dissolution of highly specialist knowledge as a precursor to observation' (*ibid.*, p. 350). This deconsecration of the lone, privileged expert and the corresponding focus on networks and collaboration prefigures the mindset that would give rise to the welfare state.

Even after the outbreak of the Second World War, when there was a shortage of paper, and publishers were severely restricted in the number and type of books they were allowed to produce, books about birds continued to sell in huge numbers. A common theme in these books is that birdwatching is a democratising pastime, something that everyone can take part in, regardless of their social standing or education. Fisher's 1941 book *Watching Birds*, which sold more than three million copies, has an example:

> *All sorts of different people seem to watch birds.*
> *Among those I know of are a late Prime Minister,*
> *a Secretary of State, a charwoman, two policemen,*
> *two kings, one ex-king, five Communists, four*
> *Labour, one Liberal and three Conservative*
> *Members of Parliament, the chairman of a County*
> *Council, several farm-labourers earning sixty*
> *shillings a week, a rich man who earns two or three*
> *times that amount in every hour of the day, at least*
> *forty-six schoolmasters, and an engine-driver.*
> *(Fisher, 1941, p. 13)*

In this chapter, I shall be asking two questions from this extract and then linking those questions to birdwatching practice in *The Archers*. The first is: where are the women? The charwoman is definitely female but what about the rest? Perhaps a Communist or possibly one of the MPs, but otherwise women are invisible, or at best shadowy. This absence of women from birdwatching discourse is also evident in fiction of the period. *Adventure Lit Their Star* (Allsop, 1972), for example, first published in 1949, is a lightly fictionalised account of the little ringed plover's struggle to establish itself as a breeding bird in the United Kingdom in the 1940s. No women take part in the main human activity, which is birdwatching. Just two appear in the text: one is a nurse in the sanatorium where the main character is a patient and the other is his mother. In a happy coincidence, this patient is called Richard Locke; he is not, however, a doctor like his Ambridge namesake but an RAF pilot who has been invalided out of the war due to TB. Locke's success in discovering the little ringed plovers and subsequently protecting them from harm is described in the book as 'a vindication of himself' (Allsop, 1972, p. 144), and it is strongly implied that this is a reassertion of the masculinity which was threatened when he was sidelined from military action and became dependent on his female carers. Both the exclusion of women from involvement in birdwatching, and the suggestion that Locke's rescue of the birds is a sign that he has broken free of dependence on women set up a link between masculinity and ornithology.

Before considering whether birdwatching in Ambridge is similarly gendered, I turn my attention to the issue of class. With regard to the quotation from Fisher, above, my second question is: how classless is this really? Fisher says in his preface that he has written his book for 'ordinary people' and not 'the privileged few' (1941, p. 11), and the list of people he knows who are birdwatchers does indeed draw on a wide range of backgrounds. However, these 'all sorts of different people' are defined in Fisher's writing by either their occupations or their social standing — a king and some farm labourers, for example. Rather than erasing class boundaries, this kind of taxonomy has the effect of reinforcing them. A similar dynamic is at work in the other fictional book I refer to, *The Awl Birds* (Stanford, 1949). The protagonist is another damaged serviceman, a sapper called Derick Gloyne, this time defending breeding avocets. He succeeds, but only with the help of an old family servant, John Blowers, who secretly disables an egg collector's car. This is how the reader learns of what Blowers has done:

> *'I put my owd missus' sugar ration in it. that's*
> *wunnerful good stuff, a sowljer told me, if you don't*
> *want a car to goo. Then I comes across to look*
> *for you.' ... And this, thought Derick, was the 'igno-*
> *rant' yokel, to whom no one gave any credit for*
> *shrewdness. (Stanford, 1949, p. 88)*

Gloyne's assumption that Blowers is viewed universally as an ignorant yokel with little intelligence betrays his own deep-seated prejudices. Additionally, the phonetic rendering of Blowers' accent separates him from other local characters in the book, such as the estate agent, whose speech is transcribed in Standard English. The book finishes with the 'yokel' being invited into the big house for a tot of rum, an incident which recalls Matthews' reference in the last Academic Archers publication (Courage et al., 2017) to Lynda Snell's 'class positioning' over her offer to Susan Carter of a glass of sherry (2017, p. 106). It is difficult for the reader of today to avoid a sense that Gloyne's attitudes are shot through with condescension.

Turning now to the ornithologists of Ambridge, an explicit link between birdwatching and gender was made in the run-up to the Great Borsetshire Bird Race (GBBR) of 2015. Shortly before competition day, Lynda discovered that Robert had spent their flood insurance money on a telephoto lens to help him see the birds more clearly. Initially she was angry, but had a change of heart when Robert explained how insecure he felt as a result of Jim's constant mocking of his birdwatching prowess. 'You don't know what it does to a man,' he said forlornly. 'I'm starting to lose confidence in telling common waders apart.' Jim, however, was unimpressed by Robert's equipment: 'Big telephoto lens, small ticklist,' he told Carol Tregorran, adding unconvincingly that he himself did not have a competitive bone in his body.

Lynda's role in relation to the birds of Ambridge has also tended to be gendered. Despite her interest in the local flora and fauna and her enthusiasm for co-opting them into her campaigns (think, Route B and the Brown Hairstreak butterfly), until very recently she has rarely been found behind a pair of binoculars. Instead, she has been cast in a more maternal role. When she discovered that peregrines were trying to nest on the roof of St Stephen's, she campaigned unsuccessfully to have a special ledge installed for them to stop the eggs smashing on the ground. Similarly, in the GBBR, while the male team members were focused on finding a route that would allow them to spot the maximum number of birds, Lynda found herself in charge of monitoring food and toilet breaks and enforcing good manners. 'We can't just march in, use the facilities and march out again' she says in response to the men's suggestion that they could stop at a handy pub or café. There are echoes of Locke's fussy and restricting mother in *Adventure Lit Their Star* here.

Further examples of traditional divisions being enforced in the GBBR can be found in the make-up of the teams. Jim, captain of the Bull Birders, has said all along that he has a 'secret weapon' to rival Robert's new telephoto lens. This turns out to be Molly Button, who has confided in him that she recently spotted a red kite over the village. So a female is included on Jim's team, but she is one of *The Archers'* famous silent characters; thus anything she has to say about birds must be reported by a man. We are back to the shadowy presence of women on the edge of birdwatching discourse that I highlighted in my discussion of Fisher's 1941 book. Meanwhile Robert, captain of the Ambridge Aviators, has Will Grundy as the third member of his team. Will has been recruited partly as a driver but also, the programme tells us, because of his expertise with woodland birds. Unlike Jim and Robert, whose knowledge of birds is acquired with the help of expensive equipment and books, Will is here cast in quasi-Romantic style as a man whose acquaintance with nature stems from the fact that he spends his days working outdoors for Brian Aldridge. This is a class-bound portrayal: Will as gamekeeper versus Robert as the Squire of Ambridge Hall and Jim as learned professor.

I have called Robert a squire but of course we all know that he's not. He and Lynda live in Ambridge Hall because of his previous success as a self-made entrepreneur in the world of IT. With that business having failed, he is now described in *The Archers*' character profiles as a 'high-class odd job man'. This, I would argue, is the real reason why Jim, retired history professor steeped in classical literature, and father of a veterinary surgeon, is able to keep up his constant mockery of Robert. Highly educated and enjoying considerable status because of his title, he can be confident that he will always have the last word on birdwatching, just as he would have done in the 1940s. In this example, birdwatching in Ambridge can be seen to reinforce very traditional boundaries of class and gender.

Certainly in terms of gender, this is surprising because women have a strong presence in *The Archers*. From Alice Carter, the high-flying tech specialist, to the latest arrival, the feisty and ambitious vet Anisha Jayakody, they are most often portrayed as independent and successful. Older women, who are so often sidelined, if not invisible, in contemporary culture, often drive the plot forward and can be seen subverting the traditional gender roles that they grew up with. This raises the possibility that the marginalisation of women in birdwatching discourse is so pervasive that the scriptwriters have failed to notice it. Class is a little more complex but certainly listeners do not usually encounter Will in the guise of romanticised son of the soil. He is far more likely to be heard engaging in passive aggressive present-buying for son George as a way of flaunting his superior income to brother Ed. However, once he moves into the realm of birdwatching, the kinds of traditional class assumptions that prevailed in mid-twentieth-century England suddenly take effect.

It could be argued that the GBBR and Jim's teasing of Robert, for example, are simply opportunities to inject some humour into *The Archers*, providing a light-hearted counter-balance in episodes that are focused on weightier issues. At the time of the GBBR, Ambridge was still reeling from the floods and the Rob and Helen storyline was gathering pace. However, the marginalisation of women in birding discourse is not a light-hearted issue for women who seek to be treated as serious ornithologists. Mya-Rose Craig, for example, is a 14-year-old birder who has seen 4400 birds on seven continents, is a qualified bird ringer and has already organised two conferences to encourage more black, Asian and minority ethnic young people to get involved in nature conservation. She has written powerfully about her experiences of sexism in birding. At the age of seven, she appeared in a television programme and afterwards was made the subject of abuse on social media. She writes:

> *If I had been a boy, being out birding at the weekends would have been acceptable and people would not have been clambering to say that I was 'clearly' uninterested in birds. A boy would have reminded male birders of their own childhood and would have been seen as normal. As a girl, I was unfairly labelled as 'bored and unhappy'. (Craig, 2015)*

When she was 11, some middle-aged birders set up a secret Facebook group and posted 150 comments about her 'including a sexual remark by a university lecturer' (Craig, 2015).

She concludes her blog post: 'To get on in nature conservation in the UK, as a girl you have to be five times better than the nearest boy. So that's what I try to do' (Craig, 2015).

Additionally, the kind of dualistic thinking that can be seen at work in the GBBR can have far-reaching environmental consequences. The storyline perpetuates a conception that activities such as mapping, driving and species identification, which might be described as scientific or cultural, belong with men. When Lynda is given responsibility for seeing that those men are appropriately fed and toileted, she is being assigned a domestic role that connects with the work women do after childbirth to ensure that children are nursed and socialised. The men are dealing with issues of the mind, Lynda with concerns of the body. This has its roots in the Cartesian separation of mind from body and by extension of culture from nature. Within this separation, women have historically been associated with nature because of the assumption that their role in reproduction renders them more corporeal than men (Soper, 1995, p. 98). Ecocritics, who study the relationship between literature and the environment, seek to expose this kind of dualistic thinking because it results in a conception of human–nature relations that militates against ideas of ecological interdependence. The privileging of mind over body and culture over nature leads to the widespread, anthropocentric assumption that the value of anything inheres only in its relation to human beings. Such an attitude is in direct opposition to ecological thinking, which emphasises the importance of recognising the interconnectedness of human and nonhuman life if we are to have any hope of solving the current environmental crisis.

In her chapter of the previous volume of Academic Archers essays, Walton makes the point that *The Archers* is a type of environmental literature 'which has the potential to profoundly influence its listeners' attitudes [to] human-nature relations and ecological interdependence' (Courage et al., 2017, p. 130). The GBBR has the unfortunate effect of validating a way of conceptualising human–nature relations that relies on ideas of separation rather than interdependence. As I have demonstrated, it separates groups of people according to class and gender; in addition it divides human from nonhuman in a way that reduces the nonhuman to a mere cipher in the story. The premise of the GBBR — to spot as many birds as possible — is completely anthropocentric: the birds only have meaning as ticks on a page. To succeed in the race, it is not necessary to know anything about the bird in question apart from the name it has been given in a human taxonomical system. In other words, the birds exist only in terms of their usefulness to a group of human beings. They also have no importance as individuals: for the competing teams, one red kite would be as good as another (and when, towards the end of the competition, the red kite turns out to be a pheasant, it is no good at all).

Recent developments in Kirsty Miller's storyline stand in welcome contrast to the reductive approach of the GBBR. It has been easy to forget that Kirsty entered *The Archers* as an eco-warrior. Her narrative arc has been dominated by being jilted at the altar by Tom Archer and her work in the Grey Gables health club is a long way from the volunteering she used to do for Borsetshire Wildlife Trust. At that time, she demonstrated considerable birding skills, although it is notable that that side of her character faded with the disappearance of wildlife expert Patrick Hennessey and the ending of any tension over whether the two of them really were going to stay 'just good friends'. Now, after a traumatic late miscarriage, Kirsty's story has begun to open a space that allows for a more nuanced and complex representation of the relationship between humans and nature in general, and humans and birds in particular.

Since her miscarriage, Kirsty has been drawn back into work that brings her into closer contact with nature, first by helping Jill Archer with her bees and then by organising the dawn chorus walk. This taps into a lively current debate about the potential of nature to benefit human wellbeing. The charity Mind, for example, recently funded more than one hundred 'ecotherapy' projects to give people living with mental health problems the opportunity to get involved with 'green' activities, and the subsequent evaluation by the University of Essex reported that participants showed significant improvements in a number of areas such as mood and social engagement (Bragg, Wood, & Barton, 2013). The dawn chorus walk was an opportunity for Kirsty to reassert agency over her life, and in addition it provided many examples of interconnectedness. These included the connections between Ambridge and the wider community, since it was organised in aid of a local miscarriage charity, and between people from different parts of the village: the Thwaites and Tracy Horrobin, for example, are not normally seen together. Then there was intergenerational connection, as Henry Archer reported to Jim on his progress in identifying birdsong, and, importantly, the connections between humans and birds, as I shall go on to discuss. In addition, the episode was part of BBC Radio 4's wider involvement in International Dawn Chorus Day, a worldwide celebration that has so far involved events in more than 80 countries (IDCD, n.d.).

In contrast to the GBBR, in which nature and culture were kept apart, the dawn chorus walk in *The Archers* was an example of 'natureculture', a term used to describe 'the continual interpenetration and mutual constitution of the human and nonhuman worlds' (Garrard, 2012, p. 208). Birds play a hugely important role in human culture. They are woven into the mythologies of many ancient civilisations and can be found on countless human artefacts: penguins on the spines of books, eagles on church lecterns and falcons on numerous pieces of military equipment, to name just a few. Part of the reason for their fascination is that they are both like and radically unlike us. They walk on two legs, they make a kind of music, and their nests can be so carefully crafted and cosy that they seem the epitome of domesticity. And yet they can fly, and in this they embody ideas of wildness and freedom that are in stark contrast to the earthbound nature of humans. They are rich sources of meaning and metaphor for humans trying to explain the world around them.

The dawn chorus is a bird event that is particularly full of meaning for humans. Because of its musicality, and because it is loudest when the dawn is sunniest, it tends to be associated with joy (although not in Brian's case. 'Wretched birds woke me,' he complained to Adam Macey). What Lynda called 'the full panoply of early morning birdsong' has a transformative power. In his book on finding joy in nature, McCarthy writes that it even 'clothes suburbia in wonder' (2015, p. 203). Principally, though, it speaks of new beginnings: 'Begin again, it says, again' writes Tim Dee (2017), ornithologist and co-presenter of BBC Radio 4's dawn chorus broadcast. New beginnings were a central theme of *The Archers*' dawn chorus episode. There was Kirsty, tentatively starting to rebuild her life after the shock of losing first Tom as a husband and then their baby. There was also the new freedom for Helen embodied in the announcement that her decree absolute had come through. This might sound as though birds risk being reduced to ciphers again, used simply as repositories for human meanings, but a consideration of what the dawn chorus actually signifies for birds shows that the programme was not being so simplistic. The song, almost exclusively from male birds, has two basic messages: phrased politely, these are 'please get out of my space' or 'please come and mate with me'. They are messages about territory and coupling and on one level underscore the fact that although Kirsty may be starting again, her nest is empty; and that although Helen appears to be free, her erstwhile mate has been fiercely territorial in his claim on the children and may prove to be again. On a lighter note, the birds' repeated assertions of their territorial claims were echoed in another of the episode's storylines as Kate Madikane and Alice Carter jostled for a better position under the new Home Farm partnership agreement.

This is a long way from birds being reduced to ticks on a list. The dawn chorus episode invited listeners to engage more fully with what birds can mean in our lives. The stories we tell about animals are important, especially at a time of environmental crisis. As Macdonald has written:

> ... *the more time spent researching, watching and interacting with animals, the more the stories they're made of change, turning into richer stories that can alter not only what you think of the animal but also who you are. (2017)*

Many scientists believe we are on the verge of a sixth mass extinction event, most of it driven by human activity. In the light of this, an awareness of the multiple ways in which the lives of different species are connected and entangled is more important than ever. The way that human–animal relations are represented in texts like *The Archers* can play a crucial role in increasing this awareness.

The dawn chorus walk also demonstrated another welcome difference from the GBBR: all the birdwatching that listeners heard was being done by women. Lynda, for example, was meticulous in attempting to distinguish garden warbler from willow warbler, and the list she was keeping was a personal record aimed at helping her to understand the birds better, not part of a competition. Although she checked some information with Robert, he was never directly in earshot, and even more unusually, Jim did not speak either. The episode seems to have opened a way for a much more egalitarian approach to birdwatching in Ambridge, albeit with one important exception, which I will now briefly consider.

Birdwatching discourse of the 1940s was not only gendered and class-conscious; like much contemporary literature relating to the countryside it was also deeply embedded in ideas of national identity. As an example, Fisher's book, published in the middle of the Second World War, describes birds as 'part of the heritage we are fighting for' (1941, p. 9). The prominent scientist and birdwatcher Julian Huxley claimed that birds were actually expressions of the British countryside: '... the yellow-hammer's song seems the best possible expression of hot country roads in July, the turtle-dove's crooning of midsummer afternoons ... the robin's song of peaceful autumn melancholy' (1949, p. 7). As Macdonald has argued, writing like this created 'a specifically British identity for the field naturalist' (2002, p. 60). It is beyond the scope of this chapter to examine the relationship between birdwatching and ideas of national identity, but historically there has been a complex and often deeply problematic relationship between certain constructions of the countryside and some ideas of what it means to be British. A large part of Mya-Rose Craig's work as a British Bangladeshi birder is aimed at countering this and encouraging more young people from black, Asian and minority ethnic (BAME) backgrounds to feel birdwatching and nature conservation are areas they can get involved in. In this context, it is crucial to point out that despite the unexpectedly high turnout for Kirsty's dawn chorus walk, no mention was made of BAME characters. Where were Usha Franks and Anisha, for example?

In conclusion, the GBBR and the dawn chorus walk represent two very different accounts of birdwatching practice in Ambridge. It is to be hoped that future episodes will follow the model of the dawn chorus walk, both in its increased inclusiveness and in the space it opened for a richer, more nuanced representation of human–nature relations.

ACKNOWLEDGEMENTS

My thanks to Dr Samantha Walton of Bath Spa University for insightful comments on a draft of this chapter, and to Emily Baker (this volume) for alerting me to the way that Kirsty and Helen are often linked sonically with blackbird song (see also review by Jennifer Aldridge).

REFERENCES

Allsop, K. (1972 [1949]). *Adventure lit their star: The story of an immigrant bird*. Harmondsworth: Penguin.

Bragg, R., Wood, C., & Barton, J. (2013). *Ecominds effects on mental wellbeing: An evaluation for Mind*. Retrieved from https://www.mind.org.uk/media/354166/Ecominds-effects-on-mental-wellbeing-evaluation-report.pdf

Craig, M. (2015, December 2). *Letter to BBC Wildlife magazine on sexism in nature conservation* [Web log post]. Retrieved from http://birdgirluk.blogspot.co.uk/2015/12/letter-to-bbc-wildlife-magazine-on.html

Dee, T. (2017, May 6). *BBC Radio 4 on international dawn chorus day* [Web log post]. Retrieved from http://www.caughtbytheriver.net/2017/05/06/radio-4-international-dawn-chorus-day-2017-tim-dee/

Fisher, J. (1941). *Watching birds*. Harmondsworth: Penguin.

Garrard, G. (2012). *Ecocriticism*. Abingdon: Routledge.

Huxley, J. (1949). *Bird watching and bird behaviour*. London: Dennis Dobson.

IDCD. (n.d.). *About international dawn chorus day*. Retrieved from http://idcd.info/idcd/

Macdonald, H. (2002). 'What makes you a scientist is the way you look at things': Ornithology and the observer 1930–1955. *Studies in History and Philosophy of Biological and Biomedical Sciences*, *33*(1), 53–77.

Macdonald, H. (2017). *What animals taught me about being human. New York Times Magazine*, May 16. Retrieved from https://www.nytimes.com/2017/05/16/magazine/what-animals-taught-me-about-being-human.html?_r=2

Mass Observation. Retrieved from http://www.massobs. org.uk/

Matthews, P. (2017). Lynda Snell, class warrior: Social class and community activism in rural Borsetshire. In C. Courage, N. Headlam, & P. Matthews (Eds.), *The Archers in fact and fiction: Academic analyses of life in rural Borsetshire* (pp. 103–110). Oxford: Peter Lang.

McCarthy, M. (2015). *The moth snowstorm: Nature and joy*. London: John Murray.

RSPB. (n.d.). *About the RSPB*. Retrieved from https://ww2. rspb.org.uk/about-the-rspb/

Soper, K. (1995). *What is nature?* Oxford: Blackwell.

Stanford, J. K. (1949). *The awl birds*. New York, NY: Devin-Adair Company.

Toogood, M. (2011). Modern observations: New ornithology and the science of ourselves, 1920–1940. *Journal of Historical Geography*, *37*(3), 348–357.

Walton, S. (2017). Cider with Grundy: On the community orchard in Ambridge. In C. Courage, N. Headlam, & P. Matthews (Eds.), *The Archers in fact and fiction: Academic analyses of life in rural Borsetshire* (pp. 129–138). Oxford: Peter Lang.

REVIEW BY JENNIFER ALDRIDGE, HOME FARM, AMBRIDGE, BORSETSHIRE

Ever since my granddaughter, Phoebe, went to the University of Oxford to study PPE I've felt myself hankering after the intellectual life. Sadly, it wasn't that easy for women of my generation to follow their own path in the way my girls have done. So when I found my interest piqued by some of the references in this chapter to the ancient meanings that birds can have for humans, I did a little research myself. Did you know that peacocks have been associated with bad luck in relationships? It makes you wonder whether it's such a good idea for Kenton and Jolene to have them at The Bull and from what I gather, Justin Elliot and Toby Fairbrother might agree. And the other day I was over at Bridge Farm and Henry was so proud that he could identify the bird that often bursts into song around Kirsty and Helen. It's a blackbird and that did make me a little bit concerned because although I suppose you could understand it as being a sign of freedom, there's also an association in folklore between blackbirds and misfortune.

The one thing that irks me though is the point that Ms Dobson makes about Will sometimes appearing a bit like a gamekeeper from the early twentieth century. Jim said that would make me Lady Chatterley. He thought he was being amusing, but I didn't think it was at all fair.

CHAPTER THREE

THE AMBRIDGE PARADOX: CAKE CONSUMPTION AND METABOLIC HEALTH IN A DEFINED RURAL POPULATION

Christine Michael

ABSTRACT

The nutritive properties of various dietary components and their effects on health are regularly debated in the scientific literature and popular media. The study of the regular consumption of cake in relation to the risk of developing metabolic disorders is however an exciting new development in the field. This chapter suggests that cake consumption is amongst a number of factors that may explain The Ambridge Paradox: *the extremely low incidence of metabolic disorders such as obesity and Type 2 diabetes observed in a small Borsetshire village. The chapter identifies 10 dietary and lifestyle habits observed in this population that may be beneficial for cardiovascular health, acting through a variety of mechanisms. Key amongst these may be the synergic properties of several biochemical components of cake, especially the phenolic compounds in varieties with a fruit-based element, such as lemon drizzle. The chapter concludes that the dietary and lifestyle habits of the Ambridge cohort show promise as a model for improving the metabolic health of wider populations. In particular, it suggests that cake consumption may be a promising therapeutic supplement to prevent and even treat metabolic disorders.*

Keywords: Ambridge; cake; lemon drizzle; dietary habits; metabolic disorders

A MIRACULOUS ANOMALY?

What lessons for wider public health can we learn from the dietary or lifestyle habits of one particular ethnic or geographically segregated group of people? Attempts to answer this question are often made by means of observational studies and are published frequently in scientific literature. Popular interest in the results also regularly leads to newspaper headlines such as 'Now fizzy water makes us fat' (Howarth & Adams, 2017) or 'Does eating chocolate make you clever?' (Hodgekiss, 2012).

This chapter is presented in the spirit of this legitimate area of endeavour, but ignores any constraint of academic rigour or the scientific method. It is based on a 20-year observational study of the inhabitants of Ambridge, a small village in the English county of Borsetshire. Specifically, it explores what may be termed an 'epidemiological anomaly' that appears to be unique to Ambridge and that may have valuable lessons for improving the metabolic health of the wider population.

Previous studies have established that, considering its size, Ambridge is a 'disproportionately risky place to live' (Bowman, 2017, p. 121), with a higher than average incidence of serious accidents and suicide (Stepney, 2011).

However, observation of the cohort suggests that when it comes to the incidence of chronic metabolic disorders, such as obesity and Type 2 diabetes, inhabitants of Ambridge are at considerably less risk than the population as a whole.

Research by Diabetes UK and the NHS shows the rapid growth of obesity and diabetes diagnoses in recent years. One quarter of UK adults are obese, and levels have trebled in a generation (NHS Choices, 2015). Approximately 3.5 million people have been diagnosed with diabetes, of which 95 per cent have Type 2 diabetes — an incidence that doubled between 1996 and 2016 (Diabetes UK, 2016).

The prevalence of obesity and Type 2 diabetes in the United Kingdom is often referred to in the popular press as an 'epidemic' or a 'time bomb'. Yet this phenomenon appears to have passed Ambridge by; in the observed cohort there is not a single known diagnosis of Type 2 diabetes. Indeed, it is believed that the only Ambridge inhabitant ever to have had diabetes was Walter Gabriel, whose favourite tipple, the oxymoronic 'diabetic beer', was stocked at The Bull. Mr Gabriel died in 1988 at the age of 92 (Davies, 2016).

There is also little evidence that obesity poses a threat to public health in Ambridge. It may be inferred — from his nickname 'Fat Paul' — that only one local individual is known for being significantly overweight, and even he is not an Ambridge resident.

This apparent absence of chronic metabolic disorders is even more remarkable when the age of the Ambridge cohort is considered. Age is a significant risk factor for developing obesity and Type 2 diabetes; research shows that prevalence rises sharply over the age of 40, with most cases occurring in the 60 to 80 age group (Diabetes UK, 2016).

A full demographic profile of the population of Ambridge is unfortunately not available. In its absence, analysis for this chapter has identified a cohort of 90 individuals whose birth years are known or can be guessed with reasonable confidence. This indicates that the Ambridge cohort has a median age of 50 (lower quartile: 29, upper quartile: 68) — considerably older than the population of the United Kingdom as a whole, which has a median age of 40 (lower quartile: 21; upper quartile: 58) (ONS, 2016).

When the dietary habits of this group are also taken into account, the absence of metabolic disorders looks not just unusual, but miraculous. The Ambridge cohort frequently consumes cake, sausages, cheese, pies, flapjacks and scones — all energy-dense foods, high in fat, sugar or salt, that are typically associated with the incidence of obesity and Type 2 diabetes.

So here we have it: *The Ambridge Paradox*. Despite an ageing population and a high intake of fat, sugar and salt, the Ambridge cohort shows a zero incidence of Type 2 diabetes.

The question arises: how can this observed phenomenon be explained? At this point, readers will no doubt call to mind the famous 'French paradox'. This term was first used in the 1980s to describe a similar anomaly — that although the typical French diet is high in fat, the incidence of coronary heart disease is relatively low.

In trying to explain this observation, researchers focused on other aspects of the French lifestyle, especially the consumption of red wine, as a mitigating factor against the development of heart disease (Simini, 2000).

Following the example of the French paradox, let us consider the elements of diet and lifestyle in Ambridge that may explain the robust metabolic health of this cohort, by acting as mitigating factors against their risk of developing obesity and Type 2 diabetes.

'GRAN'S FAMOUS LEMON DRIZZLE'

Anyone familiar with Ambridge will be aware of the important role that cake plays in village life. This reaches its peak at events such as the Flower and Produce Show and the village fete, where competitive cake-making is celebrated. But home-made cake is also eaten daily as a snack, accompanies nearly all informal gatherings and is used both to smooth the path of difficult social situations (i.e. as a 'peace offering') and to mark any occasion from a birthday to a wake.

It can therefore be assumed that the Ambridge cohort consumes far more cake than the approximate UK national average of 6 kg per head per year (Mintel, 2013; ONS, 2016). We can further infer that many Ambridge inhabitants are amongst the 5% of consumers who bake cakes several times a week, rather than the 49% who say they never bake (Statista.com, 2015). It will also be noted that lemon drizzle cake is especially popular, both for personal consumption and competitive display.

As stated at the outset of this chapter, this pattern of cake consumption is perhaps the most compelling dietary factor that may influence metabolic health in this cohort. It also shows the closest parallel to the French paradox. In that case, attention focused on resveratrol, a phenolic compound found in red grapes and therefore in red wine, as a mitigating factor against the unhealthy effects of dietary fat.

Studies reviewed by Rafiq et al. (2016) have established that phenolic compounds similar to those found in red wine are also present in zest extracted from lemon peel, which readers will recognise as a key ingredient in lemon drizzle cake.

And here, an intriguing possibility presents itself. Fukuchi et al. (2008) found that mice fed a high-energy diet supplemented with lemon zest did not gain weight, while a control group that consumed the same amount of calories without lemon zest gained weight as expected. This was attributed to the disruptive effects of phenolic compounds on fat cell metabolism.

Does this finding suggest that lemon drizzle cake could be a mitigating, or even a preventative factor in the development of metabolic disorders? If so, further study of the Ambridge cohort could lead to a major breakthrough in public health strategy.

'COFFEE? I'VE MADE A FRESH POT'

Regular observers of Ambridge will know that its residents are enthusiastic coffee drinkers. Coffee is drunk at all hours of the day and freshly brewed, which is generally higher in caffeine, is often chosen over instant, even on occasions when time is at a premium, such as at breakfast.

From this we can infer that coffee consumption in Ambridge is significantly higher than the UK average of 1.71 cups per day (Gimoka, 2015). Studies have shown that drinking around seven cups of coffee a day is strongly associated with a lower risk of Type 2 diabetes (van Dam & Feskens, 2002), which suggests that coffee consumption deserves further research as a mitigating dietary factor.

'ONLY SOUP AND A SANDWICH'

A bowl of home-made soup and a sandwich is a very popular lunch choice in Ambridge. It is often presented with an air of apology as if it is not a 'proper meal', but research suggests that nutritionally, it has nothing to apologise for.

Regular soup consumption has been shown to be associated with a reduced risk of overweight and obesity (Zhu & Hollis, 2013). Home-made soup using root vegetables, which is often eaten in Ambridge, also contains dietary fibre, as does bread, especially wholemeal varieties — although we cannot assume that all Ambridge residents favour wholemeal over the white sliced loaf.

Nonetheless, as we see from Kaline, Bornstein, Bergmann, Hauner, and Schwarz (2007), dietary fibre from wholegrains, vegetables and pulses has a preventative effect against glucose intolerance and its progression into Type 2 diabetes.

This suggests that frequent meals of soup and sandwiches may play an important role in metabolic health.

'I'VE BEEN BAKING ALL DAY …'

As we have already seen, Ambridge residents spend more time baking cakes than the UK average. But this also applies to the amount of time spent cooking at home in general. It is not unusual for women in this cohort to spend whole days in the kitchen, often engaged in high-energy activities such as hand-mixing puddings or making bread. On average, people in the United Kingdom spend 5.9 hours per week cooking (Statista, 2014). We can confidently estimate that Ambridge residents spend twice as long as this in the kitchen.

Activity analysis shows that a 150-pound woman expends approx. 140 calories per hour when cooking (MyFitnessPal, 2017). Consequently, we can estimate that the Ambridge cohort expends at least 800 more calories per week in food preparation than the general population. Since a typical home-made lemon drizzle cake contains 400 calories per slice

(Ramsay, 2007), this suggests that this cohort can consume two extra portions of cake per week without any metabolic effect whatsoever — and potentially, while benefiting from the 'prophylactic phenols' in their slice of lemon drizzle.

'I'M JUST ABOUT TO START ON LUNCH'

The preference of Ambridge residents for home cooking rather than relying on pre-prepared meals may in itself be a mitigating factor against their above-average consumption of cake. Research by Tiwari, Aggarwal, Tang, and Drewnowski (2017) has shown that the diets of people who eat home-cooked meals on most days of the week are more likely to meet healthy-eating guidelines than those who often eat out. Conversely, people who eat more than one or two takeaway meals per week that are high in calories, fat and salt increase their risk of developing obesity or Type 2 diabetes, according to public health specialists (National Charity Partnership, 2017).

With no fast-food outlets within walking distance, the Ambridge cohort has historically had little access to takeaway meals. In recent years however, the growth of home delivery services has led to an increase in availability, and choices such as pizza and Indian meals have become more popular, especially with younger residents. It is to be hoped that this will not be to the detriment of their future metabolic health.

'SUPPER'S ON THE TABLE'

Another noteworthy aspect of meal-time behaviour in Ambridge is that meals are frequently eaten at the table, where family members converse with each other rather than using electronic devices. This is in contrast to a survey (Red

Tractor, 2013) that found that six out of ten family meals in the United Kingdom are eaten in front of the TV. A relevant point here is that Ambridge residents are extremely light consumers of media, showing little or no interest in, or awareness of, television or radio programmes. While this may limit their value as members of a pub quiz team, it may well benefit their metabolic health. A study by Tumin and Anderson (2017) found that families who frequently ate home-cooked meals and switched off the TV when eating them were significantly less likely to be obese than those who usually ate while distracted by a screen. However, this study does not consider the nature of meal-time conversations. Close observation of the Ambridge cohort might reveal, for example, whether an amicable chat or an awkward confrontation about a family member's choice of partner has a better physiological outcome.

'I'VE STARTED ANOTHER BATCH OF BORSETSHIRE BLUE'

The role of dairy products — especially full-fat varieties — in the diet often provokes controversy amongst nutritionists. As Borsetshire is traditionally a dairy farming area, we can assume that Ambridge residents consume at least the average amount of dairy products per year. We can also infer that they often eat full-fat cheese, yogurt and ice cream, as an artisan producer has a thriving business in the village. Bridge Farm's Borsetshire Blue and Sterling Gold cheeses have won awards at regional food events.

Research by Ericson et al. (2015) has found that regular consumption of full-fat cheese and yogurt may reduce the risk of developing Type 2 diabetes by more than 20%. This seems counter-intuitive, but Ericson et al. suggest that the particular type of saturated fatty acids found in high-fat cheese may have a preventative effect. As blue cheese and Cheddar-type cheeses are high-fat varieties, this suggests that they may well have a role as mitigating factors in the Ambridge cohort's diet.

'RACE YOU TO THE TOP OF LAKEY HILL!'

The local beauty spot known as Lakey Hill is a cultural as well as a geographical landmark in Ambridge. It is often the site of significant conversations or encounters, especially of the romantic kind. Indeed, 'to be taken up Lakey Hill' is a rite of passage for many young people in the village.

At first sight, the presence of Lakey Hill promises to be quite a powerful mitigating factor against cake consumption, because living at altitude is linked to a lower risk of metabolic disorders, as Lopez-Pascual et al. (2017) have shown.

However, the research notes that the benefits of high-altitude living are observed at 1500 feet or more above sea level, whereas Lakey Hill is only 771 feet high, rendering this a less fruitful avenue for study than might have been hoped for.

'I JUST POPPED ROUND ...'

A further aspect of the Ambridge lifestyle that should be considered here is Non-Exercise Activity Thermogenesis, known as NEAT. This is defined as the amount of energy expended on everyday tasks, not including sports.

Levine (2002) notes that agricultural and manual workers have high NEAT, which is clearly relevant to the Ambridge cohort, where a significant number of residents are involved in the farming industry. However, the culture of NEAT runs more deeply in Ambridge than in many similar communities.

We have already observed that Ambridge residents spend more time on NEAT devoted to cooking than the national average. They also have a preference for intensive and competitive gardening, which is beyond the scope of this study.

However, one activity that no observer of Ambridge can fail to notice is the amount of energy expended in unnecessary walking. The Ambridge postman is redundant as birthday cards are always delivered by hand. Messages that could be texted or emailed are always relayed face to face. Villagers seem unfamiliar with the concept of 'phoning ahead' to check whether a neighbour is at home, so often have fruitless journeys that expose them to unwanted encounters with people they were trying to avoid. And residents quite often walk long distances just to ask when a relative will be home for supper or if they would like a coffee.

All this casual activity may not contribute to the efficiency of village life, but it may well have a positive effect on residents' metabolic health. Levine (2002) has found that people who live in a culture where NEAT is the norm tend to be leaner than those who are more sedentary, and that NEAT may be a key factor in helping to maintain and reduce body weight. This certainly seems to be the case in Ambridge.

'LISTEN TO THAT DAWN CHORUS!'

As may be expected in farming country, the Ambridge cohort tends to be early risers. Those who work with livestock have no choice, and family members who support them also get up early to provide breakfast and prepare for the day. Many villagers enjoy activities that involve an early start, such as bird-watching, while the lack of late-night entertainment in the village also contributes to a culture of 'early to bed and early to rise'.

Maukonen et al. (2017) examined the food choices of groups of 'early birds' and 'night owls'. They found that people who stay up late and have a lie-in tend to eat less protein overall, and eat more sugar in the morning and more sugary and fatty foods in the evening, while those who get up early and go to bed early tend to make healthier food choices throughout the day.

It appears that living in a culture where early rising is the norm may have a beneficial effect on the metabolic health of the Ambridge cohort.

DISCUSSION: THE AMBRIDGE EATWELL PLATE?

To return to the question we posed at the beginning of this chapter: what lessons for public health can we draw from *The Ambridge Paradox*? So far we have observed that the Ambridge cohort presents an epidemiological anomaly. Available evidence suggests that this ageing population, with some very questionable dietary habits, should be at high risk of obesity and Type 2 diabetes. Yet we see hardly any evidence of obesity, and no incidence of Type 2 diabetes, in this group.

In attempting to explain this anomaly, which we term *The Ambridge Paradox*, we have noted the population's above-average consumption of cake, and made the ground-breaking suggestion that lemon drizzle cake in particular may have a preventative effect against metabolic disorders, rather than contributing to them. We have further examined other components of the Ambridge diet, and lifestyle habits such as unnecessary walking, competitive cooking, early rising, eating family meals and avoiding television. Although it has not been possible to explore all of the potential variables and confounding factors that may affect the cohort's metabolic health, it seems that some tentative conclusions can be drawn from the evidence available.

Research so far suggests there is merit in replacing the current dietary guidelines with a new Eatwell Plate, incorporating the entire Ambridge cohort's preferred food groups, namely cake (specifically lemon drizzle, but including flapjacks and scones), cheese, soup, coffee and sandwiches. Thought should also be given to introducing a new version of the well-known slogan '5 a day', referring not to portions of fruit and vegetables, but to slices of lemon drizzle cake. It will be noted that while the proposed new Eatwell Plate is somewhat unorthodox, the Ambridge lifestyle habits that have been observed as possible mitigating factors have been widely researched and are generally accepted as making a positive contribution to public health.

It is also worth considering that there is more to health than simply the absence of illness. If the public as a whole were to take the dietary patterns of Ambridge as a model and eschew fruit and vegetables in favour of cake and cheese, it would be reasonable to expect a noticeable improvement in the national mood and sense of wellbeing.

REFERENCES

Bowman, D. (2017). From Dr Locke's boundaries to Carol's confession: On medical ethics in The Archers. In C. Courage, N. Headlam, & P. Matthews (Eds.), *The Archers in Fact and Fiction* (pp. 121–128). Peter Lang.

Davies, K. (2016). In H. Niklaus (Ed.), *The Archers: The official calendar*. Danilo Promotions Ltd.

Diabetes UK. (2016). Prevalence of diabetes. Facts and Stats. Diabetes UK. October, pp. 2–4. Retrieved from

https://www.diabetes.org.uk/Documents/Position%
20statements/DiabetesUK_Facts_Stats_Oct16.pdf

Ericson, U., Hellstrand, S., Brunkwall, L., Schulz, C.-A.,
Sonestedt, E., Wallstrøm, P. ... Orho-Melander, M. (2015).
Food sources of fat may clarify the inconsistent role of
dietary fat intake for incidence of type 2 diabetes. *American
Journal of Clinical Diabetes*. April. doi:10.3945/
ajcn.114.103010

Fukuchi, Y., Okada, M., Hayashi, S., Nabeno, Y., Osawa,
T., & Naito, M. (2008). Lemon polyphenols suppress
diet-induced obesity by up-regulation of mRNA levels of
the enzymes involved in β-oxidation in mouse white adipose
tissue. *Journal of Clinical Biochemical Nutrition*, *43*(3),
201–209. doi:10.3164/jcbn.2008066

Gimoka. (2015). *Coffee in the UK infographic*. Gimoka Coffee
UK. December 28. Retrieved from http://www.gcoffeepod.
com/en/coffee-news/11_coffee-in-the-uk-infographic

Hodgekiss, A. (2012). Does eating chocolate make you
clever? *Mail Online*. November 21. Retrieved from http://
www.dailymail.co.uk/health/article-2235932/Does-eating-
chocolate-make-clever-New-research-suggests-help-win-
Nobel-prize-.html

Howarth, M., & Adams, S. (2017). Now scientists say fizzy
water makes us fat. *Mail Online*. May 16. Retrieved from
http://www.dailymail.co.uk/health/article.../Now-scientists-
say-fizzy-WATER-makes-fat.html

Kaline, K., Bornstein, S. R., Bergmann, A., Hauner, H., &
Schwarz, P. E. (2007). The importance and effect of dietary
fiber in diabetes prevention with particular consideration
of whole grain products. *Hormone and Metabolic Research*,
39(9), 687–693.

Levine, J. A. (2002). Non-exercise activity thermogenesis (NEAT). *Best Practice & Research, Clinical Endocrinology and Metabolism, 16*(4), 679–702.

Lopez-Pascual, A., Bes-Rastrollo, M., Sayón-Orea, C., Perez-Cornago, A., Díaz-Gutiérrez, J., Pons, J. J., ... Alfredo Martínez, J. A. (2017). Living at a geographically higher elevation is associated with lower risk of metabolic syndrome: Prospective analysis of the SUN cohort. *Frontiers in Physiology*, 7. doi:10.3389/fphys.2016.00658

Maukonen, M., Kanerva, N., Partonen, T., Kronholm, E., Tapanainen, H., Kontto, J., & Mannisto, S. (2017). Chronotype differences in timing of energy and macronutrient intakes: A population-based study in adults. *Obesity, 25*(3), 608–615. doi:10.1002/oby.21747

Mintel. (2013). *Small cakes are the icing on the UK cake market: Volume sales of small cakes overtake large cakes.* June 12. Retrieved from http://www.mintel.com/press-centre/food-and-drink/uk-cakes-market-trend

MyFitnessPal. (2017). *Calories burned from cooking or food preparation.* Retrieved from http://www.myfitnesspal.com/exercise/calories-burned/cooking-or-food-preparation-47

National Charity Partnership. (2017). *'Takeaway culture putting families' health at risk.* April 5. Retrieved from http://tescocharitypartnership.org.uk/about/news/article/takeaway-culture-putting-families-health-at-risk

NHS Choices. (2015). *Britain: 'The fat man of Europe'.* Retrieved from http://www.nhs.uk/Livewell/loseweight/Pages/statistics-and-causes-of-the-obesity-epidemic-in-the-UK.aspx

ONS. (2016). *Overview of the UK population: February 2016.* Office for National Statistics. Retrieved from

https://www.ons.gov.uk/peoplepopulationandcommunity/
populationandmigration/populationestimates/articles/
overviewoftheukpopulation/february2016

Rafiq, S., Kaul, R., Sofi, S. A., Bashir, N., Nazir, F., &
Nayik, G. A. (2016). Citrus peel as a source of functional
ingredient: A review. *Journal of the Saudi Society of
Agricultural Sciences*. in press. doi:10.1016/j.
jssas.2016.07.006

Ramsay, T. (2007). *Lemon drizzle cake*. BBC Good Food.
Retrieved from https://www.bbcgoodfood.com/recipes/
4942/lemon-drizzle-cake

Red Tractor. (2013). *Research reveals that Britain is a nation
of dinner table dodgers*. Retrieved from http://www.redtractor.
org.uk/media/news/research-reveals-that-britain-is-a-nation-of-
dinner-table-dodgers

Simini, B. (2000). Serge Renaud: from French paradox to
Cretan miracle. *Lancet*, *355*, 9197. doi:10.1016/S0140-6736
(05)71990-5

Statista. (2014). *Number of hours spent cooking per week
among consumers worldwide, by country*. June. Retrieved
from https://www.statista.com/statistics/420719/time-spent-
cooking-per-week-among-consumers-by-country/

Statista. (2015). *Frequency of baking at home in Great
Britain*. Retrieved from https://www.statista.com/statistics/
303158/frequency-of-baking-from-scratch-great-britain-uk/

Stepney, R. (2011). A series of unfortunate events? Morbidity
and mortality in a Borsetshire village. *BMJ*, *343*, d7518.
doi:https://doi.org/10.1136/bmj.d7518

Tiwari, A., Aggarwal, A., Tang, W., & Drewnowski, A.
(2017). Cooking at home: A strategy to comply with

U.S. dietary guidelines at no extra cost. *American Journal of Preventive Medicine*, *52*(5), 616–624. doi:10.1016/j.amepre.2017.01.017

Tumin, R., & Anderson, S. E. (2017). Television, home-cooked meals, and family meal frequency: Associations with adult obesity. *Journal of the Academy of Nutrition and Dietetics*. in press. doi:10.1016/j/jand.2017.01.009

van Dam, R. M., & Feskens, E. J. M. (2002). Coffee consumption and risk of type 2 diabetes mellitus. *Lancet*, *360*: 1477–1478.

Zhu, Y., & Hollis, J. H. (2013). Soup consumption is associated with a reduced risk of overweight and obesity but not metabolic syndrome in US adults: NHANES 2003–2006. *PLoS ONE*, *8*(9), e75630. doi:10.1371/journal.pone.0075630

PEER REVIEW BY CHRISTINE BARFORD, THE LODGE, AMBRIDGE, BORSETSHIRE

As one of the keen bakers of Ambridge I'm thrilled to learn that my 'offerings', as my friend Peggy calls them, don't seem to be causing any ill effects and might even be good for you.

I hadn't realised that lemon zest was such a healthy ingredient, and perhaps now I'll add it to more of my recipes. Peggy will be happy to test them for me; my ginger and basil scones left her quite speechless, I remember. I must confess to a naughty habit though. If I burnt a cake, I'd mix it up with cat food and slip it into Bill's dinner. Peggy couldn't work out why he got so portly, and I couldn't bring herself to tell her, especially after he was killed so tragically. But I've learned my lesson. Peggy's new cat, Hilda Ogden, won't get a bite — not that she'll let me near her. Lively little thing.

I've always thought that people in Ambridge eat quite healthily; it's how our parents brought us up. And of course in the war, there wasn't very much to go round. I was 12 before I saw my first banana! I think of it every time I make my signature banana and Marmite muffins.

This research will definitely encourage me to do more baking and try more adventurous recipes. I see that blue cheese is also a healthy ingredient; I'm sure it would go really well in my cinnamon teacakes …

SECTION TWO

EDUCATING AMBRIDGE

CHAPTER FOUR

AMBRIDGE AS METAPHOR: SHARING THE MISSION AND VALUES OF A 21ST-CENTURY LIBRARY

Madeleine Lefebvre

ABSTRACT

21st-century libraries are a community hub, providing entertainment, learning, information sharing and idea incubation. A place for all, they can be a locus for activism and the civil society. In an era when UK public libraries are under threat, the interwoven stories of Ambridge promote those values. In the Big Society, volunteers were to fill the roles of library professionals. Ambridge too has its many volunteers yet recognises the rightful place of trained professionals.

Keywords: Public libraries; volunteers; professionals

As a university chief librarian and a trustee of a public library, I have been struck by how many elements of a modern library have echoes in Ambridge, home of *The Archers*, and decided to explore these links. I began my study by searching for references to libraries and librarians in *The Archers*. In *The Archers Miscellany* (Toye, 2010) we are reminded that in 1982, a mobile library came to Ambridge bi-weekly, alternating with stops in Penny Hassett. The librarian always ate lunch in The Bull. Toye also told us that Shula Hebden-Lloyd 'seriously considered becoming a librarian' (Toye, 2010). More recently, Bert Fry referred to a poetry contest at the Borchester Library, which he was planning to enter.

Public libraries today have expanded far beyond places to check out novels and non-fiction. They have become community hubs. They often provide entertainment for all ages. They are places for learning, information sharing, and collaboration. They are a place for knowledge transfer and idea incubation, especially with the growth of makerspaces. Bookable public meeting rooms in the Library are often the focus of activism and the civil society since they are common spaces open to all. Most have coffee shops or cafes either in the Library or nearby. Moreover, since they are places that foster the meeting of minds, they are often the catalysts for romance.

If we look at Ambridge as a community hub, there are several examples where the villagers meet socially or for a specific societal purpose. The village shop, for example, is the locus of much information sharing and debate. The Bull is an obvious place for socialising or for gathering to analyse the cricket team's performance and strategy (the cricket ground itself is another community-gathering place). The village hall hosts meetings but was itself a catalyst that brought the community together for rebuilding after the flood. St Stephen's Church isn't just a place of worship, either: it is an essential community refuge in difficult times. The farm shop serves to link the general populace of Ambridge and visitors with the core occupation of the village — farming.

Entertainment can be found in many forms and many locales in Ambridge. The Bull's landlords are entertainers themselves: Jolene is a country singer, Kenton Archer is the stalwart of every pantomime, while Jolene Archer's daughter Fallon Rogers, although she has branched out beyond The Bull, is also a singer. Every public library keeps a calendar of events, and so it is with *The Archers*. The annual pantomime and the turning on of the lights around the village green are highlights of the Christmas season. The spring and summer calendar has the cricket fixtures and the village fête, while at the end of the season is the Flower and Produce Show, sure to be the subject of much intrigue and disagreement. The harvest festival and supper is an opportunity to bring the community together to celebrate the fruits of the farmers' labour. In November, Ambridge celebrates Guy Fawkes Night, and the bonfire on the village green, which is itself a focus of the community. Although not strictly in Ambridge, Loxfest at Loxley Hall was an ambitious undertaking that led to major storylines.

Learning, information sharing and collaboration are hallmarks of modern libraries. These elements are clearly in evidence in Ambridge society. For example, the farmers lend one another specialized equipment, and often lend a hand at drilling or harvest time. They provide and seek advice from one another. Open Farm Sunday allows them to give the general population insight into what farming entails. It could be argued that village shop manager Susan Carter, referred to by Alistair Lloyd in a 2017 episode as 'the village radio', considers information sharing her calling. In his keynote address to the 2015 Conference of the Chartered Institute of Library and Information Professionals, Lankes stated 'To be … a librarian is to be someone who believes they can change the world for better through knowledge'. Could this describe Susan's motivation? Retired professor Jim Lloyd is a walking reference library, always willing to share his knowledge, while Lynda Snell is a natural leader and force for learning in Ambridge. She is the driver of the Christmas pantomime and other events, and she is well versed in Council issues and bylaws. Many libraries provide online training through the Lynda.com platform — is the same, unusual spelling of Lynda significant?

Libraries are a focus for knowledge transfer and idea incubation. Many examples of these activities can be found in the Ambridge community. The Flower and Produce Show leads to both collaborative and competitive activities. Christine Barford valiantly tries to create the perfect scone, while Jill Archer bakes and bakes … and bakes. Carol Tregorran creates wine and herbal teas. The Grundys have developed their cider and encourage others to sample their various brews in their cider hut. Helen Archer is known for her yoghurt and Borsetshire Blue cheese. Makerspaces are becoming a feature of larger public libraries: they provide the tools to enable individuals to develop their creativity, ingenuity and fabrication skills. In Ambridge, Bert Fry created the egg mobile from an old caravan, Eddie Grundy built a shepherd's hut for Lynda from old bits and pieces of scrap and Toby Fairbrother created his gin still.

Activism and the civil society have their place in the library and feature in Ambridge. In the past, Tom Archer led the GM protests, while Lynda and some members of the Archer family worked to oppose Berrow Farm's anaerobic digester and Damara Capital's Route B proposals. Eating places abound in Ambridge and environs: Bridge Farm Café, Grey Gables and Lower Loxley. However, many conversations and plot drivers happen over tea, coffee and meals in residents' kitchens and dining rooms as well. Libraries are also documented as places for the meeting of like minds and romance (Lefebvre, 2005). Romance — some more successful than others — is a constant thread in Ambridge. Where there is a dichotomy between Ambridge and UK public libraries is in the role of volunteers versus professionals. Ambridge residents have a strong volunteer ethos, yet they value the expertise of trained professionals. Some examples are the vets, Alistair Lloyd and Anisha Jayacody, Usha Franks the lawyer, Richard Locke the doctor and the many trained farmers. Note how the residents scoff at amateurs such as Toby.

In recent years UK public libraries have been under threat, as some Councils divert funding from libraries and close them in favour of 'community libraries' run by volunteers (Ballinger, 2017). This approach appears to be a holdover from the Cameron government's Big Society. The underlying and erroneous message is that libraries are little more than shelves of old books that can be run like a charity shop. There is little understanding of the essential community role that libraries play. Nor is there recognition that librarians are trained professionals who — like the professionals of Ambridge — shouldn't be replaced by well-meaning volunteers.

REFERENCES

Ballinger, L. (2017, February 6). *One in 10 Welsh libraries run by volunteers*. Retrieved from http://www.bbc.com/news/uk-wales-38742310

Lankes, R. D. (2015). Keynote address. *Chartered Institute of Library and Information Professionals conference*.

Lefebvre, M. (2005). *The romance of libraries*. Lanham, MD: Scarecrow Press, Inc.

Toye, J. (2010). *The Archers miscellany: The first official trivia collection from Britain's best-loved radio drama*. London: BBC Books.

CHAPTER FIVE

WE DON'T NEED NO EDUCATION? THE ABSENCE OF PRIMARY EDUCATION IN *THE ARCHERS*

Grant Bage and Jane Turner

ABSTRACT

The primary school in any rural village is a significant and vivid institution. Its classrooms, playground, buses, staffroom, governing body, PTA committee, religious celebrations, educational visits and community events are a focus not just for village pride but for parental and social aspirations and tensions. Village schools are special local spaces, in which the bite is keenly felt of national education policies. They are sources and sites of friendships, rivalries and divisions amongst both children and adults; places where celebrations and disappointments occur on a daily basis; an important local employer and reliant on a range of committed volunteers. Village schools are genuinely lively and dramatic places.

But not in The Archers. *The mostly invisible children of Ambridge simply board a bus to Loxley Barrett aged five, then mysteriously alight aged 11 at Borchester Green or the fee-paying Cathedral School. During those primary years Ambridge's children, parents and listeners seem blissfully unaffected by tests, snow, bullying, crazes, curriculum change, poor teachers, brilliant teaching assistants, academisation, Ofsted inspections, fussy governors, budget crises or any other rural educational reality.*

In this chapter we consider why primary education, a topic that dominates the lives and conversations of real village families from all backgrounds, seems to be of such insignificance to the inhabitants of Ambridge?

Keywords: Children; education; primary; school; village

INTRODUCTION

In 1891 the British parliament legislated to ensure that every child in England would receive free and compulsory education between the ages of five and ten. It was a political, legislative acknowledgement that the world had changed. A modern nation needed its masses to be educated, and that process started with primary schooling. Sixty years and two world wars later *The Archers* was conceived. As a radio soap opera it was hoped that it might play a different, but similarly modernising, mass educational role. For security and geopolitical reasons and as the Cold War threatened to heat up, Britain needed to maximise its self-sufficiency in food. Radio stories of everyday rural folk might just play their part in achieving that strategic aim, both by inspiring country-dwellers to produce more food and by informing the urban majority about how that was done.

Since 1891 primary schools have been ubiquitous in British rural and urban life, and since 1951 *The Archers* has become a staple of the British Broadcasting Corporation (BBC). Nearly seven decades later, how has the relationship between those primary-educated masses, the village of Ambridge and its characters developed? Such a question is of broader cultural significance than as a mere corner in listeners' imaginations, or as a footnote in the fantasy that is our favourite radio village. For as this 2014 Church of England report expounded:

> *It is a commonly-held view that having a school within a village strengthens and enhances the community ... The school is one of the state's last remaining structural points of contact with rural communities. (Church of England National Education Office, 2014, p. 6)*

Does that hold true in Ambridge?

PRIMARY EDUCATION IN ENGLAND

Since 1891 primary education has been a standard ingredient of English childhoods: by 2017 there were over 4.5 million children in English state-funded primary schools (DfE, 2016b), numbers that currently increase each year.

Children arrive in English primary schools following what is termed the Foundation Stage. Between the ages of three and five education is provided in many different forms, but thereafter the educational experience of children and their families becomes increasingly standardised. State school pupils attend school for six to seven hours a day, 38–40 weeks a year. In primary education the major goals are achieving basic literacy and numeracy for all pupils, as well as establishing foundations in science and other subjects. Children's entitlement to learning was statutorily outlined in the primary National Curriculum, introduced in 1988 to ensure pupils in state schools received a broad and balanced education. The current primary curriculum for English primary schools consequently includes Information Technology, Religious Education Design and Technology, History, Geography, Art, Music and Physical Education, as well as the core subjects of English, Mathematics and Science. Children are assessed in the core subjects at the ages of seven and eleven.

As well as fulfilling a vital and standardising educative role on an individual and national level, primary schools in England also play a major and communal part in spiritual, moral, social and cultural development. Within their primary schools children are encouraged to learn how to make friends, how to collaborate, to tolerate, to compete and to share. They develop independence and agency. Primary schools develop social capital, by strengthening and enhancing communities. They provide a local focal point where children grow up, families meet and joint activities take place. Primary school parents raise funds, listen to children read, help with cookery, art and PE, compete and encourage at sports days, govern, attend school plays and assemblies and chat amongst themselves at the school gate. Many are employed as teachers, teaching assistants, mid-day meal supervisors, cooks, cleaners and administrators. Most primary school buildings are used for a wide range of other purposes beyond the school day: pupil discos, adult quiz nights, community meetings, faith and flower arranging classes, as polling stations and for sports, recreation and community fund-raising events.

Over the last 150 years primary education has, gradually but steadily, come to play a major role in social, cultural, and economic urban and rural life in England. The amount of money spent on primary education in England has increased massively and is now over 25 billion pounds per year (Chantrill, 2017). During the last decade, as the number of primary school-aged children has risen but school budgets have come under growing pressure and scrutiny, outcomes from and inputs into English primary schools have also become matters of heightened political profile and contention. As expenditure has tightened in the face of national financial austerity, buildings have still had to be maintained or renewed, teachers' salaries paid, teaching resources bought and children kept safe. Increasing and pressurising public demands have still had to be met from politicians, industry, inspectors, communities and parents, all anxious to see children learn and achieve more. Sometimes those demands have been measured and mediated through supposed national calibrations of academic achievement in subjects, via the construction of school league tables; and at other times through the setting for individual children of more ambitious developmental, behavioural, physical, linguistic and social targets for improvement.

Whatever the final expression of the country's educational anxieties, national and local political intervention in primary education became commonplace after the 1988 introduction of the national curriculum. Political parties have on occasions used state primary schools as an ideological playground: and successive national governments have accordingly changed curriculum content, increased accountability demands and imposed different inspection frameworks. Education has become a key area of political contention, with parties' proposals and promises about organisation, class size, selection, sex education, special educational needs, testing and school meals, to name but a few, offered to the electorate in return for votes. Such issues are discussed in local and national newspapers, hustings on actual and metaphorical door steps, at elections and regularly in between.

Yet for the most part, they are rarely discussed in Ambridge. Indeed for some aspects of the above, never in Ambridge. As we will explore in the rest of this chapter, the fictional community of Ambridge is currently and educationally, a rather strange place.

PRIMARY EDUCATION IN AMBRIDGE

It hasn't always been like that. For a brief spell during the late 1960s and early 1970s Ambridge witnessed an extended episode of radical social engagement with education. In 1969 Jill Archer, who, to this day, has consistently been the only voice in Ambridge for universal educational entitlement, decided to stand for the Rural District Council and campaign against the threatened closure of Ambridge village school. Much to her surprise she was elected, but threats to the school persisted. In early summer of 1971 there was a new proposal to close the school, sparking several protest meetings, before another reprieve. In June 1973 Jill and the rest of the village heard that Ambridge's primary school was finally to close; and from then on Ambridge became part of Loxley Barrett School's catchment area.

How Ambridge children were subsequently transported to the neighbouring village does not appear to be documented, though the 'school bus drop off and pickup' is now part of the Ambridge village timetable. Interestingly, the use of the Ambridge School building post 1973 is unclear at best. According to the 1975 map of Ambridge (Gallagher, 1975) the school was between the village shop and St Stephen's church. A more recent map (Moore & Bedow, 2000) shows 'the surgery' in this location. Yet as has been noted elsewhere (Perkins, 2017), property size and location in Ambridge is not always fixed. In the intervening years after its closure, this covetable piece of Ambridge real estate mysteriously disappeared, despite being potentially ripe for domestic conversion. Around the same time both Woodbine and Honeysuckle Cottage also apparently changed their locations.

Back in the real world, subsequent decades saw a patchwork of local government proposals for what amounted to further significant closures of small English rural schools. Often these generated vociferous responses in local communities and sometimes even in national media. A 2008 article in the *Daily Telegraph* entitled 'Without a school, a village won't live long' saw Rowan Pelling claim that:

> *Anyone who has attended a village primary school can tell you that the institution is integral to the healthy pulse of rural life. A village without a pub or post office is limping along, but one without a playground ringing with children's laughter is in its death throes. (Pelling, 2008)*

Meanwhile, since 1973 the village of Ambridge has continued to thrive, despite the absence of Pelling's playground sound track; although in 2001 there was another brief foray into arguments about educational provision. At around that time the BBC's scriptwriters responded (as claimed by its members at least) to the provocations of an *Archers* online forum:

> *... it is good to see the script writers follow our advice (of some months ago) and bring the local school into the picture a bit more. We had been saying we didn't hear enough about school and its social influence in the village. (Clarke, 2001)*

The resultant storyline postulated the potential merger of five village schools, including Loxley Barrett, with Hollerton

Primary School. Lynda Snell, Siobhan Hathaway and Pat Archer were highly audible in Ambridge's campaign to lobby the Local Educational Authority, the District Council and the County Council. That campaign was supported by Archers' David and Ruth, Shula Hebden-Lloyd and Kathy Perks, along with Brian Aldridge's tractor driver and 'those people from Glebelands'. Despite a major confusion in the campaigners' understanding of how state education is managed (a District Council hasn't any authority when it comes to education and the County Council is the Local Education Authority), the Ambridge campaign was success- ful. Educational arguments prevailed over social concerns and financial pressures. Luckily Loxley Barrett had the better Ofsted inspection report and so was saved. Interestingly though, less than 12 months later the school's Ofsted rating was cited by Brian and Jennifer Aldridge as one of the rea- sons for moving eight-year-old Ruari away from his village friends at Loxley Barrett, to a distant boarding school. There, at least (Radio 4 listeners could now sleep easy) the young Ruari would be made to complete all his homework.

The closure of Ambridge's village school over 40 years ago and the subsequent threat to Loxley Barrett in 2001 were authentic script lines. They reflected similar changes and the sporadic but continuing loss of primary schools, in the real English villages that Ambridge in the noughties was designed to mirror (Todman, Harris, Carter, & McCamphill, 2009). Since those two forays, there has been little primary educa- tion action in Ambridge. Yet the pressures on rural primary schools have continued to grow (CoE, 2014 op. cit.; Hill, Kettlewell, & Salt, 2014). These and a host of other 'real world facts' make the primary educational aspects of current Ambridge life now appear dangerously inauthentic.

Each year, for example, the English government's Depart- ment for Education publishes detailed figures about the school workforce employed in English state-funded compulsory education. The June 2016 report described three main groups of school employees:

- The equivalent of 457,000 full-time teachers, just over half of whom were in primary or (far fewer) nursery schools.

- As well as teachers, the report describes how schools also employed the equivalent of 263,000 full-time teaching assistants, 174,500 of whom worked in primary or nursery schools.

- There was in 2015–2016 the equivalent of 238,000 other full-time members of staff working in English schools as caretakers, cleaners, administrators, receptionists, managers, receptionists and in other miscellaneous roles. Of these 105,000 were in primary or nursery schools (DfE, 2016c, p. 5).

In terms of gender balance, at the time of writing, four out of every five English state school employees are female; a figure which tends to be even higher in the primary sector where for example 85% of teachers (approximately 195,000 full time equivalents) are women (*ibid.*). Given these proportions there at least 419,000 full-time equivalent female employees working in English nursery or primary schools; although the number of individual women in that workforce is actually far higher, for we know from other government statistics (Office for National Statistics, 2016) that at least 40% of the UK's 14.5 million working women, do so on a part-time basis (for men the equivalent proportion is around 13% working part-time). We do not know, because the statistics are not compiled in that way, exactly how many individual women earn their living in English state-funded primary or nursery schools. Yet, if there are at least 419,000 female full-time equivalents, and an average of 40% of women work on a part-time basis, then by any means of calculation there are well over half a million individual women working in that sector.

Which makes it slightly odd, to say the least, that in Ambridge there are none: full-time, part-time or any-time the primary school employee figure is still a fat (or should that be a thin), zero. Not only does Ambridge's female workforce boast a statistically unlikely absence of anybody paid to do something in a primary or nursery school; nobody in Ambridge even volunteers for the same. Although accurate and up-to-date figures are hard to arrive at, in 2014 there were approximately 300,000 volunteers needed for English primary and secondary school governorships alone (Richardson, 2014). That figure excludes all the other volunteers who helped with school reading, sports, music, paint pot-washing, gardening, visits, fund raising or other general duties.

In Ambridge volunteering is generally embraced. Kirsty Miller does it for the wildlife trust, David for the National Farmers Union, Shula for the church and Lynda, rather promiscuously, does it for practically everything else. Hayley Tucker, previously a nanny, did lead sporadic school visits to Lower Loxley Hall before she moved to Birmingham. But as of May 2017 who in Ambridge works in or volunteers for education? Once again, it is the blind-eyed zero. Indeed amongst Ambridge inhabitants the only paid or voluntary educators and helpers are has-beens. Jim Lloyd used to be a professor of classical history, and Kathy used to be a teacher of secondary domestic science. Both have now thought better of it, opting for alternative sources of income and job satisfaction. Following retirement Jim is a volunteer in the village shop, a highly competitive ornithologist and a general genius at crosswords. Kathy now earns her metaphorical corn as an employee at the Grey Gables health club; a venue mercifully clear of adolescents who on the whole, Kathy discovered, were not that bothered about cooking.

EDUCATIONAL INAUTHENTICITY IN AMBRIDGE

Primary education in *The Archers* has two purposes and both are dramatic, rather than educationally authentic. Indeed authenticity is often a casualty of these dramatic ends. Loxley Barrett school's failure to follow statutory safeguarding procedures (DfE, 2016a) during 2016, for example, allowed estranged and strange-looking step-father Rob Titchener to talk regularly to Henry through the playground fence. This breach of legal care requirements caused consternation to primary education-savvy correspondents to Mumsnet and the national press. How the school was getting away with neglecting the safety and wellbeing of a vulnerable and traumatised child? Throughout Helen Archer and Rob's nationally gripping coercive control storyline the role of Henry's local schooling was never to offer the support or guidance to the family, that an actual English primary school would almost certainly have done. Rather (and perhaps inauthentically) the school provided a mere backdrop against which Rob could further undermine Helen (Henry's missing reading books, not being allowed to collect him from school), or as a pretext to explore Henry's understandable behavioural problems, also simplistically blamed on Helen. So much for the (conspicuously absent) nurturing skills of Loxley Barrett as a small village school: despite such skills regularly being hailed in real small village school prospectuses, which typically portray themselves as organisations in which each child and family is individually known and cared for.

The Helen and Rob storyline also demonstrated the other dramatic use of primary education in *The Archers*: to reinforce character traits, especially those influenced by class. Rob and Ursula Titchener's scheming to send Henry to board at Rob's old prep school not only showed their joint desire to damage the relationship between Henry and Helen but also served as grandparental reinforcement of the snobbery and distaste that Rob himself showed towards Emma Grundy's 'working class brats'. This use of primary education choice as a class identifier and divide had been used previously, for example when Brian and Jennifer assumed that Ruari would go to private school. The only question they seriously considered was whether he should be a day boy or a boarder. Nor did either parent see any need to talk about Ruari's future educational needs with his current teacher at Loxley Barrett. Instead, educational expertise was sought from someone considered to be of an equivalent social standing as the Aldridges, namely Elizabeth Pargetter of Lower Loxley Hall. Rather ironically of course, as a teenager Elizabeth had been expelled from her own independent secondary school.

The Archers is a radio drama that, despite having officially lost its original agricultural educational purpose in 1972, still prides itself on its research and accurate reflections of real rural life (BBC, 2017). So why does it present such an inadequate and inauthentic picture of children's education, in contemporary rural communities? One potential answer lies in pragmatics. Child actors are time consuming to work with and difficult to script. It is sometimes opined that the animals in *The Archers* sound more genuine than its children. For example, few real five year olds invariably answer 'all right then mummy' when told to put away their toys. Perhaps such compliant infant diction is part legacy from the show's original and rather po-faced 1950s public educational mission? If so, and being well into a new millennium, it could now be varied. Contemporary scriptwriters can safely assume that Radio 4 listeners have first-hand experience of children in primary education: as pupils, as relatives of a primary pupil, through employment or volunteering. Because they cannot make that assumption of their listeners' expertise in silage or sausage-making, ironically they sometimes seem to take more care about trying to explain those processes 'as they really are'.

Another explanation for *The Archers* educational inauthenticity could be that modern primary education is now rather complicated. Even professional educators struggle with the jargon, the proliferation of acronyms and the constant and confusing flow of policy changes. Hard-pressed BBC scriptwriters might be excused for not keeping up. Or might primary education be just too boring for Radio 4 thrill-seekers? To most of its audience *The Archers* represents dramatic escapism from everyday life. Listeners perhaps don't want to be reminded about the routines of excessive homework, the mad scrambles to make fancy dress costumes, or attend yet another dull fund-raising sale of largely unappetising cakes, at their real local primary school next weekend?

Or even more subversively, is actual English rural primary education, which really does throw together children and families of diverse social, cultural, economic and academic backgrounds, just too contentious, co-operative or competitive for *The Archers*? How could the clear and long established demarcations of social class, income and behaviours, on which so much of the structure and appeal of *The Archers* 'timeless' storylines depend, be maintained if all of Ambridge's children were offered equal opportunities? If all their parents and carers queued together at parents' evenings? If education was used less to school children into a preconceived place in a hierarchical world, and more to liberate their minds and realise their potential? The outcomes could prove disastrous for *The Archers*: an historic village would be drowned and its many boundaries dissolved, in a flood of social mobility.

These critiques of inauthenticity are in the end, affectionate. As audience and as fans we connive with the pretence. We collude with Ambridge's continuities, we suspend our disbeliefs and like children ourselves, we treat *The Archers* as playtime. Yet how much richer might that play be, and how many opportunities could be opened, were the scriptwriters merely to consider one of the many dramatic opportunities offered by rural primary education? Ambridge has its vicar, vet and lawyer, its publicans and proprietors, its farm owners, managers and workers, its consultants and entrepreneurs, its land owners and land agents, its poachers and its gamekeepers, its adolescents and retirees. Surely it could manage to host a male primary teaching assistant, breaking some moulds; a vivacious and untrustworthy head teacher, from a school rivalling Loxley Barrett; a vainglorious school governor from Ambridge, determined to protect the local primary school from acquisition by a chain of academies; or even just a parent, making an idiot of themselves at sports day?

Closing Ambridge's village school in 1973 was a fateful move. Not just for the imaginary village that hosted it, and the imaginary children who attended it, but for the imaginative wellsprings from which everything in Ambridge flows. It may have been an 'authentic' decision at the time, in the sense that many village schools across Britain shut during that decade. Yet it now means that the BBC's scriptwriters have to work even harder at making Ambridge feel and sound like an authentic English village: a community with many children who still have to attend primary school, and in all probability likely to contain at least one inhabitant who works or volunteers in that school. We don't need no education? Hardly. This is Radio 4!

REFERENCES

BBC. (2017). *The Archers: Frequently asked questions*. Retrieved from http://www.bbc.co.uk/programmes/articles/ 5xGwGj4NgfGRJ1B2mFqg6QM/frequently-asked-questions

Chantrill, C. (2017). *UK public spending*. Retrieved from
http://www.ukpublicspending.co.uk/government_
expenditure.html

Church of England's National Education Office. (2014).
*Working together: The future of Rural Church of England
schools*. Retrieved from https://www.churchofengland.org/
media/2088313/future%20of%20rural%20schools%
20report.pdf

Clarke, M. (2001). *UK media radio archers*. Retrieved from
https://groups.google.com/forum/#!msg/uk.media.radio.
archers/krzZ7kno9iA/DfTWyJd8r_AJ

Department for Education. (2016a). *Keeping children
safe in education: Statutory guidance for schools and
colleges*. Retrieved from https://www.gov.uk/government/
uploads/system/uploads/attachment_data/file/550511/
Keeping_children_safe_in_education.pdf

Department for Education. (2016b). *Schools, pupils and
their characteristics*. Retrieved from https://www.gov.uk/
government/uploads/system/uploads/attachment_data/file/
552342/SFR20_2016_Main_Text.pdf

Department for Education. (2016c). *School workforce
in England November 2015*. Retrieved from
https://www.gov.uk/government/uploads/system/
uploads/attachment_data/file/533618/SFR21_2016_
MainText.pdf

Gallagher, J. (1975). *Twenty five years of the archers*.
London: BBC.

Hill, R., Kettlewell, K., & Salt, J. (2014). *Partnership
working in small rural primary schools: The best of both
worlds*. Reading: CfBT.

Moore, C., & Bedow, D. (2000). *Ambridge and Borchester District: The definitive map of the archers on BBC Radio 4.* Dorchester: Magnetic North for the BBC.

Office for National Statistics. (2016). *Public Sector Employment UK.* Retrieved from https://www.ons.gov.uk/employmentandlabourmarket/peopleinwork/publicsectorpersonnel/bulletins/publicsectoremployment/dec2016

Pelling, R. (2008). Without a school a village won't live long. *The Telegraph.* Retrieved from http://www.telegraph.co.uk/comment/3554326/Without-a-school-a-village-wont-live-long.html#disqus_thread

Perkins, C. (2017). Mapping Ambridge. In C. Courage, N. Headlam, & P. Matthews (Eds.), *The Archers in fact and fiction* (pp.89–102). Oxford: Peter Lang AG.

Richardson, H. (2014). Many schools 'short of governors'. *BBC News.* Retrieved from: http://www.bbc.com/news/education-25591616

Todman, P., Harris, J., Carter, J., & McCamphill, J. (2009). *Better together: Exploratory case studies of formal collaborations between small rural primary schools. DCSF Research Report RR162.* London: DCSF. Retrieved from https://www.gov.uk/government/uploads/system/uploads/attachment_data/file/222027/DCSF-RR162.pdf

PEER REVIEW BY NIC GRUNDY, GREENWOOD COTTAGE, AMBRIDGE, BORSETSHIRE

Do you know, I often ask myself how something so big in our family life, can matter so little to other people in Ambridge? As a mother of four children, school dominates my life. There is always something: homework, homework, more home-work and then tests (the pressure these kids are under honestly, poor Mia had to do that bonkers phonics test reading nonsense words!) Then there's the projects (I think Joe enjoyed the oral history project more than Jake), making costumes for performances, dress up days (thank goodness for Mumsnet is all I can say), sports days, football matches and outings. I'm back and forwards to Loxley Barrett like a yo-yo, especially now Poppy's started nursery. It would be SO much easier if there was still a primary school in Ambridge. It's a big thing for small children to get a bus every day when they first start. And to be honest I'd enjoy waiting at the school gates every day and making friends with the other mothers. You miss stuff otherwise — like gossip about the teachers and other people's children. I heard there was trouble about that business with Rob talking to Henry. Reckon they hushed it all up ...

But the children are happy at school. The teachers work their socks off and were so lovely to Jake and Mia when they joined. I don't know why they get so worried about Ofsted. George loved Loxley Barrett too, until he left for Borchester Green last September. I know other families like the Aldridges and Pargetters don't send their kids there, but Will and I didn't really give it a second thought. The Grundys go to the local comprehensive. And do you know, I wouldn't mind a job at Loxley Barrett myself once Poppy's full time. I reckon being a teaching assistant would really suit me. I could keep an eye on Kiera too. She can be QUITE the little madam, don't you know ...

CHAPTER SIX

EDUCATING FREDDIE PARGETTER: OR, WILL HE PASS HIS MATHS GCSE?

Ruth Heilbronn and Rosalind Janssen

ABSTRACT

Research suggests that parentally bereaved children are likely to experience lower academic success and may need long-term support through tertiary education. Gender matters — boys bereaved of fathers and girls bereaved of mothers are at increased risk. Boys also exhibit higher levels of emotional and behavioural issues following bereavement. Age is another factor and exam results of children bereaved before the age of five or at twelve are significantly more affected than those bereaved at other ages. Circumstances affecting these achievements concern the relationship between the child's emotional state and how it plays out in behaviour and motivation in school.

Significantly, Freddie Pargetter, the subject of the chapter, has a twin sister, Lily. The twins had just turned 12 when their father was killed. Comparing the twins' General Certificate of Education (GCSE) results fits the research patterns — Lily managed well and Freddie did not. Freddie recognises that the academic environment of Felpersham Cathedral School did not support him well and chooses Borchester FE College to continue his studies. This choice raises controversy in the family, indicative of well-rehearsed, real-world educational arguments. Social media responses to other Archers *plot lines reveal the extent of how educational issues in the programme resonate with listeners.*

Keywords: Educational achievement; childhood bereavement; behaviour; GCSE assessment

INTRODUCTION

In this chapter, we focus on the examination results of two Ambridge youngsters, Lily and Freddie Pargetter. We can read their educational lives thus far in terms of three crucial dates. They are twins, born on 12 December 1999. Their parents are Elizabeth and Nigel Pargetter, living in Lower Loxley Hall. In a dramatic episode on 2 January 2011, while taking down Christmas decorations at the Hall, Nigel met with a fatal accident. To the dismay of his many fans, he fell off the roof, emitting a blood-curdling scream. Fast forward to 25 August 2016 and the publication of the twins' GCSE results, these are a shock to Elizabeth: Freddie has failed his maths, a subject he needs to go on in education. He will need to retake. In contrast, his sister Lily has passed this exam and gained secure GCSE grades in all her subjects. Bereavement and educational research can throw light on these very different results.

BEREAVEMENT STUDIES

Bereavement studies suggest that parentally bereaved children are likely to experience lower academic success through all phases of education and may well need long-term support through school and into tertiary level (Akerman & Statham, 2014; Haine, Ayers, Sandler, & Wolchik, 2008). Not surprisingly, the nature of the death is significant. Factors dictating their impact are whether the child expected it, and the extent to which it leaves them feeling powerless (McCarthy, 2007). Nigel's death was sudden and unexpected and this might well be a factor in Freddie's achievement.

Gender plays an important role: boys bereaved of fathers and girls bereaved of mothers are at increased risk (Abdelnoor & Hollins, 2004a). Haine et al.'s (2008) review confirms that boys typically display higher levels of negative externalising behaviour, while girls display more internalising problems. Dowdney (2000) indicates that boys exhibit higher levels of emotional and behavioural issues following bereavement. Age is also significant. Abdelnoor and Hollins (2004b) discovered that the exam results of children bereaved before the age of five or at twelve were significantly more affected than those bereaved at other ages. Significantly, Lily and Freddie had just turned 12 when their father Nigel fell off his roof in December 2011.

In August 2016 Freddie discovers that he has failed to get a C grade in maths and English. He therefore fits the research pattern of boys bereaved of fathers, and he conforms to the age pattern. Lily, a girl bereaved of a father and not a mother, also conforms to the research, in having done decidedly better than her brother with her secure A and B grades. Felpersham Cathedral School does not offer resits and will not accept any student for the sixth form without a grade C in maths. (It would be cynical to observe that Freddie's additional maths lessons with Iftikar did not seem to have done him very much good.)

What are the implications of his childhood bereavement on Freddie's possibilities for success in future life? Akerman and Statham (2014), who incorporated new findings from the 1970 British Cohort Study, depressingly report that for men, the main long-term impact was found to be raised unemployment. The good news is that any impact was found to be limited when family background was considered, and with the range of privileges bestowed by his Lower Loxley upbringing, Freddie is likely to end up better off than most in this regard.

Akerman and Statham's (2014) extensive literature review was funded by the Department of Education. It was undertaken on behalf of the independent Childhood Wellbeing Research Centre and our own Institute of Education was one of several partners. The authors conclude by recommending that schools, where children spend a large part of their daily lives, should support the emotional wellbeing of bereaved children by means of specific intervention programmes. It would be interesting to know what if any provision the Cathedral School had put in place for the Pargetter twins.

MOTIVATION AND ENVIRONMENT

Achievement is influenced too by a complex number of factors (Fredricks, Blumenfeld, & Paris, 2004). Motivation is particularly significant (Meece, Anderman, & Anderman, 2006; Wigfield & Eccles, 2000). There is also a known connection between motivation being related to self-belief, self-esteem, confidence and academic achievement (Bandura, Barbaranelli, Caprara, & Pastorelli, 1996). As Covington (2000) states:

> *Based on the accumulating research it is concluded that the quality of student learning as well as the*

> *will to continue learning depends closely on an*
> *interaction between the kinds of social and academic*
> *goals students bring to the classroom, the motivating*
> *properties of these goals and prevailing classroom*
> *reward structures. (p.171)*

Freddie may not have responded well to the Cathedral School's ethos and 'prevailing classroom reward structures' and this will have affected his achievement. Predictably, students who are engaged in school achieve better than those who do not by many measures (Bandura et al., 1996; Caraway, Tucker, Reinke, & Hall, 2003). In contrast, students who are disengaged from school and learning are more likely to perform poorly and engage in problem behaviour (Finn, 1993).

We know that the way students experience their environment at school affects their engagement and the social, instructional and organisational climate of schools influences this engagement and hence their academic achievement (Patrick, Ryan, & Kaplan, 2007). Engagement in school is influenced by an interrelation of several factors. Wang and Holcombe's 2010 longitudinal study of a representative, ethnically diverse, urban sample of 1046 students in a US school built on previous work that had isolated three factors influencing student engagement in school — behaviour, emotion and cognition. The first, behavioural engagement, includes how positively or negatively students act in school and are involved in learning (e.g. participating in extra-curricular activity). This had been studied among others (Finn, 1993). The second, emotional engagement, represents a student's affective reactions and sense of identification with school, previously studied by various researchers including Skinner and Belmont (1993). The third, cognitive engagement, refers to a student's self-regulated and strategic approach to learning, previously studied by Fredricks et al. (2004) and others. Wang and Holcombe are able to show, as we might infer from our own experiences of emotional situations, that 'these three components are dynamically interrelated within individuals and are not isolated processes' (Wang & Holcombe, 2010, p. 534).

School culture and school climate evidently have an influence on how these three factors inter-relate (MacNeil, Prater, & Busch, 2009) and again we would expect that being in school can be experienced differently by different students. We know that the Cathedral School attended by the twins stressed an academic curriculum and we can surmise that the environment was characterised by a degree of formality and an ethos of high academic achievement. Cathedral schools tend to promote a particular ethos. We have looked at the value statements on the webpages of a number of cathedral schools and find the following is typical. This school is in Llandaff, Cardiff:

> *First class academic teaching, excellent facilities and an extensive co-curricular programme, underpinned by high quality pastoral care and the school's Christian ethos, give Cathedral School pupils the opportunity to reach their full potential, both academically and personally, in a vibrant and supportive environment. (Llandaff, 2017)*

Given that a sense of engagement and participation in school life is important to achievement, the Wang and Holcombe study is useful in concluding that:

> *the presence of competitive learning environments (performance goal structures) decreases school participation, undermines the development of sense of school belonging, and diminishes the value*

> *students place on school. In turn, this leads to lower*
> *academic achievement ... A focus on comparison,*
> *competition, and relative ability in middle school*
> *seems to be behaviourally and emotionally*
> *detrimental for students. Such an emphasis ignores*
> *students' needs for a safe, supportive environment to*
> *develop their competencies and to believe that they*
> *can determine their success and succeed. (Wang &*
> *Holcombe, 2010, p. 651)*

The researchers follow up this comment with some remarks that are, we think, particularly pertinent to Freddie's case:

> *If and when a student is concerned that he or she*
> *does not 'measure up', on goals for performance, his*
> *or her senses of belonging and commitment to the*
> *school may be eroded ... This may be particularly*
> *true during adolescence because youth are increas-*
> *ingly self-conscious and more sensitive to social*
> *comparisons of their competencies to those of their*
> *peers. (*ibid.*)*

FREDDIE AND LILY MOVE ON

Perceptions of schools and school environments then are significant. Different kinds of schools may suit different children. Freddie and Lily make their post-16 educational choices. Freddie chooses to go to Borchester Further Education College, a college in the state sector. Lily decides to take his lead and go to Borchester College too. Here we might specu-late on how the atmosphere at the Cathedral School did not support Freddie, when he needed understanding. Freddie, by voting with his feet, has shown that the Cathedral School, with its emphasis on academic achievement, was probably too narrow and restrictive for him to thrive, demanding conformity to norms not compatible with his needs. A further education college in the state sector has a more diverse intake and is more inclusive in its pedagogy, because of the range of students it needs to cater for. Therefore, it must be more tolerant of 'aberrant' behaviour and 'low' achievement. The educational environment influences students' feelings of self-worth, and we think that in a more inclusive environment, Freddie might benefit from a virtuous circle in which tolerance towards him enables raised self-esteem, which in turn helps him to engage with his studies in the way outlined above, affecting his behaviour, emotion and learning, that is the behavioural, emotional and cognitive domains.

Given the information from the research on bereavement, on motivation, perception of school environment and our knowledge of Freddie as an adolescent, we may see his case as indicative of wider issues about education, some of which centre around the question — what is education for?

THE AIMS OF EDUCATION

The Cathedral School or Loxley Barrow, followed by Borchester College? We are plunged into the pertinent debate about independent versus state education. Proponents of independent education commonly talk about the importance of individual achievement and defenders of state education frequently mention wider social values of common school education, where there is no 'creaming off' of some children, along class or achievement lines. Many writers, particularly in the philosophy of education, have pointed out that education looks very different depending on the values that underpin its aims. If we believe that individual achievement is the primary outcome, the school curriculum and pedagogy will be one that helps individual achievement, and is likely to be based on examination achievements and the pursuit of individual goals of 'excellence'. Whereas, if we start from a different perspective and ask what kind of society we hope for and which human qualities we wish to nurture and develop to promote that kind of society, we get a different view of school and the school curriculum. Education in these schools would still include promoting practical capability, academic achievement and preparation for employment, but would take as its foundation the importance of human relationships, of developing together in a social environment, of developing habits of sympathy and imagination for others and the planet.

Pring (2007) analyses the history of state education in the United Kingdom, and the philosophical arguments underlying this debate suggest three different ways in which educational values are supported and justified. Recognising that this exists is important, because the kind of justification given, the ethical basis of education, affects the kinds of schools we value and promote. To some extent too, different ways of learning tend to be promoted in different models of schools. Our current curriculum model of subject divisions, rather than project based-learning, comes down to a view that 'intellectual excellence' — a term we owe to the Cardinal Newman, an important Victorian writer — relies on individuals working on their own, through a prescribed curriculum:

> *The tendency, at its worst, has led to the mere*
> *'transmission of knowledge', learning that becomes*
> *disconnected from the cultural experiences that*
> *young people bring with them to school and with*
> *which they need to be logically connected.*
> *Newman's words have been echoed many times*
> *in the shaping of educational provision and*
> *judgements. (Pring, 2007, p. 513)*

This question about the transmission of knowledge in academic subject areas, and the extent to which education should draw on children's interests and experience, runs through contemporary educational philosophy. Two philosophers illustrate this well — John Dewey and Anthony O'Hear. Dewey was writing from the end of the nineteenth to the mid-twentieth century and his views are drawn on today by a substantial number of educationalists. He favoured education based on engaging a child's interest, and promoted the 'common school' where all pupils are educated together. O'Hear was influential in the 1990s. He wrote strongly in defence of 'traditional learning' and tells us that 'education … is irretrievably authoritarian and paternalistic … imparting to a pupil something which he has yet to acquire … The transmission is inevitably between unequals' (O'Hear, 1991, p. 5). He roundly condemns Dewey's influence, stating that 'it is highly plausible to see the egalitarianism which stems from the writings of John Dewey as the proximate cause of our educational decline' (*ibid.*).

We see these debates currently in England with the attempt to return to grammar schools, selecting by competitive examination, and in SATS testing at age seven and eleven. Many parents and teachers think this a narrowing of the curriculum to what can be easily assessed, which leads to a down grading of practical subjects, the arts and the humanities, essential to the 'education of sympathy'. Passions run high in such debates, and this fervour can be found in and around Ambridge.

AMBRIDGE, EDUCATION AND SOCIAL MEDIA

Borchester College

Freddie's choice of Borchester College has caused some family discussion. We have been here before in 2005 with the story of A Level study choices when Alice Aldridge, now a highly qualified and high flying engineer, herself chose Borchester College for her A Levels. She was vehemently opposed by her father, as the Guardian's education correspondent reported:

> *Not since 1998, when Tony Blair ordered the then Home Secretary Jack Straw to investigate the imprisonment of Coronation Street's Deirdre Rachid, has a soap opera caused such a furore. The Archers' Brian Aldridge reacted with snobbish fury last week to the announcement that his youngest daughter, Alice, intended leaving her independent school for a further education college.*

> *'Borchester College?' exploded Brian. 'Has she been on the horse pills? It's sheer madness. The college is full of Neanderthals ... Have you driven past it lately? Half of the students don't appear to have opposable thumbs'. He then claimed the only facilities it had was to teach 'advanced hairdressing and media studies'. (Hill, 2005)*

The article pointed out that Brian's outburst coincided with the week that the Association of Colleges mounted its campaign to reduce the funding gap between schools and colleges. Hill cited educationalists who were dismayed at Brian's comments. Here are three of her pertinent remarks (Hill, 2005):

1. Anne Piercy, vice-principal of Stafford College (based near Ambridge in the Midlands) said 'His ill-informed criticism is hurtful to those who study and work at further education colleges and could have a very serious impact by dissuading people from choosing a learning environment which may be enormously beneficial to them'.

2. Claire Boxall, communications manager at Mid-Kent College in Chatham, is concerned that Aldridge's views could 'reinforce the derogatory opinions that people already have of colleges. We draw students from rural areas very similar to those in Ambridge and this sort of coverage is not helpful'.

3. A head of faculty, at Stoke College told Hill, 'I am horrified: we all know that Brian is both opinionated and frequently wrong, but for the casual listener, it puts further education in a bad light'.

This was all picked up in Leighton Andrew's blog, who commented that:

> *Instead of these ludicrously neurotic responses*
> *[of Brian] I hope that FE college heads... would*
> *understand that the right way to react is to praise*
> *his daughter's independence of mind and her*
> *confidence in the FE sector. In fact, they should be*
> *out there hiring the actress now for their recruitment*
> *campaigns. (Andrews, 2005)*

The independent/state debate in this *Archers* plot line was as relevant to 'real-world' education choices as our current Freddie storyline and is similarly indicative of class. Both Elizabeth, the twins' mother, and Brian, who is Alice and Ruairi's father, aspire to provide an exclusive education for their children and view the public sector as not good enough for them. Although the class issue is not discussed in these stories, it is there, with its echoes of 'excellence' pursued on the one hand by adherents of private education, and the different conception of education in the idea of 'the common school' advocated by Dewey and his adherents. The discussion reminds us about the class issue and the value implications for individual students of the choices made about where they should go to school and college. Notably, Alice stuck to her guns and went on to achieve very good A Level results at Borchester College.

Generations Disagree

Comments in Ambridge reflect divergent family generational opinions. When the twins reach transfer age the question is 'Cathedral School or local comprehensive?' In her review of our chapter Jill Archer reminds us that at that time she stated, 'What's wrong with Borchester Green?' Elizabeth, born in 1957, is at the tail end of the second baby boomer generation, a cohort famed for their capacity to ignite generational conflict (Bristow, 2015). Elizabeth took to the virtual space of social media with her adamant message that her twins 'will go to Borchester Green over my dead body'. People were quick to respond as witnessed by the 49 posts on the Felpersham Cathedral School Mumsnet (2010) thread. Lizzie's initial posting is worth quoting in full:

LoathsomeLizzieP Wed 08-Dec-10 21:13:42

Can anyone help? DH [Darling Husband] was planning in sending DD [Darling Daughter] and DS [Darling Son] to Mercer College, but I am unsure whether boarding would suit them, particularly DS. We live about 10 miles from Felpersham and are considering the Cathedral School — do any MN'ers have any experience of it? Exam results seem good, but are the facilities and extracurricular opportunities as good as an Independent School? Also worried about entrance exams, DH has arranged extra tutoring, but concerned about DS, particularly in Maths. Should we keep the option of

> *Mercer College open, and what other independent*
> *schools in the area can be considered? Other local*
> *state schools are not up to standard, DC's [Darling*
> *Children] will go to Borchester Green over my dead*
> *body. (Mumsnet, 2010)*

Before the hour is up, she is back again in full sail with
yet more to say:

> *LoathsomeLizzieP Wed 08-Dec-10 21:36:47*

> *From my experience I boarded at independent*
> *school and found that it was the intangible things,*
> *social skills and the like, that really helped me to get*
> *on in life, as like DS I am bright but wasn't the most*
> *academic. My oldest brother [Kenton Archer] was*
> *a bit of a brainbox but went to the local grammar*
> *and has never really achieved much. This is what*
> *makes the decision so difficult — it is not just a case*
> *of exam results. My niece [Pip Archer] went to*
> *Borchester Green, having met some of her friends*
> *there I wouldn't have my DCs go near the place!*
> *(Mumsnet, 2010)*

Moving on six years, to 25 August 2016, we find that we
have come full circle. Freddie's only option is now Borchester
College.

'Twas Ever Thus

Another social media example draws on some of the themes
of this chapter. This is 21 May 2011 — a blog written by
Clare Tupling, a sociologist from Teeside University, called
Education and Society. Through her recounting the story of
Ruairi Donovan and his transplanting to Ambridge after the

death of his mother, she raises a number of real-life issues
in education. Her analysis stands on its own and needs no
commentary. It is illuminating in its coverage of the issues:

> *Borsetshire must have more than its fair share of*
> *private schools and privately educated pupils if*
> The Archers *are anything to go by. We know this*
> *because school choice, once again, features in the*
> *storyline. Ruairi Donovan has been through a lot in*
> *his short life. He is the son of Brian Aldridge from*
> *his extra-marital affair with the lately departed*
> *Siobhan Hathaway/Donovan .... The decision about*
> *his schooling then, was that, if possible he should*
> *attend, the local primary, Loxley Barratt. It would be*
> *too traumatic to be packed off to boarding school so*
> *soon after losing his mother and being transported*
> *to Ambridge. They had missed the application for*
> *school places, and, as the fictional school at Loxley*
> *Barratt was fully subscribed, they had an anxious*
> *wait over that summer to see if a place became*
> *available. They were in luck. Ruairi has settled.*

Fast forward nearly four years, such fears have evapo-
rated, and now boarding is being seriously considered for this
eight year old. In other words, Brian and Jennifer are perus-
ing the education market place. They appear to have an
abstract notion that private is better than state. They are not
so much dissatisfied with Loxley Barratt as convinced that it
is not good enough for Ruairi, referring to some unsubstanti-
ated claim that his teacher wouldn't expect him to complete
all his homework. Brian and Jennifer are articulate, why
don't they exercise their cultural capital by speaking to
Ruairi's teacher to find out what this story is really about?
Educational expertise is not wholly trusted by Brian and

Jennifer. Instead they are engaging in a class-based process of school choice. Brian did remark that it is an increasingly competitive world out there; he wants Ruairi to have the edge. In other words, he wants to ensure, understandably, the reproduction of his social class advantage (Tupling, 2011).

CONCLUSION

When hackles are raised in blogs and on Mumsnet about Ruari or Alice, or the education of the Pargetter twins, we are connected with live educational controversy. The heated discussions over education that take place from time to time around tables in Ambridge and surrounding areas, over tea and lemon drizzle cake, are typical of those that happen in families and education departments throughout the land.

Freddie Pargetter's GCSE results in maths and English disappointed his mother and caused him grief, could be linked to a number of factors that we have discussed in this chapter. Being bereaved at a crucial age was likely to be the underlying factor that led to others, such as his lower self-esteem, which in turn had a knock-on effect on his engagement with school. We can only hope that this is now behind him and we have every confidence in Borchester FE College.

REFERENCES

Abdelnoor, A., & Hollins, S. (2004a). The effect of childhood bereavement on secondary school performance. *Educational Psychology in Practice, 20*(1), 43–54.

Abdelnoor, A., & Hollins, S. (2004b). How children cope at school after family bereavement. *Educational and Child Psychology, 21*(3), 85–94.

Akerman, R., & Statham, J. (2014). Bereavement in childhood. *The impact on psychological and educational outcomes and the effectiveness of support services*. London: Childhood Wellbeing Research Centre (CWRC). Retrieved from http://www.cwrc.ac.uk/news/documents/Revised_Childhood_Bereavement_review_2014a.pdf

Andrews, L. (2005, February 20). *Ambridge, Borchester College and the FE sector*. Retrieved from https://leightonandrews.wordpress.com/2005/02/20/ambridge-borchester-college-and-the-fe-sector/

Bandura, A., Barbaranelli, C., Caprara, G. V., & Pastorelli, C. (1996). Multifaceted impact of self-efficacy beliefs on academic functioning. *Child Development*, *67*(3), 1206–1222.

Bristow, J. (2015). *Baby boomers and generational conflict*. New York, NY: Palgrave Macmillan.

Caraway, K., Tucker, C. M., Reinke, W. M., & Hall, C. (2003). Self-efficacy, goal orientation, and fear of failure as predictors of school engagement in high school students. *Psychology in the Schools*, *40*(4), 417–427.

Covington, M. (2000). Goal theory, motivation, and school achievement: An integrative review. *Annual Review of Psychology*, *51*, 171–200. Retrieved from http://annualreviews.org/doi/full/10.1146/annurev.psych.51.1.171

Dowdney, L. (2000). Annotation: Childhood bereavement following parental death. *Journal of Child Psychology and Psychiatry*, *41*(7), 819–830.

Finn, J. D. (1993). *School engagement and students at risk*. Washington, DC: National Center for Education Statistics.

Fredricks, J. A., Blumenfeld, P. C., & Paris, A. H. (2004). School engagement: Potential of the concept, state of the evidence. *Review of Educational Research*, *74*(1), 59–109.

Haine, R. A., Ayers, T. S., Sandler, I. N., & Wolchik, S. A. (2008). Evidence-based practices for parentally bereaved children and their families. *Professional Psychology: Research and Practice*, *39*(2), 113–121.

Hill, A. (2005, February 20). *Motor mouth of the Archers upsets real life college heads*. Retrieved from https://www.theguardian.com/media/2005/feb/20/radio.furthereducation

Llandaff. (2017). *Welcome to the cathedral school*. Retrieved from http://www.cathedral-school.co.uk/

MacNeil, A. J., Prater, D. L., & Busch, S. (2009). The effects of school culture and climate on student achievement. *International Journal of Leadership in Education*, *12*(1), 73–84.

McCarthy, J. R. (2007). "They all look as if they're coping, but i'm not:" The relational power/lessness of "youth" in responding to experiences of bereavement. *Journal of Youth Studies*, *10*(3), 285–303.

Meece, J. L., Anderman, E. M., & Anderman, L. H. (2006). Classroom goal structure, student motivation, and academic achievement. *Annual Review of Psychology*, *57*, 487–503.

Mumsnet. (2010, December 8). *Felpersham Cathedral School*. Retrieved from https://www.mumsnet.com/Talk/secondary/1101283-Felpersham-Cathedral-School

O'Hear, A. (1991). *Father of child-centredness. Policy Study No. 126*. London: Centre for Policy Studies.

Patrick, H., Ryan, A. M., & Kaplan, A. (2007). Early adolescents' perceptions of the classroom social environment, motivational beliefs, and engagement. *Journal of Educational Psychology, 99*(1), 83–98.

Pring, R. (2007). The common school. *Journal of Philosophy of Education, 41*(4), 503–522.

Skinner, E. A., & Belmont, M. J. (1993). Motivation in the classroom: Reciprocal effect of teacher behavior and student engagement across the school year. *Journal of Educational Psychology, 85*(4), 571–581.

Tupling. (2011, May 21). *Ruairi is too bright for Loxley Barrow*. Retrieved from https://educationandsociety. wordpress.com/tag/the-archers/

Wang, M.-T., & Holcombe, R. (2010). Adolescents' perceptions of school environment, engagement, and academic achievement in middle school. *American Educational Research Journal, 47*(3), 633–662. doi:10.3102/0002831209361209

Wigfield, A., & Eccles, J. L. (2000). Expectancy–value theory of achievement motivation. *Contemporary Educational Psychology, 25*(1), 68–81. doi:10.1006/ ceps.1999.1015

PEER REVIEW BY JILL ARCHER, BROOKFIELD FARM, AMBRIDGE, BORSETSHIRE

This chapter has reminded me of why I was so cross when the twins went to the Cathedral School in Felpersham. The authors quote Claire Tupling and I recommend you look at another posting she made in her *Education and Society* blog.

That was back on 12 December 2010. Toby Fairbrother found it for me when he knew I was writing this review (not that this will change anything I feel about that young man). My immortal words were, 'There's nothing wrong with Borchester Green'. I wrote it because my grandchildren, twins Freddie and Lily Pargetter, were receiving extra tuition to ensure they passed the entrance exam to the Cathedral School.

At the time they were attending our local state primary school in Loxley Barrett, so I'm very pleased that the authors discuss the private versus state school debate since this is my bugbear. I didn't go to a private school and I hate the snobbery connected with the idea that if you pay for education it will be better for your children. Far better to have education based on cooperative values which the authors write about. The world is in a sorry state and it would be better for us all if children were educated together, and learnt tolerance for one another.

The authors link my grandson Freddie's GCSE result in maths to poor Nigel's accident, falling off the roof at Lower Loxley. Freddie lost his father at a crucial time in his young life, around the twins' twelfth birthday. So, there's evidence that boys who lose their fathers are especially at risk of not doing too well at school, and at this precise age as well.

Academic achievement certainly isn't everything. After all, had I gone to university (not easy in my day) and not studied domestic science at college, I might never have met Phil, which I did when I was demonstrating the 'Household Drudge' machine at the village fete in 1957.

And if Freddie doesn't get his GCSE maths, he can always come and help me with my bees.

CHAPTER SEVEN

PHOEBE GOES TO OXFORD

Felicity Macdonald-Smith

ABSTRACT

This chapter examines Phoebe Aldridge's experience of applying to and being accepted by the University of Oxford and attempts to establish how far she is typical of applicants from the state sector as a whole, by a consideration of the following aspects: geographical area, family circumstances, subject and College choice, motivation and previous academic performance.

Keywords: University; Oxford; state school; background; academic

It is common to see media comments castigating Oxford and Cambridge universities for not admitting more state sector pupils; it is much rarer to see portrayals in dramas of young people applying to Oxford or Cambridge, or indeed to any

university. However, Phoebe Aldridge, a state school appli-
cant from what used to be described as a 'broken family', has
now begun her studies at Oxford, and her application may
be seen as a case study in 'widening participation' (WP). WP
refers to attempts, as part of UK government education
policy, to increase the proportion of young people in higher
education from groups which are currently under-represented,
for example those from neighbourhoods with low participation in higher education, or from schools with below national
average GCSE scores and/or above national average eligibility
for free school meals.

This chapter reviews some aspects of Phoebe's experience
of the Oxford application process and compares it with
that of applicants from the state sector as a whole. In 2015
Oxford had the lowest proportion of state school entrants
out of the 24 Russell Group universities, at 55.7% (Turner,
2017, para. 4).

Following William Barras' paper from the first Academic
Archers conference, I am assuming that Ambridge is situated
in the general area of the West Midlands. The University of
Oxford website (University of Oxford, 2016) provides statistical data on undergraduate applications and admissions
each year, including by UK region: the latest figures available are for entry in 2015. The West Midlands acceptance
rate of 18.8% comes nearly at the bottom of the list; the
only region which is lower is Northern Ireland (17.1%).

Both Oxford and Cambridge have 'link College schemes'
which give schools and colleges all over the United Kingdom
a direct way of staying in touch with the Universities; school
students are invited to visit Colleges, and staff and current
undergraduates regularly visit schools. Keble is the Oxford
link College for Warwickshire and Birmingham, and Oriel
is the link College for Worcestershire. There was no mention
on air of Phoebe visiting either of these Colleges, nor even of

her attending a general Oxford Open Day (usually held in July). This might be because she only decided to apply after getting her AS results — anecdotal evidence suggests this is fairly common amongst state school applicants, for whom good AS grades may provide the necessary confidence boost to encourage them to apply to a top university.

A glance at the forums on the *Student Room* (Student Room Forums: Choosing an Oxford College, 2017) however shows that a great deal of soul-searching about College choice is usual during the application process, so it is surprising that listeners have never heard which College or Colleges interviewed her, and which one made her the offer of a place.

It is also assumed that Borchester College is a further education (FE) or tertiary college, rather than purely a sixth form college, since as well as A Level students (Phoebe, Lily Pargetter), other young characters are attending for the purpose of GCSE resits (Freddie Pargetter), and key skills or day release courses (Johnny Phillips). Strangely, Borchester College does not appear on the list of applications and acceptances from UCAS-registered schools and colleges on the University of Oxford website, so the college's success rate in getting students into Oxford is unknown. Oxford does not provide a breakdown of its admissions statistics by school type, since it believes that:

> *[...] school type is a crude and sometimes misleading indicator of disadvantage (University of Oxford, 2016).*

However, the Cambridge acceptance rate for FE/Tertiary colleges in 2015 was 15.6% (University of Cambridge, 2016).

Both Oxford and Cambridge will consider 'extenuating circumstances' which may have affected applicants' previous academic performance. These may include health problems, family situations or disrupted teaching. Although Phoebe does not suffer from material disadvantage (presumably her grandparents, at least on the Aldridge side, have made sure of that), her family situation is clearly not ideal. Abandoned by her mother, Kate Madikane, as a small child, while Kate was 'finding herself' in Africa, she settled into family life with Roy and Hayley Tucker, only for Kate to return and compete with Hayley for her affections. Following a holiday in South Africa with Kate, Phoebe stayed on to spend an academic year at school there (Year 9), which ended traumatically when she discovered Kate's extramarital affair. Roy and Hayley split up during her GCSE year, and Kate then returned to Ambridge to set up her alternative therapy business and disrupt Phoebe's study routine during her A Levels.

Clearly Phoebe would be justified in letting Oxford know about any or all of these life events, and one can only hope that Borchester College kept the admissions tutor of her Oxford College fully informed of the distractions she suffered during her A Levels (e.g. Kate expecting her to help with the yurts on the morning of one of her maths exams).

A recent article on the *Guardian* website described the Politics, Philosophy and Economics (PPE) course as 'the Oxford degree that runs Britain':

> *More than any other course at any other university [...] Oxford PPE pervades British political life. From the right to the left, from the centre ground to the fringes, from analysts to protagonists, consensus-seekers to revolutionary activists, environmentalists to ultra-capitalists, statists to libertarians, elitists to populists, bureaucrats to spin doctors, bullies to charmers, successive networks of PPEists have been at work at all levels of British politics [...] since the*

degree was established 97 years ago. (Beckett, 2017,
para 4)

When talking about Phoebe's application to read PPE (13 September 2015), Jennifer Aldridge claimed that it is the most competitive subject of all, and on the Oxford website it is listed as one of the most over-subscribed subjects. The University points out that applying for one of these subjects can adversely affect applicants' success:

State applicants' success rate is affected by subject
choice: UK domiciled state school students apply
disproportionately for the most oversubscribed
subjects. On average, 34% of UK domiciled state
school applications between 2013 and 2015 were
for the five most oversubscribed subjects at Oxford.
This compared to just 29% of independent school
applications. (University of Oxford, 2016)

For entry in 2015 the acceptance rate for female applicants in PPE was 13% (15% for males). In view of this, it may not have been a realistic choice for Phoebe, who had not shown a particular interest in politics up to this point.

Finally, and most importantly, is Phoebe's academic ability good enough for PPE at Oxford? She did well at GCSE (7 A*s, 2 As and 'a couple of Bs'), and 'sailed through' her AS levels (21 August 2014 and 21 August 2015). Her final grades at A Level were A*AAA including A* in English; her other subjects included History and Mathematics. She therefore exceeded the standard offer conditions of AAA for PPE, but her results were still probably not above average for such a competitive course.

Overall, the drama gave an accurate portrayal of the application and admission process, including Phoebe's understandable nerves about the interviews and her boyfriend's stereotypical reactions ('you'll change', 'they're all posh'). Perhaps she will go on to be the first Archers character to gain a first-class degree from Oxford.

REFERENCES

Barras, W. (2017). Rural voices: What can Borsetshire tell us about accent change? In C. Courage, N. Headlam, & P. Matthews (Eds.), *The Archers in fact and fiction: Academic analyses of life in rural Borsetshire*. Oxford: Peter Lang.

Beckett, A. (2017). *PPE: The Oxford degree that runs Britain*. Retrieved from https://www.theguardian.com/education/2017/feb/23/ppe-oxford-university-degree-that-rules-britain

Student Room Forums. (2017). *Choosing an Oxford College*. Retrieved from https://www.thestudentroom.co.uk/showthread.php?t=85158

Turner, C. (2017). *Oxford University bucks national trend and accepts fewer state school students, figures show*. Retrieved from http://www.telegraph.co.uk/education/2017/02/02/oxford-university-bucks-national-trend-accepts-fewer-state-school/

University of Cambridge. (2016). *Undergraduate study/application statistics*. Retrieved from http://www.undergraduate.study.cam.ac.uk/apply/statistics

University of Oxford. (2016). *Undergraduate admissions statistics 2015*. Retrieved from https://www.ox.ac.uk/about/facts-and-figures/admissions-statistics/undergraduate

SECTION THREE

THE GEOGRAPHY
OF AMBRIDGE

CHAPTER EIGHT

GET ME OUT OF HERE! ASSESSING AMBRIDGE'S FLOOD RESILIENCE

Angela Connelly

ABSTRACT

In March 2015, following unseasonable heavy precipitation, the River Am burst its banks flooding the village of Ambridge and causing one death and numerous injuries. The lines between fiction and reality became blurred when the BBC offered updates about the weather situation in Ambridge through social media. However, in fiction, as in reality, memories are short; recent village gossip in Ambridge has been dominated by other matters including a certain murder trial and the mix-up with Jill Archer's chutney. The flood has come and gone.

In this chapter, I will examine the response to, and recovery from, the floods in Ambridge in order to ascertain what lessons have been learned, and whether enough has been done to make Ambridge more resilient to future floods events. I will show how the programme raised important issues in relation to flooding management in England today, and focus upon the increasing responsibilisation of citizens, the tension which exists between framing the flood response in terms of 'resilience' or 'vulnerability', and the need for people to find someone or something to blame for their misfortune. I conclude that The Archers *could play a critical role in maintaining flood awareness in the future.*

Keywords: Flood risk management; flooding; flood resilience; vulnerability

INTRODUCTION

In early March 2015, the River Am burst its banks. Initially flooding sacrificial agricultural land, the waters soon rose to cause devastation in the village. It was a 'flash' flood, which means that it departed very quickly, leaving one death and numerous injuries in its wake. My interest, as a researcher on climate change resilience, was particularly heightened as the Ambridge event occurred soon after a similar incident hit the south of England in 2013/2014 and cost the UK £1.3 billion in economic damages (Environment Agency, 2016). Less than a year after the Ambridge disaster, Storms Desmond, Eva and Frank paralysed the north of England over the Christmas period. Flood events seem to be increasing in frequency and consequences. However, we cannot be certain when, where and how high the next flood will be. Hence, floods are sometimes explained away as an 'act of God' or, as one UKIP councillor suggested of the 2013/2014 floods, we might blame UK government legislation to allow same-sex civil partnerships for inciting God's wrath.

Leaving the religious allusions to one side, flood risk management is a highly complex affair. Over recent years, approaches to flood risk management have swung from an emphasis on 'defence' towards 'risk management' (Butler & Pidgeon, 2011; Johnson & Priest, 2008). Despite costly investments in defensive infrastructure, such as the Thames Barrier, the increasing frequency and intensity of individual floods has led to recognition that large flood defences cannot be the sole response. This is exacerbated by climate change projections that suggest that extreme flood events will increase in intensity and frequency in the future. Policy rhetoric now emphasises 'living with water' and, thus, increasing resilience where the emphasis is on 'bouncing back' as efficiently as possible from a disaster. The European Floods Directive (2007), for example, promoted catchment-based management and the provision of risk information, such as maps and early warning systems. As part of a more holistic flood risk management strategy, citizens are encouraged to take more responsibility for protecting themselves and their assets. Yet there remain tensions between the two approaches particularly amongst citizens who continue to believe that the state should protect them and their livelihoods from floods (White, Connelly, Garvin, Lawson, & O'Hare, 2015).

The shift from defence to living with risk through resilient approaches raises three important issues. Firstly, the perception of risk varies between individuals and, related to this, many citizens are unable to become the model of the resilient property owner that policy seems to applaud. Secondly, it can be argued that floods are no more a 'natural' disaster than they are an act of god and, consequently, communities often seek to blame someone or something for the events that have befallen them. Thirdly, portrayals of responses to floods tend to be framed in different ways and often emphasise a 'Blitz Spirit' that may be overplayed and difficult to sustain.

The Ambridge 2015 flood touched upon all of these issues and this chapter draws on examples from the event to illustrate each of them in turn. Ultimately, the aim is to assess the way that Ambridge residents were, with the risk management authorities, able to prepare for, to respond and to recover from the flood. The chapter draws on extensive online documentation of the floods and brings in examples from other flood events to illustrate the points. The research materials include radio broadcasts which relayed the events in real time (Beal, n.d.), material from the BBC website including a map and blog (Perkins, 2016) and tweets from unofficial character handles as well as listeners.

RISK PERCEPTION

We are, as the sociologist Beck (1992) pointed out, living in the 'risk society', where a belief in technology and human mastery of nature has given way to a fixation on the 'unknown and unintended' consequences of risk (p. 24). Given the uncertainty, many governments have sought to divest themselves of that risk and do so through the provision of risk information. It is believed that providing such information will allow citizens to make decisions on the likelihood and probability of risks and, in doing so, undertake measures that protect them from potential risks. Ultimately, this reflects a neoliberal approach to hazard management where citizens are increasingly responsibilised. However, this approach tends to treat these citizens as consumers and as equally rational decision makers (Eakin, Eriksen, Eikeland, & Øyen, 2011).

Yet sociologists continually show how the understanding of risk is complex and, given this complexity, individuals and organisations will interpret risk in different ways. Individual worldviews and/or ideological preferences are important variables when considering attitudes towards conventional risks since 'individuals perceive a variety of risks in a manner that supports their way of life' (Wildavsky & Dake, 1990, p. 57). Even though the risk of a plane crash is relatively low, some people fear flying but those who must travel are more likely to be able to find reasons to pacify any nagging doubts.

There were a number of incidents during the Ambridge flood where residents responded differently to the impending flood. Charlie Thomas of Damara Capital and David Archer of Brookfield Farm were aware of flood alerts and were quick to begin to respond the floodwaters. David, along with his wife Ruth and his brother Tony, had pitched in to help farmers in Worcestershire who had been affected by flooding in the previous year, which may explain David's attentiveness to these matters. However, others displayed a nonplussed attitude. Fallon Rogers pointed out that the fields that flooded first were floodplain anyway and had been under water the year before. She enlisted Jack 'Jazzer' McCreary's help to take photographs of the rising water in order to send to mother Jolene and step-father Kenton who were holidaying in Australia. Such an act was particularly worrisome given that a teenager, Harry Martin, had died the previous year in the south of England because he had gone out to take pictures of a storm event. Later, Fallon remained upset because people were ignoring the Bull's karaoke night in order to address the rising waters: 'Ambridge doesn't flood', floundered Fallon, whilst others around her, fortunately, took a different view. A few hours later, the BBC reported that a frightened Fallon tweeted 'get me out of here!' (BBC, 2015).

Similarly, Jill Archer and Caroline Sterling, who were attending a talk in St Stephen's Church, were surprised and perplexed at the sight of Hillary Noakes bursting into the building. Hillary had been lying on her sofa enjoying an afternoon snooze and awoke with her ankles wet. Not quite believing that Grange Spinney had flooded, Jill and Caroline wondered why she had not simply telephoned her neighbours. Such responses are common when people have not experienced an event before and have not been prepared for the situation.

As with any catastrophe, rational decision-making skills are compromised when an extreme weather event occurs. Even when people have insurance to cover the costs of replacing damaged goods, a price cannot be put on the emotional attachment that people have to things such as family heirlooms and photographs. Floods can also threaten an individual's 'ontological security' whereby the home is seen as a place of safety, perhaps unduly so, in an emergency situation (Giddens, 1991; Harries, 2008). This was seen in Ambridge when Clarrie Grundy assisted Lynda Snell in evacuating Ambridge Hall. Lynda was trying, belatedly, to move valuables upstairs and was caught by surprise at the entry of water to her home. Nevertheless, Lynda attempted to save her Coalport figurines and Easter cactus — which was just about to bloom — rather than saving herself despite the highly sensible Clarrie telling her that 'don't be silly, it ain't safe' and 'don't be daft, we have to leave'.

Other factors that moderate risk perception include previous experience of a risk, in this case a flood. Even individuals that self-identify as natural optimists will often become pessimistic and believe a risk to be higher than it actually is when they have been exposed to it before. Similarly, the presence of a catastrophic event can, unconsciously, lead to individuals to make the risk 'absent' as the continual psychological fear proves to be too much for them to continue their daily lives (Bickerstaff & Simmons, 2009). In any case, flood memories are, notoriously, short (McEwen, Garde-Hansen, Holmes,

Jones, & Krause, 2017) with the need to resume normal life as quickly as possible and to push the memory of a catastrophic event to one side. However, references to the flood event have become conspicuous by their absence despite the reappearance of Stefan. Certainly, Ambridge's residents have had other matters on their mind including an attempted murder, kidnapping and another Lillian affair; however, one wonders whether the residents are embracing the return to 'normal' too much.

A NATURAL DISASTER?

It is questionable the extent to which so-called natural disasters are, in fact, natural at all. A hazard — such as a flood — may be naturally occurring, but the disasters that arise from them, in terms of loss of life and assets, are very often caused by societal choices since 'human systems place some people more at risk than others' (Bankoff, 2010). Why, for example, do planners permit building on flood plains when avoidance reduces the exposure of a property and therefore the chance of flooding having severe consequences? Distinctions between 'natural' and 'manufactured' risks are therefore very difficult to make (Beck, 2009). The result is that communities who have been inundated with floodwaters will begin to apportion the blame elsewhere soon after the event. People naturally ask whom or what was responsible and what could be done differently in the future. This 'blame discourse' is a recognised phenomenon and stems from a belief that we can 'control' floods and that disasters are 'preventable' (Rose, Proverbs, Booth, & Manktelow, 2012).

Of course, the vast majority of *Archers* listeners, and Stefan the farmworker, were aware that Rob Titchener's deliberate blocking of a culvert to save Berrow Farm had contributed to the flooding of the village; however, Ambridge residents were not. The BBC reported that Eddie Grundy blamed a new housing development which, he claimed, had altered the water flows: 'I reckon it's all them new houses in Hollerton ... the rain ain't got nowhere to go'. Others resorted to fatalism, believing that nothing could have prevented the flood. Both Brian Aldridge and Kate Madikane were quick to point out that it was, well, just a lot of rain that caused the flood. Such fatalism and denial can be counter-productive in enhancing resilience as denial means that certain individuals are less likely to take preventative action against the future risk of floods (Bubeck, Botzen, & Aerts, 2012; Lin, Shaw, & Ho, 2008).

The blame discourse, therefore, functions in two ways: seeking verifiable causes can help people to make sense of their situation but it can also divert attention away from personal responsibility to prepare for a flood. That said, no one can excuse Kenton for blaming his brother David for the flood and arguing, bizarrely, that it was David's attempt to bring him and his finances down. In reality, Kenton really should have obtained adequate flood insurance as part of the necessary flood preparation measures.

THE BLITZ SPIRIT?

Policymakers are often quick to point to an indefatigable spirit that seems to rise during crises, a so-called 'Blitz Spirit'. Not long after the 2014 floods in the south of England, the then Prime Minister David Cameron said that: '... in the toughest of times we are seeing the best of Britain. It will take time, but together we will deal with these floods, we'll get our country back on its feet and we will build a more resilient country for the future' (Cameron, 2014).

The language of resilience is, in this sense, used to frame events in a much more positive way than identifying places as 'vulnerable' and 'risky'. The framing of disasters, particularly in the media, then falls between emphasising 'resilience' or 'vulnerability' (Furedi, 2007). Resilience captures the ability of individuals and communities to respond well to adversity. However, vulnerability framings tend to stress the long-lasting impacts of disasters on individual and collective psychological health as 'a rhetorical idiom that tacitly situates people and their experiences within the context of powerlessness and a lack of agency' (Furedi, 2007, p. 250).

Both the resilience and vulnerability framings could be applied to the Ambridge case study. Resilient actions were evident in both flood response and recovery. Whilst Ambridge, like many rural areas, is physically vulnerable owing to a lack of access routes, residents were able to pull together to respond to the flood situation. For example, when Ambridge was cut off from outside help, residents were unable to receive sandbags from the local council headquarters. Yet, PC Harrison Burns was on hand to coordinate a response that used items to hand to fashion make-shift flood defences. Following the flood, David stepped up to head the Ambridge Flood Action Group (FAG), after an interpersonal spat with Jennifer Archer. The group met with key institutions such as the Environment Agency in terms of understanding flood reports. Ambridge residents, it could be said, are reasonably well-educated with seemingly disposable amounts of time. Not only could the FAG call on the help of Jim Lloyd, a retired professor, and even Lillian Bellamy, not known for her civic spirit, stepped up to support the group. One Twitter wag wondered if Lillian's official role in the FAG would be 'Assistant Secretary to the Head', or FAGASH for short (Wallington, 2015). Flood Action Groups are an important part of the agenda to learn to live with floods as they can help the authorities on the ground by encouraging preparation for flooding and in supporting recovery.

On the other hand, whilst the Blitz Spirit was much evidenced, the model was challenged with outright individualism and, in some cases, powerlessness to cope with the aftermath of the flood. As noted above, Rob Titchener had only the interests of Berrow Farm at heart when he blocked a culvert. Similarly, Christine Barford's house was burgled whilst she had been temporarily displaced. Extreme situations can often mean that people fend for themselves and this was seen in New Orleans after Hurricane Katrina in 2005 where US Civil Defense Authorities were called in because of looting and other misdemeanours (Sims, 2007). Of course, those vulnerable to floods include older people and children, tenants and others who cannot access insurance (Kazmierczak, Cavan, Connelly, & Lindley, 2015). Freda Fry, an Ambridge elder, lost her life after attempting to drive through floodwaters to find her husband Bert. After becoming trapped, she was rescued and taken to hospital where she contracted pneumonia and, subsequently, had a heart attack. It is therefore important to understand the vulnerability in an area as well as emphasising the key aspects which may make it more resilient.

CONCLUSION: A FLOOD-RESILIENT AMBRIDGE?

This chapter aimed to explore the way in which Ambridge's flood spoke to many of the academic issues around flood risk management in the United Kingdom today. We saw a variable response to the risk and a tension between community resilience and individualism. As the months have worn on, there has been a noticeable decline in any mention of the flood and very little recorded evidence of the FAG meeting on a regular basis. More worryingly, there are no accounts of practical resilience measures that could be undertaken in order to prepare for a future flood and to reduce the vulnerabilities inherent in the village.

Rural areas are disproportionately disadvantaged compared to urban areas in terms of flood defence allocation since the cost-benefit ratio is skewed towards protecting areas with more assets. However, they remain physically disadvantaged in terms of access routes to and from the village. This is counter-balanced by Ambridge's relatively tight-knit community of mostly well-educated residents. There is a high amount of social and community capital that can be capitalised upon to help Ambridge residents to respond to and recover from floods. We have seen this already with the Ambridge FAG who kept the pressure on authorities to stop the intrusion of a new road potentially altering their flood risk.

Ambridge property owners should consider a range of further measures that can be taken in order to help them prepare for future flooding. We saw that the distribution of sandbags was not possible due to vehicular access during the Ambridge flood. In any case, sandbags do not perform well in test situations. Recent years have seen the development of new technologies that are smarter, such as door guards, flood doors, and air brick covers, which can all be applied to properties in order to increase their flood resilience. This is a developing market in the United Kingdom and there is a lot of mistrust surrounding the products, what they can do and how they behave during a real flood event (Connelly et al., 2015). However, they work for smaller floods and slow down the rate of water entry into a property when floods exceed 600 mm. Local entrepreneurs may not have spotted this business opportunity immediately, although Toby may wish to look into the enterprise should the gin business fail to succeed.

In Ambridge, the FAG certainly needs to meet more often that it seems to. Combined with the property level measures described above, it would be prudent to host 'dry run' flood response events in order to check that Ambridge's residents are prepared for any future floods. Further mapping work could be undertaken by the local council in order to identify where vulnerable people in the village and places, such as St Stephen's Church and Grey Gables, should be identified as being key resilience centres. This information should be shared with the FAG in order to fit into their response plans. The Ambridge FAG should also encourage residents to prepare personal flood action plans for each property.

The Ambridge flood event characterised many of the debates surrounding the practicalities of flood risk management to date. Ambridge was fortunate to contain enough community capital that gave residents the capacity to cope with the flood event but more could be done to prepare the village for any future flood inundation. The chapter has tried to identify other practical measures that Ambridge's residents may wish to undertake. Of course, we can only ever speculate about how much Ambridge's residents have learned from the 2015 flood: the true test, of course, would be the occurrence of another flood.

REFERENCES

Bankoff, G. (2010). No such things as "natural disasters": Why we had to invent them. *Harvard International Review*, 24. Retrieved from http://hir.harvard.edu/article/?a=2694

BBC. (2015). *UK Weather warning: Borsetshire* [The Archers Blog]. Retrieved from http://www.bbc.co.uk/programmes/

articles/4gnZ0YZDdJW2NHHZ1vYz00y/uk-weather-warning-borsetshire

Beal, A. (n.d.). *BBC Radio — The Archers Omnibus podcast catch up service*. Retrieved from http://www.adrianbeal.com/archers/

Beck, U. (1992). *Risk society: Towards a new modernity*. London: Sage.

Beck, U. (2009). *World at risk*. Cambridge: Polity Press.

Bickerstaff, K., & Simmons, P. (2009). Absencing/presencing risk: Rethinking proximity and the experience of living with major technological hazards. *Geoforum, 40*(5), 864–872.

Bubeck, P., Botzen, W. J., & Aerts, J. C. (2012). A review of risk perceptions and other factors that influence flood mitigation behavior. *Risk Analysis, 32*(9), 1481–1495.

Butler, C., & Pidgeon, N. (2011). From 'flood defence' to 'flood risk management': Exploring governance, responsibility, and blame. *Environment and Planning C: Government and Policy, 29*(3), 533–547.

Cameron, D. (2014). *Statement by the Prime Minister on the storms and flooding affecting the United Kingdom*. Retrieved from https://www.gov.uk/government/speeches/david-camerons-statement-on-the-uk-storms-and-flooding

Connelly, A., Gabalda, V., Garvin, S., Hunter, K., Kelly, D., Lawson, N. … White, I. (2015). Testing innovative technologies to manage flood risk. *Proceedings of the ICE - Water Management, 168*(2), 66–73.

Eakin, H., Eriksen, S., Eikeland, P.-O., & Øyen, C. (2011). Public sector reform and governance for adaptation: Implications of New Public Management for adaptive capacity in Mexico and Norway. *Environmental Management*, 47(3), 338–351.

Environment Agency. (2016). *The costs and impacts of the winter 2013 to 2014 floods*. Bristol: The Environment Agency. Retrieved from https://www.gov.uk/government/uploads/system/uploads/attachment_data/file/501784/The_costs_and_impacts_of_the_winter_2013_to_2014_floods_-_report.pdf

Furedi, F. (2007). The changing meaning of disaster. *Area*, 39(4), 482–489.

Giddens, A. (1991). *The consequences of modernity*. Cambridge: Polity Press.

Harries, T. (2008). Feeling secure or being secure? Why it can seem better not to protect yourself against a natural hazard. *Health Risk Society*, 10(5), 479–490.

Johnson, C. L., & Priest, S. J. (2008). Flood risk management in England: A changing landscape of risk responsibility. *International Journal of Water Resources Development*, 24, 513–525.

Kazmierczak, A., Cavan, G., Connelly, A., & Lindley, S. (2015). *Mapping flood disadvantage in Scotland 2015*. Edinburgh: The Scottish Government. Retrieved from http://www.gov.scot/Publications/2015/12/9621/downloads#res490788

Lin, S., Shaw, D., & Ho, M. C. (2008). Why are flood and landslide victims less willing to take mitigation measures than the public? *Natural Hazards*, 44(2), 305–314.

McEwen, L., Garde-Hansen, J., Holmes, A., Jones, O., & Krause, F. (2017). Sustainable flood memories, lay knowledges and the development of community resilience to future flood risk. *Transactions of the Institute of British Geographers*, *42*(1), 14–28.

Perkins, C. (2016). Mapping Ambridge. In C. Courage, N. Headlam, & P. Matthews (Eds.), *The Archers in fact and fiction* (pp. 89–102). New York, NY: Peter Lang.

Rose, C. B., Proverbs, D. G., Booth, C. A., & Manktelow, K. I. (2012). 'Three times is enemy action'–flood experiences and flood perceptions. *WIT Transactions on Ecology and the Environment*, *159*, 233–242.

Sims, B. (2007). 'The day after the hurricane': Infrastructure, order, and the New Orleans Police Department's response to Hurricane Katrina. *Social Studies of Science*, *37*(1), 111–118.

Wallington, N. [@Drwallington] (2015, 26 April). Lillian joins the Flood Action Group as Assistant Secretary to the Head. Or FAGASH, for short #thearchers' [Twitter Post]. Retrieved from https://twitter.com/Drwallington/status/592265921214971904

White, I., Connelly, A., Garvin, S., Lawson, N., & O'Hare, P. (2015). Towards best practice in property level flood protection. *Town and Country Planning Journal*, February, 74–79.

Wildavsky, A., & Dake, K. (1990). Theories of risk perception: Who fears what and why? *Daedalus*, *119*(4), 41–60.

PEER REVIEW, STEFAN (LOCATION PROTECTED)

It could all have been so different. Perhaps I should have confronted Rob and stopped him from blocking that culvert. That would have stopped Ambridge from flooding and saved everyone from the sight of Joe Grundy in a tiger onesie. I tried to talk but no one seemed to notice. Who would listen to my voice? I don't even have a surname. It must have all seemed so plausible when Rob bribed me to get as far away from Ambridge as possible. But I came back to frighten him. I'll never go away. That said, I'm a bit worried about where my next job will come from. With all this Brexit business, I might not be able to get another casual job in rural England (Ha! God knows where they think they will get the cheap labour from). Perhaps my next stop should be Minnesota …

CHAPTER NINE

AFTER THE FLOOD: HOW CAN AMBRIDGE RESIDENTS DEVELOP RESILIENCE TO FUTURE FLOODING?

Fiona Gleed

ABSTRACT

Flooding is a frequent problem in the United Kingdom, with 1.8 million people living in homes that are likely to flood at least once in 75 years (Sayers, Horritt, Penning-Rowsell, & McKenzie, 2015). In 2015, the River Am burst its banks, resulting in up to 1 metre of flooding in Ambridge and causing significant damage and disruption to the village. A '4Ps' approach is proposed to predict, prevent, protect from and prepare for flooding. Applying this model to evidence from Ambridge allows strategies for a flood resilient community to be explored.

Keywords: Flood resilience; community resilience; built environment; catchment management; risk management

INTRODUCTION

In February 2015, the village of Ambridge in Borsetshire was subject to flooding on a scale unprecedented in living memory, or at least its broadcast history. The River Am burst its banks, resulting in up to 1 metre (m) of flooding in Ambridge. A year after the flood, some properties were still being renovated partly as a result of drying times, which have been noted as a factor in extended recovery times (Pitt, 2008). By exploring these events in more detail, strategies to improve flood resilience can be developed, for Ambridge and beyond.

Whilst the concept of flooding is familiar, it is difficult to define as it depends on our expectations of the space that water should occupy in the landscape. Generally, for water to be considered as flooding it is likely to be in an inconvenient place at infrequent and unpredictable times. Large volumes of water may overflow on to seasonal water meadows and coastal roads may regularly be submerged by tides without either being considered as flooding. However, where water enters homes or business premises, blocks transport routes or affects prime agricultural land even small volumes are likely to be described as flooding.

HIERARCHY OF RESILIENCE

Until recently, the emphasis in preventing flooding has been to defend property by providing physical channels and barriers to keep water in defined areas. In response to a number of severe floods and with a growing recognition that the climate is changing, this has moved towards a risk management approach with an emphasis on resilience to allow rapid recovery (Johnson & Priest, 2008). A hierarchy of responses is proposed to Predict, Prevent, Protect and Prepare for flooding. This is analogous to the '4Ps' approach of Pursue, Prevent, Protect, Prepare used in the United Kingdom for Serious and Organised Crime, with prediction substituted for pursuit. At the highest level, the requirement is to predict the likelihood, location and severity of flooding. This relies on analysis of historic patterns of rainfall and an understanding of the landscape but must be modified to consider the effect of changes in climate and land use. By understanding the areas that are most vulnerable to flood events and the depth of water anticipated, informed decisions can be made on the location of new development and investment in flood protection.

In order to prevent flooding, water needs to be kept within recognised watercourses and storage, whether natural or artificial. This can be achieved by changing land use to increase the volume absorbed and reduce runoff, increasing the capacity of watercourses through dredging or raising banks, and by providing additional volume in floodplains, ponds or tanks. Whatever degree of prevention is provided there will always be a residual risk. A variety of methods can be used to protect property by excluding or diverting water. During construction floor heights can be set above anticipated flood levels, flood proofing can be built in to openings and plumbing, or radical approaches such as allowing the whole building to float up on the rising water can be incorporated.

But with shorter timescales, the main option available is to prepare for flooding. This may be through tangible actions such as moving possessions upstairs, installing barriers or stocking up with food, water and other consumables, but it can also include intangible arrangements like checking flood warnings, alerting neighbours and reviewing potential evacuation routes. In developing the resilience of Ambridge, we need to consider all levels of this hierarchy.

PREDICTING PATTERNS OF FLOODING

There are a number of different sources of natural flooding, which can occur independently or interact.

- Coastal flooding arises primarily from tides but with significant influence from weather systems. The highest water levels are experienced when a particularly high tide coincides with low pressure and on-shore winds;

- Fluvial flooding involves water in rivers and streams, with high flows causing water to overspill the banks or forge new channels;

- Surface water flooding is a result of water that is running over land. This is usually pluvial flooding as a direct result of rainfall but can also include melt-water after snow and water overflowing from drains that have become surcharged or blocked;

- Groundwater flooding occurs when the water table rises, reaching the surface in low lying areas or flowing in to underground structures such as basements and tunnels.

Floods may also result from failure of designed systems, such as reservoirs, water supply and sewers. To determine flood risk for a given location, the geography of the area, records of previous flooding and predictions of climate trends are used to determine the likelihood of each mechanism, separately and in combination (Sayers, Horritt, Penning-Rowsell, & McKenzie, 2015).

The county of Borsetshire is close to Birmingham, remote from the coast and well upstream of tidal effects. A Borsetshire

Map (BBC, n.d.) shows the River Am flowing north from Hollerton to join the River Perch in Borchester. The village of Ambridge is at a historic crossing point where a bridge was built to cross the river, which flows from East to West at this point. The Ambridge Map (BBC, n.d.) shows there are now two bridges with the roads meeting at the top of the triangular green, forming an 'A'. The majority of the village lies to the North of the river but the Church and Brookfield Farm are to the South, separated by fields and Heydon Berrow. Little information was found about the geology although there has been recent mention of a spring becoming active. However an archaeological map of Ambridge, produced circa 1980 (Smethurst, n.d.), provides information about topography with contour lines showing land falling steeply from Heydon Berrow in the South East down towards the River Am. Reports from the 2015 flood event (BBC, 2015) are primarily for low lying land close to the river, affecting properties below the 300 m contour and making roads impassable. There were some reports of high flows further from the river, in particular at Berrow Farm on the Eastern flank of Heydon Berrow.

Taken together, the geography and history suggest that the primary concerns are fluvial and surface water flooding. Groundwater flooding may also have contributed. At 300 m above sea level, and miles inland, coastal flooding can be discounted. Both fluvial and surface water flooding derive within the rainfall catchment area. The River Am catchment is bounded by the Hassett Hills in the west, but the eastern watershed is less well defined with road and rail corridors modifying natural drainage paths. Records of rainfall and river flows can be used to assess the probability of flooding but need to be modified to account for future trends in weather systems and development. In the national Climate Change Risk Assessment (Sayers et al., 2015) a number of scenarios are considered for rainfall intensity, predicted to increase as the global climate becomes more energetic, and population growth, which not only increases the number of people potentially at risk but also drives changes in land use. These in turn affect drainage routes and infiltration rates. Overall, risks are expected to increase significantly within the next 10 years, requiring adaptation to limit damage.

PREVENTION IS BETTER THAN CURE

In order to limit flooding, measures can be taken to reduce the volume of water or to increase the capacity of watercourses. A combination of engineered and natural approaches can be used, depending on the context. Engineered approaches have been preferred in the recent past with networks of drains and culverts used to contain and direct water. More natural approaches can increase infiltration, improve connectivity and provide storage (Dadson et al., 2017) and are gaining in popularity. This type of approach could work well in Ambridge, with schemes like Adam Macy's herbal leys underway and Brian Aldridge proposing to plant native woodland on his newly acquired land. If this Riparian Woodland can be extended to sub-catchment scale it could achieve significant reductions in peak flows (Dixon, Sear, Odoni, Sykes, & Lane, 2016).

Regular and appropriate maintenance is needed for both engineered and natural approaches. This can be as simple as taking time to sweep leaves away from drainage gullies or may require a detailed management plan to balance the demands of biodiversity and flood risk reduction. Additional work is required after flood events as high water levels and changed flow paths leave debris in their wake. At Berrow Farm, culverts had been maintained before the flood and were cleared by Ed Grundy afterwards. However, during the flood event they were not fully operational as Rob Titchener had blocked them to divert water away from the dairy. The displaced water could have increased flows in the River Am, exacerbating flooding downstream in the village.

PROTECTING PROPERTY, PEOPLE AND PETS

There will always be some residual risk of flooding and further measures are needed to protect people and property. This can be achieved at a variety of scales from substantial walls along miles of river banks to boards for an individual door. Larger defences can be obtrusive, blocking views and access to the river all the time in order to provide a larger channel on rare occasions. However, there can be scope to provide protection within other development. For example, the new relief road could be designed to include embankments and drainage that divert water as well as traffic.

Protecting one area will affect others, with potential to cause flooding elsewhere both upstream and downstream. It is fairly intuitive that with more water flowing on past a protected area there is an increased potential for flooding downstream. However higher water levels, enabled by defences, can also cause water to back up and cause flooding upstream. Protection as well as prevention therefore needs to be considered at a larger scale. In England, this is achieved using Catchment Flood Management Plans (CFMP) for specific rivers and coastal regions within each of 10 River Basin Districts (Environment Agency, 2009). Consequently, protection is required at a smaller scale for particularly critical or vulnerable areas. Within Ambridge, there are a number of homes and businesses that should be a priority to improve the resilience of the village as a whole.

Brookfield Farm was inundated during the flood and the storyline emphasised the potential impact on the business if milk production was compromised by contamination or power outage. However, there is also potential for contamination from farms. Slurry is the most obvious pollutant but there may also be stores of agrichemicals, such as fertilisers and pesticides. And whilst milk is considered a pure and healthy product, it too can cause significant environmental problems in watercourses. There is therefore scope to design a localised protection for the farm. This could include constructing landscaping bunds, improving existing walls and obtaining specific barriers to close gaps in the perimeter that are needed for routine activity such as vehicle and stock movements. As the dairy facility includes underground spaces for milk pumps and tanks, there would also need to be water pumps to remove water that had risen within the ground or found other routes through.

The Bungalow, currently occupied by Bert Fry, would be a high priority; its proximity to the river suggests a high likelihood of flooding whilst a single storey increases the potential severity of an incident. Flood proof doors, non-return valves for plumbing and covers for airbricks could have been incorporated during refurbishment, reducing the marginal cost, but can also be retrofitted if this opportunity was overlooked (Joseph, Proverbs, Lamond, & Wassell, 2011). Bert should also be able to take advantage of Flood Re (2017), a Government-backed scheme to ensure that affordable insurance is available for existing homes in flood risk areas.

Flood Re is limited to domestic properties so The Stables, which is the base for Shula Hebden Lloyd's livery stables and Alistair Lloyd's veterinary practice as well as their home, would not qualify. This increases the incentive to be proactive to limit damage in any future flood events. A combination of measures would be needed, tailored to the layout and purpose of the various buildings. Hopefully the investment in equipment and premises following Anisha Jayakody joining the practice will benefit from robust and resilient defences built in to the fabric. Demountable barriers could be obtained to ensure that the stable yard remains dry, protecting livery horses from the stress of evacuation and providing an additional layer of defences for the surgery and any pets being treated on the premises.

The Bull and the Village Shop both play important roles in village life but have particular vulnerabilities. Pub cellars are below ground, making them more vulnerable and consideration needs to be given to emergency evacuation routes as well as stock protection. The shop stockroom is above ground but includes large quantities of perishable goods, which are particularly vulnerable to water ingress. For these properties, careful detailing and specification of materials can minimise water damage, reducing time required to recover (Escarameia, Tagg, Walliman, Zevenbergen, & Anvarifar, 2012) and reopen to support the community.

BE PREPARED

Flooding is an unusual risk as there is a significant variation in probability depending on location; those affected tend to be clustered and it is possible to predict incidents hours if not days in advance. These factors make us less aware of flooding than other risks but also allow more scope for action when an event is imminent.

In 2015/2016, 20,000 homes across the north of England were flooded in a series of events. This was the highest total since 2007 when 48,000 homes were flooded. For comparison, the most recent data available shows 474,000 burglaries from dwellings in England and Wales (ONS, 2017) and

31,300 fires in dwellings in England (Statistics Unit, 2016). Based on the 2011 Census data (ONS, 2013) there are 22.1 million households in England and 1.3 million in Wales, so these equate to a probability of domestic burglary of one in fifty, and a probability of domestic fire of one in seven hundred. The Climate Change Risk Assessment (Sayers et al., 2015) estimates that there are currently 2.8 million UK residential properties at some risk of flooding. This means that the majority of the population have a flood risk less than one in one thousand, so less risk of a flood than a fire. Of these properties, 1.8 million have a flood risk greater than one in seventy-five and the most vulnerable of these are more likely to experience a flood than a burglary in any given year. These comparisons may be more useful in encouraging householders to make appropriate preparations than the use of return periods or the likelihood scales suggested as an alternative in the National Flood Resilience Review (Environment Agency, 2016).

Preparation for individuals includes becoming familiar with predictions and taking action to protect their homes. Resources to support this are available from organisations like Know Your Flood Risk (2017). Understanding of the implications of increasing paved area and the benefits of water butts can also help households contribute to flood prevention. Emergency plans can be made, ensuring that possessions and paperwork are positioned as safely as possible or can quickly be moved, insurance details and tenancy agreements are understood and up to date, and alerts can be received directly or via the local radio station. BBC regional news services played an important role in the Ambridge flood story, alerting residents and reporting impacts, and their local radio stations can be a vital information source where internet connections and electricity supplies have failed. Warnings also allow more detailed preparations to be made in the days and hours before a potential flood event. This could include checking on neighbours, deploying temporary barriers, moving supplies and possessions to upstairs room, and being ready to evacuate, with bags packed and plans agreed.

Flood events tend to affect not just individual homes but whole communities, such as Ambridge. Even those who have avoided direct damage to property are likely to experience inconvenience, if not peril, as a result of flooded roads, disrupted businesses and interruptions to utility services. Preparation therefore needs to take place for a wider area and a number of different timescales. In Ambridge, flood wardens had already been identified and were able to alert some residents to the imminent inundation. However, further work could be done to identify evacuation points, ensuring that people knew their location and that the venues had appropriate provisions and robust communications. This would have avoided the anxiety over Phoebe's location and could have reassured Freda Fry sufficiently to prevent her attempt to return home.

Flood action groups can be helpful in allowing local people to contribute to their community's resilience, gathering information to inform prediction, raising awareness of the potential for long-term strategies to prevent flooding and protect property, and developing response plans for future flood events. I therefore call on you to go with the flow, and join the Resilient Ambridge Flood Team.

POSTSCRIPT

A few weeks after the 2017 Academic Archers conference, I was listening to the local radio and heard a call for volunteers to join the Avon Community Resilience Team. This has been formed by SARAID, better known for their international rescue work, in collaboration with Avon Fire and Rescue and Avon and Somerset Police. We started training in April with a view to offering support during floods in our own catchment and further afield. Other Community Resilience Teams have already been formed by SERVE ON, working with Emergency Services and Local Authorities in Wiltshire and Hampshire. With roles ranging from fund raising to flood rescue, there are opportunities for people of all ages and abilities to get involved. If you hear of a group local to you why not give it a go, or at least give a donation.

ACKNOWLEDGEMENTS

The support of my PhD supervisors Prof Pete Walker and Dr Juliana Holley at the University of Bath, and Dr Julie Bregulla of the BRE is gratefully acknowledged.

REFERENCES

BBC. (2015). Ambridge floods at a glance. *The Archers*. Retrieved from http://www.bbc.co.uk/programmes/articles/4WZj29DWJzZGkyQQS6xcQFt/ambridge-floods-at-a-glance

BBC. (n.d.). *The Archers Wallpaper* [archived]. Retrieved from http://www.bbc.co.uk/radio4/archers/wallpaper/. Accessed on February 14, 2017.

Dadson, S. J., Hall, J. W., Murgatroyd, A., Acreman, M., Bates, P., Beven, K., & Lane, S. N. (2017). A restatement of the natural science evidence concerning catchment-based 'natural' flood management in the UK. Paper presented at the Proceedings of the Royal Society A.

Dixon, S. J., Sear, D. A., Odoni, N. A., Sykes, T., & Lane, S. N. (2016). The effects of river restoration on catchment scale flood risk and flood hydrology. *Earth Surface Processes and Landforms*, 41(7), 997–1008.

Environment Agency. (2009). Catchment flood management plans. *Flooding and Coastal Change*. Retrieved from https://www.gov.uk/government/collections/catchment-flood-management-plans. Accessed on February 14, 2017.

Environment Agency. (2016). *National flood resilience review*. Retrieved from www.gov.uk/government/publications

Escarameia, M., Tagg, A., Walliman, N., Zevenbergen, C., & Anvarifar, F. (2012). The role of building materials in improved flood resilience and routes for implementation. Paper presented at the 2nd European conference on flood risk management, FLOODrisk2012, Rotterdam, The Netherlands.

Flood Re. (2017). *Flood Re exists to promote the availability and affordability of flood insurance*. Retrieved from http://www.floodre.co.uk/homeowner/. Accessed on February 14, 2017.

Johnson, C. L., & Priest, S. J. (2008). Flood risk management in England: A changing landscape of risk responsibility? *International Journal of Water Resources Development*, 24(4), 513–525. doi:10.1080/07900620801923146

Joseph, R., Proverbs, D., Lamond, J., & Wassell, P. (2011). An analysis of the costs of resilient reinstatement of flood affected properties: A case study of the 2009 flood event in Cockermouth. *Structural Survey, 29*(4), 279–293. doi:10.1108/02630801111162350

Know Your Flood Risk. (2017). *Flood guide for home-owners*. Retrieved from http://www.knowyourfloodrisk.co. uk/. Accessed on May 17, 2017.

ONS. (2013). *2011 Census: Population and household estimates for the United Kingdom*, March 2011. Statistical Bulletin. Retrieved from https://www.ons.gov.uk/peoplepopu lationandcommunity/populationandmigration/populationesti mates/bulletins/populationandhouseholdestimatesfortheunited kingdom/2011-03-21#households. Accessed on May 17, 2017.

ONS. (2017). *Crime in England and Wales: Year ending Dec 2016*. Statistical Bulletin. Retrieved from https://www.ons. gov.uk/peoplepopulationandcommunity/crimeandjustice/bul-letins/crimeinenglandandwales/yearendingdec2016. Accessed on May 17, 2017.

Pitt, S. M. (2008). *Learning lessons from the 2007 floods. Full report*. London: Cabinet Office.

Sayers, P. B., Horritt, M. S., Penning-Rowsell, E., & McKenzie, A. (2015). *Climate Change Risk Assessment 2017: Projections of future flood risk in the UK*. London: Committee on Climate Change.

Smethurst, W. (n.d.). Archaeological map of Ambridge, circa 1980 published in *The Archers: The Official Companion*. Retrieved from http://jeremymcneill.tripod.com/ambridge-map2.html. Accessed on February 14, 2017.

Statistics Unit. (2016). *Fire Statistics England, 2014/15*. Statistical Bulletin 08/16. London. Retrieved from https:// www.gov.uk/government/uploads/system/uploads/attachment_ data/file/532364/fire-statistics-england-1415-hosb0816.pdf

PEER REVIEW BY CHARLIE THOMAS, A DAMARA CAPITAL OUTPOST, SCOTLAND

Flood resilience isn't difficult. A good estate manager knows his land and takes the time to understand its hydrology. Talking to people is really useful in that, particularly people like Adam, whose family has farmed the land for years, and who has learned from experience elsewhere. But it can't be green pastures all the way. We need to get the infrastructure right and be ready to challenge people who don't respect others' safety. It's been a pleasant surprise seeing the approach in Scotland, with specific Building Regulations and an established tradition of riparian responsibilities as well as rights. The impacts of flooding shouldn't be underestimated though: it costs lives, businesses and jobs. And the way we address that is by doing what we can, when we can. Timeliness, that's the key.

CHAPTER TEN

LOCATING AMBRIDGE: PUBLIC BROADCASTING, REGION AND IDENTITY, AN EVERYDAY STORY OF WORCESTERSHIRE FOLK?

Tom Nicholls

ABSTRACT

The West Midlands region has been poorly represented in national media and especially in fictional media forms. The Archers *is therefore a very important part of representation of the region to the nation. These two representational elements — regional and national culture — are part of the BBC's duties under the Royal Charter. As such, they form a core obligation for the BBC. For many years arguments have raged over whether Ambridge is located in Worcestershire or Warwickshire. This is, of course, largely a matter of interest within the region, but does have some wider implications about narrative*

*fiction. Whilst, in one sense Ambridge and Borsetshire
are purely fictional, they simultaneously have a potential impact on the national image of the West Midlands
and especially its rural areas. This chapter will consider
both reasons to suggest that* The Archers *is specifically
drawn from the county of Worcestershire and issues of
identity formation that may arise from the representations offered by* The Archers *of the county and the West
Midlands region.*

Keywords: Worcestershire; West Midlands; identity;
public service broadcasting; broadcast drama

Trying to geographically locate a fictional radio soap opera
may seem both unnecessary and indeed to miss the point
of drama. However, there is a tradition of locating soap operas
in the UK case, either by region or by city. Thus, *Coronation
Street* (Granada/ITV, 1960–), though notionally set in
Weatherfield is always taken to be located in Salford or Greater
Manchester. *Eastenders* (BBC, 1985–) is by title clearly set in
the east end of London, though exactly where Walford is might
be open to some speculation. For *Emmerdale Farm/Emmerdale*
(Yorkshire/ITV, 1972–), parallel to *The Archers* as a rurally
located soap, the location was Beckindale village, now known
as Emmerdale village. But, perhaps for most viewers this is less
of a precise location than the North Yorkshire Dales as a setting. Why would the supposed location of *The Archers* matter?
I'm going to argue that in terms of representation in national
broadcasting that it does both for the West Midlands as
a whole, but especially for Worcestershire in particular, this is
a rare opportunity for representation. The extent to which this
might be part of identity formation will also be considered,
fraught though these claims can be.

Whilst many visual aspects of the television soap opera locate it immediately — the underground station for example in *EastEnders* — radio as an aural medium is more restricted in immediately imbuing a drama with a detectable location. This also means that the idea of the location can be easily built up in the audience's imagination with publicity photos taken on set and on location in the geographical area for television. But for radio drama this causes problems when it clashes with the listener's imagination. This is more of an issue when photographs of the cast members or the characters appear, creating a mismatch with their voice characteristics and the image they create, than with the images of locations. Ambridge in *The Archers* can be located through the use of accented voices and dialect, descriptions of the landscape, characters mentioning actual towns and cities, references to the agriculture of the region and aspects of regional culture. One could argue that some of these properties are not just restricted to a specific region, but taken in combination they could signify one.

There has been some discussion about the range of character voices in *The Archers*. It is generally assumed that characters divide between those with Standard Received Pronunciation and regional accents (Alice and Chris Carter exemplify this range.) As William Barras (Courage et al., 2016, p. 25) points out, these do not always follow a logical distribution in families, especially true of Pip of the Archers at Brookfield. The range of accents within *The Archers* is consonant with those extant in Worcestershire. First and foremost the series does not largely make use of a 'Mummerset' accent which might connote the West Country. Instead the mixture of Birmingham, South and North Worcestershire, Gloucestershire borders and Welsh accents reflect the everyday mix of speech in the county. Based on a notion of 'rhotic' speech being deployed by some characters in the programme, the location based on past research (*ibid.*, p. 20) might be expected to be in the South West. However, the generally accepted location of the series is in the West Midlands, possibly straddling the Worcestershire/Warwickshire border.

Beyond the accents themselves are the values attributed to them. In the past a Birmingham accent indicated a suspect character — think Jack Woolley when he first arrived in Ambridge or Sid Perks as something of tearaway in earlier times. More recently Vicky Tucker was represented more positively as an effervescent Birmingham character, but one that initially villagers found hard to take (she also did not remain long enough in Ambridge to be fully transformed into a local character). But for local accents, actually closer to South Worcestershire/Gloucestershire borders I would argue, those in the Grundy and Tucker families are seen as indicators of stability and trustworthiness for the most part. For many years Walter Gabriel's 'Me Old, Me Old Beauty' was seen as the prime example of both local speech and these values of constancy. The expression itself, as claimed by Patricia Howard, niece of *The Archers* creator, Godfrey Baseley (interview, February 2017), was based on a worker at the Stockwood Stud Stables in Inkberrow, Worcestershire (Patricia is his sister's daughter who grew up on the family farm near Hanbury, Worcestershire).

Descriptions of the landscape in *The Archers* are very localised. The River Am valley and rolling countryside visible to characters from the top of Lakey Hill chime with much of the Worcestershire landscape. Whilst this clearly makes an East Anglian location unlikely, it does not really divide the Midlands from the South West or indeed much of the country. Attempts to map Ambridge over the last 50 years are discussed by Chris Perkins (Courage, Headlam, & Matthews, 2017, pp. 89–102). These tend to centre on the village rather than the region. Thus they give little indication of the wider area in which Ambridge might be set (or at least no relation to surrounding counties). This aids listeners in imagining the village or spotting factual errors when they occur in the storyline but it provides little wider knowledge of the gap between fictive world and actual places.

The mention of actual towns and cities is perhaps a more reliable guide to notionally where Ambridge is located. At one time there was not infrequent mention of Worcester and neighbouring towns. Most recently on Anisha Jayakody's arrival in Ambridge it was stated that she was living in Droitwich, Worcestershire. Birmingham is frequently alluded to as a place characters go to, never to return — Vicky, Bethany and Mike Tucker and also Hayley Tucker when she broke up with Roy. It is significant that the Metropolitan centre which Ambridge is placed in opposition to is almost always Birmingham. London does feature, but largely as an exotic location or a place to get away to. Many years ago when Jennifer Aldridge first met now-husband Brian in 1975, she mentioned that the only good thing about London was the down train from Paddington. Thus, suggesting a distance from the capital, the desirability of the countryside, and by reference to Paddington, possible locations for the fictional village. (This would suggest Worcestershire or Gloucestershire rather than further east in the Midlands).

Most commonly Ambridge has been considered to be based on Inkberrow and Hanbury in Worcestershire, perhaps partly because of Godfrey Baseley's family links in the area. In the fifties promotional photographs for the series were taken at Summerhill Farm (Patricia Howard, interview February 2017) and the surrounding district. There were also a series of events for tourists and *Archers* fans to visit Ambridge based on Hanbury. They could visit a house and take tea with characters from the soap (Interview with Patricia Howard, February 2017). In 1977 there was an

attempt to find the ideal Ambridge village as part of a newspaper campaign to boost audiences for the programme
(Smethurst, 2000, p. 144). The village of Ashton under Hill
near the Bredon Hills in Worcestershire was chosen. A whole
week's episodes were recorded in the village, but according to
Smethurst, the idea that Ambridge was based on Inkberrow
persisted within the press.

Finally, in terms of agriculture, the mixed agricultural
practice of the West Midlands is beneficial for the range of
stories that can be covered in the programme. Thus both livestock and arable farming are common in the region together
with market gardening for which the Vale of Evesham is
known nationally. Given the original function of the series, to
provide agricultural information through a drama, this has
enabled issues which some other regions would preclude.
Over the years this diverse practice has led to stories on
organic farming, GM crops, intensive dairy farms, mob grazing and more recently Adam Macy's herbal leys. The presence of both tenant farms as well as larger corporate ones has
also given opportunity to discuss a range of farming practice
within different economic contexts. In more recent years this
might be typified as the struggles of the Grundy family to
remain involved in agriculture and the entrepreneurship of
the Fairbrothers' in trying to establish poultry farming as
against the continuing conglomeration of Borcestershire Land
and Justin Elliot's Damara Capital company. Aspects of local
culture are much harder to identify in *The Archers* and one
could argue that in a globalised, transnational world this
notion of local culture and character is receding. First and
foremost amongst these would be the Grundy's cider and
perry making. Whilst these crafts are by no means restricted
to Worcestershire they are an intrinsic part of the locality.
This is partly conditioned by the climate with, the much wet-
ter western counties of the UK so whilst the West Country is

more famous for the trade, a number of established cider makers are in the region. The tradition of home cider making and fruit wines is also very much part of this region's home crafts.

All of these elements are consonant with a Worcestershire location, but clearly do not absolutely establish it. The same comparative test could be applied to a Warwickshire location to see if this produces a similar match.

One might reasonably ask what is at stake in trying to place a fictional drama serial in an actual location. I would argue that in broadcasting, especially public service broadcasting (PSB) the location, real or imaginary, of dramas is important. For the BBC and other PSBs this became a widely debated issue. In the 1990s it led to a view that broadcasting was far too London-centric. The 2003 Communications Act instituted a 25% quota for television production outside London. More precisely this was outside the M25, so only moving a quarter of commissions from Greater London. Nonetheless, the BBC also made moves to establish a major production centre in Salford and therefore to make more productions away from London, both in radio and television. Paradoxically, these changes have actually reduced broadcast production by the BBC in Birmingham since the large production centre, BBC Pebble Mill, closed in 2004 and was replaced by The Mailbox where *The Archers* is currently produced. The BBC is also mandated to consider these issues as one of its public purposes, 'To reflect, represent and serve the diverse communities of all of the United Kingdom's nations and regions and, in doing so, support the creative economy across the United Kingdom' (BBC, 2017). Communities might be defined in many ways here, but regions are much clearer. One might speculate that *The Archers* fulfils two elements here in both representing the West Midlands region and the farming and rural community. Outside the fictional realm, this also speaks to the need for a continuing concern with developing broadcast production in the nations and regions of the United Kingdom.

Ambridge also follows a fine tradition of both representing a region and representing the nation in BBC drama. Thus we have incoming characters, many now permanent features of the village who represent the constituent nations of Great Britain. This might not be immediately apparent in the case of Pat Archer who has lost her very strong Welsh accent and sense of Welsh identity over the years since her arrival in the seventies. But, for Jazzer McCreary and Anisha being Scottish is one of the things that first brings the characters together at a Burns Night. They bring a wider nation into the narrative of the village. Interestingly, Ian Craig's Northern Ireland identity has rarely been commented upon, although the character's accent makes this very apparent. Whether this reticence is about the political and cultural identity he might assume if this was pursued is pure speculation, but clearly this is an aspect of representing Northern Irish characters which is very different from representing Welsh or Scottish ones. English regional accents from outside the West Midlands are less common in *The Archers*. Here Ruth Archer must act as a prime example of an identity that develops the longer she is away from the North-East.

The Midlands region itself has always been poorly defined in the national consciousness. It is neither the South nor the North and has featured less in popular culture. So whilst, the North was the subject of Social Realist film in the 1950s and 1960s and home to some of the most famous popular music in the sixties and eighties, the Midlands had much less exposure. This is mirrored in the broadcasting representations of the Midlands, which are limited. Even when BBC Pebble

Mill was producing drama for the BBC network from 1970s to 1990s, the actual dramas produced were rarely located there. So, for example *Boys From the Blackstuff* (BBC, 1982) (set in Liverpool) was produced through Pebble Mill, as was *Howards' Way* (BBC, 1985–1990), a popular Sunday night drama set on the south coast. For radio drama, no figures are available for the proportion of plays set in each region of the United Kingdom. The Radio 4 Afternoon Drama slot features a large percentage of plays with a clearly defined regional setting. *The Archers* as such a regular representation of the West Midlands region may make this issue largely redundant for the medium.

The absence of representation is seen as important in terms of identity formation. Most discussions of identity in film and broadcasting tend to focus on the representation of the nation and national identity (Higson, 1995). Regions have not been the focus of so much research and debate in broadcasting studies although this has been redressed somewhat by Cooke's recent book (2012). The importance of mass media to identity formation is recognised at both a national and a supra national level. For the United Kingdom, PSB and film policy are partly based on this premise. For the cultural arm of the policy, producing broadcasting and film that talks about the nations and regions is a vital part of funding initiatives and policy. For the EU, identity formation has been a key issue for many years. One of the pressing issues for the Union has been how to make member nation's citizens feel part of the EU and fundamentally take on a pan-European identity as well as their national or regional one. Thus, much of the MEDIA (EU Commission, 2017) programme and other funding activity for screen has been based on this premise. This was voiced in a communication from the EU

Commission on State aid for films and other audiovisual works:

> *Audiovisual works, particularly films, play an important role in shaping European identities. They reflect the cultural diversity of the different traditions and histories of the EU Member States and regions. Audiovisual works are both economic goods, offering important opportunities for the creation of wealth and employment, and cultural goods which mirror and shape our societies. (EU 2013/C 332/01)*

It could never be suggested that the formation of identity is entirely due to consumption of media products, but clearly it is seen as an important factor in the process. Anderson (2006) considered how national identity in the United Kingdom might have been formed by the advent of a widely circulated, daily national press. Rather than identity being formed by ideas about some shared mythologised past, indicating an organic view of national identity, it was the mass media that started to provide national experience in Anderson's account. Edensor (2002) adds that it is the quotidian experiences which help to build this sense of identity. In terms of mass media this suggests that rather than the large scale broadcasting events, for example The Olympic Games, Royal Weddings and Coronations or the final of *The Great British Bake Off* (Love Productions for BBC, 2010−) it is both the everyday and the ordinary which may create this feeling of identity.

The Archers is now almost literally quotidian in the daily sense and perhaps very much quotidian, in the sense of being unremarkable for many of its episodes. But, how could one claim that *The Archers* has such an effect on its listeners.

This would certainly take some extensive empirical work on the audience that I have not carried out for this chapter. However, it can claim a mass audience, in contemporary radio terms. Ratings for radio are open to some scrutiny in terms of their methodology, but comparative figures are illuminating here. The RAJAR (2017) ratings for the programme in 2016 were 4.5–5 million listeners, 4.6 million in the first quarter of 2016 and a further 3.6 million listeners on Iplayer in March 2016. To place this in a Radio 4 context, *Today* (BBC, Radio 4, 1957–) had an audience of 6.8 million in the same first quarter of 2016 (Plunkett, 2016). *The Archers* audience has ebbed away over the years since its heyday in the mid-fifties of 20 million (Smethurst, 2000, p.64), though this was extraordinary as Smethurst points out and was a peak that occurred around the death of Grace Archer in 1955. Certainly, radio drama was more popular then. Television was only just starting to draw the audiences which *Quatermass* (BBC, 1953) and other later drama series would gather. The ratings have recovered well since its low point 2.75 million in the mid to late seventies (Smethurst, 2000, p. 144). Just for comparison, for television ratings soap operas can gain audiences of 6–10 million and dramas can reach a peak audience of around 10 million, but more usually average 5–8 million viewers. The audience, perhaps unsurprisingly given its Radio 4 home is skewed towards the older listener. The average age is 56, with 88% of listeners over 35 and 58% over 55 (Rajar in Thomas & Lambrianidou, 2008, p. 6). So, perhaps the programme is building a nostalgic image of the rural West Midlands for a very good reason.

For many years the most well-known representation of the West Midlands was the soap opera, *Crossroads* (ATV/ Central 1964–1988). It was seen to be a poor quality soap and its motel location is not a very exciting evocation of life in the West Midlands. It is remarkable how relatively few examples there were of dramas in which the narrative was set in the West Midlands. *Boon* (Central for ITV, 1986–1992) in the first series establishes the leading character's residence as in North Worcestershire. But, much of the early series of the drama took place in Birmingham with the location moving to Nottingham later in the run. The 1974 Play for Today, David Rudkin's *Pendas Fen* (BBC) is a very rare example of a drama being set in Worcestershire. However, its impact as a single play was quite limited, though it continues to gather academic interest today. Whilst it featured Worcestershire locations and indeed reference to the local landscape, this may have been distanced for viewers by the form of the play.

More recently *Peaky Blinders* (Caryn Mandabach/Tiger Aspect for BBC, 2013–) has created a new identity for Birmingham. Though the portrayal of gangsters in Birmingham and the West Midlands is not new — see *Gangsters* (BBC, 1976–1978) which was made at Pebble Mill — in the case of *Peaky Blinders* it is the post-World War One's political and social setting which drives the narrative. An important factor in the drama is the inclusion of key characters of Romany descent and especially in the first series the use of Romany language. This is a less well-known aspect of Midlands and especially West Midlands life and culture. However, the period setting and generic themes as a gangster drama may well deflect from reflection on contemporary Birmingham and the wider West Midlands. What the series certainly does emphasise is the long-standing engineering and manufacturing aspect of Birmingham.

The other key strand of more recent television fiction set in the West Midlands is comedy. Four recent situation comedies, *Home Time* (Baby Cow for BBC, 2009), *Cuckoo* (Roughcut Television for BBC, 2012–), *Raised by Wolves* (Big Talk Production for CH4, 2013–) and *The Job Lot* (Big Talk Productions for ITV 2, 2013–2015) demonstrate this shift. Further than this, each one is very much rooted and located in its setting. Thus, in *Home Time*, based on a woman returning home to Coventry having lived in London for 10 years, the location is emphasised by humour. The joke about the group of friends planning a weekend away from Coventry, 'What, you mean Leamington Spa?', only fully works with the dual knowledge of the geography of the region and the stereotypical image of each place. In *Cuckoo*, the Lichfield setting is less part of the humour, but is referred to and seems to suggest an everytown in its ordinariness. In *Raised by Wolves* the clue is in the title, Wolverhampton. Again, there is less direct reflection on the city, but certainly frequent mention of it and location shooting around the city. For *The Job Lot*, set in a West Midlands Job Centre there is a less precise sense of exact location, but the use of regional accents indicates this. All in their way contribute to an image of the West Midlands not just as a place of humour but as varied and lively.

Godfrey Baseley speaking in 1971 claimed that 'The BBC has too many townies at the top. They've lost touch with the country' (Smethurst, 2000, p. 131). This was uttered in 1971 when the programme was bringing in more dramatic storylines, such as a plane and a train crash in one week, in an attempt to attract listeners. Whether he was right or not, he certainly touches upon the rural representation of Ambridge. It could be argued that over and above its precise geographical location, it represents an idealised, English rural village. However, I think it is possible to place *The Archers* not only firmly in the West Midlands region, as I've outlined above, but also very probably in Worcestershire. Godfrey Baseley's own life experience may be also significant. Baseley was born in Alvechurch near Bromsgrove in North Worcestershire and spent much of his life in the area. He has strong links to

Hanbury through his sister's family farm. In an interview with his niece Patricia Howard, she claimed that he often visited them at the farm and that in the early days of the series he would ask the family to keep a farm diary as part of the agricultural research for *The Archers*. This familial link continued more recently when Patricia's son was asked to advise on the mob grazing storyline.

What can we conclude about the location of *The Archers*? Shortly after I gave my paper at the Academic Archers conference at University of Lincoln (February, 2017), it was suggested online that I might be chasing the mythical village of Brigadoon in trying to locate *The Archers*. I appreciate the point, but Ambridge surfaces so much more frequently that I think its assumed location may matter. For a region of the United Kingdom that rarely features in popular culture, opportunities for representation are important. For Worcestershire those opportunities are very much rarer than for the West Midlands conurbation. Of course in part this is purely local pride, the feeling that our place is not being missed out. But for the BBC it is part of their role and if we return to the notion of Radio and TV drama as being very widely consumed (sometimes referred to as the National Theatre of the airwaves or the real National Theatre) then there is something at stake in the representations offered. Especially so in a world in which typically US representations predominate (certainly in film, slightly less so in television drama and admittedly much less so in radio). For many listeners Ambridge is simply an 'Everyday story of country folk' as opposed to metropolitan folk yet for some an image of the West Midlands, perhaps Worcestershire, is built up by the programme. Its veracity may be debateable at times but for more than 65 years, it has made an impact upon the nation.

REFERENCES

Anderson, B. (2006). *Imagined communities: Reflections on the origin and spread of nationalism*. London: Verso.

BBC. (2017). *Our public purposes*. Retrieved from http://www.bbc.co.uk/aboutthebbc/insidethebbc/whoweare/publicpurposes

BBC Trust. (2013). *Public purposes and purpose remits*. Retrieved from http://www.bbc.co.uk/bbctrust/governance/tools_we_use/public_purposes.html

Communications Act. (2003). London: TSO.

Cooke, L. (2012). *A sense of place: Regional British television drama, 1956-82*. Manchester: Manchester University Press.

Courage, C., Headlam, N., & Matthews, P. (Eds.). (2017). *The Archers in fact and fiction*. Oxford: Peter Lang.

Edensor, T. (2002). *National identity, popular culture and everyday life*. Oxford: Berg.

EU Commission. (2013). *Communication from the commission on state aid for films and other audiovisual works, 2013/C 332/01*. Retrieved from http://eur-lex.europa.eu/legal-content/EN/TXT/?uri=celex:52013XC1115(01)

EU Commission. (2017). *The MEDIA sub-programme of creative Europe*. Retrieved from https://ec.europa.eu/digital-single-market/en/media-sub-programme-creative-europe. 26th May 2107

Higson, A. (1995). *Waving the flag*. Oxford: Oxford University Press.

Plunkett, J. (2016). *The Archers audience slips despite domestic abuse storyline*. Retrieved from https://www.theguardian.com/media/2016/may/19/the-archers-audience-domestic-abuse-radio-4-today

RAJAR. (2017). *The organisation*. Retrieved from http://www.rajar.co.uk/content.php?page=about_organisation

Smethurst, W. (2000). *The Archers. The History of Radio's Most Famous Programme*. London: Michael O'Mara Books.

Thomas, L., & Lambrianidou, M. (2008). *Radio listeners online: A case study of The Archers*. Retrieved from www.bbc.co.uk/blogs/knowledgeexchange/londonmet.pdf

BROADCAST PROGRAMMES

Boon (Central for ITV, 1986–1992).
   Boys from the Blackstuff (BBC, 1982).
   Coronation Street. (Granada/ITV, 1960–).
   Crossroads (ATV/Central 1964–1988).
   Cuckoo (Roughcut Television for BBC, 2012–),
Eastenders (BBC, 1985–).
   Emmerdale Farm/Emmerdale (Yorkshire/ITV, 1972–).
   Home Time (Baby Cow for BBC, 2009).
   Howards' Way (BBC, 1985–1990).
   Peaky Blinders (Caryn Mandabach/Tiger Aspect for BBC, 2013–).
   Pendas Fen (BBC, 1972).
   Quatermass (BBC, 1953).
   Raised by Wolves (Big Talk Production for CH4, 2013–).

The Great British Bake Off (Love Productions for BBC, 2010–).

The Job Lot (Big Talk Productions for ITV 2, 2013–2015).

Afternoon Drama (BBC Radio 4, 1967–).

The Archers (BBC Radio 4, 1950–).

Today (BBC, Radio 4, 1957–).

PEER REVIEW BY CLARRIE GRUNDY, GRANGE FARM, AMBRIDGE

Let's get this clear, we're from Borsetshire. I mean really suggesting that we live somewhere else, 'bloomin' ridiculous', as Eddie would say. But, then we do go to Worcester sometimes and even to Birmingham once in a while. We had a chat about this last night and, not surprisingly, Eddie's roots came up. Joe always claims there's been Grundys on the land in Ambridge for generations, so if he's right then Grundys are Borsetshire through and through.

But, we've always welcomed people from outside the county. We're not inward looking here. Pat, Ruth and Ian they're all good friends. Jazzer and Anisha too. Well, almost everyone really. Where was Rob originally from? Course we might be a bit wary about Brummies moving in, but then Jack Woolley was a real gent and Hayley was lovely too. Vicky too, once you got used to her. Anyway, it's not a matter of where you are from. It's how you act once you are in Ambridge. I don't know about popular culture forming who you are. I mean look at Eddie, all that Country and Western didn't make him feel any more American and any less Borsetshire. Though, I suppose it did turn his head.

'Course we're country folk, not townies. You can tell some city folk aren't cut out for this life. Hazel Woolley or Lilian's boy, James for example. But, they move on. Above all we're Ambridge and proud of it. Worcestershire's all well and good but it's another place entirely.

SECTION FOUR

POWER RELATIONSHIPS

CHAPTER ELEVEN

A CASE STUDY IN THE USE OF GENOGRAMS TO ASSESS FAMILY DYSFUNCTION AND SOCIAL CLASS: TO THE MANOR BORN VERSUS SHAMELESS

Louise Gillies and Helen M. Burrows

ABSTRACT

Families conduct their affairs through processes that are built upon those of previous generations and also social capacities such as culture, class, oppression and poverty. The media has played a part in stereotyping the lower classes through their portrayal on the television pro-grammes such as Benefits Street *and* Jeremy Kyle *and tabloid newspaper stories. This chapter is a case study of two families who are at the opposing ends of the social scale, the Horrobin/Carter and Aldridge families. The two families were chosen due to them being linked by marriage in the younger generation. Through the use of genograms, we explore how the families differ in their attitudes towards relationships within their individual families, and also how they relate to each other as separate family groups. Despite the many differences, there are also a number of key similarities, particularly regarding the key females in the families, in terms of family background and snobbery. We also show that there is little family loyalty in the more privileged family and a power differential between the two families (oppressors vs. oppressed) in terms of the crimes committed.*

Keywords: Family dysfunction; social class; genogram; *The Archers*; social class; oppression

INTRODUCTION

Our individual worlds are coloured and shaped by the familial experiences that make up our formative years and beyond. The family life cycle can be used as a framework to explain the individual behaviours based upon the previous coping mechanisms of the family, management of the present issues and the aspirations of the future — we are all basically the products of our families. Families do not develop their processes in a vacuum, and behaviour towards each other, and those outside the family network, arises from the wider cultural network. Family is still very much embedded in a local, cultural context, therefore, to understand the issues of dysfunction within a family context, we must also consider the family's culture, influenced by aspects such as class (McGoldrick, Gerson, & Petry, 2008, p. 53), life circumstances, loss and migration and local and societal political and economic situations (McGoldrick et al., 2008, pp. 50–54).

This chapter is a case study of two families who live in the village of Ambridge, Borsetshire, but come from very different ends of the social class spectrum, making them an ideal case study of family dysfunction and social class. The Aldridge family are representative of the privileged class, whilst the Horrobin/Carter family are of the lower class, struggling to make ends meet and from 'the wrong side of the tracks'. Despite living such contrasting lifestyles, the two families have a connection — Alice (née Aldridge) and Christopher (Chris) Carter surprised their parents (Brian and Jennifer Aldridge and Neil and Susan Carter, respectively) on their return from a trip to Las Vegas in the summer of 2010 with the announcement of their marriage. The reactions of the two sets of parents could not have been more different, yet both show a great deal of snobbery, demonstrating a correlation between social status and human merit from opposite ends of the spectrum. For Susan, the marriage to an Aldridge was another rung up the social ladder and something to be proud of. The Aldridge parents were a little more dismayed:

> Brian: There's only one thing for it Jenny, for the sake of our sanity we're going to have to look on this as Alice's... starter marriage

> Jenny: Marriage is not like a mortgage, Brian, it's a serious commitment. Ohh... what the hell has she done

It is upon this background that we shall explore family dysfunction through the use of genogram mapping, focussing on the following aspects: social status and social climbing; sexual relationships — marriages, extramarital affairs, domestic abuse; parenting — paternity, illegitimacy and abandonment; criminality — a comparison of the oppressors and the oppressed; opportunity — expanding horizons, education.

WHAT IS A DYSFUNCTIONAL FAMILY?

Whilst many apparently dysfunctional incidents may happen in any 'normal' family, what defines a family as 'dysfunctional' is the fact that this is the normal script of their lives — not just one-off incidents. So where do we find these dysfunctional families? We can often identify them in the media — for example, if we watch *Benefits Street* (Channel 4, Love Productions) or *Shameless* (Channel 4, Company Pictures) — and we might identify most of the participants on *The Jeremy Kyle Show* (ITV1, ITV Studios) as coming from stereotypically dysfunctional families. But is this a fair representation? We would argue that much dysfunctionality in families is actually hidden — and in fact in Ambridge can be found in unexpected places. Might those who appear to be 'to the Manor born' be as dysfunctional as the inhabitants of the council houses — or even more so?

Why does this matter? Casey (2012, p. 46) argues that parents and families, as the main influence on their children's lives, will 'determine their significant relationships as they grow up — and the ways in which those children go on to parent their own children'. Whether 'high' or 'low' born, family functioning is likely to spread from generation to generation. As Wade et al. (2016, p. 135) clearly demonstrate 'Adverse Childhood Experiences (ACEs), which include family dysfunction and community-level stressors, negatively impact the health and wellbeing of children throughout the life course'. Thus, to understand the 'everyday story' of the families whose lives we follow on a daily basis and to understand how the stories of those families might unfold over the coming years, we need to look at their backgrounds, understand how they have come to be, where and who they are, and we can then start to think about what the future might bring.

GENOGRAMS

As discussed in the Introduction, we will be looking at both family and individual behaviour through the framework of the family life cycle. Families are not static, and relationships and boundaries ebb and flow over time causing changes in boundaries and individual roles through the creation and redefining of family subsystems (Carter & McGoldrick, 1999, p. 2). The family structure itself is socially constructed, and who is included within the family is dependent on many factors, personal and cultural (Ross, 2006). One thing remains the same though, being born into a family brings with it ties and obligations, and it is virtually impossible to completely leave a family behind due to emotional baggage and shared history (McGoldrick, 2016, p. 3).

The genogram is an established tool used to map health, emotional relationships and dysfunction within families (McGoldrick et al., 2008, p. 3). With a near-standardised format, it is increasingly used by healthcare professionals, social workers, family therapists and social scientists in therapy and research to locate persisting intergenerational dysfunctional patterns of behaviour. The genogram is similar to a family tree in that it is a graphical representation of family information providing a simple visualisation of complex intra-family relationships within a whole family context. Taking the idea that family is a socially constructed concept, the genogram includes not only biological members but also more informal yet key relationships beyond the immediate blood ties, such as sexual bonds, friendships and work relationships. The genogram also indicates the psychosocial aspects of relationships, denoting patterns of functioning: conflict, closeness and pathological attitudes. The genogram is supplemented with a family chronology of key events and changes. This allows easy view of key behavioural patterns.

Relevant aspects of this case study are shown in the genograms of the Aldridge and Horrobin Families in Figures 1 and 2,

Figure 1. Genogram Showing the Key Relationships Within the Aldridge Family.

Aldridges - key relationships

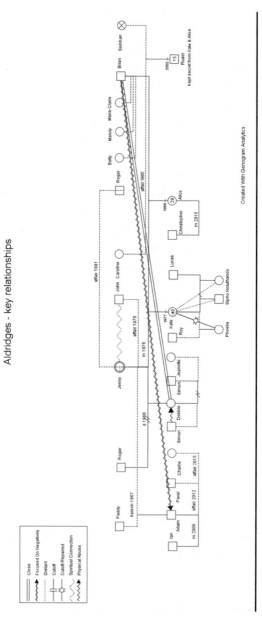

Created With Genogram Analytics

Figure 2. Genogram Showing the Key Relationships Within the Horrobin Family.

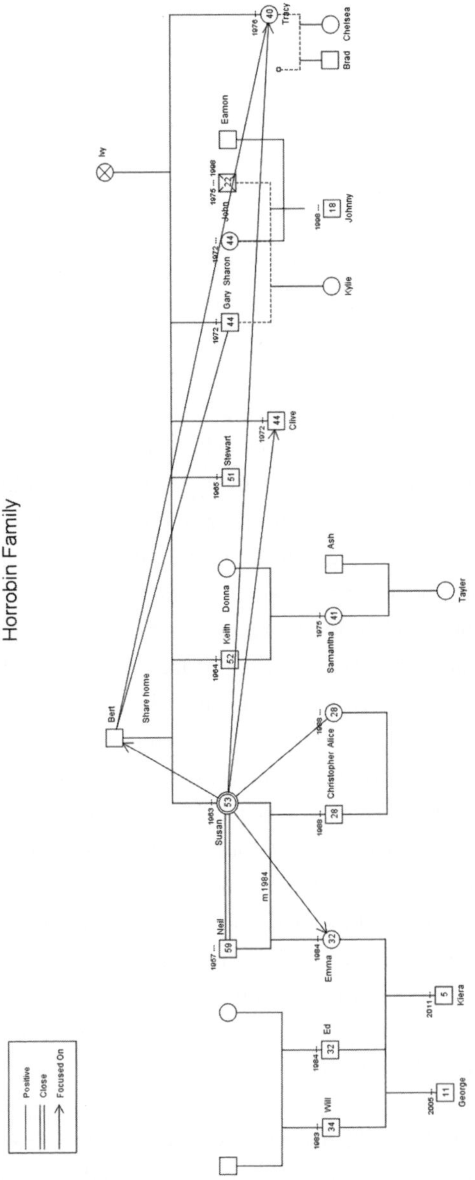

Horrobin Family

respectively, with commentary provided in the rest of this chapter.

THE CASE STUDY

Climbing the Social Ladder

Both the key women in these families, Jennifer and Susan, had poor upbringings — Jennifer was brought up in a pub, Susan in a council house. However, there were two major differences. The first relates to parental stability. Taillieu, Brownridge, Shareen, & Affifi's (2016) explanation of the features of family dysfunction, where any person 'reporting that a parent or other adult living in the household had a problem with alcohol or drugs, went to jail or prison, was treated or hospitalized due to mental illness, attempted or completed suicide was coded as having experienced family dysfunction in childhood' (pp. 4–5) fits Jennifer (and her brother Tony Archer) as children of Jack Archer, an alcoholic who was hospitalised through mental illness, far more closely than any of the adult Horrobins when they were growing up. Bert and Ivy Horrobin presented as stable parents, so it may have been other factors which led to their children having difficulties in their lives. Secondly, although Jennifer and Susan had similar social status during their formative years, Jennifer has married into wealth and a higher class. Climbing the social ladder is a trait that is particularly important to the British, and those with a stronger upward social trajectory have been shown to have increased eudaemonic wellbeing compared to those who stay at the same social level or move downwards (Vanhoutte & Nazroo, 2016). Susan exemplifies this desire to 'better' herself and has gained psychologically in terms of owning her own self-build home and the introduction of an Aldridge into her family. Susan has been desperate not to be tarred with the same brush as the rest of her family, despite staying loyal to them, and these small steps up the social ladder afford her a degree of happiness.

Sex, Lies and Secrets

Jennifer has a colourful romantic history, with many boyfriends and two marriages. Dalliances included cowman Paddy Redfern and Nelson Gabriel. Her first marriage was to Roger Travers-Macy, who came from a family of money and breeding, both indicators that typically convey prestige and high status. Interestingly, Jennifer's sister Lillian Bellamy had an affair with Roger prior to this. Following their separation, Jennifer caused more gossip in the village, this time with Gordon Armstrong and the following year (1975) met her current husband Brian (married in 1976). However, despite the marriage lasting for over 40 years, it has not been a loyal marriage and both Jennifer and Brian have struggled to remain faithful to each other.

John Tregorran fell in love with Jennifer, who fled when he declared his love for her. This appeared to be very much a cognitive affair for Jennifer, who worked with John on local history and a landscape survey of the village. The time that they spent together was the subject of much village gossip and concern for their respective spouses, who put a stop to further opportunities for relationship development. There also followed an affair in 1991 with ex-husband Roger, causing daughter Kate Aldridge to run away.

Jennifer's husband Brian is a true philanderer and has had multiple affairs and liaisons during their 41 years of marriage. Conquests include Caroline Bone (now Sterling) (1985) who he was so obsessed with, finding it difficult to give up the relationship even when wife Jennifer found out. This resulted in Brian and Jennifer having Alice in an attempt to re-cement their marriage. Further flirtations followed, including Betty Tucker (unreciprocated), pony club instructor Mandy Beesborough, and twin town delegate Marie-Claire Beguet. However, the affair that rocked the marriage the most was with Siobhan Hathaway, the much younger wife of the local doctor. The result of this affair was a much longed-for son Ruairi Donovan, born in 2002. Siobhan resettled in Germany with a new partner, taking Ruairi with her; however, following her death from cancer in 2007, Jennifer has played a big hand in bringing Ruairi up with Brian in the family home (although he is most often away at school). Ruairi had been a secret from the Aldridges' two younger children until this time. Not only was Ruairi to become a constant reminder of Brian's infidelity but it would also mean that everyone in the family and the village knew about his affair.

Family of origin experiences have impact on the romantic relationships of the offspring (Bryant & Conger, 2002) and are related to an individual's infidelity history in terms of beliefs as well as behaviours. So how does this affect the next generation of Aldridges — Adam (Macy), Debbie, Kate and Alice?

Of their children, both Adam and Kate have been unfaithful during their marriages and relationships. Adam's marriage to Ian Craig has been put at risk twice, firstly in 2012 with Pawel, a Polish fruit picker, and more recently in 2015, with estate manager Charlie Thomas. Kate's marriage to Lucas Madikane ended following an affair, and we know that this wasn't the first time she had strayed. Whilst we do not know if Debbie has been unfaithful herself, she has certainly been the mistress of an older lecturer whom she married. Divorce followed when he was caught having an affair with the head of his department.

It seems clear that for the Aldridge offspring, fidelity does not come easy, and with parents displaying the behaviour of Jenny and Brian, it could be seen as being the 'norm' within this particular family. Research has shown that offsprings are more likely to have been unfaithful to their partner if their parents had been unfaithful, the behaviour of the parent being closely linked to the behaviour of the offspring (Cui & Fincham, 2010; Weiser, Weigel, Lalasz, & Evans, 2015). Furthermore, parent satisfaction has been shown to be related to offspring relationship satisfaction (and ergo fidelity) (Atkins, Dimidjian, & Jacobsen, 2001). Brian had not been subtle in his desire to have a biological son and has a difficult relationship with stepson Adam, particularly in terms of acceptance of Adam's sexuality. His relationship with step-daughter Debbie is very different, and he is very close to her and respects her opinion on most things.

Alice got married at the age of 22, a key age for the Aldridge women, however this was not a shot-gun wedding and she has not been pregnant as far as we're aware. She is, however, very much her own woman. She enjoys male attention and when then-boyfriend Chris was left feeling insecure over the attention she was getting from male admirers, Alice told him that he should feel proud and want 'other guys' to be jealous of him. The issue of trust was broached during this time (2008) when Chris was worried that it would always be the same, 'there's always going to be richer, smarter, better looking guys'. It was also acknowledged that he knew Jenny did not think he was good enough for Alice. Alice reiterated that Chris had nothing to worry about. A year after the marriage, there was another incident in which Chris was convinced that Alice was having an affair, this time with her university housemate, Charles 'Chaz' Forster. It took a lot of persuasion before Chris believed Alice that there was nothing going on between her and Chaz, who had by this time declared his love for her and had arranged for them to run away together. Chris was later involved in an accident, and this cemented his relationship with Alice, leaving them with the strongest marriage (at present) within the Aldridge clan. Chris is very much playing the part of Susan's son — her desire to climb the social ladder ringing with insecurity.

Contrast the Aldridges and their complete lack of loyalty towards each other with the Horrobins. Bert and Ivy were married for a long time. Susan and Neil have been married for over 30 years and have remained faithful to each other, despite the trials and tribulations that they have faced. When Susan was in jail (see below), Neil was invited to stay overnight at the Travis farm in order to 'help with morning milking', yet he firmly rebuffed Mo Travis' advances. His relationship with Susan was, and still is, solid. There is both loyalty and trust within the marriage, and they are satisfied with each other. Indeed, enduring marital relationships are linked to overall wellbeing and life satisfaction (Berscheid & Reis, 1998).

Susan's daughter, Emma Grundy, also shows the same loyalty to her husband as her mother, although this may not be immediately evident. She elicited a similar disappointment as the Aldridge parents to the Alice/Chris marriage announcement when she told Susan and Neil that she was marrying into the Grundy family (Will Grundy), at a time when she had more chemistry with the brother she didn't marry (Ed Grundy). Emma and Ed eventually did get together and despite suffering from the implications of extreme poverty, Emma has proved herself to be resilient and tough, recently taking on a third job in a bid to give her two children a better life, much to her husband's anguish. Yet despite the hardships that they have been through, and continue to struggle with, Emma and Ed are solid as a couple. Like Susan and Neil, they can rely on each other.

Issues relating to domestic abuse are seemingly quite rare in Ambridge as a whole, however, three women in the Archer family (from whom the Aldridges are descended) have suffered at the hands of an abusive partner. Debbie Aldridge suffered from violence at the hands of her then-boyfriend Simon Pemberton. Her aunt (Shula Hebden Lloyd) had also faced a violent attack from Pemberton and encouraged Debbie to report the assault. Pemberton escaped with a £200 fine at that time. Domestic abuse is now taken more seriously (Garcia-Moreno, Zimmerman, & Watts, 2017), but it is interesting that there seemed to be a communication shutdown regarding the two older women and lack of help towards the well-documented abuse of their cousin/niece Helen Archer, particularly in the case of Shula who had an idea of the kind of manipulative person Helen's (then) husband was, and who had been so encouraging of her other niece in reporting her abuse.

Parenting

Jennifer gave birth to her first child, Adam Macy, in 1967 at the age of 22. Her pregnancy shocked the village at the time and Jennifer refused to name the father, even to her parents. Laura Archer guessed that the father was Paddy and whilst Jennifer did not deny it, the truth wasn't made clear until 2015. Jennifer was something of a hippy, and daughter Kate has followed her mother down this path. She too had an 'illegitimate' child at the age of 21, Phoebe, and claimed that she wasn't sure who the father was. After giving birth in a tepee at Glastonbury, Kate was planning to take the baby to France. Roy, the potential father, stepped in with a prohibited steps in order to keep Kate in the United Kingdom and subsequent paternity testing showed him to be Phoebe's father. A little over a year later, Kate's itchy feet resulted in Roy looking after Phoebe full time as Kate could not cope with the baby alone. In a similar situation, Emma (Susan's daughter) found herself pregnant and was unsure which of the Grundy brothers the father was. Despite marrying Will, she hoped the father was Ed and she and Ed planned to run away together but are thwarted by baby George's lack of passport. Roy advises Will on his legal rights as presumptive father which eventually lead to contact and access, albeit not without a struggle. Whilst Emma has gone on to prove herself in the maternal stakes, and Jennifer is helping to bring up Brian's love child, Kate has had further maternal issues and has now abandoned her two younger children with their father in South Africa. Kate is something of a flighty Edina Monsoon character (*Absolutely Fabulous*, BBC), whose bored, selfish ways and jealousy have caused further disruption and issues with Phoebe, who has grown up in a secure household with her father and stepmother.

Susan is possibly the most responsible of all the women in the two families and not only brought up Chris and Emma, but has been something of a lynchpin to the entire Horrobin family, providing shelter for her sister and children, brokered an arrangement for her brother, Gary Horrobin, to live with their father after Ivy had died and helped out brother Clive Horrobin when he was on the run from the police.

Criminal Activity — High Jinks or Miscreant Behaviour?

One of the most evident features of the children of Bert and Ivy has been criminal activity. Maybe we should not be surprised at this — attitudes towards lone mothers (like Tracy Horrobin) and people living on 'sink estates' (though whether you'd class Ambridge's council houses as a 'sink estate' is debatable) often equate them with 'the criminal classes' (Cook, 1997) and this can be a self-fulfilling prophecy. Of Ivy and Bert's six children (Susan, Keith, Stewart, Clive, Gary and Tracy), Clive's criminal record maybe the best documented. Born in 1972, he was barely 21 when he was remanded in custody for the armed robbery at the Ambridge village shop and escaped whilst still on remand. It was during this escape that big sister Susan (then aged thirty) hid him, resulting in her also receiving a custodial sentence for perverting the course of justice. Susan ended up having 10 days added to her sentence after she too absconded from prison to go to Mark Hebden's funeral in 1994. Clive later added to his criminal career when in 1997 he assaulted George Barford, and further, set fire to the Barfords' house in 2004. He appears to have spent much of his adult life in prison; out in the community in 2012 he was sent back after breaching the terms of his licence by entering Ambridge to confront and threaten his sister, Tracy, and his brother Keith's wife, Donna.

Keith appears to have started off well enough, with a second-hand car dealership, however, as the business started to fail, he struggled to keep up with his wife's spending habits. He got involved in some very dodgy dealing with stolen vehicles, and tipping off his shadier friends about farm machinery kept insecurely enough to be taken away. This all went predictably and horribly wrong when Adam was assaulted during the course of machinery thefts, and as part of the intimidation by the gang of David Archer (sole witness to the assault on Adam), Keith was forced into an arson attack on one of Brookfield's barns. Stewart, Gary and Tracy seem to have avoided criminal activity, and in fact little seems to be known about Stewart at all, though there is some suggestion that he was the driver of the speeding car that made Caroline Bone's horse throw her, resulting in the death of Mark Hebden. Gary and Tracy, however, have fallen into fairly common stereotypical 'underclass' roles, with Gary losing contact with his only child (Kylie Richards, Johnny Richards/Archer's half-sister) and living an apparently passive 'ne'er-do-well' life at home with his dad, and Tracy bringing up her two children, Brad and Chelsea, alone.

The Horrobins, then, appear to have developed dysfunctional behaviour, with no strong family history to lead into it. In looking at the other side of the class divide, I will focus on Jennifer. Jennifer was not born into a wealthy family, but has climbed the social ladder. She has achieved economic stability, but it is clear to see that her family's functioning has been far from stable, as discussed in the previous sections.

Bad behaviour and criminal activity have also been a feature of the Aldridge family lives. Jennifer lied about her age as a 16 year old and was thrown out of her flat in Walsall after a rowdy party. Brian assaulted an employee, Jack Roberts, after sacking him in 1978, and Jennifer threw a garden rake at Mike Tucker after he took up Roberts' case — Jennifer's mother, Peggy Wooley (née Archer), commented that Jennifer had become 'more violent' since taking up with Brian, which suggests at least some history of violence before that. Kate has been trouble most of her life, from running away and being expelled from school, to breaking and entering, vandalism, and allowing herself to be carried in a stolen vehicle, to abandoning all three of her children at different stages (and indeed across continents). In the wider family, Matt Crawford, as (now ex-) partner to Jennifer's sister Lillian, has spent time in prison, was suspected by many listeners to have killed his brother Paul, and has added fraud, theft of the contents of the Dower House and abandoning Lilian, to his misdemeanours in recent years.

Jeroslow (2011) proposes that we need to look to class and power differentials related to poverty to explain crime and delinquency in recent years criminal activities, and

I would suggest that the differences between the histories of the Aldridges and Horrobins demonstrate that quite well. Whereas the Aldridge family 'crimes' can be seen as those of entitlement and power, the Horrobins' can be seen as related to oppression and poverty in their different motivation and contexts. Cook (1997), Macdonald and Shildrick (2010) and McCarthy (2011) all suggest that the social class of a person committing a crime has a significant impact on the perception of that crime by other people, including the criminal justice system, and can affect the response to and punishment of that crime.

Jennifer, Brian and Kate have all got away with their activities to a greater or lesser extent in terms of formal criminal action, however, the implications for the future wellbeing and mental health of their children may be serious. The future mental health of Kate's children, Phoebe, Noluthando and Sipho is particularly worrying — 'Maternal emotional unavailability in early life predicted suicide attempts in adolescence' (Weich, Patterson, Shaw, & Stewart-Brown, 2009, p. 392).

Opportunities

All the Aldridge children have had good educational opportunities. Debbie and Alice have postgraduate degrees and Kate has an advanced diploma. Phoebe is currently reading for a degree at Oxford. The Carter children did not go to university and this resulted in Chris feeling very insecure when Alice was studying in Southampton, as discussed above. The Aldridge children have also had extensive opportunities for work and travel. Both Adam and Kate have lived and worked in Africa (Kenya and Johannesburg, respectively) and Debbie is based in Hungary. Alice had a job offer in Canada, which put pressure on her marriage. By the time Chris decided to go with her, Alice had made her mind up to stay in Ambridge.

CONCLUSION: SOCIAL CLASS STEREOTYPING — *TO THE MANOR BORN* VERSUS *SHAMELESS*

The Carter/Horrobin family have little in the way of income and education, and provide us with a stereotypical representation of the lower classes as villains. As onlookers, we are not surprised that the Horrobin family contains so many miscreants. This is, in part, due to cultivation theory in which our perceptions of the real world are skewed to match the 'reality' portrayed within the media (Gerbner, Gross, Morgan, & Signorielli, 1986). The news media has been shown to underrepresent the most sympathised-with groups (the working poor and elderly) and over-represent the least sympathised-with groups, such as the working-age unemployed. This in turn has led to a distorted view of the lower classes and a subsequent drop in sympathy for their plight along with a warped association of traits and behaviours (Gilens, 1996). Media portrayals have developed the stereotype that the lower classes have neglectful parents, are lazy, linguistically poor and uneducated and prone to substance abuse (Gorski, 2015). Indeed, on looking at their genogram, it does seem that a number of the Horrobin family conform to some of these stereotypes.

But this is very far from being the whole story. What we see in the middle-class Aldridge family is that loyalty is an issue with widespread adultery (at least two generations), jealousy, bigotry, favouritism and child abandonment. This is coupled with children who are illegitimate and have numerous half-siblings. We also have to question what Jennifer has to gain by staying with a philanderer like Brian.

In contrast, the Horrobin marriages appear to be strong and have survived numerous traumas and hardships, yet adultery is rare. In the one case in which it did happen (Emma), there were difficulties and doubts leading up to the first marriage, and she appeared to be swept along to a point at which she could not turn back. She has since settled down into a solid marriage with her current husband. Both Susan and Emma very much want the best for their children and work hard to provide them with opportunities.

We have shown through the use genograms that family dysfunction is not the preserve of the lower (poorer) classes. The main differences between these two families is the loyalty that the Carter/Horrobins have towards each other, and that Jennifer married into money which enabled her to escape the cycle of poverty and provide her children with a better standard of living and opportunities, which would have been harder to obtain if she had not done so.

REFERENCES

Absolutely Fabulous. (1992–2012). [TV programme]. *BBC1/2*. French & Saunders Productions.

Atkins, D. C., Dimidjian, S., & Jacobsen, N. S. (2001). Why do people have affairs? Recent research and future directions about attributions for extramarital involvement. In V. Manusov & J. H. Harvey (Eds.), *Attribution, communication behavior, and close relationships* (pp. 305–319). Cambridge, England: Cambridge University Press.

Benefits Street. (2014). [TV programme]. *Channel 4*: Love Productions.

Berscheid, E., & Reis, H. T. (1998). Attraction and close relationships. In D. T. Gilbert, S. T. Fiske, & G. Lindzey

(Eds.), *The handbook of social psychology* (pp. 193–281). Boston, MA: McGraw-Hill.

Bryant, C. M., & Conger, R. D. (2002). An intergenerational model of romantic relationship development. *Stability and Change in Relationships*, 57–82.

Carter, E. A., & McGoldrick, M. (Eds.). (1999). *The expanded family life cycle: Individual, family, and social perspectives*. Boston: Allyn & Bacon.

Casey, L. (2012). *Listening to troubled families*. London: Department for Communities and Local Government. Retrieved from https://www.gov.uk/government/uploads/ system/uploads/attachment_data/file/6151/2183663.pdf. Accessed on April 29, 2017.

Cook, D. (1997). *Poverty, crime and punishment*. London: Child Poverty Action Group [CPAG].

Cui, M., & Fincham, F. D. (2010). The differential effects of parental divorce and marital conflict on young adult romantic relationships. *Personal Relationships*, *17*(3), 331–343.

Garcia-Moreno, C., Zimmerman, C., & Watts, C. (2017). Calling for action on violence against women: Is anyone listening? *The Lancet*, *389*(10068), 486–488.

Gerbner, G., Gross, L., Morgan, M., & Signorielli, N. (1986). Living with television: The dynamics of the cultivation process. *Perspectives on Media Effects*, 17–40.

Gilens, M. (1996). Race and poverty in America public misperceptions and the American news media. *Public Opinion Quarterly*, *60*(4), 515–541.

Gorski, P. C. (2015). *Reaching and teaching students in poverty: Strategies for erasing the opportunity gap*. New York, NY: Teachers College Press.

The Jeremy Kyle Show. (2005-present). [TV programme]. *ITV1*. ITV Productions.

Jeroslow, P. (2011). Anthropological theories of crime and delinquency. *Journal of Human Behavior in the Social Environment, 21*(3), 255–269.

Macdonald, R., & Shildrick, T. (2010). The view from below: Marginalised young people's biographical encounters with criminal justice agencies. *Child and Family Law Quarterly, 22*(2), 186–199.

McCarthy, D. (2011). Classing early intervention: Social class, occupational moralities and criminalization. *Critical Social Policy, 31*(4), 495–516.

McGoldrick, M. (2016). *The genogram casebook: A clinical companion to genograms: Assessment and intervention*. New York: WW Norton & Company.

McGoldrick, M., Gerson, R., & Petry, S. S. (2008). *Genograms: Assessment and intervention*. New York: WW Norton & Company.

Ross, S. M. (2006). *American families past and present: Social perspectives on transformations*. New Jersey: Rutgers University Press.

Shameless. (2004-2013). [TV programme]. *Channel 4*. Company Pictures.

Taillieu, T., Brownridge, D., Shareen, J., & Affifi, T. (2016). Childhood emotional maltreatment and mental disorders: Results from a nationally representative adult sample from the United States. *Child Abuse and Neglect, 59*, 1–12.

Vanhoutte, B., & Nazroo, J. (2016). Life course pathways to later life wellbeing: A comparative study of the role of socio-economic position in England and the US. *Journal of Population Ageing*, 9(1-2), 157–177.

Wade, R., Cronholm, P. F., Fein, J. A., Forke, C. M., Davis, M. B., Harkins-Schwarz, M., … Bair-Merritt, M. H. (2016). Household and community-level adverse childhood experiences and adult health outcomes in a diverse urban population. *Child Abuse & Neglect*, 52, 135–145.

Weich, S., Patterson, J., Shaw, R., & Stewart-Brown, S. (2009). Family relationships in childhood and common psychiatric disorders in later life: Systematic review of prospective studies. *British Journal of Psychiatry*, 194, 392–398.

Weiser, D. A., Weigel, D. J., Lalasz, C. B., & Evans, W. P. (2015). Family background and propensity to engage in infidelity. *Journal of Family Issues*. p.0192513X15581660.

PEER REVIEW, BY CLIVE HORROBIN, ADDRESS WITHHELD

Them Aldridges think they're something special. They have had it coming to them with their airs and graces. It's not right that they get away with murder and I'm always being banged up for things that aren't my fault. They look down their toffee-noses at us lot and this just goes to show that they're slippery as eels. That Jennifer Aldridge only puts up with her husband because she knows which side her bread's buttered on. She thinks none of us know what goes on, but our Susan's got a gob on her like the Mersey Tunnel. That lot only get away with it all because they can afford fancy lawyers.

Us lot are honest, not sneaky and conniving like them Aldridges. We stay true to our own and watch each other's backs, 'though Tracy and Donna need to take a leaf out of our Susan's book. She's a good 'un despite thinking she's better than the rest of us. Thinks she's royalty now her Chris has married that Aldridge girl.

I've been unlucky and judged harshly when it's clearly not my fault, and this proves it. I agree that it's because I'm oppressed that I've had to do some of the things that I've done. People see us Horrobins and judge us harshly because we're not rolling in it and have to make ends meet somehow. Can I keep a copy of this and show it to my brief?

CHAPTER TWELVE

KINSHIP NETWORKS IN AMBRIDGE

Nicola Headlam

ABSTRACT

Kinship structures in Ambridge have been analysed using social network analysis (SNA) showing a network of a 'small world' type with 75 individual people linked by birth or marriage. Further, the network shows four major cliques: the first two centred on Aldridge and Archer matriarchies and the second where through the marriages of the third generation the Grundies, Carters, Bellamies and Snells connect together. The chapter considers the possible futures for kinship networks in the village, arguing either a version of the status quo or The Headlam Hypothesis *through which Archers assume less importance and the strength of the weak ties in the network assume more prominence.*

Keywords: Kinship; networks; SNA; clique; family

INTRODUCTION

Brillat-Savarin's quote 'show me what you eat and I'll show you who you are' (Medland, 2017) can reasonably be modified for academic interests: Show me your research and I'll show you who you are. Network diagrams — maps of points and lines showing how people or things connect together and illuminating on the power relationships between people — excite some people and leave others cold. I embrace this Marmite quality and have been fascinated by the possibilities of networks in visualising and explaining social life. I learnt the specific quantitative techniques for use on my PhD and have sought to apply them to most spheres of social life I have come across since. I was delighted when the paper on genograms (Gillies & Burrows, 2017) showed genogram mapping techniques for exploring the qualities of various family relationships in Ambridge. The more visual methods that can be brought to bear in analysing power relations the better. This is called social network analysis (SNA), a mathematical tool for interrogating the networks of human and non-human interactions and is used in this chapter to render the invisible networks of kinship in Ambridge as visible. In order to construct a network you need two things: nodes (dots, points), a set of people or things which are connected in some ways that can be measured and ties or edges (the ways they link together).

> *Networks constitute the new social morphology of our societies, and the diffusion of networking logic modifies the operation and outcome in process of production, experience power and culture. (Castells, 1996)*

If then, networks as so key in modifying production, experience, power and culture then a complex social world, such as we see in Ambridge, needs a method capable of rendering some of these complexities legible. SNA maps can introduce pattern and structure for complex social realities.

IT TAKES A VILLAGE: KINSHIP NETWORKS IN AMBRIDGE

You lot really are all related aren't you?
(Rob Titchener)

Popularised by Hillary Clinton in the mid-nineties 'it takes a village to raise a child' has been in very common circulation as a way of articulating connectedness and social interaction as a corollary to more individualised conceptualisations of action as the preserve of people, who function within systems as more or less rational and autonomous economic agents:

> *Wherever human association is examined, we can see what can be described as thick spots — relatively unchanging clusters or collections of individuals who are linked by **frequent interaction and often by sentimental ties**. (Freeman & Webster, 1994) [author emphasis]*

These 'thick spots' of 'frequent interaction' and 'sentimental ties' are very much in evidence in the village of Ambridge. Its clusters and collections can be viewed as a matriarchy as the two main cliques have senior female members, Peggy Wooley and Gill Archer who were sister-in-laws at a point of time and with large families, and they exercise the most connected kinship power in Ambridge. However, they are afforded this status not by their gender per se but by their advanced age. Ambridge then may more properly be viewed as a gerontocracy — ruled by the old. In this sense Ambridge reflects the demographics of the UK aging society with assets held in the older members. The inter-generational asset transfer of forms of capital from Peggy and Gill provides some of the context for plotlines of more and less intensity, which, arguably can only intensify over the next decade as, inevitably Peggy and Gill die, settling the inheritance politics of the village and dissolving the extant matriarchal power structure. The ways in which forms of capital are circulated within a lifetime only frame their roles in life chances and access to power and authority between generations.

Viewing inter-generational transfer and the perishability of forms of capital as important may offer a way through critiques of wider forms of capital rather than non-material as less important than material and economic forms. This matters as the role of economic explanations and models have held sway for a long time at the expense of more social or cultural explanations.

The interactions between forms of capital in Ambridge are particularly intense, unusually for late capitalism there are strong connections with the land ('The Land' said Bran Aldridge poetically recently, as some more characteristically Machiavellian property deal was brokered) as well as to more usual forms of fungible and fiduciary wealth stand in for 'The Land' and it has been argued that Ambridge retains some similarities with a feudal system due to the strong connections between land and work for some of the main protagonists. (Byrne, 2017).

Ambridge has a bounded outer edge. In its kinship networks only the characters from *The Archers* link together. This requires that decisions be taken as to. For example, do we include dead characters? There is a very key hinge connecting the Brookfield and Home Farm clans which only functions if you map the earlier generations of Dan and Doris, Dan's Brother Jack, Peggy's first husband and Dan's sister Christine, without whom the strong links between Archers and Aldridges do not make sense.

In exploring the kinship networks of Ambridge we discuss each of the main 'elementary families' — viewed for these purposes as cliques within the larger network. We see how they are linked and consider not just for 'emotional satisfaction' according to Bott, but the mechanisms for forms of intergeneration capital and how far the cliques are able to transmit both cultural capital and assets through the generations depends on the kinship network and strategies for 'Socioemotional Wealth Preservation'. This is a serious real-world public policy issue. For example, 'the bank of mum and dad' assumes a key role in housing of younger people within the current housing crisis of affordability and access to mortgage finance. This can be clearly seen in Ambridge as we see more affluent families playing a role in the housing of their offspring. Kate living on the fringes of Home Farm affords her the option of building her holistic health business on the premises.

The precise methodological steps I have taken to generate these kinship networks are as follows:

1. Ethical clearance obtained from all villagers

2. Nodes are defined — and the edges of the network decided upon.

3. Data are generated — for kinship networks. These are generally settled fact, except in outlying cases of disputed parentage, for example, George Grundy who has tie to both Ed and Will or multiple marriage/cohabitation, for example Kenton Archer

4. Algorithms for centrality are applied

5. Maps are presented and analysed

Figure 1. The Kinship Structure of Ambridge in 2017.

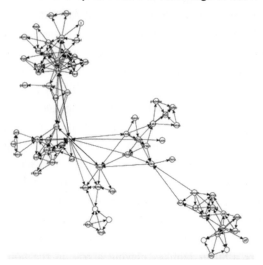

Figure 1 shows the full kinship structure of Ambridge. The first finding of the network analysis is that it shows 75 people all connected with one another by birth or marriage by no more than four degrees of separation. It includes deceased relations as the main family cliques are linked by ancestry. The whole network is one of a Small World type, with distinct family groupings, and shows a high degree of cohesion which would suggest frequency of interaction between characters. The 'thick spots' or 'cliques' within the main network can be viewed as follows (Figure 2).

Each circle (below) delimits a discrete familial cliques defined as

1. Aldridges/Home Farm Archer Clique

2. Archers Brookfield Branch Archer Clique

Figure 2. Kinship Network with Cliques.

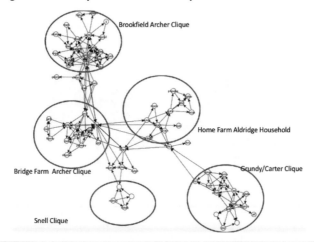

3. The Grundy/Carter Clique

4. Bellamy/Snell Clique

The first two cliques are long-established families. The other cliques cross a number of small nuclear families who have become linked with the Archers and Aldridges through marriages of the third generation. These cliques are more peripheral to the overall network but have great promise in the future of the village. We go on to explore the cliques in more detail before a discussion of how durable these structures may prove to be.

CLIQUE 1: ALDRIDGES AND HOME FARM ARCHERS

In **Figure 3**, the system of relationship of the largest clique in the village is presented. This network may reasonably be

Figure 3. Aldridges and Home Farm Archers.

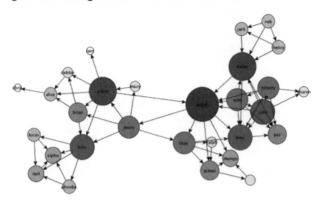

described as the tribe of Peggy, as she is the matriarch. Shown here are 29 members spanning four generations and covering the Aldridge/Bridge Farm Archer extended network (Table 1).

As discussed the clique is centred around Peggy, whose marriage to The Two Jacks, Archer and Woolley, has led to her having independence and considerable assets, which she has deployed to more and less divisive effect in recent years. Her decision to privilege her grandson Tom at the expense of his father Tony was a major plotline causing significant bad feeling. I have not included Hazel, Peggy's step-daughter in the network as she is universally loathed and estranged from the village although she is a rich vein of interest through her landholdings in Ambridge.

There are three main constellations of actors grouped around Peggy's three children; Jennifer, Tony and Lilian (though we will look at Lilian separately in the chapter). Whilst this clique supports 10 households three are not in Ambridge: Kate's South African children, Debbie in Hungary

Table 1. First Major Family Clique — Aldridges and Home Farm Archers.

Size of clique	29 people
Generational structure	Four generations
Household structure	10 households
	7 within Ambridge
	○ Peggy (and Christine Barford)
	○ Brian, Jennifer and Ruari
	○ Adam & Iain[a]
	○ Kate (in Home Farm cottage)
	○ Lilian & Justin (The Dower House)
	○ Pat and Tony, Helen, George and Jack[a]
	○ Johnny & Tom (1 The Green)[a]
	3 beyond Ambridge
	○ Phoebe in Oxford
	○ Madikanes in SA
	○ Debbie in Hungary

[a]Denotes recent household formation or disturbance.

and Phoebe at the University of Oxford. (I hope her research career will go on the DPhil level where I am available to supervise her doctoral career).

Home Farm family

Marital fidelity and the legitimacy of offspring have long been a core function of bourgeoisie marriage, not so much in the Home Farm Aldridges. Brian Aldridge has, over four decades in Ambridge, operationalized a highly differentiated set of mating strategies which may have threatened to fragment the Home Farm Aldridge legacy through sub-optimal strategy. However, despite this for now the Home Farm finances seem secure. Where there are risks, however, to the continuing dominance of the Aldridges in Ambridge it is in the remarkably underactive mating strategies of the generation of Adam, Debbie, Ruari, and Alice and Chris Carter. This lack of fecundity is countered by Kate who has two separate families (beyond the village). The inheritance politics of the Aldridge clique only intensify after a family meeting where shares in the farm were allocated according to input in the farm recently.

Bridge Farm Family

Pat and Tony's son and daughter have been struggling in the mating game. Helen's disastrous coupling with Rob Titchener has her returning to the fold of the family for the foreseeable future and recently, following wounding liaisons with Brenda and Kirsty, Tom Archer is foreswearing affairs of the heart for now. Purely from a household perspective the Bridge Farm Archers seem bad at forming stable households/couples beyond the farm. It may be that John's son Johnny from Leeds may offer some possibilities in the mating department but until then Pat and Tony have an inter-generational household for the foreseeable future (**Figure 4**)

CLIQUE 2: BROOKFIELD ARCHERS

Despite having their name above the door (as it were) the Brookfield Archers, or the tribe of Gill, are the second order clique within the structure of Ambridge. There are fewer members in the Gill clique than the Peggy one and are yet to

Figure 4. Brookfield Archers.

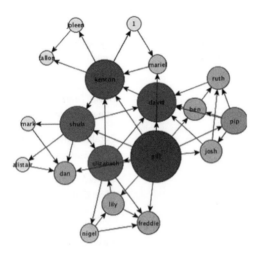

deliver a fourth generation. As befits their land-owning status the clique supports four independent households: Brookfield, Lower Loxley, The Stables and The Bull (Table 2).

The 4th generation of Brookfield Archers are yet to emerge because Gill is 10 years younger than Peggy.

Brookfield

It is fair to describe the relationship of David and Ruth as quite rocky over the years. Despite their closeness as business partners and husband and wife there has been a restlessness and resentment expressed and acted upon by Ruth, who often seems miserable in Ambridge. It may be that this has echoes in the reticence of the children of this marriage to commit to partners themselves. In short Pip, Josh and Ben, for quite different

Table 2. Second Major Family Clique — Brookfield Archers.

Size of clique	18 people
Generational structure	3 generations
Household structure	4 within Ambridge
	○ Brookfield
	David, Ruth, Gill, Pip, Josh, Ben
	○ Lower Loxley
	Elizabeth, Freddie, Lily
	○ The Stables
	Shula & Alistair
	○ The Bull
	Kenton & Jolene
	Fallon & Harrison
	Beyond Ambridge
	Meriel in NZ

reasons was unable to appear as their Bridge Farm cousins in the relationships department. Indeed the weight of expectation from her parents and grandparent as regards Pip's poor choices of companion make the future of the farm omnipresent in her romantic life. Josh is currently in entrepreneurial mode — in the mould of the sausage king years of his older cousin Tom — and Ben is currently a silent character.

Pargetters: Lower Loxley

The marriage of Elizabeth to lord of the manor Nigel was a significant step from land-owning farming family to landed gentry, that the marriage produced the twins Lily and Freddie offers great possibilities for the Pargetter side of the family.

Bull branch: Kenton and his many links

By virtue of his serial monogamy there are a number of routes through which Kenton's branch of the family might grow. Indeed his daughter Meriel in New Zealand and step-daughter Fallon, whose cohabitation with PC Harrison Burns appears to be generally successful. Between these, Kenton, by virtue of his long cohabitation with Kathy Perks, was also a father-figure to Jamie Perks, though both he and his mother have been silent for several years now.

The Stables

Dan born through IVF was a strong 80s storyline — there is a great potential for him and Dorothy to have children. Shula may be the first grandmother within her generation of Brookfield Archers however a military career does not promise their return to the village for some time yet.

The role of the Aldridges and Archers in Ambridge has been of settled and bourgeois land-owning families. Their connectedness as 'cousins' underpins the routine co-operation necessary for life to run smoothly. However, as has been argued, the principal role of families of this type is as regards their ability to transmit capital across generations. Such concerns are not so in evidence with the 'lower status' families in Ambridge who are more intimately connected with day-to-day life for extended periods with multi-generational family formations from necessity. The trials of the whole Grundy clan in making the rent on Grange Farm every month are frequently referenced and Ed and Emma and their children have lived with both sets of in-laws — Carters and Grundies.

CLIQUE 3: GRUNDY/CARTER

The 'Tribe of Joe'

The longevity of the matriarchs of the other clans in the village is not reflected in the Grundies. Joe is the titular head of the Grundy Clan, of whom there are four generations. It was Neil Kinnock who argued in the 1980s that *The Archers* ought to be renamed 'The Grundies and their class oppressors' as the perpetual money worries and precarity of the clan as regards both land and labour are a counterpoint to the upward curve of the Archers and Aldridges. The Grundies are linked to the Carters by virtue of Emma's marriage to Ed, sealing many decades of fondness between the families.

Casa Nueva

As much as snobbish Susan celebrated going up in the world through Christopher's marriage to Alice Aldridge her lifelong friendship with Clarrie and Eddie had already been cemented via Emma joining the Grundy family, initially by marrying Will and then leaving him for his brother Ed. These two marriages put Susan in a key brokerage role as the marriages of her offspring place her at the edges of both Grundy and Aldridge cliques.

CLIQUE 4: BELLAMY/SNELL CLIQUE

Dower House

Following her break-up with Matt, Lilian has been as much of a permanent fixture in her sister Jennifer's kitchen as the extraordinary fixtures and fittings purchased with such fuss to fit the place out. For now, however she and fiancé Justin have returned to the Dower House. Both Jennifer and Lilian have operationalised strategy of which Jane Austen would approve — securing their status and wealth through marriages. It is often ignored that they are the children of the 'black sheep' of the Archer Clan, Jack, a heavy drinker and erstwhile publican.

The Snells

The incorporation of Robert and Linda Snell into the kinship network of the village represents their acceptance having been incomers. The elopement of James Bellamy with a Snell creates connections between these families and the linking of Lilian to Linda as grandparents to Mungo offer significant potential for intrigue and interest in Ambridge. Despite living 'in London' James and Leonie, with their offspring of Mungo represent the sole conventional (normative) nuclear family in their generation. Should they ever decide to return to Ambridge this could disrupt power dynamics significantly (Table 3).

THE FUTURE OF NETWORKS OF THE VILLAGE

We have seen in this chapter that kinship structures in Ambridge have the following features of being small worlds, linked by birth and marriage and that by virtue of this closeness and cohesion it is not hard to see why the village shop would do well to keep a wide range of greetings cards in stock at all times. In this discussion section, what are we to read from the current network structures and what trends may be reasonably extrapolated? The results from exploring

Table 3. Comparison of the Ambridge Cliques, 2017.

Clique	Wooley/ Aldridge Bridge Farm Archers	Brookfield Archers	Grundy	Bellamy/ Snell
Status	1	2	3	4
Size	29 living	18 living	12 living	8 living
Generational Structure	4 generations	3 generations	4 generations	4 generations
Household Structure (beyond Ambridge)	10 households (3)	5 households	3 households	5 households (2)

consequences of networked power in Ambridge is divided for clarity into two possible futures: the first Scenario 1: Archers and Aldridges (status quo) and the second, Scenario 2: recombining the network of other characters where *The Headlam Hypothesis* argues that '*The Archers* are dead but long live the network'.

Scenario 1: Archers and Aldridges (Versions of the Status Quo)

For the existing matriarchies to have more enduring power then we need to see more offspring (or any?) from the various branches of the family. It is quite extraordinary that there are quite so many childless people in their thirties, forties and fifties in Ambridge. In terms of Brookfield Archers it may be the wildcards of Meriel, and Fallon who are our best hope as so far no Brookfield Archers, Pip, Josh or Ben show any skills in the dating department. Pip is disastrous for now and we may have to look to her younger brothers for next generations of Archers. There is of course the possibility that Dan and Dorothy could offer the possibility of great-grandchildren for Gill but unless it brings them back to the village rather than following a military career this does not serve to enhance the prestige of the future for the tribe of Gill.

There is another path to maintaining the centrality of *The Archers* but it is based on a whole series of rather fanciful assumptions. These are that: both Jill and Peggy die; Alice and Chris have two children; Leonie and James have two more (and return to the village); Phoebe marries Freddie; and that no one else reproduces (!) Under this scenario kinship structure is transformed isolating both Brookfield and Bridge Farm Archers. It would create a whole new matriarchy with network centrality for Lilian! As outlandish as this sounds, unless the Brookfield or Home Farm offspring sort themselves and their marriage prospects out then the centrality of the tribe of Gill is threatened. So watch very carefully if Phoebe shows any more than a passing interest in Freddie.

Scenario 2: The Headlam Hypothesis

It may be that the future kinship structure of the village rests on Mungo — who stands out as the only legitimate offspring of married parents in his generation. Watch very carefully for any sign of James and Leonie moving back to Ambridge as this move would displace the existing clans and place Lilian and Lynda at the centre of the network. Similarly should Alice and Christopher Carter have children the granny power of Susan and Jennifer makes them of increased importance and centrality. Susan, as already described sits between the

Grundy and Aldridge clans by virtue of the marriages of her two children, this key brokerage role may result in her centrality in generations to come. It will be fascinating to see how the kinship networks of Ambridge adapt to the inevitable loss of Gill and Peggy, and to compare the SNA structures of the future.

REFERENCES

Bott, E. (1971). *Family and social network*. (2nd ed.). (Originally published, 1957). New York, NY: Free Press.

Byrne, P. (2017). The medieval world of the archers, William Morris and the problem with class struggle. In *The Archers in fact and fiction: Academic analyses of life in rural Borsetshire*.

Castells, M. (1996). The network society.

Clinton, H. (2007). *It takes a village*. Simon & Schuster UK.

Freeman, L. C., & Webster, C. M. (1994). Interpersonal proximity in social and cognitive space. *Social Cognition*, *12*(3), 223–247. doi:10.1521/soco.1994.12.3.223

Gillies, L., & Burrows, H. M. (2017). A case study in the use of genograms to assess family dysfunction and social class: To the Manor Born versus Shameless. In *Custard, culverts and cake: Academics on life in the archers*. Bingley: Emerald Publishing Limited.

Medland, A. (2017). Culinary coercion; nurturing traditional gender roles in Ambridge. In *Custard, culverts and cake: Academics on life in the archers*. Bingley: Emerald Publishing Limited.

PEER REVIEW BY HAZEL WOOLLEY, ADDRESS WITHHELD

I never knew why my darling daddy got himself entangled with the troglodytes of the shire. *The Archers* and Aldridges and whatnot are more like hobbits than rabbits — As Dr Headlam points out they aren't very fecund are they? All inbred no doubt. Imagine being able to trace 75 people all connected by blood or marriage. Horrors! And so enmeshed with one another preventing sensible business transactions. Look at all that nonsense over my flat and the village shop! This is a gene pool that is all shallow end in my opinion.

I see that the good doctor has omitted me from her sociograms and focusses on the possibilities of dynasties of Grundies and Carters, Snells and Bellamies displacing Peggy and Gill's ghastly and unpromising offspring. Well we shall see. There was never any love lost between myself and my stepmother Peggy and the notion that she has high status in Ambridge is absolutely laughable, she is all genteel pretensions and gradations of good China. What tosh! She was a penniless single mother who drove her first husband to drink and had nothing until she got her claws into my daddy, and now with her meddlesome largesse she dares to spend HIS hard earned money on indulging the useless next generation. Although she has been generously provided for in her lifetime she wants to check the small print of the family trusts before getting over-excited about gifts to cat's homes or her awful relations. Kinship networks indeed — what sentimental nonsense.

CHAPTER THIRTEEN

GOD IN AMBRIDGE:
THE ARCHERS AS RURAL
THEOLOGY

Jonathan Hustler

ABSTRACT

Rural theology is explained here as a form of practical theology that seeks to interpret the rural context in the light of the central themes of Christian theology and vice versa. If Christian theology can be understood as concerning belief in God and the understanding of human relationships with God, the created order, and each other in the light of that belief, rural theology expresses that in the light of the lived experience in a rural context, which for these purposes is the daily bulletin from Ambridge. The author draws on his experience of teaching in the Cambridge Theological Federation to reflect on three recent examples: the recent changes at Brookfield in response to the perennial issue of the milk price lead us to ask who benefits from the production of higher quality food; the care for the land and Adam Macy's reforms at Home Farm point us to issues about sustainability and responsibility; and the cohesion of a community with shared values and its treatment of Rob Titchener asks questions about the limits of inclusion. As with much practical theology, the outcome of the reflection is in ethical action and some further ethical questions, which, as the example of Jim Lloyd's philosophical conversations with Alan Franks illustrate, are not the monopoly of the Church.

Keywords: Theology; rural; food; land; community; redemption

My first appointment as a Methodist minister was in a village in Buckinghamshire. Having never before lived in a settlement that boasted no bank, that only had three buses a day, and where the minimal approach to street lighting left me stumbling from the car to the back door of the house, my sole preparation for rural life was quarter of a century's exposure to *The Archers*. I became convinced of the fundamental veracity of life in Ambridge. The saga of the bearers of a few surnames interweaving their family trees with regular (and sometimes surprising) injections of fresh blood from elsewhere, the plight of the village shop that has ceased to be commercially viable, the school suffering a falling roll and eventually closing, the dependence on the motor car and the urgent needs of seventeen-year-olds to learn to drive, the camaraderie that sees the loaning of expensive equipment between farmers, the struggle to field an eleven for a cricket match, the annual cycle of pantomime, flower and produce show and fete, and the role of the parish church in marking the seasons were at least in part all replicated in the villages in which I ministered, though the moment of clearest insight was when a church warden stood up at an harvest supper to sing 'The Village Pump', as once Tom Forrest used to do.

For many years, Tom was church warden at Ambridge (Toye & Flynn, 2001, p. 143).The church which the latter day Tom Forrests of the British countryside hold office is (if not in vacancy) served by a parish priest (often now by a priest who holds several benefices); that priest will have received a theological education somewhere. If she or he had any inkling when in initial training that they would be serving in a country parish, or if they had at a later date undertaken continued development when changing appointments, they may well have studied rural theology. Where rural theology is taught it has tended to be to ordinands and much of what is written in journals of rural theology has tended to focus on questions about the role of the Church in the countryside. The 2017 issue of *Rural Theology* for instance contains four main articles, three of which are in one way or another concerned with the life of the church in the countryside. Tillich's (1953, p. 3) insistence that theology 'as a function of the Christian Church, must serve the needs of the Church' can become over-limiting.

Rural theology, even when taught to those in training for ordained ministry, is more than the consideration of the needs of the church in the rural context and informs more than pastoral practice. If theology is an academic discipline that asks questions about the nature of God, about how belief in God informs our understanding of the universe, and about what it means to be human in the light of our understanding of who God is, rural theology can be understood as specifically asking those questions in the context of the countryside and village life. That is not to criticise those who write about how multi-parish benefices can best operate, what patterns of Christian mission encourage increased church attendance in small communities or how inflexible spaces can best be used for modern worship; these are important issues for many rural clergy and probably occupy more of Alan Franks' waking moments than Usha would wish. It is rather to say that those matters of pastoral practice are surface questions about how (in theological terms) the people of God are enabled to live out their faith which is informed by the theological understanding gained from the exploration of those core questions (so Tillich was right after all).

Rural theology, then, belongs to the broader field of practical theology which Pattison and Lynch (2011, p. 410) define as beginning with lived experience and adopting an interdisciplinary approach as it engages with the sacred texts, creeds, traditions and doctrinal writings of a religious tradition. For our purposes, the lived experience is the daily insight into life in Borsetshire. The trials and tribulations of the Archers, the Aldridges, the Carters and the Grundys can through disciplined reflection help to inform our understanding of God, the universe, and what it means to be human, and, critically, vice versa: theology offers a prism through which the events in Ambridge can be interpreted.

Practical theology takes a number of forms and its students find themselves exposed to a number of different methods but most if not all of them are essentially dialogical or cyclic. Green's (2009, p. 19) emphasis on 'doing' theology is typical: 'I have found it helpful to think of the process as a circle, cycle, or even better, a spiral, which moves around continually from action to reflection and from reflection to action.' Browning (1996, p. 7) argues that all theology is or should be practical but that the method that he proposes specifically 'goes from present theory-laden practice to a retrieval of normative theory-laden practice to the creation of more critically held theory-laden practices'. What is implied here is that theology does not simply enable us (or perhaps more accurately the community of faith) to know more about a situation but to examine the way in which our faith has informed our response to a situation by reviewing the fundamentals of that faith and responding afresh to the situation. Whilst few of us have any opportunity to shape events in Ambridge (however loudly we have shouted at the wireless to urge Pip to dump Toby, Tom to stop being so arrogant, Oliver and Caroline to have mercy on the Grundys, or Jill to tell David to let go the apron strings), a theological approach to our listening places their actions on a wider map, shaping our understanding of the world we share, and perhaps influencing our own behaviour.

Although theology is usually written (or, as Green maintains, done) by and for the Church, the concerns that it reflects are those of all humanity. It is significant that Jim Lloyd's caustic scepticism about the Christian faith (as shortly after moving to the village he described Shula's church attendance as 'talking to an imaginary friend') has mellowed into philosophical discussions with Alan Franks; the task of theology as I present it here can offer insights to those who do not share the faith premise on which the venture is based for two reasons. The first is that the themes that emerge are those which concern all those who live in Ambridge (either in Borsetshire or in their minds as they listen): the questions that I seek to explore in this chapter about food, about soil and about how we treat the outcast and offender are fundamental to all who eat and walk on the earth and keep company with others. The second reason is that Ambridge is at least a nominally Christian place. In fact it is a largely Anglican place. Usha Franks appears to be the only adherent to a non-Christian religion in the village (unless

one counts Kate Madikane's eclectic and esoteric paganism).
Joe Grundy's no longer mentioned Methodism and the late
Siobhan Hathaway's Catholicism are the only other denomi-
national allegiances of which we have been aware.
Consciously or not, the teachings of the Christian faith have
shaped the ways in which the residents of Ambridge behave.

ALL GOOD GIFTS...

One of those ways is to celebrate a harvest festival and still to
make the harvest supper a major occasion in the autumn calendar. That Alan Franks is the one who organises the supper
ties it to the worship of the Church which gives thanks to
God for God's bounty. A key question is rural theology asks
what it means to believe that God provides God's creatures
with the means to sustain life, a question that forms part of
the doctrine of creation. As Young (1976, p. 13) points out,
for all that Christian theology is centred on what Christians
understand to be the revelation of God in the life, death, and
resurrection of Jesus Christ, the doctrine of creation 'seems
an obvious place to start any serious thinking about the
Christian faith.' Young points out that the Bible, the Creeds
and even the 39 Articles of the Church of England all begin
with God as creator.

From day to day, the practical concern in thinking about
the notion of God as creator is not about whatever primor-
dial events brought the universe to birth but about the fact of
creation and the benefits that human beings derive from it;
the theist believes that creation has been ordered so that creatures are fed and life maintained by God's action or (general)
providence. The fundamental nature of this belief in the
Judaeo-Christian tradition is indicated by the first words that

Scripture records God saying to the first human being —
'You may eat....' (Genesis 2v16).

'You may eat...' was a message that the Atlee government
wanted to communicate in the late 1940s. The genesis of
The Archers in 1948 was, as is well known, in the desire of
the BBC to assist the Ministry of Agriculture to encourage
farmers to make the reforms deemed necessary to feed a
growing population that was still struggling with rationing:
most of those who know about *The Archers* beginnings are
aware of the story of Henry Burtt's interjection in Godfrey
Baseley's discussion on how that desire might be met —
'What we need is a farming *Dick Barton*' (Smethurst, 1996,
p. 12). *The Archers* has faithfully chronicled changing methods in food production in the subsequent 67 years. Such
changes (as chronicled by, inter alia, Harvey, 2006) have
involved the use and overuse of pesticides, the increased con-
finement of animals, the development of new breeds of both
beast and crop, the deployment of new forms of pesticide and
a move away from patterns of crop rotation. Alongside the
growth of factory farming and a belief amongst many farmers (with Brian Aldridge as their champion) that efficient food
production can best be accomplished through large-scale
enterprises, there has also been a renaissance of small-scale
production and an emphasis on local produce.

A key question that recurs in Ambridge is about the quality of food that is being produced. In January 2016, Ruth
Archer returned from her sojourn in New Zealand full of
ideas about the future of the farm. She had been considering
the perennial question of the milk yield and the difficulty that
Brookfield had in maintaining it. She pointed out that that
yield was not an end in itself: the end should be the profit
that the farm looked to make and there were other ways to
make a profit than by pushing up the milk yield. Ruth argued
for a smaller mixed herd which would produce higher quality

milk (which would therefore command a higher price). This 'not quantity but quality' argument echoes several other debates that *The Archers'* characters have had down the years. Oliver Sterling began producing milk from Guernseys believing that it tasted more like milk should taste than that which he could buy in the shops; he would have been unaware of the echo of Mary Pound's assertion that 'in good milk you should be able to taste the grass' (Toye & Farrington, 2013, chapter 1, section 4). The desire to offer quality food has been at the heart of the Bridge Farm enterprise since the conversion to organic began. Tom Archer was prepared to sacrifice his organic credentials when he threw in his lot in a short-lived partnership with Brian Aldridge; he was not prepared to cut the percentage of meat in his sausages. Hassett Hills lamb and the Brookfield beef are both marketed as quality local products. The recurrent motif is that people want not just food but good food, not simply to be fed but to eat well; it is a motif that not only informs farming practices but also the patterns of eating out in Ambridge. The Feathers or Grey Gables seems more appropriate to a special occasion (or the deeper pocket) than 'just The Bull'.

The American Methodist theologian Hauerwas (2012, p. 1) argues that the essence of the ethicist's task can be summarised in a simple question: 'Do you like to eat?' For Hauerwas, this is a question about habit; he argues that we need to understand the nature of our habits in order to explore what it means to live a good life or to be a moral being. But Hauerwas' interrogative can be taken in a different way by emphasising the *like* in the question. Do you enjoy what you eat? Theology that argues (as most theology does, following Augustine) that the creator is good and that fundamentally creation is good (and that where creation is evil that is to be understood as an absence of the intended good) also argues that creatures are therefore created to delight in that good creation. That means that human happiness and well-being cannot be divorced from the moral imperative (on which the Christian tradition has no monopoly) that human beings should behave well. McCabe (2005, p. 5) summarised the position: 'In the tradition from which I speak, which we may call the tradition of Aristotle, understood with the help of Aquinas, it is thought proper to praise those actions and dispositions that lead to and are constitutive of that human satisfaction in which happiness consists.' The moral imperative to live well can have more than one meaning: to live well can mean to live as one who enjoys the good things in life or to live as one who does good things. McCabe and Hauerwas in different ways refuse to divorce the two.

This leads us further to reflect on two ethical questions that arise from that argument that God wants human beings to be good by delighting in God's goodness: first, how do we define 'good'? By what criteria do we judge that since the herd was replaced at Brookfield the milk is higher quality? Or, Sterling Gold might not be to everyone's taste; it may well be that Tracey Horrobin's children prefer the mass-produced cheddar we assume that they are fed. Even to raise these questions is to venture into a social, political, and ethical minefield, where some general rules might help but where every contention is subject to debate. Aquinas' definition of 'good' as 'useful, worthy, and desirable' (McDermott, 1989, p. 19) only takes us so far, though it does indicate that the current debates are critical to our understanding. Harvey contends that much industrially produced food is neither useful (in that its nutritional content is less than the human body needs) nor worthy (in that modern diet can be linked to an increase in reported diseases, implying that in some ways food has proved positively harmful) (Harvey, 2006,

pp. 31–40). Moreover, he argues (*ibid.*, p. 1) its lack of flavour rules out its being desirable.

The second ethical question we are forced to ask by this
argument is 'for whom is "higher quality food" good?' The
question can be focussed on the issue of milk production
and the pasture-fed, mixed herd at Brookfield. Is this good
for the consumer who gets a fuller flavour (surely a subjective argument)? Is it good for the farmer who might get
something nearer to the cost of production at the farm gate?
This was, after all, Ruth's key argument in agitating for the
changes. Or is it good for the cows that spend more time on
grass? Christian ethicists (such as McCabe) have in recent
decades encouraged Christians to be alert to the ethical
issues created by our reliance on other species. Harvey
(2006, p. 198) again seems to drink from a similar well
when he argues that the fundamental issue about industrial
food production is that it is reliant on a reductionist scientific approach which 'works by looking at the effect of a
single measure or action taken in isolation'. The apparently
simple idea of 'good food' covers a complex of ethical issues
about the relationship between human beings and the rest of
creation.

ADAM — MAN OF THE SOIL

That leads us to the second issue: the relationship of human
beings to the rest of creation. Brookfield is not the only farm
to have been through significant change in the last couple of
years, though as Toye and Farrington (2013, chapter 1, section 4) point out change has been a constant feature of life in
Ambridge: 'As time marches by, incremental adjustments to
daily life follow in their wake. Ultimately these add up to
some substantial step changes that have shaped the lives of

those in Ambridge and beyond.' From time to time, the farmers of Ambridge decide that they need to do more than simply to accept incremental changes and significantly alter their practice. The decision of Tony and Pat Archer to farm organically might be the most drastic of such moves but Brian's decision to move out of dairy, Tom's move to persuade Tony and Pat they could run a successful dairy with no cows, and David and Ruth's decision no longer to keep pigs at Hollowtree are all examples of the adaptability that is clearly a necessary feature of modern farming. One of these moves in 2015 was at Home Farm and on the estate land that Home Farm is contracted to manage. Adam Macey was able to persuade both Brian and Charlie Thomas that in the aftermath of the flood something needed to be done about the erosion of the soil on the land he farmed. For far too long he argued (and we recognise the echoes of Harvey's arguments in *The Killing of the Countryside* (Harvey, 1998)) crop yields have been kept artificially high by pumping chemical fertiliser into the soil which is now depleted of natural goodness and simply a sponge to soak up nitrates. He held up a handful of soil to show Charlie how lacking in life it was. Adam's answer was to move away from the dependence on chemical fertilizers so we who live in cities were introduced to herbal leys and no till agriculture, the means by which he intended to restore the rich ecosystem that every spadeful of earth should be.

That it was Adam who voiced these opinions is music to the theologian's ears. Adam is the name that the Hebrew Bible gives to the first human being, who was made from the ground ('adamah). This identification with the earth in which our crops are grown has been a fundamental theme in the Judaeo-Christian understanding of what it means to be human; 'dust you are and to dust you shall return' is also taken from the early part of the book of Genesis and echoes around churches on Ash Wednesday as believers are reminded of their mortality.

In the most famous of all Christian prayers (the Lord's Prayer) Christian believers ask that God's will be done on earth — and the Greek word is 'gē' which has the range of meanings that the English word 'earth' has. It can mean 'the earth' as opposed to 'the heavens' or 'land' as opposed to 'sea' but it can also mean earth as the ground which is tilled or earth as the soil that runs through Adam's fingers. In other words, the soil in which seeds are planted is not in theological terms simply a resource for human beings to exploit for their own needs and which can be used to the point of exhaustion but something to which they are related and which the Christian belief system avers has a key place in God's purposes. Preserving the quality of our soil is not simply ecologically sound; it is fundamental to who we are. Such thoughts have been fundamental to a number of recent theological developments as Christians have, admittedly late, come to recognise the urgency of the concerns of those who have urged greater environmental awareness. Pope Francis (2015) argues in *Laudato Si'* that human beings cannot behave as though somehow we are separate from our own environment. We are, the Pope avers, part of the very eco-system that we have damaged. He complains that human activity 'is actually making our earth less rich and beautiful, ever more limited and grey' (Francis, 2015, chapter 34). Similarly, Spencer and White (2007) tie the issues of the environment which concern them into the notion of a shared planet. The interconnectedness of humans and humus, of Adam and the soil, is a fundamental of theology, rediscovered in dialogue with the modern ecological movement.

THE DEFENESTRATION OF ROB TITCHENER

Adam's no till system did not impress everyone. Rob Titchener was planning to ask the board of Borchester Land to pull the plug on Adam's experiment, but Rob is now, we believe, far away on the other side of the Atlantic and the collective view of the village is 'Good riddance'. The Rob and Helen story was one which created a great deal of comment on social media, much of which was hostile to Rob. But we might ask when Rob came to be universally seen, in Linda's phrase, as 'a dreadful excuse for a human being'. It is worth recalling that it was not only to Susan that he was a hero after the flood (when none but Charlie and Stefan knew of his dastardly deeds); whilst Helen was in prison opinion remained divided, but the tide turned rapidly after the trial and Rob became a pariah. A key moment was when the cricket team refused to let him play; that he was the star batsman of the 2015 season counted for naught and his attempts to advise PC Harrison Burns (who had maintained strict neutrality during the trial) were politely but firmly rejected. Rob was no longer wanted in or by the team and the team was representing the village; it was a pointed act of exclusion of someone who had offended against the norms and values of the local society.

A third theme of rural theology is community: how do (and how should) human beings relate to each other? The notion of community implies belonging, and therefore exclusion as well as inclusion, or as Volf (1996) argues, differentiation. There is always a degree of heterogeneity in any human society, but there are also limits to inclusion. Volf's arguments were developed from his own experience as a Croat who had experienced the horrors of war in the Balkans as those who had co-existed became enemies as one side sought

to exclude the other. It is a pattern that was tragically replicated in other conflicts in the late twentieth century, but it is
not the only narrative of exclusion. What is fascinating about
the Rob story is that he appears always to have been on the
edge, that he never quite belonged. When Volf offers his first
definition of exclusion as 'cutting of the bonds that connect,
taking oneself out of the pattern of interdependence and placing oneself in a position of sovereign independence. The other
then emerges as an enemy that must be pushed away from
the self and driven out of its space as a nonentity...' (Volf,
1996, p. 67), he describes the inner being of Rob that
emerged as his self-composure unravelled. *The Archers* were
scorned by him as of no significance; his claim that he had
demeaned himself by ever playing for the Ambridge XI was
more than mere petulance. There were always hints that Rob
viewed himself as the outsider; that he was willing to live in
Ambridge and to profit from doing so but never really to
embrace the village. His marriage to Helen can be understood
as a sign of his outsider status.

For the Christian theologian, marriage belongs to society
as a whole. The Methodist Church's 1946 statement on marriage began 'Marriage is much more than a concern of the
individual — it is of vital importance to the community'
(Methodist Church, 1995, p. 79). That fundamentally public
understanding of marriage is reflected in the rites and practices that surround a wedding. The Church will insist that the
marriage be celebrated publicly (with the provision that those
who would object have the opportunity to do so by the reading of banns or a parallel process which implies that those
who are to marry are known in the locality); the marriage
marks a development of relationships within a community
(so the practice of the two families occupying sides of a
church can be seen as kin groups in the village coming
together); a known public figure (for these purposes often a

priest) leads the witnessing of the couple's commitment (not only sacerdotally but in England as the registrar's deputy, i.e., a civic functionary); it is applauded by the community in which it is celebrated (as in many ceremonies the priest will literally invite the congregation to clap but also in ways that the community itself develops, sometimes spontaneously as when Kirsty made her tragic journey in public procession); marriage represents and contributes to the cohesion of the community. That Rob and Helen chose to register their union many miles away on the Isle of Wight was a negation of all those expectations, in a way that somehow Alice and Chris Carter's impulsive American marriage was not: the stranger remained a stranger even when he married into the eponymous clan. His employment also pointed to Rob's identity as an outsider. The comparatively short-lived mega dairy that was Berrow Farm always seemed an unwelcome imposition of industrial scale animal husbandry. Debbie Aldridge expressed a more profound truth than she realised when at the Hunt Ball she told Rob that she regretted it ever having been established as it brought him to the village.

In the July 2016 newsletter of the Rural Theology Association (RTA) Caroline Pinchbeck lamented that we had heard little from Alan Franks in the Helen and Rob saga. Alan may well be a member of the RTA and seems to have taken the hint as in subsequent weeks we heard about his attempts to minister to Rob, but he made little headway. He returned to Usha from one conversation admitting that he found talking to Rob frustrating as the man seemed to have no empathy with anyone else. Alan was not attempting to pathologise Rob's attitude but was asking himself a theological question as he confessed that his faith that everyone was capable of redemption had been shaken. Whatever lay behind Rob's unsympathetic attitude, Alan could not reach him. We heard a dedicated Christian priest wrestle with the idea that there might be limits to grace.

Alan's fundamental conviction that there is no one beyond redemption places him on one side of a theological debate that has rumbled in the Church of England and other Protestant denominations in Britain since the sixteenth century. It pits a stricter form of Calvinism (which maintains that God has predetermined who shall be redeemed) against an Arminian belief (after the Dutch theologian, Jakob Arminius (1560–1609)) which contends that 'God's grace is universally available to humankind and that in no sense did God foreknow, elect, or predestine those who would be saved and those who would be lost.' (Cracknell & White, 2005, p. 100). The implication for Alan of placing himself in the Arminian camp is that Rob need not be an outsider, though his attempt to introduce to Rob the concept of forgiveness (which Alan maintained was the way to begin to approach the future) was swiftly rebuffed. Human society should, in Christian terms, reflect the generosity of God's love and forgiveness. Good priest that he is, Alan grounds the limits (or the openness) of human community in his espoused theological position and exercises his ministry on that basis.

It is rare for the listeners to *The Archers* to get so clear an invitation to reflect on an explicit theological statement, but the opportunities for the practical theologian to review her or his thinking and practice that are offered six days a week are considerable. Pattison and Lynch's description of those writers who 'in an increasingly secularised Britain.... use practical theology to describe a practice of normative analysis and critique of the action-guiding worldviews, assumptions, and behaviours prevalent in contemporary society that does not simply draw on the concepts, values, and beliefs of the Christian church' (*ibid.*, p. 410) might also be applied to those who listen (religiously?) to *The Archers*.

REFERENCES

Browning, D. S. (1996). *A fundamental practical theology.* Minneapolis, MN: Fortress Press.

Cracknell, K., & White, S. J. (2005). *An introduction to world methodism.* Cambridge, MA: Cambridge University Press.

Francis. (2015). *Laudato Si'.* Vatican. Retrieved from http://w2.vatican.va/content/francesco/en/encyclicals/documents/papa-francesco_20150524_enciclica-laudato-si.html

Green, L. (2009). *Let's do theology* (Revised ed.). London: Continuum.

Harvey, G. (1998). *The killing of the countryside* (Kindle ed.). Random House.

Harvey, G. (2006). *We want real food.* London: Constable.

Hauerwas, S. (2012). *Habit matters: The bodily character of the virtues. The Silver Jubilee Von Hugel Institute Lecture.* Retrieved from http://www.vhi.st-edmunds.cam.ac.uk/resources-folder/papers-files/Paper-hauerwas

McCabe, H. (2005). *The good life.* London: Continuum.

McDermott, T. (Ed.). (1989). *St Thomas Aquinas: Summa Theologiae. A Concise Translation.* London: Methuen.

Methodist Church in Britain. (1995). The law of marriage and divorce (1946). *Statements of social responsibility.* London: Methodist Church Division of Social Responsibility.

Pattison, S., & Lynch, G. (2011). Pastoral and practical theology. In D. F. Ford & R. Muers (Eds.), *The modern theologians* (pp. 408–425). Oxford: Blackwell.

Rural Theology Newsletter. (2016). Retrieved from http://
campaigns.ablosmedia.com/t/ViewEmail/r/
C0B9AC523ED985B72540EF23F30FEDED/
9B50E530B5D4B0F7981D23A7722F2DCD#toc_item_2

Rural Theology. (2017). Volume 15. Retrieved from http://
www.tandfonline.com/toc/yrur20/current

Smethurst, W. (1996). *The Archers: The true story*. London:
Michael O'Mara.

Spencer, N., & White, R. (2007). *Christianity, climate change
and sustainable living*. London: SPCK.

Tillich, P. (1953). *Systematic theology* (Vol. 1). London:
Nisbet & Co.

Toye, J., & Farrington, K. (2013). *The Archers: The
Ambridge chronicles* (Kindle ed.). London: BBC Books.

Toye, J., & Flynn, A. (2001). *The Archers Encyclopaedia*.
London: BBC Books.

Volf, M. (1996). *Exclusion and Embrace*. Nashville:
Abingdon.

Young, N. (1976). *Creator, creation and faith*. London:
Collins.

PEER REVIEW, BY ALAN FRANKS, THE VICARAGE, AMBRIDGE, BORSETSHIRE

The author offers a strong case for explicating what busy
rural clergy do automatically. In response to his first point
I would only argue that his definition of the *cui bono* is rather
limited and we need to ask the broader questions, not only
about the good of the planet (which he does in making his

second point) but also for the good of wider society. I spend much of my life frustrated by the dissonance between the quality and quantity of food in Ambridge and the needs at the food bank. Having a vegetarian diet (and being persuaded by those Christian theologians who argue that no Christian should eat meat) would give the author a different perspective.

The author's identification of the prevailing theological persuasion of St Stephens as open is spot on though the implicit comparison with situations of inter-communal violence is unnerving. I would like to see those who teach rural theology help their students to see how a small community can be enabled to put its own concerns in context.

CHAPTER FOURTEEN

SOME CORNER OF A FOREIGN FIELD/THAT IS FOREVER AMBRIDGE: *THE ARCHERS* AS A *LIEU DE MEMOIRE* OF THE FIRST WORLD WAR IN BRITAIN

Jessica Meyer

ABSTRACT

The history of the memory and commemoration of the First World War in British culture has long been the subject of academic debate. In particular, numerous studies have explored the significance of place, both local and national, to the creation and continuity of commemorative practices across the past 100 years. The current years of the centenary provide a particularly useful point of reference for exploring the development of cultural memory of the First World War in Britain, while the village of Ambridge forms a unique case study of local and national commemorative practices.

This chapter examines two forms of commemoration represented in The Archers, *the episodic marking of Remembrance Sunday across a 30-year period from 1996 to the present, and the community's engagement with national commemorative events in the centenary year 2014. It locates both these forms of commemoration in Nora's (1996) concept of* lieux de memoire, *the key symbolic elements of community memorial heritage, and Hobsbawm's (1983) definitions of invented traditions as those which are imposed upon communities rather than emerging organically from them. In doing so it argues that place functions as the key element of Ambridge's role as a* lieu de memoire *of the war, in contrast to people whose stories appear as invented traditions, particularly in 2014. It concludes that the programme ultimately maintains its ability to function as a* lieu de memoire *across the period, not only for the community of Ambridge, but also for the wider national community of* Archers *listeners.*

Keywords: Ambridge; First World War; commemoration; centenary; lieux de memoire; place

In October 2012, then Prime Minister David Cameron laid out the government's plans for the centenary commemoration of the First World War: 'Our ambition is a truly national commemoration ... I want a commemoration that captures our national spirit, in every corner of the country, from our schools to our workplaces, to our town halls and local communities' (Cabinet Office, 2012). The government pledged funding for the three commemorative strands: the renovation of the Imperial War Museum (IWM) in London as a commemorative monument; a programme of national events on key dates including Britain's entry into the war and the first day of the battle of the Somme; and an educational programme based on sending school groups to the battlefields and war cemeteries of the Western Front (Cabinet Office, 2012).

In his speech, however, Cameron also asserted 'a truly national commemoration cannot just be about national initiatives and government action, it needs to be local too' (Cabinet Office, 2012, para. 29). To tell local stories, the Heritage Lottery Fund was empowered to provide funding for projects based in, and undertaken by, local communities (First World War: then and now, n.d.). A similar dual imperative shaped the commemorative practices of the BBC. The overarching aim of the corporation's World War One commissions has been to tell the national and international story of the war through local voices, as in Jeremy Paxman's *Britain's Great War* (2013), and places, as in the BBC's *World War One at Home* project. 'Each World War One at Home story focussed on a place — airfields, hospitals, schools, churches, town squares, theatres, high streets — to show how events there influenced a global conflict' (World War One At Home, 2014). The result was a series of projects across the country which explore subjects such as the first Zeppelin raid in Great Britain at Yarmouth and the use of an elephant to replace delivery horses recruited into the armed forces in Sheffield. Just as the strands of national commemoration had, from the start, been focussed on the places where memory is seen to reside — the IWM and the battlefields — so local commemoration came to focus on locale as much as individuals, with the former informing understanding and memory of the latter.

The significance of place that these centenary practices reflect is unsurprising given its roots in the commemorations of the war from 1919 onwards. The creation of war memorials in communities across the country in the years after the war as *foci* for annual commemorative events helped to cement specific sites within clearly defined communities as the locus of war remembrance (King, 1998). This in turn has been reflected in academic histories of the memory and commemoration of the First World War. Studies such as King's *Memorials of the Great War in Britain* (1998) and Connelly's *The Great War, Memory and Ritual* (2001) have examined the ways in which local war commemoration was 'a socially comprehensive creative activity' which served as 'an instrument for creating desired forms of co-operative social relationship' (King, 1998, pp. 246–248). The physical nature of this commemoration has been noted by Winter in *Sites of Memory, Sites of Mourning*: 'Remembrance is part of the [European] landscape'. The damage that war wrought on the landscape influenced 'The construction, dedication and repeated pilgrimages to war memorials in the interwar years [which] provided a ritual expression of ... bereavement' (1980, p. 6). As a result, Europe, including Britain, has remembered the First World War in terms of specific, identifiable, imaginable places and close-knit communities which draw on traditional cultural tropes for their articulation and representation.

Winter's argument about the local community nature of the commemorative practices that these landscapes of memory enabled draws on the theories of Nora relating to French cultures of memory in which *lieux de memoire*, or sites of memory, are defined as 'any significant entity, whether material or non-material in nature, which by dint of human will or the work of time has become a symbolic element of the memorial heritage of any community' (1996, p. xvii) This can include, as Winter's analysis demonstrates, both places where commemoration occurs and the people who undertake the rituals of commemorative practice. Nora, however, sets such entities in contrast to what Hobsbawm and Ranger have defined as 'invented traditions', histories and rituals created to impose and enforce hegemonic structures of power. The involvement of official institutions in the structuring of memorials can result in the homogenization of the memories they symbolize in ways which rob them of their cultural and community meaning (Hobsbawm & Ranger, 1983).

By these definitions, *The Archers* as a whole can, on the one hand, be defined as a very British *lieu de memoire*, forming as it does a repository for 60 + years of historical memory of rural Britain. The importance of the audience and its engagement with the programme, from the enthusiasm for Phil and Grace Archer's romance in the early years through to the passionate support for Helen Archer as she suffered Rob Titchener's coercive control, serve as clear demonstration of the programmes place in the national community and conversation. On the other hand, given the Reithian underpinnings of Ambridge, with its role of educating a national audience about a range of social, cultural and political issues, this everyday story of country folk can be interpreted, and indeed often has been by critics, as an invented tradition. Criticisms of the Helen and Rob story line as a soap opera, designed as much to educate audiences about new laws on coercive control in domestic violence as to drive the drama, are only the most recent example.

Given the length of time over which *The Archers* has been broadcast, and the BBC's wider role in reflecting and shaping national commemorations of the First World War during the centenary years, the programme's representation of commemorations serve as an excellent case study by which to examine both the programme's dual status as a site of memory and an invented tradition and the place of the First World War in contemporary British memory. This chapter, therefore, looks at two forms of commemoration that occur within the programme, the annual marking of Remembrance Sunday across a period of 20 years and the references made to the centenary commemoration of the First World War throughout 2014. In doing so it will argue that, in representing national sites of memory in a local context, spaces of commemoration in *The Archers* function more effectively than people as symbols of our shared cultural memory of the war.

To begin with the recurring theme of Remembrance Sunday, which is generally, if somewhat erratically, marked in *The Archers* by comment on the annual church service, often within the specific space of St. Stephen's churchyard. In most years, this forms the primary marking of remembrance, although it does not occur every year and the intensity of commemorative practice varies. Thus in 1996 the minutes silence is marked, while in 2007 Nigel Pargetter speaks during the service of visiting his Great-Uncle Rupert's grave at Ypres, while separately Kathy Perks forces Jamie to observe the silence. In other years, the wars remembered have been other twentieth century conflicts, with Peggy Wooley in particular giving voice to memory of the Second World War, particularly the experiences of the Home Front, while the struggles of contemporary ex-servicemen were the focus in 2010 (McCartney, 2014, p. 308). The poppy appeal is also a recurrent theme, particularly at the turn of the century.

All these elements follow wider cultural patterns in the shifting emphases within the culture of commemoration throughout Britain. As both McCartney and Todman have demonstrated, commemorations of the First World War have never been static, but have always changed in response to the 'generational experience ... contemporary cultural, social, economic and political concerns' of the participants (McCartney, 2014, p. 3; Todman, 2005). What is interesting is the extent to which the Ambridge commemorations occupy a specifically religious space, occurring predominantly in both temporal and spatial proximity to religious sites and practices. Thus even as the national practice might be said to be becoming more secular, even commercial, as the British Legion seeks to monetize memorial practice through newly invented traditions such as the unveiling of the poppy campaign, *The Archers* reasserts, if not annually then regularly, the links between commemorative practice and the established religion and faith that underpinned the lives of both those who served in the war and those who supported and remembered them in its immediate aftermath. In doing so, it supports Winter's argument that First World War sites of memory drew on 'a complex traditional vocabulary of mourning, derived from classical, romantic or religious forms' which 'faced the past, not the future' (Winter, 1995, p. 223). Through the invocation of space and ritual, the marking of Remembrance Sunday reflects and reinforces symbolic practices both within the drama and for the community of listeners.

Where Remembrance Sunday in *The Archers* can thus be seen as a *lieu de memoire* of the First World War, part of a tradition of commemorative practices that reflect both the origins of ritual practice and contemporary cultural variations, the multiple commemorations across 2014 have generally been less successful, particularly those which focussed on people rather than places. Within what was an extremely busy year, even by Ambridge's standards, the repeated reference to the commemoration of the centenary of the outbreak of the war on 4th August often felt somewhat contrived. Neil

Carter and Lynda Snell's discussion of the Lives of the First World War website on 20th January, for instance, is clearly designed to relay information rather than drive any plot or subplot forward, despite the suggestion in the discussion of the potential creation of a local version on the village website. Indeed, the local website fails to develop as a subplot across the year, and the contrived nature of the story line is reinforced by the types of the stories which Lynda's research turns up. These stories, particularly those relating to women, reflect some of the dominant narratives of the BBC's World War One at Home project, which specifically identifies women and 'Trailblazers: People who changed the world around them' as key themes (World War One at Home, 2014).

What underlines the nature of the stories as invented traditions is the extent to which they reinforce common myths of wartime life rather than emerging as more organic stories of village history. Thus Diane Chambers' great-aunt not only worked in Felpersham Munitions Factory, but also played for their women's football team. The discovery of John Benjamin's Borsetshire Agricultural Worker's Alliance lapel badge initially appears as a more original and relevant reflection on the impact of war on everyday country folk. However, Robert Snell's comment that it was of a type which 'became very popular once the white feather campaign started — to show you weren't shirking' (O'Conner, 2014, January 23), places it squarely in mythic narratives of 'khaki fever', the image of young women attracted to volunteers in uniform, popularised by the press in the early years of the war and shaming recruitment practices, such as the well-known poster 'What Did You Do in the Great War, Daddy?' (Gullace, 2002). While such badges did have a function in identifying men undertaking reserved occupations, their relationship to white feather campaigns is less clear. Most historians who have examined the campaign in detail have drawn on sources which appear to show that the practice, where it occurred, was more common in urban centres than rural areas (Cohen, 2001; Gullace, 2002). Similarly, Jim Lloyd's claim that women's war work was 'what got them the vote' (O'Conner, 2014, 23 January) owes more to dominant cultural myths of the war than recent historical scholarship. While Arthur Marwick most influentially argued that the war marked a watershed for women in British society (Marwick, 1965), younger generations of feminist scholars have nuanced this assertion through studies of women whose wide range of wartime work formed important part of the story of the war that is only starting to be uncovered. Braybon wrote in 2003, a decade before the centenary, that 'an obsession with "the" impact of war on women makes them appear to be passive victims, rather than active agents — and, I would add, as mere symbols rather than individuals', with stories of their own (2003, pp. 104–105). Braybon's own work (1981), along with that of scholars such as Thom (1997), Woollacott (1994), Grayzel (2002), Watson (2004) and Andrews and Lomas (2014), has shown how women's agency as contributors to the war effort in the factories, fields and home extended well beyond playing football and winning the vote. These histories uncover women's wartime roles as individuals, not just symbols of gender liberation and the widening suffrage.

If we take Hynes' (1990) definition of myth as being 'not a falsification of reality, but an imaginative version of it, the story of the war that has evolved, and has come to be accepted as true', then the stories *The Archers* sought to tell about the history of the war through the Lives of the First World War storyline, namely that of people associated with the Borsetshire in the war, reflect dominant mythic narratives. While myths of the war do undoubtedly develop organically through communal repetition and reification, and in doing so become *lieux de memoire* themselves, the forcible insertion of these particular mythic stories into the narrative of both Ambridge's past and its present-day commemorations transforms them into invented tradition. They become, in Hobsbawm's (1983, p. 1) formulation, an 'attempt to establish continuity with a *suitable* historic past' (author's emphasis).

Yet one of the 2014 storylines does enable Ambridge to become a *lieu de memoire* of the war, namely the decision to use the 'Your Country's Call' recruitment poster as part of the Save campaign at the village fête (Figure 1). This is one of the three posters mentioned in the discussion, the best known being the oft-adapted 'Your Country Needs You' image of Kitchener pointing his finger at the viewer, which Kenton suggests superimposing David's face on. The 'Your Country's Call', however, resonates more deeply with the fête committee as a symbol of the historical memory of the war in Ambridge. It is a symbol of what we imagine Ambridge looks like as well as, in Kenton's words, 'what they [the soldiers of the Great War] were fighting for' (2 July 2014). Unlike the Kitchener image, the poster has direct resonances with the contemporary storyline. As Jill Archer notes, the Save campaign is motivated by the same impulses as many of the men who enlisted: 'at heart they were fighting to preserve a particular way of life' (2 July 2014). Extensive scholarship has demonstrated that among British troops 'Motivations for enlisting in 1914 were myriad, but many soldiers felt a duty to preserve their home, family and way of life. ... [W]hile initial motivations could fall by the wayside in the face of war experience, for many soldiers the protection of home and family remained a powerful motivating force to the end of the conflict, helping to justify sacrifice rather than encouraging interpretations of death as tragic waste' (McCartney, 2014, pp. 302–303).

Figure 1. Your Country's Call: Isn't This Worth Fighting for?, Liddle Collection, Special Collections, University of Leeds, LIDDLE/MUS/AW/115. *Source*: **Reproduced with the permission of Special Collections, Leeds University Library.**

The poster, therefore, serves to unify contemporary concerns with a historic reality, one which was reflected at the time in what Grieves (2008, p. 23) has identified as 'the propinquity of place' in minor war poetry, the 'intimate relationship [which] arose between a precisely depicted still-tranquil "home" and a reticent or private expression of patriotism'. *The Archers* picks up this theme again on 4 August, when Jill reads Wilfred Owen's poem *Futility* (1918) as part of the memorial service at St. Stephen's, again locating a national narrative in a particular local space, that of Anglican worship. Owen can in no way be described as a minor war poet, but the agricultural imagery of the poem which clearly influenced its choice can be found in many other verses of the period, such as Edward Thomas's *As the Team's Head Brass* (1916) or E. A. Mackintosh's *In Memoriam* (1916). The natural landscape of Britain was of huge importance throughout the war to the articulation of the values being fought for, and after the war to the ways in which the conflict was remembered. The use of *Futility* within a space already identified with commemorative practice through Remembrance Sunday services, like the poster, serves to locate *The Archers* in the historic arc of war commemorations far more effectively than confected associations of imaginary football teams and agricultural associations, however closely they ally with the dominant myths of the home front at war.

Place and its evocation through ritual practices is, therefore, of primary importance to the effectiveness of *The Archers* as a site of memory. It is in the imagined spaces of this imagined community — whether St. Stephen's and its churchyard or the entire village and its surrounding landscape — that form the symbolic links to the past that are crucial to genuine sites of memory. By contrast, the stories of people, so central to the conception of the Lives of the First World War project and the BBC's focus on family stories, function as invented traditions, impositions of national myths on a community, albeit one with national resonances, which has its own stories of memory and commemoration to tell.

As we approach the culmination of the centenary commemorations, Ambridge retains its ambiguous identity as both a *lieu de memoire* of the war and a vehicle for invented traditions of commemoration. On the one hand, the stories of historical people inserted at points throughout 2014 failed to take hold as subplots, while the people of the present have faced more pressing issue to concern themselves with in relation to current political, social and agricultural conflicts than battles long ago. Where the historical struggles intersect with the modern era, an organic form of commemorative practice has the potential to emerge, transforming space into a site of memory. At the same time, the sites themselves, here St. Stephen's and the village itself, continue to act as the *loci* of historic memories, shaped by the rituals of the seasons, including Remembrance Sunday. Here commemorative practice is reified by time and cultural acceptance as a *lieu de memoire*. Ambridge and its church, a community and space of great significance to the national psyche, have thus become symbolic elements of our memorial heritage, making them important sites of memory in the centenary period. As long as the village itself remains part of British cultural heritage and imagination, it will continue to form a significant *lieu de memoire* of one of the twentieth century's defining conflicts.

REFERENCES

Andrews, M., & Lomas, J. (Eds.) (2014). *The Home Front in Britain: Images, Myths and Forgotten Experiences since 1914*. Basingstoke: Palgrave Macmillan.

Braybon, G. (1981). *Women Workers in the First World War: the British experience*. London: Croom Helm.

Braybon, G. (2003). Winners or Losers: Women's Symbolic Role in the War Story. In G. Braybon (Ed.), *Evidence, History and the Great War: Historians and the Impact of 1914-18* (pp. 86–112). Oxford: Berghan Books.

Cabinet Office. (2012, 11 October). *Speech at Imperial War Museum on First World War centenary plans*. Retrieved from https://www.gov.uk/government/speeches/speech-at-imperial-war-museum-on-first-world-war-centenary-plans

Cohen, D. (2001). *The War Come Home: Disabled Veterans in Britain and Germany, 1914-1939*. Berkeley. CA: University of California Press.

Connelly, M. (2001). *The Great War, Memory and Ritual: Commemoration in the City and East London, 1916-1939. Royal Historical Society Studies in History*. London: Boydell & Brewer, Ltd.

First World War: then and now. (n.d.). Retrieved from https://www.hlf.org.uk/looking-funding/our-grant-programmes/first-world-war-then-and-now

Grayzel, S. (2002). *Women and the First World War*. Harlow: Longman.

Grieves, K. (2008). The propinquity of place: Home, landscape and the soldier poets of the First World War. In J. Meyer (Ed.), *British Popular Culture and the First World War* (pp. 21−46). Leiden: Brill.

Gullace, N. F. (2002). *"The Blood of Our Sons": Men, women, and the renegotiation of British citizenship during the great war*. Basingstoke: Palgrave Macmillan.

Hobsbawm, E. (1983). Introduction: Inventing tradition. In E. Hobsbawm & T. O. Ranger (Eds.), *The Invention of Tradition* (pp. 1−14). Cambridge: Cambridge University Press.

Hobsbawm, E., & Ranger, T. O. (Eds.) (1983). *The Invention of Tradition*. Cambridge: Cambridge University Press.

King, A. (1998). *Memorials of the Great War in Britain: The symbolism and politics of remembrance*. Oxford: Berg.

Marwick, A. (1965). *The Deluge: British society and the First World War*. London: Little, Brown.

McCartney, H. B. (2014). The First World War Soldier and his Contemporary Image in Britain. *International Affairs*, *90*(2), 299–315. doi:10.1111/1468-2346.12110

Nora, P. (1996). From lieux de mémoire to realms of memory. In P. Nora & L. D. Kritzman (Eds.), *Realms of Memory: Rethinking the French Past. Vol. 1: conflicts and divisions* (pp. xv–xxiv). New York, NY: Columbia University Press.

O'Conner, S. (Ed.). (2014). *The Archers. [Radio broadcast]*. Birmingham: BBC Radio 4.

Paxman, J. (2013). *Britain's Great War*. London: Viking.

Thom, D. (1997). *Nice Girls and Rude Girls: Women workers in World War I*. London: I.B. Tauris.

Todman, D. (2005). *The Great War: Myth and memory*. London: Hambledon and London.

Watson, J. S. K. (2004). *Fighting Different Wars: Experience, memory, and the First World War in Britain*. Cambridge: Cambridge University Press.

Winter, J. (1995). *Sites of Memory, Sites of Mourning: The Great War in European cultural history*. Cambridge: Cambridge University Press.

Woollacott, A. (1994). *On her Their Lives Depend: Munitions workers in the Great War*. Berkeley, CA: University of California Press.

World War One At Home. (2014). Retrieved from http://www.bbc.co.uk/programmes/articles/1ml2vCqtv2zQy3SxcGzvLS5/about

PEER REVIEW, BY PROF JIM LLOYD, GREENACRES, AMBRIDGE, BORSETSHIRE

In this, the third year of commemorations of the centenary of the First World War, it is hard not to approach any article on the subject without a certain element of war weariness. Certainly, Meyer's argument treads some well-worn paths in the debates over contemporary understandings of the war as a moment of cultural disjuncture or continuity. Yet her location of the commemorative practices of Ambridge over not merely the centenary but the past two decades within the wider national picture brings an entirely new perspective to local histories of the war and its legacy.

I do take some issue with the primacy she gives to place over people in her argument. The voices of the people of Ambridge are, surely, more central to the identity of the village in the modern era than established religious practice. However, her linking of the village's commemorative practice to poetic rural imaginings is acute and convincing. This chapter undoubtedly would have been improved by an extension of the argument to include the significance of Classical imagery, as argued to so superbly in Elizabeth Vandiver's *Stand in the Trench Achilles* (2010). Nonetheless, it offers an important and entirely original addition to local studies of the memory of the First World War in Britain.

SECTION FIVE

—

AMBRIDGE ONLINE

CHAPTER FIFTEEN

'AN EVERYDAY STORY OF COUNTRY FOLK' ONLINE? THE MARGINALISATION OF THE INTERNET AND SOCIAL MEDIA IN *THE ARCHERS*

Lizzie Coles-Kemp and Debi Ashenden

ABSTRACT

In this chapter, we explore to what extent storylines about the internet and social media are absent or marginal in The Archers. *In particular, we examine these storylines to better understand how the inhabitants of Ambridge interact online and how their online activities intersect with their real-world experiences. We compare what happens in* The Archers *with the moral panic that often characterises narratives of technology use and find a striking contrast that we argue supports a broader way of understanding and characterising practices of online safety and security. We analysed four social media-related* Archers' *storylines from the last 24 months. Our analysis shows that* The Archers *storylines enable us to look at human—computer interaction in relief so that instead of only looking at how people use technology we can also see the context in which it is used and the usually unseen support structures.* The Archers *narratives also provide a rich picture of how the fixed space of the physical world interacts with virtual space. In the broader context, the social media storylines provide us with an understanding of how connecting, care receiving and care giving take place in both fixed space and virtual space, and how these co-connected relationships of care receiving and care giving contribute to a form of security more expansive than technologically enabled data protection.*

Keywords: Digital technology; social media; security; safety; community

INTRODUCTION

In this chapter, we explore to what extent storylines about the internet and social media are absent or marginal in *The Archers*. In particular, we examine these storylines to better understand how the inhabitants of Ambridge interact online, and how their online activities intersect with their real-world experiences. We compare what happens in *The Archers* with the moral panic that often characterises narratives of technology use and find a striking contrast that we argue supports a broader way of understanding and characterising practices of online safety and security in everyday life.

We start by looking at *The Archers* from the real-world perspective of rural internet connectivity and the social media response to its storylines. After exploring two different ways of understanding everyday security we focus on three themes that illustrate the contribution that we believe *The Archers* makes to our understanding of online safety and security which we summarise as follows. Firstly, *The Archers* storylines enable us to look at human–computer interaction in relief so that instead of only looking at how people use technology we can also see the context in which it is used and the usually unseen support structures. Secondly, *The Archers* narratives provide a rich picture of how the fixed space of the physical world interacts with virtual space. Thirdly, social media storylines provide us with an understanding of how connecting care receiving and care giving take place in both fixed space and virtual space, and how these co-connected relationships of care receiving and care giving contribute to a form of security more expansive than technologically enabled data protection. We conclude by reflecting on how these themes contribute both to the drama's storylines and to our understanding of online safety and security.

THE ARCHERS, THE INTERNET AND SOCIAL MEDIA

The Archers has always had a social policy emphasis, initially focused on post-war agricultural community issues. It has covered major social topics over the decades, most recently with a storyline on domestic violence. One social topic that fits *The Archers* social policy focus is the issue of internet access and connection speeds in Ambridge. This is an everyday social as well as an everyday technology issue that affects many rural communities in the United Kingdom. While internet availability is similar in both rural and urban areas across the United Kingdom, rural internet connectivity has significantly lower connection speeds. A rural village will have an average of 9 Mbit/s (UK Government, 2016) whereas the average urban speed is 26 Mbit/s. Access in rural communities may well be to use a dongle to access broadband via a mobile signal where it takes '4 mins and 49 secs to download the Sheep Society web page' (Farrington et al., 2015, p. 46). The same study suggests that, 'over 1 million people in Britain are potentially excluded from, or at best find it challenging to participate in, what is generally regarded as "normal" online social, commercial, creative and civic life, because they live in deep rural areas' (Farrington et al., 2015, p. 53). The response to this problem has included real-world campaigns in rural communities to try and improve speeds and some groups are implementing DIY broadband (using their own tractors to dig trenches, negotiating their own deals between farmers to cross land for example (Kleinman, 2016).

The community activism dimension to the DIY broadband story cited in the previous paragraph shows how technology can move to the centre of a rural storyline whilst retaining a social impact focus. It offers an engrossing everyday story of empowerment where communities are finding their own solutions to the pressing problem of internet connection speeds. It is, however, only in community narratives such as *The Archers*, that interwoven implications of such a technological intervention and the concomitant community and individual responses can be explored. We argue that our analysis of the digital media storylines found in *The Archers* indicates that a storyline of DIY broadband would be likely to include implications of faster broadband for digital use within the Ambridge communities, the emergent security and safety issues and the community responses to these issues, including a variety of digitally mediated forms of community care. In such a story a more expansive interpretation of security and safety is likely to be presented including not only technological know-how but also the wider links between digital usage and financial, health and housing securities for example.

CONNECTING SPACES AND COMMUNITIES: MAKINGS AND SAYINGS OF AN *ARCHERS* UNIVERSE

Social media is threaded through the fabric of the listening culture that surrounds *The Archers* as we can see through the response to the Helen Archer and Rob Titchener storyline, as well as the live tweets during broadcasts, dedicated twitter accounts both official (@bbcthearchers) and unofficial (@dumteedum), podcasts, plot summaries and in-depth discussions about the storyline in popular online forums, such as Mumsnet. This strong social media response from listeners indicates that social media and its usages are of interest to sections of *The Archers* listening audience. However, when social media appears in an *Archers* storyline, it is typically not centre stage but a side issue and always characterised as a mundane everyday activity. It is used as a narrative device to weave together fixed spaces, where face-to-face interaction takes place and day-to-day physical activities such as farming are performed, with virtual spaces found in social media and on the wider internet.

Roy Tucker's online dating storyline not only demonstrates how social media offers a way to connect with people you would not normally meet but also helps to augment everyday relationships as Kirsty Miller and Jack 'Jazzer' McCreary provide support for Roy's online dating. Taken at face value, the use of social media in *The Archers* primarily offers a means of connecting worlds. For example, social media is used in *The Archers* storylines as a way to bring the outside world, people away from Ambridge, into the narrative. It offers the characters the ability to communicate beyond their village community. Social media is also used to connect the world of *The Archers* with the worlds of *The Archers* listening community, by offering listeners a means of conversation with scriptwriters. As the editor of *The Archers* explained, it was discussion on social media that pushed the Helen and Rob storyline on as it became clear that listeners were ahead of the plot from the very beginning (Greenslade, 2016) and that the scriptwriters needed to keep up. However, social media offers *The Archers* a lot more than a technique to connect worlds both to and within a storyline; social media presents both the listeners and the inhabitants of Ambridge with an opportunity to reflect on how the real world and the online world intersect and contribute to the narrative of collective care and support that is central to *The Archers* narrative. It is this notion of support that is of particular importance when understanding digital technology use in its broader context and where *The Archers* presents an opportunity to explore how an individual's safety and security can be augmented by social media and how social media can constructively support daily life. It is this positioning of social media that offers an alternative to the moral panic framing that often accompanies social media use.

TWO TALES OF EVERYDAY SECURITY

We found it interesting to see that the scriptwriters have not as yet taken the opportunity to characterise social media use in the programme in terms of moral panic (Cohen, 2002). The Ambridge flood storyline demonstrated this is a resilient community that establishes and maintains security of both the individual and the collective through relationships. Social media as a communicator, an augmenter of kin and friendship networks is a sympathetic narrative to the theme of community resilience. Given this characterisation, we argue that *The Archers* has a considerable contribution to make to a social policy that speaks to an everyday security that recognises the role social media can play in the development and management of trust relationships grounded in everyday routines.

This characterisation differs strikingly with the more typical characterisation of social media as a cause for social concern. Moral panic or widespread social concern about the use of the internet and social media often reflect the assumptions of a particular community and tend to revolve around safety and security issues and practices. Just as there have been no storylines about internet connectivity neither have there been storylines focusing on moral panics nor cautionary tales related to security and the use of the internet. Examples of such narratives could have included identity theft, cybercrime, cyberbullying or cyber fraud. Such narratives, however, typically characterise the individual as isolated, vulnerable and without recourse to support from kin and friendship networks and, of course, this is at odds with the typical narrative arc of *The Archers*.

A moral panic or cautionary tale is, however, not the only way in which social media usage and use of the internet in general can be framed. Security theorist McSweeney (1999) argues for a broader framing of security, one that includes the freedom to live free from fear as well as protection from harms. It is this framing of security as freedom from fear that is the most dominant in *The Archers*. The notion of living free from fear is linked to the fundamental idea of ontological security, the sense of each being secure in the other (McSweeney, 1999; Roe, 2008). In order to live life free from fear, we need to have a strong sense of ontological security that is, as *The Archers* storylines show, largely created through our relationships founded on basic trust and the use of everyday routines. A sense of biographical identity is also important to ontological security where an individual has a clear picture of who they are and where they have come from and this, again, is a key tenet of *The Archers* universe. An individual's ontological security keeps feelings of chaos at bay and social media can both contribute to an individual's ontological security as well as disrupt it. *The Archers* storylines have largely presented a picture of positive social media use that supports an individual's everyday life. The social media use is typically presented in storylines as being grounded in a strong sense of biographical identity and supported by a kin and friendship network that is able to absorb any unsettling effects of social media use. Our analysis of *The Archers* storylines has led us to conclude that this is achieved by a focus on the social networks that support human—computer interaction, narratives that link fixed and virtual spaces and storylines that, at times, link the giving and receiving of care with the use digital and social media.

HUMAN–COMPUTER INTERACTION IN RELIEF

Instead of the usual focus on how an end user engages with technology *The Archers* gives us the opportunity to look at this scenario in relief as the web of relationships between the technology users and the non-user or supporting user is fore-grounded. This foregrounding of the web of relationships into which technology usage is woven, is perhaps the strongest contribution that *The Archers* makes to the social media debate. Kirsty becomes Roy's 'dating advisor' helping him to 'get back out there'. While Kirsty's support is not obvious to anyone interacting with Roy online she is playing a key role in determining how he projects himself and refuses to allow him to give up when he is demoralised at his lack of success, saying, 'you can't give up now… it's early days yet'. In the virtual world, Roy works out how well his job stacks up against other online daters, and Kirsty challenges the veracity of the statistics that he cites, pointing out that he can't believe the self that is projected by others. She points out that he must move from connecting to messaging and then meeting to develop a full sense of the person he has shown an interest in. Roy is supported by an extensive community of supporting users in Jazzer, Tom Archer, Kirsty and Phoebe Aldridge who all advise and encourage. Kate Madikane reports to Alice Carter that as Roy has become more confident he is 'swiping away, left, right and centre'. Linda Snell, however, expresses a similar point of view to Jolene Archer suggesting that he is just as likely to find someone in community activities than he is by putting his 'faith in a dating app'.

This brings us to an examination of where competence lies in social media use in Ambridge and how competences circulate and are shared (Watson & Shove, 2008). Competences include skills, know-how and techniques (Shove, Pantzar, & Watson, 2012). Social policy regards digital inclusion or exclusion as a binary discussion of access to technology and individual skills to use technology. *The Archers*, however, demonstrates that this is only partly what makes an effective technology user. In *The Archers*, digital competences circulate between those who know how to use social media and have experiences to share and those who are new to it, but these competences are shared within the context of community knowledge about the real-world context in which such competences will be used. This support is an interesting aspect because it demonstrates how experiences in virtual space and fixed space interactions are mediated by communities and linked in a way that is often ignored when we think about online skills.

As we can see in the online dating storyline, Kirsty has the knowledge of how to use online dating apps. She tells Roy that he will need 'a decent profile first' and her comment on his photograph, 'No-one's ever going to swipe right on that' suggests that she has experience of using Tinder, as does her comment that looking online at night is a 'good time for the drunk and lonely'. Kirsty's character is implicitly tapping into the experience of the listeners in the assumption that they will know what she is making reference to. Kirsty demonstrates a 'cosmopolitan knowledge' (Shove et al., 2012, p. 50) and an experience of online dating apps that is then localised as she tempers it with her understanding of Roy's everyday life.

FIXED SPACE AND VIRTUAL SPACE

Just as the real-world of social media influences the fictional world of *The Archers* so the storyline of Roy's online dating experiences is a good example of how fixed space interacts with virtual space to create and shape Roy's identity in both spaces. Kirsty takes control of Roy's online presence and understands the importance of managing his profile and his photograph online. Roy struggles with the idea that his projected self will be at odds with his real self, he asks, 'isn't it cheating?' and says, 'it all seems so false'. Kirsty has a no-nonsense response to his concerns with 'yeah, well welcome to 21st century dating'. The fact that it takes three episodes to take and choose a photo demonstrates how much care Kirsty is putting into Roy's projected image (right the way through to hiring Holly the dog as an accessory) and underlines that the world of social media is not merely digital but also virtual, a space into which alternative identity narratives can be projected (Miller, 1995; Robinson, 2007). Such performances happen in a different space to the fixed space interactions in everyday life but is an accepted fiction by both the person who projects and the person who views.

In a very practical way space is important in the transmission of social media practices. As Shove et al. (2012) point out, social geography limits and constrains practices. While the internet is global we may choose to limit our online connections because of fixed-space constraints. We see Kirsty showing Roy how a location-based dating app limits who he will interact with. It is this very feature, of course, that causes him, much to his disgust, to be matched with Tracy Horrobin. In a similar way, Roy's online dating experience is mediated through past fixed-space experiences of others. Jazzer insists that Roy should take his advice with online dating and who to choose because he is 'in the know' and has been doing online dating for a while. Not only that, even though Roy is reticent to engage in online dating he is encouraged by a panoply of other characters in fixed space, including his daughter Phoebe. While Roy is embarrassed to admit that he has been looking at dating sites and says it got a 'bit addictive', virtual space gives him a freedom that was lacking in his fixed-space affair with Elizabeth Pargetter. Kirsty sets his reluctance and embarrassment at online dating in context with her lack of patience and her exclamation — 'it's not internet porn!'.

It is Roy's sense of safety and security in his fixed space that also helps him to absorb his mistake in texting the wrong message to the wrong woman. Roy's sense of safety and security in the fixed-space relationships that surround him give him the confidence to take his online dating mis-steps in his stride. In this particular narrative, *The Archers* storyline uses to great effect the multi-layering of the virtual and fixed spaces. The listener is encouraged to stay one step ahead here so that we hear Roy talking to Jolene in The Bull but in the background we can also hear a number of text alerts. Roy is distracted — being in two worlds at the same time. Eventually Jolene asks, 'what's with all these texts Roy?' It is at this point that we see a different side of Roy. His sense of safety and security in his relationship with Jolene and in the collective relationship he has with the Ambridge community (of which The Bull is symbolic) means Roy feels empowered to admit that he's engaged in online dating with 'not just one woman' and reveals that he has a spreadsheet to manage his dates. Jolene and Rex Fairbrother help him recover from his mistake by discussing it in fixed space and help him to put it into perspective with alternatives as Jolene suggests, 'instead of using these fancy apps...do it the old fashioned way'. It is possible to believe that if this had happened to him while he was online on his own late at night (the time for the 'drunk and lonely' as Kirsty pointed out) his reaction would have been very different from his response in the pub to his friends, 'Do you know what? I'm not even going to look'.

CONNECTING, CARE RECEIVING AND CARE GIVING

Framed in the context of *The Archers*, the story of social media safety is less one of data protection and more one of care giving and care receiving — of being and remaining to be secure within each other. As Fisher and Tronto (1990) have suggested, 'caring can be viewed as a species activity that includes everything we do to maintain, continue, and repair our "world" so that we can live in it as well as possible'. From this perspective, we can argue that sharing and supporting through social media is one means of giving and receiving care. Care receiving and care giving also connect to the concept of being secure within each other because it offers forms of protection found in relationships as Roy's online dating storyline shows us.

For many in Ambridge social media will be woven into the fabric of everyday lives and they do not worry about it unduly. The majority of the Ambridge communities are portrayed as feeling safe and secure within their relationships with each other in both fixed and virtual space and this engenders a resilience that enables them to weather mishaps and adverse events that occur in both fixed and virtual space.

One storyline that strongly illustrates these points is the Helen and Rob storyline. It is interesting that during her pregnancy, Helen made no reference to Mumsnet. Clearly, Helen fits the Mumsnet demographic and indeed Mumsnet was certainly very vocal about Helen and her experiences. One possible interpretation for this absence is that Helen was not on Mumsnet quite simply because she didn't need to be — she has strong family connections close by and close friends to help her. Another interpretation is that Helen is on Mumsnet but it isn't newsworthy in everyday conversation.

Although the virtual type of care giving is likely to be present in Helen's life, it is the fixed-space care giving that was to the fore in the Helen and Rob storyline. For example, when Helen goes on her 'pamper day' we can see the positive benefits of caring and connecting that help to make Helen more secure and safe in her surroundings. Kirsty is trying to care for Helen but is blocked by lack of presence and contact. Similarly, at the family dinner we see the family coming together and reminiscing about a missing care giver in John Archer (Helen's brother) while at the same time we see Tom caring for Helen when she runs out crying. He knows something is wrong, saying, 'I'm here if you ever need to talk'.

The narrative of security grounded in trusted relationships, community solidarity and everyday routines fractures however, when faced with isolation and silencing. Rob isolates and silences Helen cutting her off from family and friends and in this way increases her feelings of insecurity by disrupting her everyday routines and rupturing her biographical identity and therefore, her sense of self. He does this through a strategy of marginalisation that cuts her off from her *Archers* identity and gaslighting Helen to the point of disrupting her everyday routines making it easy for Rob to engulf Helen in a sense of chaos and dread. Nowhere is this more apparent than in Rob's campaign to persuade Helen to stop driving which disrupts her identity as an independent, capable woman and inhibits her ability to maintain relationships with friends and family. At the family dinner, we see the effect of Rob's gaslighting in more detail. Helen has already started to doubt her own state of mind so that when Pat Archer asks her if Ursula Titchener passed on Kirsty's 'phone message and whether she wrote it down, she says her 'brain's turned to mush'. Only a short time later when Rob arrives with the scan photograph she berates herself for forgetting it. Throughout this episode with the family dinner we hear others reporting on Helen's state of mind but hear little from Helen. Rob talks for her and puts words into her mouth but we rarely hear her voice directly. This silence can be interpreted as a sign that Helen's life is tipping into chaos and in so doing, her insecurities are engulfing her in dread.

Lily Pargetter's party is a good example of a more multi-layered story that brings together care giving and receiving in both fixed space and virtual space. As with all *Archers* characters, Lily is part of a network of care givers and care receivers, for example, she gives Phoebe advice and makes sure that she makes the right choices about who to talk to. In turn, Ian Craig worries about Lily's safety and whether he has 'made an awful mistake' in trying to be 'the cool uncle'. He worries about the party being advertised on Facebook, comparing Lily's party with his childhood escapades when social media did not exist. His fear is that it could end up as a 'free for all at Lower Loxley', echoing the moral panic scenario that we might normally expect to see. In reality though, he knows Lily has a 'good head on her shoulders' and, as we see, her network of friends looks after her making sure the party is not disclosed. She thinks it's 'so sweet' that Ian and Adam Macy come over to look after her that she invites them into the party so 'you can check we haven't destroyed the place'. While Ian is worried about the perils of Facebook and Instagram, Lily's kin and friendship circle have ensured that social media is managed so that Lily's party is not threatened by gatecrashers and remains a friends and family affair. This is a very different narrative to the one that is often in the press about the dangers and imminent threat of social media-fuelled aggressions.

Interestingly in *The Archers*, security breaks down when people move to the periphery of the community, just as it does for individuals when they isolate themselves online. However, *The Archers* storylines reveal the complexity of isolation and silencing and *The Archers* highlights that we need to understand the nature of particular forms of isolation and silencing in order to effectively respond to it. For example, whilst Freddie Pargetter is silent in the fixed spaces within *The Archers*, we can imagine that he is more socially connected online. The subplot to Lily's party is his re-entry into the fixed-space community. Furthermore, it is only when Freddie re-enters the fixed space that he can see his contribution to the people around him and only then do opportunities appear for Elizabeth to explore why Freddie distanced himself in the first place. The fixed space is therefore in this case the space of healing through the provision of care. The virtual space is a means of escapism (in Freddie's case escaping the identities of being the son of a dead man and living in a posh house), denial and identity performance.

CONCLUSION

Our exploration of the marginalisation of the internet and social media in *The Archers* compares interestingly with what happens in the real-world. There is no mention of the importance of connectivity or the problems of rural broadband but we do know that in the real-world rural communities are coming together to solve these problems themselves. The empowerment, however, that is indicative in these types of activities is evident in *The Archers*. This is a resilient rural community where they look after each other. The use of the internet and social media is largely a background activity and there is no cause for moral panic because the inhabitants of Ambridge have a strong sense of community and their place within it. In our example Members of the community support both Roy and Lily in different ways bringing to bear their skills where needed and sharing knowledge and expertise. We see how identities are created and shaped through the interaction of fixed space and virtual space and how even in an online environment there can be geographical and experiential constraints that shape behaviours. Through the Rob and Helen storyline we can see how social media could offer support where there is real-world isolation and silencing but the flip side of this is, as we see with Freddie, that the online world can also become a place to hide.

As our reflection has shown, it is a particular type of marginalisation of technology and social media that occurs in *The Archers*. The marginalisation is of the narrative of social media usage giving rise to a type of moral panic. *The Archers* brings into sharp relief, the shared and social conventions around technology use embedded within a tightly woven web of community relationships and offers an alternative story of technology as support to networks of solidarity and resilience that naturally occur within the Ambridge communities.

ACKNOWLEDGEMENTS

Lizzie Coles-Kemp's contribution was funded by EPSRC grant: ESSfES: Everyday Safety-Security for Everyday Services (grant number EP/N02561X/1).

REFERENCES

@bbcthearchers. Retrieved from https://twitter.com/ BBCTheArchers?ref_src=twsrc%5Egoogle%7Ctwcamp% 5Eserp%7Ctwgr%5Eauthor

@DumTeeDum. Retrieved from https://twitter.com/ DumTeeDum

Cohen, S. (2002). *Folk devils and moral panics: The creation of the mods and rockers*. New York, NY: Psychology Press.

Farrington, J., Philip, L., Cottrill, C., Abbott, P., Blank, G., & Dutton, W. H. (2015). *Two-speed Britain: Rural internet use*. Retrieved from http://dx.doi.org/10.2139/ssrn.2645771.

Fisher, B., & Tronto, J. (1990). Toward a feminist theory of caring. Circles of care. In E. K. Abel & M. Nelson (Eds.), *Work and identity in women's lives* (pp. 35–62). Albany, NY: SUNY Press.

Greenslade, R. (2016, September 12). The Archers and social media — A case of 21st century media synergy. *The Guardian*. Retrieved from http://www.theguardian.com

Kleinman, Z. (2016, December 26). The woman who built her own broadband. *BBC News*. Retrieved from http://www. bbc.co.uk/news/technology-37974267

McSweeney, B. (1999). *Security, identity and interests: A sociology of international relations* (Vol. 69). Cambridge, MA: Cambridge University Press.

Miller, H. (1995, June). The presentation of self in electronic life: Goffman on the Internet. In *Embodied knowledge and virtual space conference* (Vol. 9).

Mumsnet. Retrieved from https://www.mumsnet.com

Robinson, L. (2007). The cyberself: The selfing project goes online, symbolic interaction in the digital age. *New Media & Society*, *9*(1), 93–110.

Roe, P. (2008). The 'value' of positive security. *Review of International Studies*, *34*(04), 777–794. doi:10.1017/ S0260210508008279

Shove, E., Pantzar, M., & Watson, M. (2012). *The dynamics of social practice: Everyday life and how it changes*. Los Angeles, CA: Sage publications.

UK Government. (2016). Dept of the Environment, Food & Rural Affairs. *Rural Broadband Statistics*. Retrieved from https://www.gov.uk/government/collections/rural-living-statis-tical-indicators

Watson, M., & Shove, E. (2008). Product, competence, project and practice: DIY and the dynamics of craft consumption. *Journal of Consumer Culture*, *8*(1), 69–89. doi:10.1177/ 1469540507085726

PEER REVIEW, JOSH ARCHER, BROOKFIELD, AMBRIDGE, BORSETSHIRE

Well, I hadn't really thought about social media this way before. For me it's always been a tool, something I use to get the job done. It's really useful being able to work from anywhere — I mean I've even worked from the bus shelter before now. Of course, I know all about privacy settings and passwords — don't always use them mind you — but yeah, people of my age know what we are meant to do. I hadn't thought about any of the relationship stuff though; I'm just focused on getting my business off the ground. Sometimes the pressure of starting a new business can mean that we're a bit distracted with what we put online. We've already lost some commission because of Rex's mistake and I can see how one of us could put the wrong price on some machinery we're advertising online. I mean we're under pressure all the time. If that did happen, Debi and Lizzie are right, it would be down to how well we got on with the client as to whether it caused a problem, as well as how quickly we picked it up and reacted. Not sure about this idea of caring though — I'll have to give it some more thought. Being a successful businessman is more my thing than being a caring businessman...

CHAPTER SIXTEEN

THE IMPORTANCE OF SOCIAL MEDIA IN MODERN BORSETSHIRE LIFE: DOMESTIC AND COMMERCIAL

Olivia Vandyk

ABSTRACT

If you are running a rural business there are associated difficulties in reaching new customers, how can growth be sustained without spending huge amounts of time or money on marketing? Borsetshire needs more social media, and this chapter will illustrate how social media can help rural business. Looking at known online activity in Ambridge, it will highlight the perceived and potential social media practices of a variety of residents to give an example of what can be achieved, touching on the various networks and technology that can enhance the personal and professional lives of all,

*whether poultry smallholder or publican. The conclu-
sion that social media can help foster feelings of community suggests that the Borsetshire populace should take
immediate measures to advance their online activities.*

Keywords: Social media; community; small business;
marketing; online; smartphone

People who live in rural locations will vouch for the vital
importance of the internet not only for feelings of connectivity but also as a way of information gathering. This chapter
will focus on the role that social media plays in Ambridge —
and how it could positively affect various inhabitants, were
they to utilise it more fully. In Ambridge, many (though not
all) of the mobile phones that we hear ringing sound like previous generation cell phones with limited connectivity. We
have heard the typical early-adopter Miranda Elliot complain
bitterly about the lack of signal to use an app to find a news-
agent, but mostly we hear phones being used for calls. This is
atypical, given that two thirds of people in the United
Kingdom now own a smartphone, using it on average for
nearly two hours every day to browse the internet, access
social media and bank and shop online. This leads to the
question of what we know about online activity both in the
United Kingdom and in Borsetshire.

In total, 80% of all UK adults are using the internet daily
and, within that use, the two most common categories of
activity are finding information about goods and services and
checking social media. There is the occasional nod to this in
The Archers, such as Jennifer Aldridge showing husband

Brian details of various caterers for a big party on a phone or tablet in The Bull, but on the whole such usage is absent. Whilst we never hear about Lynda Snell having to wait in for the Ocado delivery, we know that in the United Kingdom 1 in 10 (11%) do all of their grocery shopping online, with a further 12% doing most of their grocery shopping online. Data from the Office for National Statistics shows us that the people are using social media for a wide variety of reasons and that 37% of them are checking social media 'several times' a day. The primary social networks to which I refer in this chapter are Facebook, Instagram and Twitter. Others (YouTube, Snapchat, Pinterest and LinkedIn) absolutely have their place in a social media marketing strategy but these former three are widely considered to be the main channels for Business to Consumer (B2C) communications which is the basis of all of the case studies looked into here.

Turning to online activity in Ambridge rather than United Kingdom-wide, we know that there is an official village website. Jennifer is seemingly in charge of it. This was also apparently the platform for the Save Ambridge Vale Environment (SAVE) campaign, but we hear less of that since the demise of Route B. Early in 2017, we also heard Helen Archer mention having seen a photo of the infamous New Year's kiss between Roy Tucker and Tracy Horrobin on Facebook. However, this brief mention implies a passive consumption of the newsfeed of others rather than any active sharing herself. Had Helen been a member of Mumsnet, the peer-to-peer discussion site for parents, she would have been able to ask anonymously of the relationship talkboards questions she dare not ask those close to her. For example, if she was being unreasonable to expect to be allowed to drive whilst pregnant? Or if it was unreasonable for her husband to tell her to send her maternity tops back for being too revealing or indeed any of the other behaviours that had the nation swearing at the radio. Her peers on Mumsnet would not have been backward in coming forward to ensure that she was made aware that Rob's behaviour was not normal. All of the red flags would have raised and alarm bells been set ringing long before anyone was demanding homemade custard or refusing tuna bake. The Mumsnetters would have been shouting in caps lock for her to LTB (leave the bastard).

In the United Kingdom, the average turnover per person employed by businesses based in what is defined as a rural village location is less than 50% of the national average, 'There are more registered businesses per head of population in predominantly rural areas … reflecting there being more small businesses in rural areas' (Statistic Digest of Rural England, p. 39). Therefore, ventures situated in villages like Ambridge need to use every opportunity to market themselves and increase sales. In the real world, rural businesses are making the most of opportunities presented by social media and the ability to tell their own stories. However, aside from a nod to Tom Archer's football playing pigs in 2013 and Josh's latest farm machinery-flipping racket, this is not represented in *The Archers*. In this era of digital access, other than the well-documented delay in the roll out of rural broadband, there's no excuse for this Borsetshire social media blackout. While there are a number of characters and enterprises in business in Ambridge, the four examples have excellent potential for social media marketing.

CASE STUDY: POULTRY SMALL HOLDERS

When brothers Rex and Toby Fairbrother spied a gap in the lucrative Christmas market, the Grundys found themselves with competition for the first time in years. In the face of this in November 2015, Eddie thinks perhaps last year's leaflets are looking a bit tired, and he should come into the twenty-first century on 'twitter gram'. Eddie on this occasion is right, of course and even if you don't know an iPhone from a ferret, it's easy to get online. Eddie asks Emma 'because she's good at Facebook' to build a website for the turkeys. This in addition to the many other gig-based ad hoc jobs she has, making her a wonderful personification of the thriving 'mum economy' which was worth over £7.2 billion to the UK economy supporting 204,000 jobs in 2014. Good old Emma builds a website, and Clarrie persuades her to take some lovely photos of Keira feeding the turkeys. This is wise advice as showcasing behind the scenes footage gives personality to a brand and allows people to see that it's a real-life family business — which counts for a lot. Unfortunately within the story, there certainly wasn't any mention of any other online activity by the Grundys in 2016, despite the continuing competition from Rex and Toby.

Much like waiting for the benefits of herbal leys and mob grazing to take effect, you have to invest time and effort to create a fertile online presence. It is vital to keep a website active and up to date both in terms of being found online as well as building a brand. This is where the all-important content marketing, that is, blogging and video diary vlogging comes in. This ensures not only that potential customers realise that you're still in business but also that the Google crawl-bots place you higher in their search index. Being on page one of Google for your relevant keyword brings huge dividends.

As Google themselves say, 'Search results, like warm cookies right out of the oven or cool refreshing fruit on a hot summer's day, are best when they're fresh.' Ensuring that you have regular new content on your website cannot be underestimated. That's not all — it is imperative to ensure that any online page has a call to action, an invitation to do more. In this case, phone us to reserve your turkey, sign up to our email list, use this code and receive 10% off. To ensure that you are making the sale it needs to be as seamless as possible for customers to contact you (in your preferred way) and do business, so keeping contact information somewhere prominent with relevant click-links is the key here. If the Grundy's were to push their online activities they would be able to sell to a much wider demographic. Similar pop-up seasonal boutiques found that some frequent posting on their business page as well as some quick-to-take photos of the kids with their product and some targeted online ads led to record sales.

As it happens, we have not heard much about the goose venture having a website. But a Facebook business page works well to brand-build: and here, engagement, that is, having conversations with your online followers is critical to keep your customers, potential and existing, coming back. Gamification, turning the conversation into a game, is a proven technique. There are three key methods — piquing curiosity, issuing a challenge or allowing a moment of fantasy — getting people to associate those aspirational thoughts with you and your brand, is a great way of engaging your customers. All of these would be excellent methods for the Fairbrothers or indeed the Grundy's to increase brand awareness and ultimately drive sales when the final purchase moment comes.

CASE STUDY: SPIRITUAL HOME

Kate Madikane's spiritual retreat at Home Farm is absolutely made for Instagram. There is currently a lot of noise about one of the newest social platforms, Snapchat, but Instagram, the beautiful photo-sharing site, remains the place to be for young and old alike. Additionally, its search facility makes customer discovery easy and it promises a huge variety of sharing opportunities. In terms of business use, Instagram users are more than happy to have business intrusion on their personal feed. Yoga and a vegan lifestyle are hugely popular hashtags on the network. Kate would easily be able to capitalise on these. Even photos taken in haste can look good once the right filter is added and the relevant hashtags can be saved, cut and pasted into the comments box in order to drive traffic her way.

In terms of her complementary therapies, using text overlay apps for inspirational quotes on a phone or even just adding comments to photos would allow her to connect with her followers. It is very quick and easy to use Instagram to run discounted promotions to fill any last minute cancelled appointments. This has many benefits — it avoids the costs of having therapists idle and potentially extends the customer base by tempting newcomers at lower prices. All of these tactics would add up to a strategy for growth.

CASE STUDY: AMBRIDGE TEA-ROOM

This is another local enterprise which would hugely benefit from online activity. In February 2017, we heard references to posters and fliers produced by Fallon Rogers for her UnValentine's event. It was a surprise to hear that Fallon's marketing strategy seems to be based on working offline in print, when the tea-room would positively shine on social media.

Like Kate's yurts, photos of the homemade cakes and upcycled furniture would glow with the shabby chic filters on Instagram, and it would be advisable to alternate between the two attractions — for example, a gorgeous Farrow & Ball painted wheel back chair followed by a styled muffin on vintage china. The beautiful pictures would be helpful if she wanted to ensure an easy sale on Facebook's Local Marketplace. This fairly recent feature allows users to browse local bargains from right within the platform by category and to find items close to them geographically. This removes the need for costly eBay fees. For Fallon, unless she has something particularly specialist, posting on eBay may prove difficult as furniture is costly to ship. With Facebook's built in local filter, she can easily arrange pickup of sold items during cafe opening hours, reducing hassle and in fact, she might even pull in some new cafe customers from those arriving to collect items and finding there's a tea-room they didn't know about.

Fallon would be well advised to collate catering themes and recipes on Pinterest boards showing her awareness of the latest trends like macaroons and artisan marshmallow, as well as sharing her recipes as Pinterest has a wonderful ability to point traffic in the right directions. Fallon could also benefit from offering a small free cake sample or similar in return for a Facebook check-in to improve her visibility among other peers. Twitter would also be an excellent network for Fallon. She could take a photo of an NCT group meeting in her cafe and tweet about it, gently reminding all and sundry that it's a baby friendly meeting place (as well we know from the visits between baby Jack, Tony Archer and Rob Titchener) for her local NCT groups.

To boost her catering bookings locally, Fallon should join #BorsetshireHour. Networking meetings held on Twitter for local businesses to chat, collaborate and create opportunities. There's a huge variety of these and taking part in them is akin to a Chamber of Commerce breakfast only without the dubious filter coffee or indeed the need to leave your premises.

CASE STUDY: THE BULL

Kenton and Jolene Archer are excellent marketers — their 2016 mid-December Twixtmas campaign was inspired. December is always busy for those in hospitality but the period between Christmas and New Year itself can often be hit and miss. The Great Escape, where locals were offered somewhere to be, far from visiting relatives and piles of left-overs, both of which may be past their best-before date, shows a brilliant understanding of their customers' needs and psyches and also a keen eye on the books.

However, if Kenton were to invest some time listing the pub's events, such as quiz nights and live music on Facebook, ensuring that they were paired with attractive imagery, he would doubtless find an increased reach in his customer base. Listing an event on Facebook allows individuals to show themselves as interested in attending. This shows up on the newsfeed of others for them to participate too, and this in turn leads their friends to learn about the event as well. They can then make an informed decision about whether they want to be part of it. If Facebook showed Tracy Horrobin as interested in going to see the Midnight Walkers playing live at The Bull, while Roy Tucker may want to give the pub a swerve that evening, whereas Susan and Neil Carter would probably be up for a night out though.

For those in the catering arena, Facebook does also provide a facility for customers to book tables online. Kenton and Jolene could easily promote and list their daily specials. A successful digital strategy for a pub like The Bull really would not need to take much time, energy or cash; a small amount of planning, a little bit of thought and lots of consistency. Simple posts such as a photo of their roaring fire to warm birdwatchers on a cold day or a cool drink in the shade of the pub garden on a hot afternoon would remind patrons to return to the warm welcome at their local, whatever the weather.

These four case studies are just the tip of the iceberg in terms of how social media can help to grow the different enterprises in the village. Bridge Farm is probably a whole separate chapter. We have recently heard that Tom had updated the site's blog with a damning allusion to Brookfield over the IBR, and it is good that they have a decent presence. But there must still be a huge amount of search engine optimisation (SEO) needed to deal with the negative results that Google would have recorded in relation to both events at Blossom Hill Cottage and the disastrous *E. coli* breakout of 2011.

The health club at Grey Gables might want to promote the aqua fit classes, and the relaunched veterinary practice certainly needs a horse of the month spot. There is ample opportunity for some astute cross-promotional collaboration, such as the Hunt Ball and other black tie events at Lower Loxley. There is not a business in Ambridge that would not hugely benefit from some well-defined Facebook advertising campaigns. Certainly the ability to effectively target your audience so precisely in terms of interests, demographics and location all for the price of a pint of Shires is putting local newspapers out of business.

Outside of the commercial arena, we know that social media is of vital importance for personal feelings of connectivity. A Kraut and Burke (2015) study found that interacting directly with friends on Facebook increased feelings of wellbeing and sociability. But despite Jennifer's best efforts with the village website, there really does not appear to be any of the useful online community building that hugely helps to oil the wheels of not only business but also life in general. For example, there is no mention of any online Facebook community such as 'Spotted in Ambridge'. These hyperlocal groups have evolved across the country. A 2013 report on these by the BBC, 'No-one knows exactly who is behind them, but in towns, villages and cities right across the UK, "Spotted In" Facebook pages are springing up — offering a kind of local information, dating site, and lost and found service all rolled into one.' This kind of group has many potential uses. The disappearance of Lynda Snell's faithful hound, Scruff, could have speedily spread around the county towards Penny Hassett and Loxley Barrett if it had been online: missing pet posts are eagerly and widely shared by fellow animal lovers. Internet sleuths may well have got to the bottom of the blocked culvert incident a lot quicker than the investigation did — use of admins and anonymous posts on groups like this has helped in many a similar situation.

For leisure pursuits, cricket captain PC Harrison Burns could more easily have recruited potential players for the 2017 season if there was an Ambridge Cricket Facebook page. These sorts of pages for clubs abound on the network and basic information is vital for member recruitment and to see what kind of commitment is needed. People are intrinsically nosy and potential players would be able to find out what time nets practice is to establish whether it clashes with bell ringing or circuit training; and in the unlikely event they don't know everyone involved, who else is in the team and if they have mutual friends. Once Harrison has established a team, he could then migrate to WhatsApp for speedy information exchange. The messaging network has over a billion users worldwide, group chats are a hugely popular part of their offering, allowing people to plan events and get-togethers in an easy to use format. This would save him lots of time ringing round to check attendance at practice and encourage camaraderie during the week between matches and training sessions.

Not all of this is immediately transferable to the audible Ambridge on which we eavesdrop. Obviously listening to somebody typing a Facebook status does not work on the radio as well as Susan disseminating gossip in the shop. Furthermore, most of us are aware that there is actually a good news filter applied to the casual glimpses into the lives of others that Facebook affords.

But there is evidence that social media does make people feel more connected and bolsters feelings of community. This is especially true of those who might otherwise feel socially isolated, such as those with young families or those who both live work in a remote area. Certainly, despite Clarrie's best intentions, Nic Grundy must be fairly lonely.

It is interesting to note that since this paper was presented in February 2017, there has been a noticeable increase in the mention of social media on the air. We can cite for example Kirsty Miller's dawn chorus walk was promoted on Facebook; Tom used the Bridge Farm blog to needle David, and Lily Pargetter invited her mother's Facebook friends to boost the numbers at her 50th birthday party. But we can see there still remains a huge gap in the social media activity in Borsetshire. These case studies demonstrate the positive effects that the application of some basic techniques would have on the businesses and the people involved. While we know that Justin Elliott had his own personal need for an Ambridge-based social secretary, a social media manager would be much more likely to reap business rewards. Ultimately, *The Archers* is a story about community; we can see that there are benefits for all the residents to be informed and connected. As social media is increasingly a crucial component of modern life, the people of Ambridge should eagerly embrace the sites that we take for granted.

REFERENCES

BBC trending. (2013). Retrieved from http://www.bbc.co.uk/news/magazine-24801698

Burn-Callander, Rebecca, *Daily Telegraph*, Mumpreneurs generate £7bn for the UK economy Retrieved from http://www.telegraph.co.uk/finance/yourbusiness/11782294/Mumpreneurs-generate-7bn-for-the-UK-economy.html

Google official blog. (2011). Retrieved from https://google-blog.blogspot.co.uk/2011/11/giving-you-fresher-more-recent-search.html

Kraut, R., & Burke, M. (2015 December). Internet use and psychological well-being: Effects of activity and audience. *Communications of the ACM, 58*(12), 94–100.

Office for National Statistics. (2016). Retrieved from https://www.ons.gov.uk/peoplepopulationandcommunity/householdcharacteristics/homeinternetandsocialmediausage/bulletins/internetaccesshouseholdsandindividuals/2016#mobile-or-smartphones-are-the-most-popular-devices-used-by-adults-to-access-the-internet

Online Grocery Retailing UK 2016 report. (2016). Retrieved from http://www.mintel.com/press-centre/retail-press-centre/29-of-uk-online-grocery-shoppers-are-shopping-for-groceries-more-online-now-than-a-year-ago)

Statistical Digest of Rural England. (January 2015 Edition). Retrieved from https://www.gov.uk/government/uploads/system/uploads/attachment_data/file/539291/Statistical_Digest_of_Rural_England_January_2015.pdf

Statistical Digest of Rural England. (March 2016 Edition). Retrieved from https://www.gov.uk/government/uploads/

system/uploads/attachment_data/file/539302/Statistical_
Digest_of_Rural_England_2016_March_edition_4apr16.pdf

WhatsApp official blog. (2016). Retrieved from https://blog.
whatsapp.com/616/One-billion

PEER REVIEW, BY KATE MADIKANE, FOUNDER AND MAVEN, SPIRITUAL HOMES, AMBRIDGE

Like Emma, I find that combining motherhood and working really can be physically and emotionally exhausting and I've perhaps overlooked this side of things. There were lots of helpful hints and tips here so I really enjoyed this chapter. Obviously my business plan was really focused on sourcing the yurts and ensuring that the interiors were of the highest quality and it had the bonus effect of imposing a wonderfully minimalist look on some of the rooms in Home Farm.

My interpersonal intentions have so far been on spiritual connections but I can see that I really need to connect online as well. I have been journalling for years, and I have Moleskines just filled with inspirational thoughts that I can use as the basis for quotes and mantras for posts. Ooh, and I could share my smoothie recipes every day as well — it's amazing what you can do with kale, even at breakfast time. What we do here is help people discover their inner beauty. We can reflect that in the outer beauty of the countryside setting of the yurts intermingling with the ancient trees of the Millennium Wood in the background. I'm sure that some of the Instagram filters will capture the radiance of the vibe that flows through all that we do here. Namaste.

CHAPTER SEVENTEEN

BEING @BORSETPOLICE: AUTOETHNOGRAPHIC REFLECTIONS ON *ARCHERS* FAN FICTION ON TWITTER

Jerome Turner

ABSTRACT

As the internet has evolved through the emergence of social media, so too have the communicative practices of The Archers *listeners. Many of them now use Twitter to comment, discuss the show or participate in the omnibus episode 'tweetalong'. Primarily, this chapter recognises the hundred-plus Twitter accounts which have been created by listeners to authentically roleplay characters, organisations, animals and even objects from the show. I frame these practices and ground the chapter in academic discourses of 'fan fiction'. Reflecting on my own activity as @borsetpolice, I look at the role and place of*

*this fan fiction from the individual practitioner's per-
spective but also the wider listener base. In this chapter,
I develop an argument that these practices contribute
towards the community of listeners online, as well as the
show itself. I explore the types of activities and accounts
involved, where they often focus around major storylines, and then reflect in detail on the individual's motivations and practice. I situate this in terms of an
opportunity to become involved in an online community
that aspires towards everyday rural ideals, and how this
can be understood as a significant affective experience
for listeners. This need for escapism into 'banal' worlds,
the desire to participate, and the sense that fan fiction is
a game that we take part in are also drawn out as
significant.*

Keywords: Fan fiction; transmedia; Twitter;
social media; audiences

On 12 September 2010, I was driving home with my family,
listening to *The Archers*. Harry Mason was starting a 'We
Love The Bull' campaign to save the pub from closure,
because landlady Jolene showed interest in selling it for rede-
velopment. The part of this narrative that really caught my
attention was Harry talking about social media — he specifically mentioned Twitter. At home I turned on my laptop,
looked for a 'welovethebull' Twitter account and found none.
Seconds later, I had registered it myself. From my experience
of listening to the show, but also following Twitter activity
on #thearchers hashtag, I knew that listeners often tweeted in

the role of *Archers* characters, and that in signing up for the @welovethebull account, I would now be contributing in my own way.

FANS AND FAN FICTION

When I first registered the @welovethebull account, it was with some understanding that others were already engaged in similar practices, those which are framed as fan fiction. However, it is important to set this in some relevant context, of fans themselves. What is a 'fan'? Sandvoss (2005) recognised the problems of such subjective classifications, when an outsider's view of casual listeners to a show such as *The Archers* might be understood as more active fan practices by those within the circle. Where Sandvoss noted that fans identified their fandom with relation to their 'patterns of consumption' (*ibid.*, p. 7), we might therefore typify an *Archers* fan partly as one using online services to ensure they never miss an episode, in contrast to those listeners who hear parts of episodes in passing during the live radio transmissions, often starting by osmosis in early childhood (Thomas, 2007).

However, it is also recognised (Jenkins, 2012; Sandvoss, 2005) that fan practices extend beyond the consumption of the texts, to others 'ranging from group interaction in the form of conventions, online discussion groups, or regular fan meetings, to the writing or creating of artwork' (Sandvoss, 2005, p. 23). We can recognise some of these activities with relation to *The Archers* listeners, such as the use of message boards or a more recent engagement through social media (Thomas, 2007, 2016). It is specifically fan fiction that I focus on here.

Fan fiction can be defined as 'creative written work' based on an existing published or produced text (such as a radio soap opera), which is then published or produced in itself (Parrish, 2010, p. 176). It is also significant in 'calling attention to itself as fan fiction' (*ibid*, p. 176). However, whilst this situates the practices within a fan community, the fan fiction can sometimes be presented as alternative to, rather than contributing to, the original source texts. This can be borne from frustrations, for example, where the third season of the CBS drama *Beauty and the Beast* was deemed to be unsatisfying to many fans, and so they created their own accounts of the relationship between the characters (Jenkins, 2012). In other situations, fan fiction is not so specifically critical but seeks to fill the 'narrative gaps' (*ibid*, p.74), such as those found in *New Moon*, the second book in the Twilight series, where eight essentially blank pages proved open invitation for fan writers on the Twilighted.net website (Parrish, 2010).

However, it is in two final studies of fan fiction that we come closer to practices as we see them on Twitter relating to *The Archers*. Firstly, Bore and Hickman's (2013) study of *West Wing* (TWW) fan fiction on Twitter demonstrates the extent to which these practices made them part of a community, especially given these practices were in place following the end of the show and thus provided fans a way of staying together online. Worth noting also is the extent to which 'by entering into dialogue with other TWW Twitter accounts, the fans become part of a fan community that has developed certain norms and values' (*ibid*., p. 232). The implication here then is that practice is learned and developed through engagement with and observation of the particular field, as per Bourdieu (Wacquant, 1989) and Giddens (1984). This is the case rather than that notion Parrish described (2010, p. 176), of contributing to an existing cannon of 'that thing' called fan fiction, or one of its recognised sub-genres (Duffett, 2013, p. 170). The fact that this is undertaken using a social tool such as Twitter develops this sense of the field rather than the fan-created text, where Bore and Hickman recognise the 'resulting output is not a coherent, linear narrative, but a sprawling, polysequential text made up of ephemeral segments' (2013, p. 234). The second example is that of Wood and Baughman's (2012) study of the US television show *Glee*, which feels closer already to *The Archers* case in the respect that these were fan practices undertaken whilst the show was still being broadcast. This allowed (similarly to *The Archers*) for those fan character accounts to interact not just in those undocumented times in between the show but during its transmission as well. Finally, it is worth noting Wood and Baughman's concerns that whilst fans contribute to the 'transmedia storytelling' (Jenkins, 2006, p. 20) of *Glee*, this might be seen as bearing beneficial relation to the original text, and so concerns of fan digital labour are introduced.

APPROACHING AN UNDERSTANDING OF TWITTER FAN FICTION

I am a fan of *The Archers*. Like other avid listeners, I grew up with the show as background noise (Thomas, 2007, 2016), sometimes resenting what I considered to be a boring show. Then in later life an element of nostalgia drew me to listen more carefully, until I could identify the characters and follow plotlines and relationships. My fan status was finally declared in realising that *The Archers* was one of a few BBC radio shows that mysteriously wasn't being podcast, and so I started an online petition. This was never recognised by the BBC themselves as far as I know but I would like to think that it contributed somehow to the podcasting, which started a few months later in 2007. Since then, I have rarely missed an episode. This context is worth noting when we consider one of the key concerns in studying fan cultures, that 'scholars failing to display an adequate level of knowledge about the fan cultures and texts they explore raise suspicion amongst their peers and fans alike' (Sandvoss, 2005, p. 5).

CONTEXTUALISING THE FIELD OF ARCHERS TWITTER FAN FICTION

In order to understand the place of Twitter in discussing *The Archers* we should take into account micro-, meso- and macro-levels of interaction. Media ethnographers such as Moores extoll contextualised accounts of media use, as well as the fine detail of interactions and communication (1993). At micro-level, the listener is sometimes tweeting about #thearchers during a broadcast, and so we can expect peaks of activity at 2 pm or 7 pm in the week and 10 am on Sundays — the Sunday omnibus show is unofficially recognised as the 'tweetalong' time. Alternatively, people may tweet whilst listening to the podcast or on iPlayer, or in fact at any time of the day when *The Archers* comes to mind and may be reflected on. Finally, they may be simply reading the hashtag, to draw themselves into the community of listeners found there. This brings us to the meso-level, the general *Archers* Twitter community. It can sometimes be hard to understand Twitter in terms of the theory of 'a field' (Bourdieu, 2010) given the sprawling and interwoven nature of interactions. However, when listeners use the #thearchers hashtag the understanding is that they are talking to those who will understand and appreciate the discussion. The hashtag can also be used as shorthand, so that referring to Toby Fairbrother by just his first name is enough without having to give context of his character, or his long surname — thankfully, given the 140-character limit. Finally, at the wider macro-level, we should of course recognise those who listen but don't discuss the show with other listeners, or who use other mediums to do so, either online or offline. The extent to which the Twitter conversations (meso) respond to or influence and inform wider discourses of the show (macro) remain to be seen, although it is worth noting the recent Radio 4 drama *Hashtag Love* that squarely referenced *Archers* tweeters, even quoting them (BBC, 2017).

RECOGNISING ARCHERS TWITTER FAN FICTION

Contextualisation of the listening and online experience means we can then situate #thearchers fan fiction within that meso-level of the hashtag 'field'. From my own experience as a listener, I was already using Twitter to discuss the show before I started to notice these character accounts. @eddie_grundy was one of these, having started in November 2009, and currently sporting an impressive 10,800 followers (at time of writing). As I became increasingly aware of them, I was impressed by their creativity but also the audience's definition and understanding of which characters were acceptable to turn into fan fiction accounts. On one hand, listener/tweeters including myself have now settled into an expectation that any new character will eventually result in Twitter account, where such norms established entirely through the productive and reproductive practices of the active audience (as opposed to the BBC) (Giddens, 1984). When Peggy Wolley took on her new cat Hilda Ogden, two separate accounts cropped up in the space of a few days. However, I am often surprised by the range and breadth of these, the extent to which not characters, animals and even objects can be given voice. I've identified 103 fan fiction accounts, partly with the aid of a pre-existing 'Twitter list'.

My own list of these 103 accounts is available online. A typology of these accounts can be set out as follows:

- Speaking characters — those based on prominent and current characters, such as @RobTitchener, @JazzerArchers, @Clarrie_Grundy.

- Prominent but silent characters — those mentioned in the show frequently but who are never voiced such as @the_fat_paul, @Sabrina_Thwaite.

- Dead characters — both humans and animals: @GhostOfNigelP, @CaptainsGhost, @SidPerksGhost.

- Places, organisations and businesses — where they feature prominently in storylines: @Soosanssmallads ('Small ads direct from the Ambridge village shop'), @AmbridgeChurch, @AmbridgeTeaRoom.

- Hyperdiegetic characters or organisations — we will explore hyperdiegesis shortly, but this fills in the blanks in what we can assume to be existing in the wider Ambridge 'universe', such as @borsetpolice, @AmbridgeLabour, @felpershamaccs (accountancy firm).

- Animals — both agricultural and pets: @WilburTSheep, @UpperClassHens, @LonelyCowArcher.

- Objects — those of significance within storylines, where they might 'bear witness' to key events: @Helens_Burner (telephone), @WorkbagOfJazzer.

There is a common thread that representations usually respond to the original *Archers* fan text by aiming for authenticity. There is a sense of playfulness in these practices, but one that usually honours the show through simulation (Bore & Hickman, 2013) rather than creating conflict or tension by introducing oppositional or alternative narratives as in some of the cases described earlier. One possible exception to this is when 'ghosts' of characters are introduced. This happened following the demise of Nigel Pargetter in 2011 (@GhostOfNigelP) but even here we might read this as reluctance to let the character go rather than directly challenging decisions of the programme makers to kill off characters.

FILLING IN THE NARRATIVE GAPS

Archers fan fiction accounts on Twitter typically demark their activity first in how they set up their account (the name, biography and profile picture used) but also in using #thearchers tag. This ensures the content is delivered to the appreciative audience and can also be understood in those terms, where just a couple of words followed by the hashtag provides context or responds to a scene currently airing. Whilst the intention with many of these accounts may have been to always stay in character and be responsive in this way, sometimes the tweets respond more generally to storylines. However, for the most part we can understand *The Archers* fan fiction (TAFF) as filling in the gaps made available by the hyperdiegetic universe of *The Archers*, where hyperdiegesis describes 'the creation of a vast and detailed narrative space, only a fraction of which is ever directly seen or encountered within the text' (Hills, 2002, p. 137). It has been argued that radio is ripe for such transmedia extension of narratives, more so than television or cinema given the lack of the visual element (Edmond, 2015). This is proven to be the case in *The Archers*, where a TAFF character's musings extend beyond the broadcast period, throughout their everyday practices, but in ways that do not dismantle or otherwise break the BBC's hyperdiegetic universe. An example of this from my own practice as @borsetpolice can be drawn from the night that Helen Archer stabbed her abusive husband Rob Titchener. As a listener I knew the audience would be waiting for the police's response, both from the radio drama and the Twitter account. However, the evening's episode did not include a call to the police or confirm that they were being called, so I tweeted this:

> *Another quiet beat tonight. Some anti social [sic] behaviour to deal with in Felpersham but that's it. #thearchers @BBCTheArchers. (Borsetpolice, 2016)*

The intention was to maintain the casual, laidback and underworked persona I'd developed for the police over time, but also provide some light and hopefully not-too-trifling relief to the high tensions of the radio narrative. There was also a sense that the police would be involved at some point, so this foreshadowed their presence as part of a long game for me to play, allowing the pace of the tweets to unfold over time. But more importantly, it was authentic in terms of the timeline and 'who knew what and when' within the cast of characters.

FAN FICTION AROUND KEY EVENTS

Before going on to talk specifically about practice, it's also worth noting that new accounts tend to emerge around major storylines when they're likely to run for weeks or even months. The most obvious example of this was the Helen and Rob domestic violence storyline, where there were several Rob accounts being run, but also Helen, their children and other new characters such as Helen's barrister (@anna-tregorran) and Helen's friend in the secure unit Kaz (@KazSurnameUnkwn). The audience's recognition of plot points and events that were key or resonated with them was expressed in their creation of accounts for Rob's colostomy stoma bag during his recovery (@bagofthedevil), Titchna Casserole Ware (@TichnaCasserole) and the mobile phone that Helen was given by friend Kirsty (@Helens_Burner).

My own @borsetpolice was inspired in 2011 by such a major storyline, with the first tweet:

> *#sattc #thearchers Borsetshire Police would like to hear any witnesses to the death of Nigel Pargetter at Lower Loxley on 02 January 2011*

Then in 2013 policing became more prominent with the introduction of local bobby PC Harrison Burns, and followers continued to rise along with the emerging Helen and Rob story through to its climax. Given this, it helps to understand the appeal by looking at my practice, especially as I see it as being typical of other TAFF activity.

BEING @BORSETPOLICE

First of all it is worth picking apart what I do when I tweet as the Borsetshire police force, to describe those practices and the micro-texts that result. This gives us a sense of how they fit into the online Twitter community and communications, the show itself, and how they contribute. I've already identified that in my case, as with others, there is a sense of being true and authentic to that action and narrative which is taking place in the radio show. Rather than 'breaking' the original text it plays into the same space (Sandvoss, 2005. p. 42). With this in mind, if a crime is committed on the programme, or the police are mentioned and active in some way, I try and tweet something to reflect that.

There are three main ways that my tweets are informed. First of all, I might be simulating how a real police force would use Twitter — not just in what they tweet but in the shape of such tweets. Accounts such as @wmpolice (West Midlands Police) are used to engage with the public, report on crime and generally communicate (Crump, 2011). So I might tweet for a witness appeal, or report on proceedings of both parochial and major in their civic impact, for example, theft of money from the church or a domestic violence case.

The second influence on the shape of activity is a more playful stereotyping of a local police force. Borsetshire Police sit around eating a lot of doughnuts and drinking tea, according to my tweets. Given that they aren't regularly called in to storylines, or weren't until the arrival of PC Burns at least, we can assume that there is a police force but that they spend most of their time at the station waiting for crimes to occur, which they rarely do. When the police are involved, storylines are often ambiguous enough that they allow for an idea of the organisation as ineffectual, vaguely oafish and possibly quite sexist too. In fact, the village often gives the impression of being 'policed' by the actions and interventions of its residents anyway, so this creates a sense of the police also being slightly redundant and oblivious as to what crimes might be unfolding around them.

Finally, my practice is informed by a sense of the Twitter audience it speaks into, that fan community that Bore and Hickman talked about, driven by authenticity and a need to stay in character. However, this is a sense of performing for an audience, rather than discussion within a community, as I have learned that other *Archers* tweeters might Like or Retweet my efforts, but do not always respond more directly in their own tweeted answers. Sometimes I will invite this by posing tweets as questions:

> *We're rewatching The Wire here at the station.*
> *Great show, now wondering whose home we could*
> *bug... #thearchers. (Borsetpolice, 2017)*

MOTIVATIONS — WHY BOTHER?

There is a sense that TAFF practitioners become part of something when they engage in these practices. On one level they join the 'cast' of TAFF practitioners, which the wider community of tweeters recognise and sometimes reference in their tweets. It is less often that these characters mention each other in their activity, starting TAFF turn-based conversations. On another level, they become part of a wider *Archers* transmedia — this is the closest the general public can come to being in the show itself. Thomas (2016) has recognised the idyllic and aspirational nature of *The Archers* universe and therefore the extent to which *The Archers* is escapist in its setting and also everyday banality. Therefore, it is hardly surprising that TAFF aspires to this also in authentic accounts, rather than '[break] with the cultural and ideological frameworks of the fan text and radically [reformulate] its substance', as in other fan fiction examples (Sandvoss, 2005, p. 42). It is also worth noting the affective motivation of creating fan fiction in this way that it is simply fun and enjoyable. In contrast to my own personal account or other Twitter accounts I run professionally, @borsetpolice allows me to play a role that differs in its expectations.

WHAT DOES *ARCHERS* FAN FICTION DO?

How can we understand the value and role of *Archers* fan fiction? I'll tackle this again by exploring from the micro-level of the practitioner, and then working outwards, through Twitter and the wider *Archers* text and audience. I've talked above about how this roleplay is escapist, in allowing me to put aside other everyday concerns and engage in the 'play' of being @borsetpolice. This is afforded by the anonymity of the

account, which was securely in place before attending the
2017 Academic Archers conference — less so now, and in the
writing of this chapter. But with that anonymity I was
afforded a certain level of cathartic release, where the police
were more blasé about certain storylines than I might have
been in my own personal reflection.

My tweets also contribute to an ongoing and indefinite
corpus of *Archers* fan fiction. There is no end to this practice, until there is an end to *The Archers* show itself (God
forbid). But while this contributes to a volume of work, it
is worth noting once again that the TAFF characters rarely
talk to each other — rather than visualise this practice as
a second mesh level of narrative, interweaving as transmedia over the top of the BBC *Archers* product, they might
instead be considered as injections of narrative. The reason
for this lack of dialogue might be revealed in the practicalities of tweeting — I only tend to converse directly with
those accounts I can remember to spell: @CSI_ambridge
and @HeatherChloeDog. The first came about following
the culmination of the Helen and Rob storyline, and its
necessary crime scene investigation, whereas the second is a
PC Burns account (run by a lady called Heather who owns
a dog called Chloe and was tweeting as such before changing focus). Given that we are all part of the same police
force, it is natural and expected that we would talk to
each other.

The contribution and the value to the audience is also
revealed in their response. As much as it allows the TAFF
practitioners to involve themselves in the show, it also affords
the rest of the tweeting audience dialogue with characters, in
a way that many prior online forms of written fan fiction
couldn't. The idea of an online police force of course invites
this, the sense that listeners have 'witnessed' crimes as they
listen to the show and can report them, even if the radio

characters don't seem to want to (as was observed in the case of Helen and Rob). The value then in giving the audience ways to cathartically respond to such storylines is significant. As my practice continues, with my follower numbers and audience increasing, this cements the idea of @borsetpolice amongst the tweeters, and I am increasingly mentioned in tweets and engaged in conversation.

Whilst it is unlikely that *Archers* fan fiction somehow makes people listen to *The Archers*, it may be that Twitter users in their everyday practice are reminded of the show when they see #thearchers appear in their timeline and so this supports the theory that fan fiction contributes to but also promotes the fan text, as Wood and Baughman (2012) suggest. If this is the case, why does the BBC not see this as valuable enough to take up this work themselves? It is not simply that the production is tied up entirely in its core output of the show, as they regularly monitor and partake in online discussion, blog additional content and have been equally playful in their creation of five parallel short series of *Ambridge Extra* (2011–2013). Should we be concerned at the digital labour undertaken for free by listeners in creating content and contributing to *The Archers*? Rather than suggesting that the BBC undervalues this input or takes advantage of their listener base, I assume it is rather through a recognition that (a) the listeners enjoy taking on *Archers* roles, (b) they are doing a good enough job that they do not damage the intellectual property of the BBC and (c) that, through their expertise as listeners, they do the job well, and this could not be improved on by the BBC themselves. Where listeners are intrinsically motivated in carrying out TAFF as a hobby, how would BBC staff be similarly motivated? How many characters could or would the BBC take on? The likelihood is that the product of such efforts would look and feel very different as a result.

WHAT CAN WE UNDERSTAND MORE WIDELY FROM FAN FICTION?

The breadth of uses for social media seems to be constantly expanding but it is perhaps unsurprising that people choose to use it in some of the creative ways I've touched on in this chapter. After all, Twitter and radio drama match up well. *The Archers* is a short radio drama at just 13 minutes per episode, but its frequency as a soap opera, broadcasting 6 days a week, means that we hear a little, but often. The fact we can now listen whenever we like via the internet means it weaves itself into our everyday practices and thoughts – users of Twitter will find this description familiar. So the idea that listeners use Twitter to perform *Archers* transmedia, punctuating these everyday drama narratives, makes complete sense to me. Where listeners appreciate the escapism offered by listening, they can go deeper by placing themselves in the space through their own performance as a character. This doesn't necessarily play into discourses of social media as a tool for communication or a 'space of flows' (Castells, 2000). However, there is a sense that I personally enjoy the control I can exercise in representing the police, where there otherwise lies a narrative gap — I am making my 'mark on the world' and being recognised for my efforts (Gauntlett, 2013, p. 224). Whilst it is often the case that we point to social media and the idea that it supports activism, societal transformation or even revolution (in the case of the 'Arab Spring'), we should not overlook these affective and enjoyable everyday experiences in the process.

REFERENCES

AmbridgeChurch. Retrieved from https://www.twitter.com/ AmbridgeChurch. Accessed on May 30, 2017.

AmbridgeLabour. Retrieved from https://www.twitter.com/ AmbridgeLabour. Accessed on May 30, 2017.

AmbridgeTeaRoom. Retrieved from https://www.twitter. com/AmbridgeTeaRoom. Accessed on May 30, 2017.

annatregorran. Retrieved from https://www.twitter.com/ annatregorran. Accessed on May 30, 2017.

bagofthedevil. Retrieved from https://www.twitter.com/ bagofthedevil. Accessed on May 30, 2017.

BBC. (2017). *Hashtag Love: Radio 4's interactive Valentine's Day drama*. Retrieved from http://www.bbc.co.uk/programmes/ articles/4n3DPQhm0bGgCm4Mf9jGKZk/hashtag-love-radio-4s-interactive-valentine-s-day-drama. Accessed on 27 2017.

BBCTheArchers. Retrieved from https://www.twitter.com/ BBCTheArchers. Accessed on May 30, 2017.

Bore, I-L. K., & Hickman, J. (2013). Continuing The West Wing in 140 characters or less: Improvised simulation on Twitter. *The Journal of Fandom Studies*, *1*, 219–238.

Borsetpolice. (2011). Borsetshire Police would like to hear any witnesses to the death of Nigel Pargetter at Lower Loxley on 02/01/2011. #sattc #thearchers. Twitter, January 5, 2011. Retrieved from https://twitter.com/borsetpolice/status/ 22649753917460481. Accessed on May 30, 2017.

Borsetpolice. (2016). Another quiet beat tonight. Some anti social behavior to deal with in Felpersham but that's it. #thearchers @BBCTheArchers. Twitter, April 3, 2016.

Retrieved from https://twitter.com/borsetpolice/status/ 716719064123580416. Accessed on May 30, 2017.

Borsetpolice. (2017). We're rewatching The Wire here at the station. Great show now, wondering whose home we could bug... #thearchers. Twitter, 26/02/17 Retrieved from https:// twitter.com/borsetpolice/status/835967018910289920. Accessed on May 30, 2017.

borsetpolice. Retrieved from https://www.twitter.com/borset-police. Accessed on May 30, 2017.

Bourdieu, P. (2010). *Distinction: A social critique of the judgement of taste*. Abingdon: Routledge.

CaptainsGhost. Retrieved from https://www.twitter.com/ CaptainsGhost. Accessed on May 30, 2017.

Castells, M. (2000). *The rise of the network society: The information age: Economy, society, and culture* (Vol. 1). Hoboken, NJ: John Wiley & Sons.

Clarrie_Grundy. Retrieved from https://www.twitter.com/ Clarrie_Grundy. Accessed on May 30, 2017.

Crump, J. (2011). What are the police doing on Twitter? Social media, the police and the public. *Policy & Internet*, *3*(4), 1–27.

CSI_ambridge. Retrieved from https://www.twitter.com/CSI_ ambridge. Accessed on May 30, 2017.

Duffett, M. (2013). *Understanding fandom: An introduction to the study of media fan culture*. Bloomsbury, USA: Bloomsbury Publishing.

eddie_grundy. Retrieved from https://www.twitter.com/ eddie_grundy. Accessed on May 30, 2017.

Edmond, M. (2015). All platforms considered: Contemporary radio and transmedia engagement. *New Media & Society*, *17*(9), 1566–1582.

felpershamaccs. Retrieved from https://www.twitter.com/felpershamaccs. Accessed on May 30, 2017.

Gauntlett, D. (2013). *Making is connecting*. New York, NY: John Wiley & Sons.

GhostOfNigelP. Retrieved from https://www.twitter.com/GhostOfNigelP. Accessed on May 30, 2017.

Giddens, A. (1984). *The constitution of society: Outline of the theory of structuration*. Cambridge, Polity Press.

HeatherChloeDog. Retrieved from https://www.twitter.com/HeatherChloeDog. Accessed on May 30, 2017.

Helens_Burner. Retrieved from https://www.twitter.com/Helens_Burner. Accessed on May 30, 2017.

Hills, M. (2002). *Fan cultures*. Abingdon: Routledge.

JazzerArchers. Retrieved from https://www.twitter.com/JazzerArchers. Accessed on May 30, 2017.

Jenkins, H. (2006). *Convergence culture: Where old and new media collide*. New York, NY: NYU press.

Jenkins, H. (2012). *Textual poachers: Television fans and participatory culture*. Abingdon: Routledge.

KazSurnameUnkwn. Retrieved from https://www.twitter.com/KazSurnameUnkwn. Accessed on May 30, 2017.

LonelyCowArcher. Retrieved from https://www.twitter.com/LonelyCowArcher. Accessed on May 30, 2017.

Moores, S. (1993). *Interpreting audiences: The ethnography of media consumption* (Vol. 8). England, UK: Sage.

Parrish, J. (2010). Back to the woods: Narrative revisions in New Moon fan fiction at Twilighted. In M. A. Click, J. Stevens Aubrey, & E. Behm-Morawitz (Eds.), *Bitten by Twilight: Youth culture, media, and the vampire franchise* (pp. 173–188). New York, NY: Peter Lang.

RobTitchener. Retrieved from https://www.twitter.com/RobTitchener. Accessed on May 30, 2017.

Sabrina_Thwaite. Retrieved from https://www.twitter.com/Sabrina_Thwaite. Accessed on May 30, 2017.

Sandvoss, C. (2005). *Fans: The mirror of consumption.* Cambridge: Polity Press.

SidPerksGhost. Retrieved from https://www.twitter.com/SidPerksGhost. Accessed on May 30, 2017.

Soosanssmallads. Retrieved from https://www.twitter.com/Soosanssmallads. Accessed on May 30, 2017.

the_fat_paul. Retrieved from https://www.twitter.com/the_fat_paul. Accessed on May 30, 2017.

Thomas, L. (2007). Online fan cultures around The Archers. In T. Ferne, B. Audio, T. Wall, A. Dubber, L. Thomas, M. Lambrianidou, M. Hills, A. Luther, & B. Klein. *Listener online engagement with BBC Radio programming* (pp. 32–55). Citeseer.

Thomas, L. (2016). The Archers and its listeners in the twenty first century. In C. Courage, N. Hadlam, & P. Matthews (Eds.), *The Archers in fact and fiction: Academic analyses of life in rural Borsetshire* (pp. 5–18). Oxford: Peter Lang.

TichnaCasserole. Retrieved from https://www.twitter.com/
TichnaCasserole. Accessed on May 30, 2017.

UpperClassHens. Retrieved from https://www.twitter.com/
UpperClassHens. Accessed on May 30, 2017.

Wacquant, L. J. (1989). Towards a reflexive sociology:
A workshop with Pierre Bourdieu. *Sociological Theory*, 7,
26–63.

welovethebull. Retrieved from https://www.twitter.com/welo-
vethebull. Accessed on May 30, 2017.

WilburTSheep. Retrieved from https://www.twitter.com/
WilburTSheep. Accessed on May 30, 2017.

wmpolice. Retrieved from https://www.twitter.com/wmpo-
lice. Accessed on May 30, 2017.

Wood, M. M., & Baughman, L. (2012). Glee fandom and
Twitter: Something new, or more of the same old thing?
Communication Studies, 63, 328–344.

WorkbagOfJazzer. Retrieved from https://www.twitter.com/
WorkbagOfJazzer. Accessed on May 30, 2017.

PEER REVIEW, TRANSCRIPT OF POLICE INTERVIEW

This interview is being recorded. Present are Officer Burns
and Mr Jerome Turner. The time is now 11.12 a.m. on 26
May 2017. This interview is being conducted under caution.
Mr Turner attended voluntarily and is not under arrest at
this time. We are here to discuss alleged criminal activity
under Section 90 of the Police Act 1996, namely that of
impersonating a police officer. Do you understand that? For
the tape, Mr Turner is nodding. Good. OK. I am now

showing Mr Turner printouts of 'tweets' dating back to 1 January 2011 through to May 2017. This shows activity from an apparently legitimate account, @borsetpolice, but of which Borsetshire Police had no knowledge until yesterday. Do you know who is responsible for this account Mr Turner? I should point out that the IP address associated with these tweets has been located to your home. OK. Perhaps most alarmingly, this account has been used in dialogue and communication with members of the public, and has risked the viability of actual criminal prosecutions, including a recent case of domestic violence. I hope you understand the severity of these claims being made against you Mr Turner. Do you have anything to say at this stage? What can you tell us about this fictional account?

SECTION SIX

THE HELEN AND ROB STORY

CHAPTER EIGHTEEN

UNDERSTANDING THE ANTECEDENTS OF THE DOMESTIC VIOLENCE PERPETRATOR USING *THE ARCHERS* COERCIVE CONTROLLING BEHAVIOUR STORYLINE AS A CASE STUDY

Jennifer Brown

ABSTRACT

The Archers *storyline of domestic abuse has raised awareness of the phenomenon of coercive controlling behaviours and marital rape. This chapter provides some context for the occurrence of partner sexual violence and focuses on profiling the antecedents of the perpetrator. Personal and family histories identify potential risk factors and include attachment problems, childhood exposure to family violence and personality disorder. These provide markers for future violating behaviours in intimate relationships. The absence of pre-ventative factors such as a positive mentoring adult and supportive school environment increases the likelihood of subsequent offending. Predictions about cessation, continuation and escalation of violence will also be discussed.*

Keywords: Domestic abuse; coercive control; partner sexual violence

INTRODUCTION

The Rob and Helen Titchener storyline in *The Archers* raised awareness of particular forms of domestic abuse: coercive controlling behaviours and marital rape. Much of the attention focussed on the victim's perspective, powerfully representing the nature and effects of undermining and insidious behaviour. This chapter takes the opportunity afforded by the story to look in more detail at the perpetrator. Rob has been labelled a 'monster', a not-uncommon descriptor given to sex offenders, and the actor himself has been subject to vilification via social media. Whilst his behaviour may be monstrous, the argument presented here is that men such as those portrayed by the Rob character are not monsters. By using his backstory some insights and understanding of why men become domestic abusers can be explored. This is not to exonerate coercion and violence but rather provides some explanation as to why this happens.

DEFINITIONS

The Home Office (2013) broadly defines domestic abuse as nonphysical abuse, threats, force, sexual assault or stalking. In 2015, the Serious Crime Act created a specific offence of controlling or coercive behaviours in intimate or family relationships (section 78) with a maximum sentence of 5 years' imprisonment, a fine or both, if convicted. The behaviour must be repeated and continuous having a serious effect. Controlling behaviour is:

> *a range of acts designed to make a person subordinate and/or dependent by isolating them from sources of support, exploiting their resources and capacities for personal gain, depriving them of the means needed for independence, resistance and escape and regulating their everyday behaviour.*

Coercive behaviour is 'a continuing act or pattern of acts of assault, threats, humiliation and intimidation or other abuse that is used to harm, punish or frighten their victim'. The specific list of behaviours in Home Office guidance includes inhibiting access to transport, electronic monitoring and rape. Marital rape was made a criminal offence in 1991.

CONTEXTUALISING THE SCALE OF THE PROBLEM

Domestic Violence

The Crime Survey of England and Wales (CSEW) estimates the incidence (i.e., recent experience) of domestic abuse, as broadly defined, is experienced by 8% of women aged between 16 and 59 annually, that is, 1.3 million per year. The equivalent figure for male victims is 600,000. Roughly speaking approximately one in twelve women said they had experienced domestic violence. The prevalence (i.e., having been incurred over a lifetime) of domestic abuse is 27.1% of women and 13.2% for men, that is, 4.5 million women and 2.2 million men, respectively. Police-recorded crime data show a year on year increase with a 43% rise in reporting domestic abuse since 2007/2008. In 2014/2015, nearly a million (943,628) cases were recorded, 13% of this number were referred to the Crown Prosecution Service and charges made in 68.9% of such cases. In all, there were 9% successful prosecutions of all recorded police cases in 2014/2015. CSEW provides more detail of the experiences of those suffering intimate personal violence. Data from 2015 ($N = 10,363$ women respondents) indicates 63% suffered emotional and financial abuse such as withholding of household finances, belittling behaviours and attempts to restrict access to family and relatives. 2.7% suffered a serious sexual assault including rape.

Rape

Figures available from CSEW for 2009/2012 estimated an average of 77,500 rape victims of which 15,670 were recorded by the police. In the same accounting period (although may not relate to equivalent cases) 2910 proceeded to court and 1070 resulted in prosecution representing about 6% of recorded cases by police. Estimating the numbers of marital rape is a little more difficult. The CSEW data report that 56% of rape victims were partners. In a survey conducted by Painter (1991), it was reported that marital rape was, on average, experienced by one in seven women from her community sample who were, or had been, married and said they had been raped by their husband or ex-husband.

Thus in terms of the *Archers* story, Helen was amongst the one in twelve women suffering domestic violence annually and within this her experience of coercive controlling behaviours is typical. If Painter's estimates are correct, Helen will be amongst the one in seven women suffering a marital rape. What is unusual is Helen stabbing her husband. Figures from ONS (2015) show that only 2% of domestic homicides were women killing men. In 77% of cases it was men killing their woman partner. This equates to one woman killed almost every day of the year.

ANTECEDENTS OF CONTROLLING AND COERCIVE BEHAVIOURS

There are a number of candidate explanations for why men engage in sexual violence: attachment style; childhood witnessing of parental domestic abuse; personality disorder; blame attribution.

Attachment Style

Problematic attachment in childhood is associated with subsequent adult sexual violence (Ward, Hudson, Marshall, & Siegert, 1995; Ward, Hudson, & Marshall, 1996).

Attachment was originally conceptualised by Bowlby and subsequently refined by Ainsworth and colleagues. Bowlby formulated the idea of an attachment system between a baby and its main caretaker that ensured the infant's protection and helps to develop positive emotional states and sense of security. Adverse outcomes may occur when attachment is dislocated partly because this disrupts the template whereby children construct expectations about people's roles in relationships. Ainsworth suggested three types of attachment: *secure* — sensitive to needs of child and caretaker responds warmly and affectionately; *anxious/ambivalent* — caretaking is inconsistent such that child become attention seeking, impulsive, tense and helpless; *avoidant* — *caregiver* is detached, lacks emotional expression and is unresponsive to the child's needs such that child becomes emotionally detached, lacks empathy and engages in hostile and antisocial behaviours.

Adult attachment styles may change especially if the person is subsequently involved in a supportive and loving relationship, whereas prolonged insecure attachments have been hypothesised to be a vulnerability factor in criminality. Thus Marshall (1989, 1993) argues that the failure to develop secure attachment bonds in childhood by sex offenders results in their failure to learn the necessary interpersonal skills and self-confidence to achieve intimacy with other adults, rather they experience a form of emotional loneliness.

Reder and Duncan (2001) proposes that fear of being abandoned and emotional loneliness acts as a precursor to violence which is used as a means to dominate others, with the abusive partner becoming mistrustful, possessive and imprisoning. The offender seeks intimacy through sex, even forcing their partner to participate. The violence serves an expressive function involving processes implicated in identity confirmation through relationships among others and between others and self. In further theoretical work, Ward et al. (1995) suggest that anxious/ambivalent attachment style is associated with controlling behaviours and a preoccupation with relationships (marked by strong sexual attraction, jealousy and contrasting emotional states) with fluctuating levels of intimacy but which are never satisfactory. On the one hand having a partner they can control tends to make insecurely attached individuals more secure. On the other, the insecure adults may relate well to needy children, relying on the child to satisfy their own unmet psychological needs. If they are unable to satisfy their intimacy in adult relationships, they may become emotionally dependent upon their relationships with children but the nurturing demands of the child can intensify their own unsatisfied dependency feelings.

Child Witness of Domestic Violence

There is a well-established literature on the adverse impacts on children who witness violence in the home. The CSEW suggests as many as two-thirds of children present in domestically violent households witness the abuse of a parent. Rosenbaum and O'Leary (1981) note that male child witnesses of household violence are more prone to conduct disorders and general signs of distress and they also found this to be a predictor of adult domestic violence. It is postulated that children originating in violent families learn how to behave and treat others by virtue of their observations thereby acting out a cycle of abuse. Social learning not only shows the child how to commit violence but also reinforces controlling outcomes for the perpetrator. Thus violence is instrumental in that it presents one way of resolving conflict and confers power to the perpetrator. Herman, Perry, and Van der Kolk (1989) found links between witnessing domestic violence in early childhood and personality disorder.

Personality Disorder

A compounding factor is personality. There is a strong link in the research literature between personality disorder (PD) and criminality (Brown, Miller, O'Neill, & Northey, 2014). The

Diagnostic and Statistical Manual of Mental Disorders criteria suggest PD is indicative of a long-standing pattern evident from childhood of disregarding the rights of others.

There are broadly three clusters of disorders: odd or eccentric; dramatic, emotional or erratic; anxious and fearful. Cluster two contains the narcissistic type which has been associated with sex offending (Francia, Coolidge, White, Segal, Cahill, & Estey, 2010). Hepper, Hart, Meek, Cisek, and Sedikides (2014) suggest that narcissistic personality traits are evident in the general population and entails grandiosity, self-inflated self-image and a desire for power coupled with a sense of entitlement and lack of regards for others. It is also associated with lack of empathy and failure to consider the effects of behaviour on others and accompanied by aggressive reactions to threat. Sense of entitlement and exploitiveness are the most toxic or maladaptive ingredients of narcissism. In the Hepper et al. study comparing offenders from nonoffenders they found that the personality trait (disposition) was more relevant that a clinical diagnosis of narcissism in their offending sample. Offending was best predicted by sense of entitlement which in turn was associated with lack of empathy.

Proulx and Beauregard (2014) looked at the profiles for men who raped their wives/partners. They identified several different pathways. They found narcissism a significant personality disorder in one of the pathways they termed hypersexual. In this pathway, the man expects his wife not only to fulfil his needs but also to admire him. If she does not, he adopts a victim stance and considers his wife selfish and that he is entitled to punish her. Associated behaviours include temper tantrums, lying and sensation seeking in other domains of their lives. Motivation was fuelled by a need for sexual gratification without limits with the goal of enhancing positive mood.

Blame Attribution

Attribution is a process through which individuals attempt to construct causal explanations for their own and other's behaviours. Gudjonsson and Singh (1988) identify internal attribution occurs when the cause of behaviour is located within the individual's personal qualities whilst external attributions are constructed when the cause is attributed to others or environmental pressures. Gudjonsson developed a blame attribution inventory which measures the degree to which people blame commission of a crime on external factors such as the victim or situational circumstances, some internal factors such as poor self-control, or a guilt attribution whereby the person is regretful or shows remorse for their criminal acts. External attributions serve the purpose of reducing guilt and anxiety and maintaining self-esteem. Blumenthal, Gudjonsson, and Burns (1999) found that those who sexually offended against adults expressed more cognitive distortion and tended to externalise blame for their criminal acts.

RISK AND PROTECTIVE FACTORS

The presence of risk factors per se does not mean that inevitably a person will use violence in their intimate adult relationships. The presence of exacerbating factors and the absence of protective factors may increase the propensity towards using controlling and coercive behaviours as a coping strategy.

Farrington (1994) found that harsh or erratic parental discipline, cruel, neglectful or passive parenting or poor parental supervision was strongly correlated with antisocial behaviours and subsequent offending. Low levels of positive parental involvement and enrolment in schools that failed to address the social and emotional needs of the child are also ancillary factors as are problematic employment records. The presence of protective factors such as participating in shared activities with family, having a positive adult (ally) in the family to mentor and be supportive, being in a safe environment at school and having a more resilient personality may mitigate adverse early experiences.

ROB'S RISK PROFILE AS A CASE STUDY

We know relatively little about Rob's backstory from *The Archers* script and much has to be conjectured from his reflections and interactions. It is reasonable to infer that his father, Bruce, is a bully and holds patriarchal notions about the role of women and whose ideas about masculinity are fairly stereotypic. From his father's own comments (and observations made by Ursula his wife and Rob's mother) Bruce demands his household is run to his command. Bruce is very condemnatory of Rob's 'blubbing' in the witness box as inimical to 'being a man'. Bruce's uncontrolled rage is vented against Helen during the trial. Rob appears to want his father's respect yet is afraid of him, as indeed is Ursula. So perhaps the inference can be stretched to suggest if not actual physical violence in the home, certainly there were expressions of anger if household arrangements were not to Bruce's exacting standards and demands on the young Rob to behave in terms of his father's model of masculinity.

Rob appears to have a rather ambivalent attitude towards his mother, alternatively calling her 'Mum' or 'Mother'. At first he was reluctant to have his parents visit, as exemplified by a dinner invitation with his prospective in-laws, Pat and Tony Archer. Did Rob actually invite Bruce and Ursula, rather he made excuses for their nonappearance by saying 'this is what they do'. Yet later he insists that Ursula stays in his marital home notionally to help Helen with her pregnancy. He is supportive of his mother's suggestion of a home birth despite Helen's previous pre-natal problems, yet is irritated by her 'fussing' when he himself is convalescing. He is compliant with Ursula's suggestion to send young Henry to his former prep school yet indicated his own dismay at being sent away to that school. Tellingly, he responds to Ursula's suggestion he move back to Hampshire by saying 'I stopped being a Hampshire boy the day you shipped me off to school'.

So here is an indication of his feelings of being let down and abandoned. When Henry, his stepson, appears to go off happily with Pat and Tony he comments 'children often hide sadness behind a smile' – a heartfelt personal recollection of dissembling from an early age. There is evidence of Rob lying as an adult e.g. his distorted account of his altercation with a hunt saboteur and his gaslighting of Helen, where he appears to set up situations designed to confuse Helen about her own behaviour or intentions.

We do not know much about his experiences at school but perhaps again not too much of a stretch to suggest he may have been lonely. He does not appear to have retained any friendships with fellow pupils, indeed, he does not appear to have any adult friends.

Rob has a fractured relationship with his brother, possibly over family inheritance, indicative of a subverted sense of entitlement. That entitlement reasserts itself for example when he insists on sick pay from Pat after his wounding by Helen. We know he is intensely competitive and boasts about his prowess at cricket and denigrates others. It is he who single handedly wins a vital match against arch rivals, Darrington, possibly by cheating. If his actions do not affect a desired result (as when Helen fails to appreciate a specially prepared meal) he becomes a petulant victim.

There is some evidence of prior criminality, for example, the assault on the hunt saboteur. There is also some suspicion of fraudulent accounting when he was manager at Berrow Farm and he admits he blocked the drains illegally to divert flood water.

His employment history seems problematic. We don't know why he left his previous employment abroad in Minnesota or Canada. He has a strong sense of how things should be done yet blames others when things go wrong (as at Berrow Farm). This is symptomatic of external blame attribution, that is, looking elsewhere to lay responsibility for outcomes rather than internalising and showing insight about his own culpability. He becomes resentful and hostile if his ideas are thwarted (as in some of his suggestions about re-equipping the farm shop).

Clearly his relationship with his former wife, Jess, is a template for his subsequent behaviour towards his second, Helen. He is not only a serial offender but also lacks any insight into his own motives and impacts of his behaviours, deflecting responsibility to both Jess and Helen. His conversations to Alan Franks, the vicar, confirm his belief in his own victim status.

His relationship to Henry and his own son, Jack, shows a degree of possessiveness. He needs them to love and admire him and through them and having a beautiful wife he creates his idealised vision of himself as complete and indeed the envy of others. With his boys and wife he can't possibly be lonely. Yet the trophy wife and dream family have disintegrated. Increasingly Rob finds himself isolated and abandoned by his fellow villagers. Christmas without his boys was miserable. He is thwarted by the family court which has reduced and restricted his access to his son.

We might represent a risk equation for Rob as follows:

Attachment deficits + childhood witnessing of domestic violence + narcissistic personality traits + exacerbating situational factors − protective factors − interventions (Criminal Justice System (CJS) or (NHS))

=

Lack of empathy + inflated self-image + overblown sense of entitlement + use of violence expressively and instrumentally + loneliness − self insight into the causes of violent behaviours.

FUTURE BEHAVIOURS

Predictions about the future behaviour in a profile presented by men such as Rob are: desistence — cessation of the violent behaviours; continuance — with same or another partner; escalation — increase in the severity of the violence.

Desistence

Walby and Allen (2004) look at the victim's perspective by analysing British Crime Survey [(BCS) predecessor to the Crime Survey of England and Wales] data. They start by suggesting that cessation may be achieved by virtue of the ending of the violent relationship is mistaken and that the picture is rather more complicated. Whilst for the majority of women leaving the violent partner stopped the violence, for a significant minority, one third (37%) of women, the violence continues and for 18% the abusive behaviour changed to another form. For 7% of women who had suffered domestic violence, the worst incident took place after they stopped living with their violent partner.

While some people can make a clean break from a violent partner, others do not or are not able to, often for reasons of continued contact with children. Of the women who did see their former partner because of children, in more than one third of the cases this had led to threats, abuse or violence, with 29% reporting that they had been threatened and 13% that they had been abused in some way.

Giordano, Johnson, Manning, Longmore, and Minter (2015) undertook qualitative interviews with 89 perpetrators of domestic violence. Twenty of these, one in five were desisters. Key to cessation of violence was finding a new partner where different couple level dynamics facilitated cessation of violence. Experience of different partners contributes to a 'relationship learning curve' in which self-reflection and taking the role of the other becomes an important basis for change. In Rob's case we see little indication of re-defining his situation rather a confirmation of external blame attribution and confirmation of himself as victim.

Continuance

Prevalence of continuation of violent behaviours towards an intimate partner has been estimated at occurring between 13% and 26% of the time by Robinson, Clancy, and Hanks (2014) on a sample of Welsh domestic violence perpetrators. Giordano and colleagues found 13% of persisters in their sample. They were characterised by continued feelings of anger, use of violence as serving expressive needs and using violence defensively, that is, against negative statements made by the partner or fighting back against a perceived violation of trust.

Escalation

Escalation of the severity of behaviours with the same partner was intimated by Walby and Allan. Feld and Straus (1989) who suggest four reasons why domestic violence might increase in severity: minor violence may normalise this as a pattern of tolerated behaviour; violence is a motivator for reducing stress or gaining power; partner using violence does expressively to support achievement of own ends; impact of normalised violence may lessen.

The form of escalation could result in suicide, murder of the abused partner or murder of his estranged family and the perpetrator's own suicide. Aldridge and Browne (2003) show that links between spousal homicide and previous domestic violence are well established. They extracted risk factors from 21 previous studies of spousal homicide and itemise the following: witnessing violence in the home by family members when a child; being married rather than cohabiting drug/alcohol abuse; possessiveness and sexual jealousy; separation (threat or actuality); personality disorder (being over controlling and more dependent featured significantly); previous domestic violence with murdered victim (about half of the victims accumulated from the studies they looked at were killed within two months and most killed within 1 year).

Murder of a partner is often accompanied by suicide of the killer (this happened more frequently when there was a history of separation and reunion and killer having previously had depressive episodes). Murder of partner, self and children (familicide) may also occur, with prior domestic violence as a key predictor. Being unemployed is a significant risk factor and possessive jealousy a significant motivation.

Yardley, Wilson, and Lynes (2014) reviewed 59 family annihilations occurring in Britain between 1980 and 2012 gleaned from newspaper accounts. They observe an increase over the decades of their research period. Most of the murders occurred during the school summer holiday and more likely happened over a weekend. Over half of the murders occurred at home rather than other locations by stabbing or carbon monoxide poisoning. A significant proportion of annihilators were unemployed and were aged between 30 and 39. They suggest that motivations are rather messy with connections between multiple reasons. They were able to identify family break up as the most common motive, which includes anger over child contact arrangements. A second significant motive is financial with the annihilator facing bankruptcy. They propose four sub types of annihilators: self-righteous, disappointed, anomic and paranoid. The self-righteous, for example, lay the blame on their former partner who is held responsible for the family's break up and murder is a means of exacting revenge. These men have an idealised view of family life which is central to their construction of their masculinity. They control the family and may have exerted that control through violence and threats. But if the family slips out of his control and moreover if they thrive without him, he will be constantly reminded of his failure and experiences this as a threat to his self-image. He is unable to accept or adapt to the fact that his idealised conception of family life is over. They will be narcissistic and dramatic and highly likely to take their own life after the murder.

INTERVENTION OPTIONS

There are a number of criminal justice and therapeutic interventions. In a brief overview Westmarland, Thorlby, Wistow, and Gadd (2014) evaluated CJS interventions as follows: arrest of offender — mixed findings; protection orders — evidence of reduced rates of re-victimisation; conditional cautioning — uncertain; second responder programmes — evidence of lower rates of recidivism; graded response — evidence some reduction in repeat victimisation. In addition evidence is ambivalent about restorative justice programme (Mills, Barocas, & Ariel, 2013). Babcock, Green, and Robie (2004) undertook a meta-analysis of educational and therapeutic interventions, for example, Deluth, Cognitive Behavioural Therapy, couples' therapy and found small treatment effects and no differences between interventions.

FINAL COMMENTS

Prior history is a strong predictor of subsequent behaviours. In the hypothetical scenario presented in *The Archers*, without some form of intervention, either therapeutic or criminal justice, the prognosis for any new intimate relationships by the Rob character is pretty bleak. More optimistically, the presence of preventative factors may avert the cycle of abuse being perpetuated in the next generation, that is, with Henry.

REFERENCES

Aldridge, M. L., & Browne, K. D. (2003). Perpetrators of spousal homicide a review. *Trauma, Violence, & Abuse*, 4(3), 265–276.

Babcock, J. C., Green, C. E., & Robie, C. (2004). Does batterers' treatment work? A meta-analytic review of domestic violence treatment. *Clinical Psychology Review*, 23(8), 1023–1053.

Blumenthal, S., Gudjonsson, G., & Burns, J. (1999). Cognitive distortions and blame attribution in sex offenders against adults and children. *Child Abuse & Neglect*, *23*(2), 129–143.

Brown, J., Miller, S., O'Neill, D., & Northey, S. (2014). *What works in Therapeutic Prisons? Basingstoke, UK*: Palgrave.

Farrington, D. (1994). Human development and criminal careers. In M. Maguire, T. Morgan, & R. Reiner (Eds.), *The Oxford Handbook of Criminology* (pp. 511–584). Oxford: OUP.

Feld, S. L., & Straus, M. A. (1989). Escalation and desistance of wife assault in marriage. *Criminology*, *27*(1), 141–162.

Francia, C. A., Coolidge, F. L., White, L. A., Segal, D. L., Cahill, B. S., & Estey, A. J. (2010). Personality disorder profiles in incarcerated male rapists and child molesters. *American Journal of Forensic Psychology*, *28*(3), 55–75.

Giordano, P. C., Johnson, W. L., Manning, W. D., Longmore, M. A., & Minter, M. D. (2015). Intimate partner violence in young adulthood: Narratives of persistence and desistance. *Criminology*, *53*(3), 330–365.

Gudjonsson, G. H., & Singh, K. K. (1988). Attribution of blame for criminal acts and its relationship with type of offence. *Medicine, Science and the Law*, *28*(4), 301–303.

Hepper, E. G., Hart, C. M., Meek, R., Cisek, S., & Sedikides, C. (2014). Narcissism and empathy in young offenders and non-offenders. *European Journal of Personality*, *28*(2), 201–210.

Herman, J. L., Perry, C., & Van der Kolk, B. A. (1989). Childhood trauma in borderline personality disorder. *The American Journal of Psychiatry*, *146*(4), 490–495.

Home Office. (2013). *Guidance on domestic abuse*. Retrieved from https://www.gov.uk/guidance/domestic-violence-and-abuse#domestic-violence-and-abuse-new-definition

Marshall, W. L. (1989). Intimacy, loneliness and sexual offenders. *Behaviour Research and Therapy*, *27*(5), 491–504.

Marshall, W. L. (1993). The treatment of sex offenders: What does the outcome data tell us? A reply to Quinsey, Harris, Rice, and Lalumière. *Journal of Interpersonal Violence*, *8*(4), 524–530.

Mills, L. G., Barocas, B., & Ariel, B. (2013). The next generation of court-mandated domestic violence treatment: A comparison study of batterer intervention and restorative justice programs. *Journal of Experimental Criminology*, *9*(1), 65–90.

Painter, K. (1991). Wife rape in the United Kingdom. Paper presented to the American Society of Criminology, San Francisco, November 20–23rd.

Proulx, J., & Beauregard, E. (2014). Pathways in the offending process of marital rapists. In J. Proulx, E. Beauregard, P. Lussier, & B. Leclerc (Eds.), *Pathways to Sexual Aggression* (pp. 110–136). Abingdon: Routledge.

Reder, P., & Duncan, S. (2001). Abusive relationships, care and control conflicts and insecure attachments. *Child Abuse Review*, *10*(6), 411–427.

Robinson, A. L., Clancy, A., & Hanks, S. (2014). *Prevalence and characteristics of serial domestic abuse perpetrators:*

Multi-agency evidence from Wales. [Project Report]. Cardiff: Cardiff University.

Rosenbaum, A., & O'Leary, K. D. (1981). Marital violence: Characteristics of abusive couples. *Journal of Consulting and Clinical Psychology, 49*(1), 63–71.

Walby, S., & Allen, J. (2004). *Home Office Research Study 276 Domestic violence, sexual assault and stalking: Findings from the British Crime Survey.* Retrieved from: http://www.lancaster.ac.uk/fass/resources/sociology-online-papers/papers/walby-hors.pdf

Ward, T., Hudson, S. M., & Marshall, W. L. (1996). Attachment style in sex offenders: A preliminary study. *Journal of Sex Research, 33*(1), 17–26.

Ward, T., Hudson, S. M., Marshall, W. L., & Siegert, R. (1995). Attachment style and intimacy deficits in sexual offenders: A theoretical framework. *Sexual Abuse, 7*(4), 317–335.

Westmarland, N., Thorlby, K., Wistow, J., & Gadd, D. (2014). Domestic violence evidence review. N8 Policing Research Partnership. Retrieved from: http://dro.dur.ac.uk/12747/1/12747.pdf.

Yardley, E., Wilson, D., & Lynes, A. (2014). A taxonomy of male British family annihilators, 1980–2012. *Howard Journal, 53,* 117–140.

INTERNET SOURCES

https://www.ons.gov.uk/peoplepopulationandcommunity/crimeandjustice/bulletins/crimeinenglandandwales/yearendingmar2016

https://www.ons.gov.uk/peoplepopulationandcommunity/
crimeandjustice/bulletins/crimeinenglandandwales/
yearendingmar2016
https://www.ons.gov.uk/peoplepopulationandcommunity/
crimeandjustice/compendium/focusonviolentcrimeandsexua-
loffences/yearendingmarch2015/chapter2homicide#focus-on-
domestic-homicides

CHAPTER NINETEEN

BAG OF THE DEVIL: THE DISABLEMENT OF ROB TITCHENER

Katherine Runswick-Cole and
Rebecca Wood

ABSTRACT

In this chapter, we consider how the character of Rob Titchener has been developed in The Archers, *moving him from hero of the hour to villain of the piece. We draw on a critical disability studies' perspective to argue that ability and disability have been crucial in turning the character of Rob from the desirable and attractive man who first arrived in the village into a national hate figure, despised by all. We begin this analysis by introducing critical disability studies and studies of ableism as fields of academic inquiry. We then draw on these resources to offer an analysis of the ways in which ability and disability were used as a narrative device to develop Rob's character. We question the ways in which ability and disability are used to denote 'good' and 'evil' in the development of characters in cultural texts like* The Archers, *and end with a plea to scriptwriters to engage differently with dis/ability and to consider the impact of the stories we tell on the everyday lives of disabled people.*

Keywords: Disability; ability; Rob Titchener; stoma; gaslighting; *The Archers*

INTRODUCTION

In this chapter, we consider how the character of Rob Titchener has been developed in *The Archers*, moving him from hero of the hour to villain of the piece. We show how he was initially constructed as able but ultimately deconstructed as disabled and reflect on what this might tell us about how disability is represented in *The Archers*. Moreover, while many listeners might not consider Rob to be disabled in the ways we conventionally conceive of it, we draw on a critical disability studies' perspective to argue that ability and disability have been crucial in turning the character of Rob from a desirable and attractive man when he first arrived in the village into a national hate figure, universally loathed.

We begin this analysis by introducing critical disability studies and enquiries about ableism as fields of academic investigation. We then draw on these resources to offer an analysis of the ways in which ability and disability were used as a narrative device to develop Rob's character (Mitchell & Synder,

2000). We question the ways in which dis/ability is used to denote 'good' and 'evil' in the development of characters in cultural texts and end with a plea to the scriptwriters of *The Archers* — and to others — to engage differently with dis/ability and to consider the impact of the stories we tell on the everyday lives of disabled people.

CRITICAL DISABILITY STUDIES AND STUDIES OF ABLEISM

Disability studies seek to expose and to challenge disablism (Goodley, 2012), which is described as 'a form of social oppression involving the social imposition of restrictions of activity on people with impairments and the socially engendered undermining of their psycho-emotional well-being' (Thomas, 2007, p. 73). Critical disability studies also reflect on how disablism intersects with other forms of marginalisation, including hetero/sexism, racism, class, colonialism and imperialism (Goodley, 2012). Meanwhile, Campbell (2009) describes ableism as 'the compulsion to emulate ableist regulatory norms' resulting in a 'network' of values, beliefs and practices through which disability is cast as a 'diminished' state (Campbell, 2001, cited in Campbell, 2009, p. 5). Campbell also argues that ableism works to construct impaired bodies as 'other': different, lesser, undesirable, in need of repair or modification and, ultimately, de-humanised (Campbell, 2009). Furthermore, Campbell encourages us to pay attention to the ways in which 'ability' appears in cultural texts – in our case, *The Archers* – just as much as 'disability' might or might not feature.

So how do notions of ableism and disablism feature in *The Archers*? How do they operate through the character of Rob, and why does this even matter? As long-term fans, our view is that *The Archers* plays a role in both reflecting and shaping public attitudes towards socio-political issues, especially as the Helen and Rob storyline brought the issue of coercive control to a level in the public consciousness in a way that, arguably, would not have happened otherwise (Kerley & Bates, 2016). Therefore, we suggest that the ways in which ability and disability are made visible, or invisible, in the United Kingdom's longest running radio soap might tell us something important about current contemporary attitudes towards these issues. Importantly, we also propose that these attitudes can and do impact on the everyday lives of disabled people in contemporary Britain.

'ABLE' ROB

We can take a moment to remember what Rob was like — or at least, how he was constructed — when he first arrived in Ambridge. At that time, he was the very embodiment of 'able' (Campbell, 2009), taking up a responsible job at the ultra-modern mega dairy and portrayed as competent, rational and self-confident. As Byrne (2017) pointed out, Rob was presented as a forward-thinking man, willing to embrace modernity, the latest farming methods and technological developments in agriculture. Moreover, although listeners speculated about why his wife, Jess, was still living in Hampshire, they were nevertheless intrigued by this capable man, with a deep, alluring voice, who seemed to be good at everything. Rob was athletic and sporty, and so was a welcome addition to the cricket team. Furthermore, he was seductive, as we saw in the effect he had on Helen where, in the early stages of their relationship, their rapport was shown to be one of a powerful, mutual sexual attraction. Even Susan Carter, who occupies the privileged position of shop manager and chief gossip-in-residence in Ambridge, described Rob as 'a bit of a catch'. In these ways, Rob was not only constructed as 'hyper-able' but as a modern man, keen to spend time with Helen's young son Henry and taking an active role in his care. Indeed, Rob was not only 'able' in every sense, but was constructed as a neoliberal ideal who is physically, intellectually and emotionally adept, sexually desirable as well as a worker making his economic contribution to the state (Goodley, Lawthom, & Runswick-Cole, 2014).

However, the scriptwriters soon began to chip away at Rob's status as an 'ideal' man, using a number of different devices that, as we will see, allude to sexism, homophobia and disablism. The Helen and Rob storyline itself moved in a much more sinister direction as Rob, in a persistent and calculated way, set out to control Helen and to deprive her of autonomy by systematically draining her self-confidence and isolating her from others. Rob convinced Helen to distance herself from her friends and family, that she should close her own shop and that she was not safe to drive, for example. This was all done in a seemingly calm and reasonable way (Pattenden, 2017), and indeed Rob's behaviour has been described as 'gaslighting' after the 1944 film *Gaslight*, in which Gregory Anton sets out to convince Paula that she has gone mad. Gaslighting has since been used to describe a particular kind of abuse in 'that makes the victim doubt her — and it is often a her — own sanity, memory and perception' (Watts, 2016, para 2). Indeed, drawing on another well-known cultural text — Shakespeare's Othello — Pattenden (2017) describes Rob as being so skilled at influencing Helen and others around her, that he resembles the master-manipulator, Iago.

As part of this process of the vilification of Rob and his dramatic fall from grace, he also loses his economic status as manager at the mega dairy as he takes the role of shop worker at Bridge Farm. Here, he is effectively preying on Pat and Tony's family business while he continues to coerce Helen into a more traditional role of a nonworking wife and mother. No longer the reasonable and emotionally sensitive man, Rob has become irrational and cruel. Helen's young son Henry, once provided with kindness and affection, is now shown to be at risk as Rob tries to separate him from his mother and mould him in his own image. The charming professional has become an economic and sexual predator, a cruel and dangerous villain, whose conception of love depends on exploitation, manipulation and rape.

At the same time, and as if his controlling and increasingly cruel behaviour towards Helen were not enough, Rob also shows signs of misogyny and homophobia. For example, he dismisses the views of a female psychologist, not just because she portrays a view of him which is to his disadvantage in the legal case, but simply on the basis that she is a woman. Further, we also see indications of a latent homophobia, such as when he refers disparagingly to Ian Craig and Adam Macy's 'lifestyle'. In these ways, Rob's misogyny and homophobia are offered, alongside his controlling nature, as a device by the scriptwriters to further compound Rob's decline from attractive hero to repellent 'villain'.

THE 'DISABLEMENT' OF ROB

While the character of Rob was initially constructed through his hyper-ability, we argue that he was deconstructed — demolished, even — through disability. As readers will know, Rob's horrific treatment of Helen over a prolonged period of time culminated in an infamous episode where Helen stabs him repeatedly. This point in the narrative not only represents the zenith of a protracted storyline involving abuse and coercion, but it also marks the moment at which Rob, having already been represented as increasingly villainous and cruel, becomes disabled too. Significantly, while listeners are told that Rob was close to death, the only substantial injury we learn about is the wound to Rob's bowel, which resulted in a temporary stoma bag being fitted. This injury, and the disablement it represents, constitutes the final demolition of hyper-able Rob.

According to the website NHS Choices, a stoma is an opening in the stomach created by an operation called an ileostomy and there are about 9000 of these procedures each year in England alone. The same website makes it clear that the impact of living with a stoma is significant for the people affected. Similarly, the Colostomy Association, which supports people with stoma, uses its web page to describe a number of problems of living with stoma including pain, odour and leakage from the bag. Having a stoma requires people to take care of their equipment in order to avoid complications, including infection. Furthermore, research shows that there can be significant impacts to people's well-being as a result of an ileostomy. In 2002, Persson and Hellström found that in the weeks that followed a stoma operation, people experienced a sense of alienation from their body and that their social, sporting and leisure activities were all impacted. In a study by Wirsching, Drüner, and Herrmann (1975), long-term colostomy was shown to result in a decrease in sexual activity and is connected with sexual and social impotence and depression. By implication — because in fact the scriptwriters are somewhat sketchy on the details — Rob is now presented as physically impaired, no longer sexually alluring and potentially impotent. The master-manipulator has ceased to be in control, having lost the power of his most intimate of bodily functions. Far from being a hyper-able man, Rob is now disabled.

DISABILITY IN *THE ARCHERS*

The Archers has a complicated relationship with disability, which usually arises in plotlines as 'narrative prosthesis', meaning that disability appears either to enable character development or to extend an aspect of the storyline. Characters in *The Archers* are only ever temporarily disabled or, if a character's impairment is permanent, that person eventually leaves (Runswick-Cole, 2017). Think about Dan Hebden-Lloyd's juvenile arthritis which, having fulfilled the purpose of enabling his mother, Shula, to get closer to Richard Locke, is no longer mentioned. Consider also Bethany Tucker — Vicky and Mike's daughter — born with Down Syndrome, leaving to go to Birmingham with her family and of whom we rarely hear any more (*ibid.*). Indeed, Rob's stoma is only temporary and is reversed before he flees Ambridge.

However and notwithstanding the temporary nature of the inclusion of disability in *The Archers*, there are significant differences to how Rob's injury and disablement were tackled compared with previous characters and storylines. Usually, when disability appears in *The Archers*, it is accompanied by what seems to be a very conscious effort by the scriptwriters to provide — sensitively — medical information about the nature of the impairment itself. Indeed, a disability storyline is almost always used as moment of raising 'awareness' among the general population. So, for example, the consultant explained gently and very carefully to Bethany's parents how life might be with a baby with Down's Syndrome, providing detailed medical information about the condition, with links for listeners to more information should we need it. Similarly, the storyline that saw Jack Wooley developing dementia was praised for its accurate information (Moreton, 2014). In a further example, when Hayley and Roy Tucker were having trouble conceiving, Lord Robert Winston, well known for his pioneering work on human fertility, turned up in person to deliver the information to them, and of course by extension, to us, the listeners (BBC, 2007).

Despite these precedents and a clear drive by the BBC to harness the significant opportunities offered by *The Archers* to inform the public and raise awareness of different health issues, there has been no such gentle medical explanation or informed counsel by an expert in the field of stoma for the listeners here. Indeed, no information about what the operation would entail, or explanation of what the consequences of living with stoma might be for Rob, were provided. Helpful links to the Colostomy Association or stoma support groups were glaringly absent, as were offers of helplines or any sense of awareness that some listeners would have stomas themselves. Rob's stoma was in fact a device, and the scriptwriters had no desire to soften the listeners' attitudes to Rob.

THE DISABLED PERSON AS SINISTER AND EVIL

In 1992, Colin Barnes produced a report in which he described 13 typologies of representations of disabled people in the media:

1. The Disabled Person as Pitiable and Pathetic

2. The Disabled Person as an Object of Violence

3. *The Disabled Person as Sinister and Evil*

4. The Disabled Person as Atmosphere or Curio

5. The Disabled Person as Super Cripple

6. The Disabled Person as an Object of Ridicule

7. The Disabled Person as Their Own Worst and Only Enemy

8. The Disabled Person as Burden

9. The Disabled Person as Sexually Abnormal

10. The Disabled Person as Incapable of Participating Fully in Community Life

11. The Disabled Person as Ordinary

12. Pitiable and pathetic

13. Object of violence and so on (Barnes, 1992, p. 2, emphasis ours).

Whilst the character of Rob might fit into more than one of these stereotypes, the most evident is number three: the disabled person as sinister and evil. Indeed, this stereotype is embedded within cultural texts in the global North, such as *Richard III*, the *Hunchback of Notre Dame*, *Captain Hook* and Darth Vader in *Star Wars*. In fact, most *Bond* villains fit into this stereotype, although perhaps the most famous is Blofeld in *For Your Eyes Only*, ultimately scooped up by his wheelchair by James Bond's helicopter and dropped down an industrial chimney to kill him. Similarly, during the agonising storyline of Rob's appalling treatment of Helen and his subsequent injury, the popular press demonised the character of Rob, often describing him as 'evil' (Borg, 2015; Brown, 2016). In the same ways, by 'punishing' Rob via a stoma at the height of his villainous status, the scriptwriters have, albeit unconsciously perhaps, merely repeated this well-worn stereotype of associating evil with disability.

THE CONSEQUENCES OF STEREOTYPES

Barnes describes disabled people's representation as sinister and evil as 'one of the most persistent stereotypes and a major obstacle to disabled people's successful integration into the community' (Barnes, 1992, p. 8). These negative representations not only serve to prolong ignorance about the lived experiences of disabled people, but to maintain their marginalised and impoverished status. As we noted above, *The Archers* both reflects and shapes contemporary cultural attitudes to a range of social issues. It has not shied away from challenging sexism, racism and homophobia, for example. Pat Archer is a noted feminist, with Ruth and Pip Archer challenging traditional gender roles. *The Archers* has tackled racism through the character of Usha Gupta and homophobia via Ian and Adam's relationship. Therefore, in arguably the most famous of fictional communities — the village of Ambridge — the failure to embrace disability in a cogent and meaningful way is an issue which urgently needs to be addressed. Disablism — the social oppression of people living with impairments — remains the missing socio-cultural analytical frame in Ambridge.

CONCLUSION

So, we end with a plea to the scriptwriters on *The Archers* and beyond, to think again about how they use disability in cultural texts and to ask: please, don't use ability and disability as a means of representing good and evil when thinking about how to develop a character; and if you want to take a moment to raise 'awareness' of living with an impairment, then do so with the support and advice of the people affected by it.

According to Pfeiffer (2000), everything is 'on a continuum, including disability' (p. 1082). There's not a clear dividing line between 'able' and 'disabled', with people in separate camps, because we will all experience disability in one way or another at some point during our life time. In the Convention on the Rights of Persons with Disabilities (2006), the importance of 'mainstreaming disability issues' is emphasised (preamble g). In other words, it's not a question of adding in a splash of disability here and there, on an occasional and ad hoc basis, but thinking about how disability issues and disabled characters can be embedded within the narrative, as part of the rich patchwork of themes and ideas that imbue this fictional series which we all love. As natural and in some senses unremarkable as Joe Grundy's ferrets, Jill Archer's lemon drizzle cake, or the church committee.

REFERENCES

Barnes, C. (1992). *An exploration of the principles for media representation of disabled people*. Halifax: British Council of Organisations of Disabled People.

BBC. (2007). *Press Release: Leading doctor has appointment with The Archers*. Retrieved from http://www.bbc.co.uk/pressoffice/pressreleases/stories/2007/01_january/02/archers.shtml

Borg, L. (2015). Rob Titchener's evil in the Archers makes for uncomfortable listening. *The Telegraph*. Retrieved from http://www.telegraph.co.uk/culture/tvandradio/11913870/Rob-Titcheners-evil-in-the-Archers-makes-for-uncomfortable-listening.html. Accessed on October 24, 2015.

Brown, D. (2016). The Archers: "I'm evil personified," says Rob Titchener actor Timothy Watson. *The Radio Times*. Retrieved from http://www.radiotimes.com/news/2016-03-29/the-archers-im-evil-personified-says-rob-titchener-actor-timothy-watson. Accessed on March 29, 2016.

Byrne, P. (2017). The Medieval World of The Archers, William Morris and the Problem with Class Struggle. In C. Courage, N. Headlam, & P. Matthews (Eds.), *The Archers in fact and fiction: Academic analyses of life in rural Borsetshire* (pp. 79–88). Oxford: Peter Lang.

Campbell, F. K. (2009). *The contours of ableism: The production of disability and abledness*. Basingstoke: Palgrave MacMillan.

Convention on the Rights of Persons with Disabilities. (2006). *United Nations*. Retrieved from: http://www.un.org/disabilities/convention/conventionfull.shtml

Goodley, D. (2012). Disentangling critical disability studies. *Disability & Society*, *28*(5), 631–644. doi:10.1080/09687599.2012.717884

Goodley, D., Lawthom, R., & Runswick-Cole, K. (2014). Dis/ability and austerity: Beyond work and slow death. *Disability & Society*, *29*(6), 980–984. doi:0.1080/09687599.2014.920125

Kerley, P., & Bates, C. (2016). *The Archers: What effect has the Rob and Helen story had?* Retrieved from http://www.bbc.co.uk/news/magazine-35961057

Mitchell, D., & Synder, S. (2000). *Narrative prosthesis: Disability and the dependencies of discourse*. Michigan: The University of Michigan Press.

Moreton, C. (2014). The Archers' Storyline that Touched the Nation. *The Telegraph*, January 18, 2014.

NHS Choices. (2004). *Colostomy*. Retrieved from http://www.nhs.uk/conditions/Colostomy/Pages/Introduction.aspx

Pattenden, A. (2017). Seeming, Seeming: Othello, The Archers and Rob Titchener. In C. Courage, N. Headlam, & P. Matthews (Eds.). *The Archers in Fact and Fiction: Academic analyses of life in rural Borsetshire* (pp. 43–50). Oxford: Peter Lang.

Persson, E., & Hellström, A.-L. (2002). Experiences of Swedish Men and Women 6 to 12 Weeks after Ostomy Surgery. *Journal of Wound, Ostomy & Continence Nursing*, *29*(2), 103–108.

Pfeiffer, D. (2000). The Devils are in the Details: The ICIDH2 and the disability movement. *Disability & Society*, *15*(7), 1079–1082.

Runswick-Cole, K. (2017). The Dis/appearance of disability in The Archers – Or why Bethany had to go to Birmingham. In C. Courage, N. Headlam, & P. Matthews (Eds.). *The Archers in fact and fiction: Academic analyses of life in rural Borsetshire* (pp. 139–138). Oxford: Peter Lang.

Thomas, C. (2007). *Sociologies of disability, 'impairment', and chronic illness: Ideas in disability studies and medical sociology*. London: Palgrave.

Watts, J. (2016). *The Archers domestic abuse is gaslighting – very real, little understood*. Retrieved from https://www.theguardian.com/commentisfree/2016/apr/05/the-archers-domestic-abuse-gaslighting-sanity-abusive-relationship

Wirsching, M., Drüner, H., & Herrmann, G. (1975). Results of psychosocial adjustment to long-term colostomy. *Psychotherapy and* Psychosomatics, *26*(5), 245–256.

PEER REVIEW, BY ROB TITCHENER
(ADDRESS WITHHELD, USA)

Words fail me – almost! What palpable tosh! Who knew disability studies existed in British universities? It was bad enough when there were women's studies courses, but in this politically correct world gone mad, why do we have to be subjected to this nonsense as well? The authors are women, of course. Self-professed 'experts', like that bloody woman, the psychologist, who denied me access to my sons. These are the sort of women who boast about buying shop bought custard so they have more time for their 'careers'.

Such utter rubbish is not worthy of a response, but just to be clear, I am neither a homophobic nor a sexist person. Adam is an inveterate philanderer and to disapprove of this does not make me homophobic, nor does the fact that I think a wife should love and support her husband make me sexist. For God's sake, I looked after Henry, didn't I? All I ever wanted was to look after Gideon. When I am part of their lives again, when justice is truly served, you can be sure that neither of my boys will adopt 'an alternative lifestyle'.

And for the record, I never was disabled – I was stabbed. If the narrow-minded rabble that call themselves the Ambridge cricket team had let me play, I would have showed them all. I am not weak. Everything, and I mean everything, is functioning just as well as it ever was here in the States.

So, thank you for your 'concern' but there's nothing to see here, you can move along now and go back to finding a new word to add 'ism' to in your 'academic' jobs.

CHAPTER TWENTY

CULINARY COERCION:
NURTURING TRADITIONAL
GENDER ROLES IN AMBRIDGE

Amber Medland

ABSTRACT

This chapter explores the queasy relationship between food and sex on The Archers. *For listeners, food provides an imaginative reference point; consumption of food hints towards characters embodiment and occupation of physical space. To the extent that these characters have boundaries, the way they approach and react to food reveals their rigidity or permeability, and the tones in which characters offer, provide, prepare, coax and force food upon one another tells us a lot about the sexual politics at play in Ambridge. In* The Archers, *women cook and men eat. Characters who rebel against this norm often subvert traditional masculinity in other ways.*

Through close reading (and obsessive listening), this chapter analyses the ways in which food allows the relationships on The Archers *to act as foils to one another. It also explores: food as metaphor; food used both to sustain and fortify the boundaries of the self and to besiege the ego boundaries of others; how characters are given weight in acoustic space; female emancipation; male helplessness; the hunger/satiety/aural claustrophobia of listeners.*

Keywords: *The Archers*; food; coercive control; sexual politics; masculinity; power dynamics; anorexia

The first five episodes of *The Archers* — broadcast in 1950 by the BBC Midland's home service — were produced with collaborative input from the (now defunct) Ministry of Agriculture, Fisheries and Food. Because *The Archers* was first imagined in the post-World-War II years of rationing and food shortages, the 'government was urging farmers to grow more food'. *The Archers* was educational and 'intended as a device by which farmers could catch up with agricultural news' (Donovan, 1991, p. 8). Conversations on the programme framed food accordingly, taking its production as their explicit subject. When, for example, in a 1952 episode, Peggy Archer/Wooley laments, 'Milk, meat and flour are all going up in price,' Dan points out that this will 'make the public realise just what it costs to produce this stuff' (Davies, 2010). *The Archers* lost its educational mandate in 1972.

Now, agricultural information about food is less important than the metaphorical heft food lends other subjects. Paying close attention to the way food is talked about on *The Archers* clues us into its way of world-making and mapping of imaginative space.

When Savarin wrote, 'Tell me what you eat, and I will tell you what you are,' he spoke to the connection between what we say, what we eat and how both are heard. Because listening to *The Archers* is a disembodied experience, we are greedy for imaginative reference points — hearing about the consumption of food gives us a sense of characters' occupation of physical space. Certain characters like certain foods, and both the particularity and recurrence here allow food to work like a *leitmotif* in classical music; each mention of a meal reminds us of the last time it was eaten and amplifies the associations we make; over time, our sense of how a character gives, takes and shares food becomes imaginatively embedded, serving to individuate characters, tease out new conflicts and strengthen the structural integrity of Ambridge as a whole.

For example, Kate Madikane will always use meat eaten in her presence as an excuse to flaunt her vegetarianism. Any mention of hummus, quinoa or tofu conjures Kate faster than the word 'yurt'. Pat and Tony Archer have similar vegetarian predilections, albeit more moderate than Kate's. Because their organic credentials have narrative significance beyond Kate's faddishness, at Bridge Farm they serve toad-in-the-hole alongside ratatouille. Kate evangelises 'global' ingredients, signalling her ambivalence about being back in Ambridge, whereas the Bridge Farm Archers prize local ingredients. Food establishes the fault-lines of future conflicts: Tom's black-pudding scotch-eggs represent his ongoing struggle to reconcile tradition and popular appetites. For this reason, and in its displacement of Helen's organic baby food, the kefir venture spells trouble. Whilst Tom is designing speedy ready-meals and rebranding, Helen focuses on her Borsetshire Blue, each batch of which takes 10 weeks to mature. All of this fosters our sense of history, of stories-within-stories, and allows fans to feel in-the-know. To a new listener, Lillian Bellamy's customary gin-and-tonic might be a whim, whereas we know it's more of a talisman. By making it clear who is eating for pleasure and who eats for survival, food also reinforces traditional class and gender roles in Ambridge — the pasties Ed Grundy, Neil Carter and Jazzer McCreary regularly eat are warm, comforting and cheap. Earlier this year, Lilly Pargetter, teenage hostess of her first party expected 'palmiers...cheese straws...anything with smoked salmon' (*The Archers*, 17 January 2017).

Food provides the emotional context of our family lives and our sex lives. Our childhood memories are laced with picnics, birthday dinners, stolen treats. *The Archers* knows this and food features in every episode. Time, in Ambridge, is measured in meal-times. We can't see light and dark in acoustic space, so instead characters' appetites work like sundials — Jazzer rarely appears without letting us know whether he's had his lunch. Within each section of a 13-minute episode, time is linear, but the pauses (aural ellipsis) mean that more happens in 13 minutes in Ambridge than we might expect. As a narrative device then, food buys time: cramming as many meals and snacks as possible into each episode increases our imaginative bandwidth.

And, in part because there is no text the listeners imagine characters from the inside out. We hear direct rather than indirect, reported, speech, so our experience is both bodily and intensely personal. We savour every mention of food because we are all intimately familiar with the vehicle of the metaphor, and engaging with food on *The Archers* can make the private experience — of over-hearing a conversation — feel communal. Twitter exploded as soon as the custard was mentioned in 'that' episode (*The Archers*, 3 April 2016) because we all had the same associations — we knew how much, just as Helen was leaving, Rob's insistence on traditional custard meant. 'Real custard' stands for Rob's boarding school ideals, his pedantic insistence on tradition and on female labour, rather than 'laziness', in service of male appetites. Custard, by then, was a public symbol of everything we hate about Rob.

There is a queasy relationship between sex and food in *The Archers*. To the extent that these characters have boundaries, the way they approach and react to food reveals their rigidity or permeability and the tones with which characters offer, provide, prepare, coax and force food upon one another tells us a great deal about the sexual politics at play in Ambridge. In general in *The Archers*, women cook and men eat. Characters who rebel against this norm often subvert traditional notions of masculinity in other ways. Ian Craig is one of the only men who cooks and one of the only gays in the village. Claude, previously chef at The Bull, was French to the point of burlesque. When men cook, they do so professionally; as head-chef at Grey Gables, Ian is of course paid, and we hear multiple references to his hours, promotions and his appreciative audience. For Ian, cooking a meal isn't an emotional transaction, and so meal-times are robbed of their romance; whether or not Adam Macy and Ian are sharing food is more of an indicator of whether Adam is being faithful than a source of mutual pleasure. Subsequently, we only hear Ian talk about food if he's reeling off a menu, and his cooking never drives the plot forward.

More men 'help out in the kitchen' in Ambridge these days, but they're not roped into the daily drudgery of turning out hot dinners in quite the same way as female characters, like Clarrie and Emma Grundy, Susan Carter and Shula

Hebden-Lloyd, to name but a few. In Ambridge, food is more likely to give men power in the business world and tempt women with power in the domestic. For example, Brookfield is sustained by Jill Archer's work in the kitchen. Her cooked breakfasts and walnut cakes and roast dinners are as important to the farm as outdoor labour. When Jill moves to Lower Loxley, briefly, the daily routine at Brookfield falls apart. When Jill chirps, 'as long as I'm useful', she means it literally — cooking is her use (function) as well as her way of helping, loving and participating in village life. At Brookfield, the women only clash in the kitchen when other territory is being negotiated: Jill's reign only bothers Ruth, her daughter-in-law (a terrible cook) when Ruth is unsure of her own role; Jill only complains about Pip's lack of self-sufficiency and goes so far as to withhold flapjacks, when she needs to express her displeasure. The power structure at Home Farm is similar — Jennifer Aldridge cooks constantly, and occasionally bakes with Phoebe, but none of her three daughters (Alice, Debby, Kate) are particularly interested.

The next generation of women on *The Archers* are also finding ways to use their culinary powers outside the home. Where before, there was only Frieda Fry, the silent cook, as we go down the generations, women too use food to make money. Helen, for example, uses an old recipe given to her (by none other than Jennifer) to produce a prize-winning money-spinning product. In 2007, Helen's Borsetshire Blue won a silver medal at the British Cheese Awards, and in 2016, at the Borsetshire Food and Drink Awards, it won Best Artisan Product. Rob Titchener, of course, recognising the empowering nature of Helen's work, was keen to master the steps of the process himself; Helen winning Best Artisan Product whilst in prison signalled the beginning of her return to power. The locales we return to in Ambridge revolve around food: The Bull; Lower Loxley; Grey Gables; various dinner tables; that sketchy coffee shop in Borsetshire and of course the Ambridge Tea Room, set up by Fallon and staffed also by Emma Grundy, who has a catering qualification. Women now can be providers as well as nurturers, or rather feeding men does not have to be the first priority. In 2014, after Lilian introduces a feast of lamb tagine, apricots, rosemary focaccia, and 'choccy torte' to Matt Crawford, we are relieved to hear her cackle, *You know I'd have done it myself if I'd had the time.* Spending time outside the kitchen — unless someone is paying you to be there — is an expression of creativity and power, or of making transactions work differently, as heard in the joy of Lillian's many lunches with Justin Elliot.

How men and women eat together reveals the ongoing negotiation of traditional gender roles in Ambridge. There are broad similarities between the culinary efforts Brian Aldridge, Rob Titchener and Toby Fairbrother would ideally like from their women. The different ways in which these men enforce their expectations allows their romantic relationships to act as foils to one another. Of course, a man who would like his wife to cook for him isn't necessarily a misogynist, and a woman who likes to feed her family isn't necessarily downtrodden. Traditional gender roles become problematic when they aren't chosen and when their performance is both expected and inflicted. As when Rob's expectation of three-hot-meals-a-day gradually displaces Helen's full-time career, then part-time career, then her setting foot outside the house without permission.

Elsewhere though, the 'who-cooks-for-who' power balance is very much in discussion. Early on in Pip and Toby's relationship, tension rises as Toby grumbles that there's not enough pasta. Increasingly, Pip becomes frustrated on returning home, having worked harder and for longer than Toby, to discover that he has ordered pizza again. But despite

Toby's performance of male helplessness in the kitchen, Pip doesn't pick up the slack or lower her expectations. Instead, when Toby ruins Christmas dinner, they retreat to bed with champagne, a different kind of compromise. In April, Chris Tucker (having previously moved countries for the sake of Alice's career) cooked dinner for Alice and Pip, before packing Alice's lunch for the next day. Pip, watching him, and heartily sick of Toby blurts out, 'You are good to her, Chris', just as Kirsty, jilted by Tom Archer says disbelievingly to Linda, 'Does Robert make your sandwiches?'

Jennifer and Brian Aldridge are perhaps the last couple in Ambridge who whole-heartedly embrace traditional gender roles. Jennifer keeps Brian in three-hot-meals-a-day, and in return, Brian pays for everything. When Jennifer wants an expensive new kitchen and Brian says no, her only way of getting what she wants is to go on strike — to refuse to cook. When Jennifer doesn't cook, Brian doesn't eat and Jennifer gets her kitchen. When Jennifer is away and Brian hears beeping in the state-of-the-art kitchen, he calls his daughter and asks her to fix it. When neither wife nor daughter can fulfil the roles Brian imagines for them, he takes Ian — his step-son as Adam's partner — upon his offer to cook dinner, and with the 'female' role filled, Brian resumes his pattern of eating, praising and opening another bottle of wine.

Brian and Jennifer's relationship isn't equal in any modern sense, but there is a form of balance, so that both can play up, play with and occasionally rebel against their roles. To send up a role, you have to be able to imagine yourself without it — so when Jennifer watches *Babette's Feast* (a 1987 film about two sisters who devote their lives to caring for their father) for inspiration before a dinner party, and then sighs, proclaiming that she identifies as she too is 'chained to the Aga', her career-minded daughter, Alice replies, 'Come on mum, you love cooking...if anyone chained you to the Aga, it's you', and Jennifer laughs along (*The Archers*, 28 July 2014). When Jennifer is irritated with Brian, she chides him, replying to his 'What about lunch before you go?' with 'Can't you get it yourself?' She frequently laments, 'All you can think about is your stomach'. Her way of loving Brian is dependent on him being the man she feeds — she finds it hilarious when he 'buys a kebab'. Last year, when Brian was worried about what to eat on a road trip, Jennifer 'joked' about him stopping off at a service station and in secret asked Ian to once again to fill her role and make an elaborate picnic.

Food gives us a sense of characters' psychological edges; what you eat tells us what you will allow into your body. How people eat when they're together tells us what they will accept from each other. Any instance of food then, regardless of context, gives us an immediate clue as to where a relationship is on the boundary between caring and controlling. Some women gain status through cooking (Jill Archer) and for others it is a weapon wielded carefully (Jennifer's strike). Encouraging others to eat can be a playful innuendo (Susan's chilli) or demonstrate a lack of respect for physical boundaries (Ursula, Rob, Helen). What we might call the healthier relationships in Ambridge retain a sense of play; Jolene and Kenton, the pleasure-seekers, hold endless themed food-nights at The Bull (pancake day) and tease each other about eating. They test and enjoy each other's appetites, Jolene accusing Kenton of 'torturing her by eating chocolate provocatively' during Lent.

For Susan and Neil Carter too, food is sexy. Here the playfulness is between Susan, however unwittingly, and her audience, in the gap between Susan's intentions and how we experience her, as when she puts Neil on a diet and only manages half a day of DIY juice-fasting herself, or when, sounding sultry, she offers him chilli and says: *Nice and hot.*

So, is it a date then? Chilli becomes a stand-in for sex, and because they're both in on the joke, we accept it. Susan speaks in self-conscious innuendo but remains oblivious of being the punch line. On hearing Susan's scenes, we often laugh, and we are laughing not-exactly-at-her, but nor are we exactly laughing with her; we are, rather, as listeners, laughing with each other. The way Susan talks about food informs how we consume her narrative; with a hefty pinch of salt. Susan draws power from food, but hers is a private kitchen, there is no trade-off, whereas Jennifer's kitchen is a public demonstration that her financial dependence on Brian pays off, tacitly, proof that all the adultery is worth it. This is of course why, to her mind, Jennifer's proffering her discarded kitchen units to Susan, is both generous and thrifty, and to Susan's, it is condescending and rude.

Each of Jennifer's parties provides the opportunity for other characters to perform their social roles: Brian is greedy and drinks too much; Kate disparages ingredients; Emma and Fallon use their entrepreneurial wiles; Jim Lloyd enjoys privately lording his knowledge, as at the recent 'land' themed evening. Rob, though absent at that particular party, is usually in Jennifer's kitchen unusually quiet and admiring. Schoolboy awe aside though, Jennifer isn't Rob's type. Rob wants a domestic goddess but he doesn't want her to have any power. So, in isolating Helen to the home and not letting her do anything, Rob neutralises the domestic as potential power-source.

Rob regularly sets up situations in which the women he professes to love (Jess, his first wife, and then Helen) cannot do other than displease him, because the basis for his pleasure is the annihilation of female will. We see the failure of Jess's house-warming, despite Jennifer's elaborate advice (poached salmon with lemon and cucumber slices, not, as Jess was thinking, avocado and wasabi mayonnaise). The Titchener's party guests sense tension, later hear the couple arguing, and leave early. Not though before Helen, like a maid-in-training, is coaxed into serving canapes by Jennifer, who does not know that Helen and Rob are already deep in an affair. The party breaks down; the salmon goes uneaten. Not long after, when Helen and Rob have moved in together, it's Helen's turn. She plans a dinner party for both sets of parents, Archers and Titcheners, but the Titchener's don't show up (we suspect they were never invited) and Helen has begun to fail at the role too.

We can map the trajectory and shifting power dynamics of Helen and Rob's relationship by what they eat together and what he forces her to eat. Rob's insistence on feeding Helen speaks to his gradual intrusion of her physical and psychic boundaries and foreshadows her eventual rape. It's only through transcribing and close-reading certain scenes that we can be sure what we are seeing, let alone hearing:

> *Helen, I feel awful I only bought one steak....*
>
> *It's easy, I'll easily rustle something up*
>
> *Oh no, I just realised I didn't get any vegetables*
>
> *Don't worry I'll just make a salad ...I can't wait for Anya to come back —*
>
> *Looking at the state of my dinner nor can I —*
>
> *Oh, I'm sorry Rob —*
>
> *Don't be silly, you've got a lot on... I'm quite happy to fend for myself...once in a while...*

(The Archers, 6 August 2014)

It's like watching a cat play with a mouse in a room with no door. Rob constantly redefines the terms of the conversation, so that although Helen is desperate to please him, she can only second-guess and irritate. The conversation above is a blueprint of many of the interactions we hear between them, the pauses growing more tense as the months go by. Rob's tipple of choice is a heady combination of professing of guilt or inadequacy, qualifying, undercutting, and pretending that none of it ever happened.

Every time they eat together, Rob has an opportunity to violate Helen's boundaries further. His expectations generally necessitate their own failure; he doesn't want her to eat and he doesn't want her to gain weight; he rapes her, but doesn't want her to look pregnant. Rob only cooks for Helen when she clearly isn't hungry. When she says she'd rather not, Rob alternates between slightly camp over-enunciation of dishes, belabouring his effort, as when he makes 'Mellazane parmiagano...home-made focaccia...and there's a mixed side-salad and limoncello baba for dessert'. Helen can only interject with praise: 'It looks delicious' ... 'You went to town' ... 'Wow'... 'It really does look amazing...'. Just as fast, it flips: Helen says that she's eaten, then says that she forgot, then pleads, 'I don't want to be greedy'. In perfect sync, Rob sighs, then accuses, 'What is going on in your head.' He makes tactical, momentary retreats ('It's nice to be appreciated') and as soon as Helen feels safe enough to ask, 'Have you...um... have you had a chance yet, Darling, to look at the bank statement on the joint account?' There's a horrible pause before Rob drops his fork and says: 'Bank statement?' (*The Archers*, 5 January 2016).

Of course, Rob never asks Helen what she wants. Every 'Tuck in' and 'Eat up' is a tug on the reigns — Rob's way of reminding Helen that he's in control, performed in such a way that he can always blame his need to protect on the fragility and vulnerability he both creates and plunders. His running commentary on her eating ('Aren't you going to finish that spaghetti?') means that by the time, at their final meal, Rob says, 'Is the custard ready?' we, the listeners, are already tense. At the beginning of the scene, Helen lies about Kirsty bringing over the tuna bake (she says it was from her Grandmother). Then, she doesn't make the custard from scratch. When Rob says 'I think this is one of the tastiest suppers you've made, it makes me wonder why you don't make it more often' and Helen replies, 'You know why' and insists on that, repeats it, says 'I did' and then 'You said you wouldn't like it, you wouldn't eat it' — that's the first stalemate. Tuna bake may seem anti-climactic, mundane even — but that's the point. As listeners, we have learnt to hear the sub-text and anticipate what Rob wants. We, like Helen, remember Rob refusing to eat tuna bake before — we hear Helen's anger and her sudden insistence on being seen. Rob swears it never happened. Helen says 'You did' and Rob says 'No I didn't' — but in Helen's utterance, Rob begins to lose his power (*The Archers* 3 April 2016). Up till this point, Rob has made listeners claustrophobic and Helen complicit. It's the way he says 'We agreed that earlier, didn't we, Darling?' or 'You should have asked me, shouldn't you?' Not real questions at all but a vocal up-turn in a sentence masquerading as asking for consent.

We experience Rob's abuse in both his occupation of acoustic space, and the way this negates Helen's speech, volume, and imagined physical presence. He forces Helen to say *Yes* while disallowing her agency. Take this scene, in which Helen takes her son Henry out of school early for a treat: an afternoon with Kirsty Miller on a steam-train. Rob catches her in the act. Later, we find out that he has installed tracking software on her phone:

*So...tell me...I just want to understand...it's a bit
more than funny...let's get this straight ...you
planned an afternoon out...an afternoon out on a
steam-train with Henry...and with Kirsty...behind
my back...deceiving me...lying to me about it and
lying to school as well...oh, Darling, the last thing I
want to do is upset you but you must admit...why
all this subterfuge?...You don't know?...it's just such
a very odd way to go about things....well then...did
Kirsty put you up to this?...but you felt you had to
be, that's what I don't understand....shhhh....
Darling, I knew this would happen... you get close
to Kirsty again and see what comes of it (*The
Archers, *2 February 2016).*

The threat, stated imploringly, is still explicit. We hear
Helen, in between clauses, crying, saying 'I don't know' and
apologising. Rob, good-cop and bad-cop, is judge and jury
both. The way he speaks has a momentum that has no need
of another person in the conversation; transcribed, the
machinery of this writing ticks along by itself, marking time
till he exhausts her.

In public, Rob is a charmer. The few times his mask slips
food is involved — it's as if he can't resist opportunities for
cruelty. Take the scene when, at a dinner, having not allowed
Helen to buy a dress she feels comfortable in, Rob remarks,
at a full table, that 'It's nice to see Helen tucking in, given
that she was worried about putting on weight'. We hear
Helen's cutlery fall to her plate. At the pub on Mother's Day,
Rob complains to David about her 'fat ankles'. Too easily,
when Rob and Helen are alone, we become acclimatised to
the misery. Scenes like this which show-case the confusion
and incredulity of David — an eminently reasonable if irritat-
ing man — are a narrative bucket of cold water. We wake

up. Elsewhere, Rob remarks constantly on Helen's 'blooming' (somehow, Rob's voice, instantly conjuring 'and gone to seed'). Rob tells Helen's mother, as if it's an endearing story, how he bought her a dress but 'she's gone up more than one dress size' (*The* Archers, 29 December 2016.). He humiliates Helen in every sense of the word, offering, or rather threatening, to cut up her food in front of Henry. When Helen goes to the bathroom to throw up, Rob sends Henry after — we hear Henry say, sounding remarkably Rob-like, 'You've been ages. We were worried about you.' Henry, a child giggling about the surprise concocted by him and 'Daddy', can have no concept of how cruel it is to order, not a chamomile tea, as Helen guesses, or a small scoop of ice-cream, but sticky toffee pudding with extra custard (*The Archers*, 31 January 2016).

Of course, we don't know whether Helen is gaining a normal amount of pregnancy weight or not. But when Kirsty sees Helen for the first time in months and says that, despite being pregnant, Helen is pale and 'seems to have lost weight', it comes as a surprise (*The Archers*, 10 January 2016). In listening to Rob, we have been complicit in eclipsing Helen's reality. When Rob tells Helen to eat he is also saying *Ignore what you think and feel, ignore your appetite — ignore your body and acknowledge mine.* ('He didn't take no for an answer,' is what both Jess and Helen say when testifying about their rape (*The Archers*, 6 September 2017; 8 September 2017). Rob's constant gaslighting severs the connection between Helen's instincts and thoughts about what things mean, and what they mean now, because he says so.

In weaponising cooking and eating as a mode of control, Rob's approach goads Helen back towards anorexia. He does not make her salads. In insisting that she eat aggressively rich food, Rob locks Helen into situations in which either *Yes* or *No* will be taken as provocation, and like Melville's

Bartleby, Helen can only say that she *prefers not to*.
Sometimes, Helen's suppressed will manifests itself in narrative twists, in which what Helen wants is brought about, though we know she is not acting deliberately, if at all. Rob and his mother, Ursula, gang up. Ursula makes bread-and-dripping by slicing bread, pouring lard over it, and putting it in the oven. Helen asks whether quite that much dripping is necessary, pointing out that olive oil would be healthier. Despite Helen's protestations, Ursula complains to Rob, and Helen backpedals. Still, when Ursula pops to the shops, entrusting the dish to Helen, and it burns, by default, Helen is culpable. Later, Ursula hisses, 'This is what they do' — they, in this case meaning anorexics. Even though this scene remained focused on Helen, and we know that she didn't ruin the dish, because Rob and Ursula are always the majority, and Helen increasingly uncertain — ghostly — we experience the flicker of doubt.

After the first time Helen collapses, Rob says, 'You haven't been eating properly, have you'. Helen replies that she's not been hungry. Rob insists, 'That's just a story you've been telling yourself', force-feeding her his own paranoid narrative (*The Archers*, 27 January 2016). It is not just outward subservience Rob wants, but narrative control. Helen's repeated phrase after stabbing Rob *He made me choose* is often interpreted as the choice between Rob and Henry. It was also a choice between Rob's reality and her own (one negates the other). In refusing to eat, Helen finds a way to refuse Rob's appetite — in denying her need for nourishment she finds a way to defy his desire for satisfaction. Not eating can be a form of passive resistance. A quiet revolution against the too-much of someone else's body. Helen is first sick after Tom encourages her to eat his black pudding (made of blood); the Doctor diagnoses Helen as anemic (not enough iron in the blood); it is only by stabbing Rob in the stomach and rupturing his bowel that Helen escapes. Even then, her control over her body is questioned, as the unflappable PC Burns remarks, 'Did you know Helen was anorexic?' as if that somehow puts her innocence in question (*The Archers*, 3 April 2016).

Bodies, as sites of giving and taking, provide the setting for fraught emotional scenes even when we cannot see them. In *The Archers,* transgression of boundaries is perhaps more acute because we are imaginatively responsible for our experience — we are implicated in the making up. Part of our shock was also relief — in finally knowing what was at the centre of the menace in his voice, the constant threat. At the trial, when Helen finally breaks down, crying, telling of her repeated rape 'I told myself it should be okay, that he was my husband, but it wasn't okay, was it?', she takes back both the story and her life, using Rob's narrative weapon of choice; in asking a question which doesn't need an answer she insists on its reality.

ACKNOWLEDGEMENTS

My thanks to Cara Courage and Nicola Headlam for creating Academic Archers; for their intellectual curiosity and generosity with it, and to Nicola, in particular, for her observation about the different experiences of hearing direct and indirect speech. Also, to Joanna Dobson for her encouragement and proofreader's eye.

REFERENCES

Brillat-Savarin, J. (2012). *Physiology of Taste* (1st ed.). New York, NY: Dover Publications.

Davies, K. *Six diamond decades — The 1950s* (2010). Retrieved from http://www.bbc.co.uk/blogs/thearchers/2010/11/six_diamond_decades_-_the_1950.html

Donovan, P. (1991). *The radio companion* (1st ed.). London: Grafton.

All episodes *The Archers,* BBC Radio 4, February 2011–May 2017

The Archers, BBC Radio 4, August 6, 2014

The Archers, BBC Radio 4, January 5, 2016

The Archers, BBC Radio 4, January 10, 2016

The Archers, BBC Radio 4, January 27, 2016

The Archers, BBC Radio 4, January 27, 2016

The Archers, BBC Radio 4, January 31, 2016

The Archers, BBC Radio 4, April 3, 2016

*The Archer*s, BBC Radio 4, September 6, 2016

The Archers, BBC Radio 4, September 8, 2016

The Archers, BBC Radio 4, December 29, 2016

The Archers, BBC Radio 4, January 17, 2017

PEER REVIEW, BY JENNIFER ALDRIDGE, HOME FARM, AMBRIDGE, BORSETSHIRE

Well, *really* — some people. This essay makes me sound so cunning…and really, all I do is keep my family happy and everyone pitches in when they have the time. You don't see me out on a tractor and I don't expect Brian and Adam in the kitchen — and that's an end to it. And Phoebe made some lovely scones the other day.

Though it is interesting, isn't it, what people like to eat and what that means. I like the idea of that. I see myself as a nice, frothy, lemon meringue. With Italian coffee, *espresso*, so rejuvenating. Or if I'm being wicked, a glass of champagne.

It was nice to see cooking for once recognised as the source of female empowerment and joy it can be. Nobody ever realises quite how hard I work. Alice gave me *Bridget Jones's Diary* for Christmas one year and when Mrs Jones — that's Bridget's mother — can't do the taxes and a tax-man belittles her she says, 'Listen, can *you* make a brioche?' I thought that was rather wonderful. We can't all be suffragettes, or go to Oxford and we don't all want to go tramping about with farm machinery, but I have encouraged all of my daughters to follow their paths — Look at Kate! Spiritual Home is flourishing, and it's my job to keep the home fires burning. And, for the record, Brian is nothing like that *horrid man*. Though, of course, I would never use shop-bought custard.

CHAPTER TWENTY-ONE

THE CASE OF HELEN AND ROB: AN EVALUATION OF THE NEW COERCIVE CONTROL OFFENCE AND ITS PORTRAYAL IN *THE ARCHERS*

Elizabeth R. A. Campion

ABSTRACT

Despite the Helen and Rob storyline initially being billed as showcasing the new offence introduced by Section 76 of the Serious Crime Act 2015, it concluded with only minimal discussion of the offence. This section briefly explores some of the flaws in the coercive control offence and its portrayal in The Archers *from a legal and criminological perspective.*

Keywords: Coercive control; domestic violence; *The Archers*

Amongst the suspense and drama of Helen Archer's trial and the events which followed, the fact that the storyline was originally 'sold' by the then editor, Sean O'Connor, as showcasing the new offence of coercive and controlling behaviour in an intimate relationship ('the coercive control offence') might have been forgotten. While no prosecution for the new offence, which was introduced in Section 76 of the Serious Crime Act 2015 and came into force on 29 December 2015, was ever brought against Rob Titchener, his storyline highlighted the insidious and pernicious effects of psychological abuse on victims and inspired a listener to begin a fundraising campaign (for 'real-life Helens') which raised nearly £175,000 for Refuge. But Rob was not alone in evading prosecution; in his first eight months in force only 62 prosecutions for coercive and controlling behaviour, while over a million incidents of domestic violence were recorded by the police during the year ending March 2016 alone. If Rob and those like him really are 'the worst kind of abuser', the coercive control offence as enacted is a flawed way of dealing with them.

Under Section 76, an offence is committed where person A repeatedly or continuously engages in behaviour towards person B that is controlling or coercive, at a time when A and B are personally connected, the behaviour has a serious effect on B and A knows or ought to know that the behaviour will have a serious effect on B. A and B are personally connected where they are in an intimate personal relationship or are family members living together, and behaviour has a 'serious effect' when it causes B to fear on at least two occasions that violence will be used against them, or causes B serious alarm or distress that substantially affects their day-to-day life (s76 Serious Crime Act 2015, subsections (1)-(3)). As the statutory guidance puts it, the coercive control offence supposedly 'closes a gap in the law' and 'sends a clear message that this form of domestic abuse can constitute a serious offence [...] and will provide better protection to victims experiencing repeated or continuous abuse.'

This is problematic in two ways. First, it will be very difficult to prove the behaviour covered by the offence, which criminalises patterns of individual incidences of insidious and manipulative behaviour which, looked at in isolation, may seem innocuous. The burden of showing that they are not will, in practice, come to rest on the victim who, having by definition been subject to a psychological war of attrition, is unlikely to be confident in their own recollection and perception of the abuse. This is likely to make it very difficult to obtain convictions even where victims are willing to go to the police (and receive a kinder reception than Helen did).

Helen had the unique advantage of having had each stage of her relationship, the gradual escalation of Rob's abuse and her progressive deterioration, broadcast to listeners; she had a loyal best friend prepared to defend her to the hilt and, apparently, a near-universally sympathetic and credulous audience both inside and outside Ambridge. But without the extreme levels of surveillance the village residents apparently tolerate without complaint on a daily basis and the extremely convincing evidence thereby produced, how can those 'real-life Helens' be expected to convince those around them and how exactly someone might have come to control, trap and psychologically devastate them?

Even if the offence can be proved and offenders convicted, 'better protection' is not achieved by locking people up after the fact, but by preventing damage in the first place through deterrence. In order effectively to deter coercive and controlling behaviour, the law must make it possible for individuals to tell criminal from non-criminal behaviour and regulate their behaviour accordingly. Section 76 effectively defines controlling and coercive behaviour by reference to its effect on the victim, which means that whether or not someone has behaved abusively will depend on how the object of the behaviour reacts to it. Not only does this ignore the collateral damage inflicted on witnesses to domestic abuse, particularly children, the severity of the crime will depend on how resilient the victim was to start with. In addition, the fact that the more effectively someone has been intimidated or gaslighted the less likely they are to come forward means the worst offenders will be least often denounced.

The effect of coercive and controlling behaviour is context dependent. As Johnson and Leone (2005) put it, 'even the nonviolent control tactics take on a violent meaning that they would not have in the absence of their connection with violence'. Many of the incidents in Rob and Helen's relationship would be unremarkable in a different setting: Rob ordering a pudding for Helen while out at a restaurant and his phone call to the school after she took Henry on an impromptu outing to the Blackberry Line would not have looked out of place in a healthy and loving marriage. Most men, in turn, can usually change their pasta bake preferences without risking perforation.

In real borderline cases it is almost impossible reliably to differentiate abusive and non-abusive conduct in advance. For example, marital rape is patently abuse, but even O'Connor refused definitively to class Rob's behaviour as sexual coercion, shortly after listeners had heard what we now know to have been one of several marital rapes perpetrated by him. Rob's behaviour also encompassed assault, harassment and attempted kidnap, a reflection of early convictions under Section 76 in which coercive control has occurred alongside crimes which carry a much higher maximum sentence than the five years under Section 76(11).

Helen's ultimate decision not to make a complaint of coercive control and the corresponding editorial decision to focus on Helen's trial for attempted murder rather than Rob's for domestic abuse, perhaps reflect the real-life flaws and potentially the impact of Section 76 of the Serious Crime Act 2015. Throughout the storyline, the existence of the offence first failed to keep Helen, Henry and Jack safe from Rob and ultimately did not allow him to be brought to justice, hindering him in repeating the cycle with unsuspecting natives of Minnesota. It would be optimistic to expect it to be any more useful for all the 'real-life Helens' out there.

REFERENCE

Johnson, M. P., & Leone, J. M. (2005). The differential effects of intimate terrorism and situational couple violence: Findings from the National Violence Against Women Survey. *Journal of Family Issues*, *26*, 322–349.

CHAPTER TWENTY-TWO

BLOOD PATTERN ANALYSIS IN BLOSSOM HILL COTTAGE

Anna-Marie O'Connor

ABSTRACT

The popularity of television shows such as CSI:(insert appropriate city here) makes everyone think they are somehow a forensic expert. The portrayal of this kind of subject on radio is of course much more complicated as each observer has an image in their own head rather than in front of their eyes. This chapter seeks to inform The Archers *listeners and other interested parties about the Blossom Hill Cottage crime scene examination — what they might expect to have seen from an evidential perspective and how the findings may inform the court as to what really occurred that fateful night. The chapter presents general information about different blood patterns that may be observed at crime scenes such as this and others, what they may (or may not) mean and a discussion about the strengths and limitations of this kind of scientific examination and interpretation. Whilst this can clearly be a serious subject, the intention is to inform and (probably) bust some televisual myths with a light-hearted edge from an* Archers *fan and fellow Tweetalonger, additionally considering online speculation about other potential evidence.*

Keywords: Blood spatter patterns; forensic; analysis; crime scene; attempted murder

On 4 April 2016 (also 3rd April if you were listening on the radio) the complainant Robert Titchener was stabbed by the defendant, when his wife Helen Titchener was in the kitchen of their home at Blossom Hill Cottage, Ambridge, Borsetshire (*The Archers*, 2016a). This chapter proposes to investigate the examination of the premises as a crime scene and consideration of the bloodstain patterns which may be expected at this and other such scenes where blood is shed. A word of warning! By its very nature, this chapter contains descriptions of blood, blood patterns, crime scene information and consideration of injuries. Proceed at your peril and in this knowledge!

In this case, the first responding officer was PC Harrison Burns. His role would have been to establish the early facts of the unfolding events, check the state of all concerned and call upon the assistance of emergency services as required (Weston, 2004, p. 28). His first concern should be for public safety whilst making every effort to preserve and secure the scene for potential examination by specialist colleagues.

It is likely that a scenes of crime officer (SOCO) or, as they are now more commonly referred to, a crime scene examiner (CSE) or crime scene investigator (CSI) would be deployed to a scene such as this, particularly when blood has been shed in an alleged assault case. The role of each of these individuals is to examine the crime scene for any visual signs of assault, to document and record what they see and to recover any relevant items as exhibits which may become useful or of interest as the investigation of the case progresses (Weston, 2004, p. 24). Their role is critical in that their initial examination and their recorded notes are relied upon throughout the case as an accurate record of how the scene appeared immediately after any alleged offence. The CSI role, however, is distinct from that of the forensic scientist, although they are seemingly commonly considered interchangeable in popular culture and in the media. Typically CSIs are civilian employees of the police service and are based at police locations throughout England and Wales (Weston, 2004, p. 24). They work in shift patterns to ensure there is scene examination cover at all times of the day and night, every day of the year. The forensic scientist is typically based at a laboratory and, whilst they provide scene attendance cover on a rota basis, they are called to examine crime scenes much less frequently than popular television drama would have you believe. In the United Kingdom, forensic science provision has been delivered by private companies since the closure of the Forensic Science Service in 2012 (House of Lords, 2010).

Serious cases such as attempted murder are allocated to a Senior Investigating Officer (SIO) whose role is to manage the progression of the case from crime scene to court, including appointing relevant expertise to expedite specific relevant roles throughout (Cook, 2016). They would make an assessment of any exhibits recovered from the crime scene and develop a forensic strategy, often in conjunction with

experienced CSEs and, when necessary with the forensic
scientist at the laboratory. They will also make the decision
regarding whether a specialist forensic scientist needs to be
called to attend the crime scene to undertake any specialist
examination for blood.

The process of examination for blood is broadly similar
whether at the crime scene or examining items recovered
from it at the laboratory. First, each begins with a visual
examination to assess whether there any stains present which
bear the typical characteristics of blood. Any suspected blood
stains are tested using a chemical presumptive test, often the
Kastle-Meyer test (Glaister, 1926) which provides a simple
colour change reaction in the presence of a particular chemical. Several varied types of this test are commercially available and those deployed either in the laboratory or at the
crime scene are a matter of preference for each organisation
and can be dependent on the test sensitivity required (Tobe,
Watson, & Nic Daéid, 2007).

BLOODSTAIN PATTERNS

For ease of narrative, this section is based on the knowledge
and professional training of the author however, scientific
documentation of blood patterns and their analyses can be
found in various core texts such as those included but not
limited to those in the reference section (Emes & Price, 2004;
James & Eckert, 1999; Wonder, 2001).

The patterns blood forms when it is shed fit broadly into
two groups — impact spatter and non-spatter groups. Note
the use of the word spatter and not splatter! Impact spatter
patterns are those which are formed when an item, commonly but not always a weapon, impacts into a source of wet
blood causing the blood to disperse. The spattered blood

travels until it either encounters a surface to land on or falls onto one under gravity. Termed impact spatter, these stains form characteristic patterns which may assist the interpretation of a forensic scientist who may be required to consider whether such patterns have arisen as the result of a particular, given set of events. When a source of wet blood is disturbed by an impact, it breaks up into smaller droplets which are then dispersed along the path of least resistance, away from the point of impact and generally in a radial pattern. The droplets can be a range of sizes, associated with their volumes which in turn is based on the amount of blood available for dispersion and on the force of the impact. Their final appearance on landing can be affected by a number of factors. For example, blood drops of the same volume may have a different appearance if they land on a porous surface such as a textile fabric versus a non-porous surface such as a floor tile. Similarly, if blood drips from an item wet with blood, the appearance of the resulting stain will be affected both by the angle at which the blood is travelling as it moves and/or the angle of the surface it lands on. Blood which drips or is projected onto a surface perpendicular to it will form round drops, which will clearly be proportional in size to the volume of blood available in the droplet to make the stain. When such droplets land on angled surface or are themselves travelling at an angle to their point of impact, they form elongated stains which narrow, widen and then narrow again along their longitudinal length. Sometimes, the volume of blood in these droplets is sufficient to cause an additional droplet to form and 'bounce' out of the original stain depositing a characteristic overall stain with the appearance of an exclamation mark. This shape and the occasional additional spot can indicate the direction of travel of such stains. Forensic scientists can use the measurement of the component parts of a complex impact spatter pattern of these stains to estimate their point of origin and this can assist in evaluating where the point of impact was when the blood was dispersed. These elongated stains can also be deposited in linear patterns as they are flung from the item which has impacted into the source of wet blood. These lines of stains can help to indicate the position the person holding the item was in and, in some cases, the minimum amount of times it was swung — all very useful in the investigation of an assault.

The description of blood so far has considered only what it looks like when it leaves the weapon and lands on another surface but it can also be important to consider the appearance of the blood remaining on the weapon. The swinging action itself will cause any remaining, still wet blood to change direction and can indicate if the weapon made further impacts after it became wet with blood. Stains such as these show very characteristic patterns, obvious to the trained eye.

Particular injuries can also produce distinctive blood patterns, the most distinctive being arterial blood spatters. These patterns, as its name suggests, result from damage to an artery. As the heart continues to pump, blood is forced at high velocity through the damaged artery leaving sprays of blood at pulse intervals on vertical surfaces — particularly if the injured person remains in a standing position. Blood from a wound such as this also produces small, regularly sized blood spots — termed arterial rain — which are commonly seen associated with arterial spatter in its characteristic wave pattern.

SCENE EXAMINATION AT BLOSSOM HILL COTTAGE

Returning again to the scene of the crime in Ambridge to consider what an attending scene of crime officer might have encountered when called to attend Blossom Hill Cottage. The blood stain patterns discussed previously, whilst interesting and perhaps firmly ensconced in the mind of the casual television drama viewer, have concentrated on those formed by impact into wet blood. It is important for any specialist forensic scientist called to interpret a scene of crime to keep an open mind and to consider what they might expect given a proposed set of circumstances. They should be guided by a non-finite number of questions:

- what might be expected given the alleged circumstances?

- what factors may affect these expectations?

- what weapons (if any) were used?

- what were the injuries sustained?

- what is the time since the injuries were sustained?

- what were the activities before and after bloodshed?

It should be clear that a stabbing is not typically an impact into wet blood and subsequently, the blood patterns described thus far are arguably less likely to be seen at a stabbing scene unless there were further activities after any blood was shed. The attending forensic practitioners would likely be considering the possible presence of non-spatter stains. These stains tend to be less dynamic in their formation than the spatter patterns previously described and are more commonly a function of something wet with blood making some direct contact with another surface. Such contact stains often have distinctive appearances due to the nature of their transfer. A simple visual reference would be a hand print or footwear mark in blood so formed by their placement onto an unstained surface after collecting blood either directly or indirectly from a bleeding wound. Hair which has become wet with blood leaves distinctive patterns when in contact with unstained surfaces and it can also produce blood spatter as droplets are flung from it upon movement. Blood naturally thickens when it leaves the body and this clotting process can also create distinctive stains. Similarly, blood can become mixed with other media creating what are termed physiologically altered blood stains (PABs). It would be common to see blood mixed with saliva for example and subsequent stains may appear dilute when deposited.

What do we know then about the crime scene at Blossom Hill Cottage? Listeners to *The Archers* were privileged in a way that real scene examiners are not in that they heard the whole series of events and saw them played out in their own heads. A real CSI or attending forensic scientist would consider in advance what they may expect to see at the scene of a multiple stabbing. They would likely know the extent of the injuries and at least an estimate of the number of wounds. They would commonly have a good idea of the time the stabbing occurred and would be updated on the condition of the complainant, as a change in their condition may have an impact on the type of case being investigated.

Rob Titchener was stabbed more than once by Helen (*The Archers*, 2016a). He was described as having defence wounds and we know that his bowel was punctured as he was forced to wear a stoma for some weeks after his initial surgery (*The Archers*, 2016c). If the stabs were sufficient to puncture his skin and cause bleeding, it should be considered where this blood may be found. If he was fully clothed and then started to bleed quite quickly after he was stabbed then the blood would first be absorbed by any clothing he was wearing. As explained, where it went next would depend on a number of factors, for example whether the first wound incapacitated him preventing his movement or whether he continued to bleed with blood seeping out through his clothing. Some of the dialogue indicated that Helen had blood on her clothing and that Rob was attended to by Kirsty Miller shortly after the attack so blood may have transferred to her clothing too (*The Archers*, 2016b). Television drama often suggests that a crime scene remains intact awaiting the arrival of forensic examination teams however, in reality, often the first people to attend may be paramedic staff whose primary focus is to preserve life. Whilst they have some understanding and responsibility to consider they are attending a potential crime scene it is unlikely to be their main focus when attending to someone with life threatening injuries. Forensic practitioners may then have to consider the possibility that the scene they are examining does not look as it did in the immediate aftermath of the events leading to the blood loss injuries. Helen's angst-ridden exclamation indicated that the homemade custard was spilled offering the real possibility of, arguably, rather unusual PABs!

It is the view of the author that the Blossom Hill Cottage crime scene would have been attended by a CSE but it is unlikely that a laboratory-based forensic scientist would have been called out to attend. From what was heard, Rob Titchener's movements were limited after he was first stabbed and so there would be a low expectation of complex impact spatter blood patterns requiring specialist examination. If any forensic evidence was gathered, it did not form a large part of the trial broadcast as it played out in September 2016 (*The Archers*, 2016d). Helen Titchener eventually gave an account of her actions in so far as she could remember. Rob's testimony was more focussed on Helen's intent and the denial of his controlling behaviour rather than disputing her account of the actions which led to his injuries — at least not those which could have been countered by any physical evidence.

It is important to note that, contrary to common portrayal on screen, it is not the job of the forensic scientist to solve the crime! Their role is to examine the evidence and consider it in the light of propositions posited by the prosecution and defence. These propositions are typically formed by the allegation and witness accounts and the scientific interpretation is supported by evaluation of relevant data and professional expertise. The forensic scientist should always consider the likelihood of the evidence given the propositions and not the likelihood of the propositions given the evidence, as the latter is a matter for the jury (Cook, Evett, Jackson, Jones, & Lambert, 1998; Evett, 1995).

OTHER EVIDENCE

Lastly, a few words to address the amateur sleuthing apparent on some social media sites! Many comments were seen regarding the examination of the knife for supporting evidence. Would the knife used to stab Rob Titchener bear Helen's fingerprints or DNA? Would it bear Rob's blood on its blade? The chance of finding blood on the blade depends on a number of factors. Contrary to popular belief, a sharp knife may actually appear to be quite clean after a stabbing event and may have very little if any blood present, particularly if only used fleetingly. This assault occurred in the Titchener marital home so the presence of Helen's fingerprints and/or her DNA might be entirely expected and therefore offer little in the way of useful evidence. The decisions to make these examinations lie entirely with the police investigation team who will consider what they need evidentially to build their case for consideration by the Crown Prosecution Service (Cook, 2016). Their requirements may change throughout the progression of the investigation and must be balanced by time and, increasingly, budget. Although, if social media is anything to go by, Borsetshire Police are more concerned with their tea consumption and doughnut quota than the investigation of missing bunting, let alone attempted murder!

ACKNOWLEDGEMENTS

The author would like to acknowledge the in-house Blood Pattern Analysis training she received when employed by the London Laboratory of the Forensic Science Service.

REFERENCES

Cook, R. [Roger], Evett, I. W., Jackson, G., Jones, P. J., & Lambert, J. (1998). A model for case assessment and interpretation. *Science & Justice, 38*(3), 151–156.

Cook, T. [Tony]. (2016). *Blackstone's senior investigating officer's handbook*. Oxford: Oxford University Press.

Emes, A., & Price, C. (2004). Blood pattern analysis. In P. C. White (Ed.), *Crime scene to court, the essentials of forensic science* (2nd ed., pp. 115–141). Cambridge: RSC Publishing.

Evett, I. W. (1995). Avoiding transposing the conditional. *Science and Justice, 35*, 127–131

Glaister, J. (1926). The Kastle-Meyer test for the detection of blood. *British Medical Journal*, 10 April 1926; 650–652. Retrieved from www.bmj.com/content/bmj/1/3406/650.full. pdf. Accessed on May 18, 2017.

House of Lords Written ministerial statement on forensic science read by Baroness Neville-Jones. (2010, 14 December). Retrieved from https://www.gov.uk/government/speeches/ forensic-science. Accessed on May 18, 2017.

James, S. H., & Eckert, W. G. (1999). *Interpretation of bloodstain evidence at crime scenes* (2nd ed.). Boca Raton, FL: CRC Press.

The Archers. (2016a). [radio]. BBC Radio 4, 3 April, 19:00.

The Archers. (2016b). [radio]. BBC Radio 4, 4 April, 19:00.

The Archers. (2016c). [radio]. BBC Radio 4, 5 April, 19:00.

The Archers. (2016d). [radio]. BBC Radio 4, 11 April, 10:00.

Tobe, S. S., Watson, N., & Nic Daéid, N. (2007). Evaluation of six presumptive tests for blood, their specificity, sensitivity, and effect on high molecular-weight DNA. *Journal of Forensic Sciences*, *52*, 102−109.

Weston, N. T. (2004). The crime scene. In P. C. White (Ed.), *Crime scene to court, The essentials of forensic science* (2nd ed., pp. 21−55). Cambridge: RSC Publishing.

Wonder, A. Y. (2001). *Blood dynamics*. London: Academic Press.

PEER REVIEW BY PC HARRISON BURNS, BORSETSHIRE POLICE, AMBRIDGE

As I'm only a Police Constable, I haven't yet had much in the way of first-hand forensic training so this has been a bit of an eye-opener for me. Still reeling from the shock of the missing bunting and arresting my Fallon's Dad, an attempted murder on my patch was almost more than I could cope with. It was important to be methodical so I think I did a good job being first on the scene, taking down particulars and trying to be authoritative and the voice of calm in the ensuing chaos. It were a right mess in there, I don't mind telling you. And fairly pungent too! I think Helen must have been baking as I could smell tuna and possibly fruit pie but there was custard everywhere! But not much blood, so now I understand why. It wasn't much fun having to give up my handcuffs for Helen to be taken away, I'll not forget that in a hurry. Can't say I was expecting this much excitement in a sleepy village compared with up North where I'm from! I was a bit apprehensive about what I might find when I went inside Blossom Hill Cottage but now, well, I'm glad I don't have to put up with that insufferable Rob Titchener on my cricket team if I'm honest. Just don't tell Sergeant Madeley I said that, alright?!

CHAPTER TWENTY-THREE

SOUNDTRACK TO A STABBING: WHAT ROB'S CHOICE OF MUSIC OVER DINNER TELLS US ABOUT WHY HE ENDED UP SPILLING THE CUSTARD

Emily Baker and Freya Jarman

ABSTRACT

In this chapter, we argue that the four songs we hear on 3rd April 2016 serve as both background music and a means of revealing the inner world of Helen and Rob.

Keywords: Background music; underscoring; intertextuality; domestic violence

As utterly iconic as *The Archers* theme music, *Barwick Green*, may be, music typically only takes us far as the 'Welcome to Ambridge' road sign; once we're in Ambridge proper, music plays far more subtle a role in *The Archers*. When background music is used, it is very often as a 'scene setting' device to locate the listener in a particular space, such as organ music in the church or wind bands at the Flower and Produce show for example. Generally speaking it is used sparingly – in any one omnibus, listeners might hear one or two moments, but rarely more, and often less. Occasionally, and with a subtle beauty, a specific track will appear in the narrative world that reveals an extrinsic layer of meaning and works as a knowing nod to the attentive listener: Neil Diamond's *Sweet Caroline* played the week Caroline Sterling revealed she had cancer (22 November 2016); Bessie Smith's *Nobody Knows You When You're Down And Out* worked as an internal roll-of-the-eyes at Shula's moaning after her sandwiches were snubbed in favour of Fallon's piri piri chicken at the cricket match (4 September 2016); Eddie's ringtone is The Wurzels' *I Am A Cider Drinker*, and so on.

When a song is played into Borsetshire it brings its own story from the off-air world. It thereby opens up intertextual meanings that extend far beyond any given song's lyrics and orchestrating a richer network of meanings that have to do with the song's history of creation, its various uses in other media forms and connotations of artist, genre and so on. Julia Kristeva's definition of intertextuality is useful in this way as she argues for texts' inherent hybridity, the continued and perpetual reorganisation of cultural fragments in that 'any text is constructed as a mosaic of quotation: any text is the absorption and transformation of another' (Kristeva, in Moi, 1986, p. 37). So, when Rob Titchener decided on the perfect music playlist for the dinner that ended with his stabbing, listeners were not just offered an unusual amount of music as a part of the sonic texture of the whole episode (only the first two and a half minutes are without music) but even had their attention drawn to it by the protagonist. In doing so, this act functioned as an invitation to interpret the music's meaning in relation to the dramatic events of the evening in the Titchener household. We suggest that the four songs we hear speak beyond the confines of Ambridge and into both 'our' world and other intertextual worlds too; they operate within the narrative world and yet come always-already saturated with multi-dimensional meaning from elsewhere. In this way, we thread a connection between lyrical expression, musical context and the resonance of the singers' biographies with those of the Titcheners.

We also explore how a cinematic world and history, touching on the conventions of the 1940s gothic film genre, is revealed through the imbrication of song, sound effect, dialogue and actor performance. This is done to enmesh the characters in sonic shadows, to reinforce the narrative of Rob's continued 'gaslighting' of Helen. Originating from Patrick Hamilton's 1938 play *Gas Light* the notion of gaslighting has become a common parlance in the twenty-first century, an era of alternative facts. Abramson defines the concept as the means by which the victims' 'reactions, perceptions, memories and/or beliefs are not just mistaken, but utterly without grounds – paradigmatically, so unfounded as to qualify as crazy' (2014, p. 2). Gaslighting is thereby noted as a gendered practice, where femininity and irrationality are seen to go hand-in-hand and therefore the 'madness' of the victim is made to seem entirely plausible (Haworth, 2014). In short, we aim to show that, within the confines of Blossom Hill Cottage, Rob uses sound and music as tools to manipulate and terrorise Helen; we argue that music sheds important light on the intricacies of their relationship as we tune in.

THE EAGLES, *LYIN' EYES*

As Rob arrives home from work, Helen ushers Kirsty away from the cottage after confiding that her plan is to leave her husband. With the stage set in the kitchen, it becomes clear that Helen is playing a dangerous game to undertake her exit strategy. She knows Rob doesn't like tuna (based on a previous, notorious event over a meal in February 2014) and yet a tuna bake is in the oven. In return, Rob is immediately wise to what appears to be Helen's testing of him and the sound of shuffling feet in the kitchen stops suddenly when she reveals the menu; we and Helen alike are similarly immediately wise to his game, as he has unwittingly declared it to 'smell delicious'. This pause in dialogue and movement underlines how this first section is essentially a complex transaction of power between the Titcheners, as each tries to gauge how much the other knows about their various deceptions.

Rob's retort is a musical one and he sets the playlist to start, deciding that The Eagles' *Lyin' Eyes* is 'perfect'. Allowing Rob to continue communicating without saying anything, the first level of meaning is that the song's refrain is a clear lyrical marker of the message he intends her to hear. But beyond this, the song adheres to all the conventions of male-centred middle-of-the-road rock; the musical codes here are all signify uncritical, specifically American, whiteness, and hegemonic masculinity. Insofar as this song speaks on behalf of Rob, it also thereby affirms the trope of the gaslighter being in play, since that trope is centered precisely on this hegemonic identity. Music magazine *Rolling Stone* called the song 'a smooth satire of LA's gold-digger culture' (Dolan et al., 2016); we would argue that the lyrics are misogynistic for their essentialist take on 'the way women are'. The song speaks for Rob's vociferous disdain for women, the notion that it is apparently innate for men to be used for financial gain. He positions himself as the hapless victim, a classic symptom of the logic of the narcissistic personality disorder with which he is later diagnosed (McCullough, Emmons, Kilpatrick, & Mooney, 2003). To Rob's mind at least, this legitimises his maltreatment of Helen and the choice of song thereby signifies not only a subject-position to which Helen finds herself subservient but also a time to which she has no direct connection. Released in 1975, it is from 'before her time', a musical texture which is synonymous with the post-hippy, ego-driven commercialism of country rock (Gittins, 2008; Hoskyns, 2006). Rob, meanwhile, has easier access to this subject-position (further enhanced by his having lived in North America for some time) and he thereby wields this power to his own end in selecting the song.

Before long, however, the balance of power becomes shaky as Rob angrily discovers Helen's escape bag on their bed. Helen tries to calm the situation by pretending it is her hospital bag. Rob is momentarily tripped up, but the song persists in the background, reminding the listener of the manipulation. The melody covers over the tension here in a way that the conversation about the tuna bake did not enjoy: that earlier moment was all the more awkward for the lack of music. In this sense, the musical aesthetic of *Lyin' Eyes* adheres to the conventions of Muzak® in that it is bland and yet designed to manipulate mood by sonically filling physical spaces (Groom, 1996; Lanza, 2003). This paradox, of music being consigned to the background to undertake highly emotional work in its general 'unheardness', is explored in the context of film music by Claudia Gorbman who writes that 'most feature films relegate music to the viewer's sensory background, that area least susceptible to rigorous judgment and most susceptible to affective manipulation' (1987, p. 12).

Whilst a comparison of the roles of music in radio drama and in audiovisual media like film or television is too complex to investigate here, such film-music scholarship models are useful in trying to unpick what is being foregrounded in Blossom Hill Cottage, and the effects that foregrounding generates. During this song, Rob's 'background muzak' is occasionally disrupted by Glen Frey's nasal-sounding lead vocal as it pokes out from the slickly produced soundworld of the song and reaches out to awaken both the listener and Rob from the soporific effects of Muzak® as a reminder of Helen's game playing. When Helen asks Rob if he will still have the shower he had gone for earlier on, his refusal, in a renewed tone of assertion, coincides with an equally assertive musical signal of a move from verse to chorus. It is as if he realises his attention has been cleverly drawn elsewhere but he is awake to what he perceives as Helen's manipulation of him. With the introduction of the chorus, the lush vocal harmonies become more prominent, bringing into audible space an iconic stamp of 70s rock, which serves, along with Rob's change in vocal timbre, to frame his regaining of power as he demands, 'Let's have supper now'.

AMY WINEHOUSE, *YOU KNOW I'M NO GOOD*

A fade out signifies a scene change and the passage of time, and we rejoin the couple over dinner. The layering of sound and the order by which sound is layered in this section speaks of a more claustrophobic and tangled atmosphere. In the first place we hear Amy Winehouse sing about the 'rolled up sleeves and skull t-shirt' of her lover, followed by a clatter of cutlery which gives way to Rob's grossly embodied chomping and breathing as he eats. He chides Helen, through full mouth, his panoptic gaze (Foucault, 1977 [1995]) ostensibly working on behalf of her worried parents; his policing operating as a merciless reminder of the public and private shame her anorexia brought to the family.

The space, of course, is its own layer of meaning, in that it constitutes the tension between the two – and Rob dominates the aural space by being the only person to speak for 30 seconds. *You Know I'm No Good* is an inspired choice to bolster the drama for three key reasons. Firstly, a characteristic of Winehouse's lyrical style is the way she deftly weaves domestic signifiers into her songs. Writing in *The Guardian*, Barton writes that this is a song that 'start[s] off like a Degas painting, naked and intimate and warmly erotic, but swiftly dissemble[s] into something sad and messy and ruined' (2011). Indeed, in terms of lyrics, this song offers some cunning clues as to the present and future of the unhappy couple: references to 'crying on the kitchen floor', 'guts churning' and, incredibly, who 'truly stuck the knife in first' can be read retrospectively as a darkly humorous foreshadowing of the climactic events. Secondly, the timing of the song gives further insight into Rob's psychological state with regards to the theme of duplicity that was introduced in and through *Lyin' Eyes*. Winehouse's song has a confessional tone, and Rob wields this over dinner to tease out an admission of game playing from Helen; the song's pronoun-heavy title functions as a means of reflecting the back and forth of power between the two. In this way, the 'voice' of the song is not clearly attached to either Titchener and the question of which one knows the other is 'no good' therefore looms large over the scene. Certainly, the scene is musically marked by the ratcheting up of Rob's manipulation of Helen, as his light voice weaves in and out of Winehouse's music in rhythm and pitch.

The third element that makes this song ideal for the drama is how Winehouse's well-documented, tabloid-fodder troubles were lurking somewhere in the mind of scriptwriter Tim

Stimpson as he went about choosing songs that would speak on behalf of Helen's inner voice. In an email exchange, Stimpson notes how an awareness of biography, lyric and melody were all used to sonically enmesh Helen:

> *I think I was keen to have female singers. I suppose I wanted the songs to be on Helen's side — for the lyrics to speak to her and not to support Rob. Paradoxically I also wanted their melodic quality to contrast with the appalling situation Helen found herself in and to play into the creation of [a] cosy domestic prison...*

(personal communication, 6 February, 2017)

The horror of a 'cosy prison' resonates with the kind of films Haworth explores in her examination of 1940s female gothic pictures. These psychological and creepy 'gaslight melodramas' (Haworth, 2014) lean on expressionistic techniques of film noir, where moody lighting smokily ensnares the heroine while their oppressors (usually a partner or spouse) are characterised as damaged antiheroes. Haworth argues that these films are symptomatic and reflective of America at the time, where traditional roles were troubled by mass conscription. She writes that 'the intimidating houses where the heroine's persecution frequently takes place function as a kind of prison, and have been linked with anxieties about the societal demands and expectations placed upon women in occupying domestic and professional roles in the years around World War II' (2014). But of course in Ambridge, Helen's cell is an aural construction in the same way that Winehouse's dark love songs are the soulful expressions of a young woman trapped by private addictions that included her manipulative relationship with her husband. The sonic shadows that represent Helen's remaining insecurities can be heard as Winehouse sings about being 'no good', or being the 'trouble' that Rob tells her that she was when she was anorexic. As Rob forces Helen to own up to playing a game with the tuna bake, a serendipitously timed drum fill stutters in time with Helen's defence of her sanity. But the revelation (as much as to herself as to him) that 'This started long before I was pregnant' proves too much, and she is soon left silent in the face of Rob's challenge.

In the end, Helen makes another attempt at resistance, playing what she believes to be the trump card of having met with Rob's ex-wife, Jess. The middle eight of the song plays here. It is devoid of lyrics and poised to land anywhere by virtue of its lack of clear harmonic direction, just as the power subtly and uncertainly shifts between the Titcheners. Sure enough, although Rob is momentarily blindsided, Helen's revelation that '[Jess] said the best thing she's ever done is to get away from [Rob]' pushes him too far, and much of the rest of Winehouse's song is obscured beneath the volume of his anger.

CORINNE BAILEY RAE, *IS THIS LOVE?*

As Winehouse's heavily processed voice fades away, a ghostly 'no good' repeats through vocal delays and the resounding effects of Rob's long-term psychological abuse are felt in a momentary gap between Winehouse and Bailey Rae's musical offerings. After so many minutes of continuous music, the quiet between the tracks is itself noticeable, and Stimpson confirms that the timing of silence can be carefully controlled and 'definitely used to underscore moments of drama' (personal communication, 6 February 2017), since music is added after the dialogue is recorded. When music does return to Blossom Hill, it does so with a darkly dramatic power, underlining a change in Rob's tone from the angry verbal abuse only moments before to a quiet intimacy. Staccato piano chords stab the beat of the song with a lazy groove and capture the listener's attention, which is already heightened due to the high drama, the change of vocal timbre and the preceding silence. Entering split seconds before Rob asks 'Don't I make you feel special?', the music and dialogue work together here in ways akin to the spoken sections of doo-wop and rock 'n' roll love songs: The Ink Spots' *Do I Worry?* (1941) is an early example; Elvis Presley's *Are You Lonesome Tonight?* (1960) is particularly famous; and the latter was successfully parodied by Mud in *Lonely This Christmas* (1974), confirming the device as a musical trope that signifies heartfelt romantic feeling and the potential for male emotional intimacy. At this moment, listening to the scene is no longer a case of eavesdropping from a distance, but being brought into an almost physical relationship with the scene as the manipulation we understand from the dialogue fuses with the terror we feel from the acting and production.

This is the kind of listening that Coulthard calls 'haptic aurality', an experience of sound as a fully embodied sense — 'in the tactile, not rationally comprehensible way' (2012, p. 19) — rather than as a simple stimulus to the ears, separable from all other sensual experience. For Coulthard, talking about music in film, silence is a particularly useful tool in the production of this haptic, bodily listening, where the viewer (or, in our case, listener) is brought into a fully embodied relationship with the aural object. Specifically, it is not really silence as such, but the impression thereof, since cinematic silence is, she writes, 'rarely total and almost always relative and complexly layered' (p. 18). Even more relevant to this moment in Blossom Hill is Coulthard's further explanation that a haptic listening can easily be underpinned by a lack of music in a film, and by 'the attention to sounds associated with the body (breath, footsteps, clothing, skin) – sounds we hear in part because [...] they are not covered by music or voice' (p. 20). Between the end of *You Know I'm No Good* and the beginning of *Is This Love?* the musical silence pricks up our ears. And, as a byproduct of that silence, we are aurally focused then not only on the dialogue between Rob and Helen but also on their breathing in particular—her sobs, and his panting as he recovers from his rage. The terror of this moment for the listener, then, is the intense experience of proximity to, and engagement with, the unfolding drama. As the piano chords enter, our skin crawls with the sound of Rob's manipulation, twisting the mood in order to lay the blame for Helen's dissatisfaction at her own feet. The chorus of backing singers neatly coinciding with Helen's subservient 'Yes' only underlines the extent to which she is one of many victims of this complex abuse, and troubles the listener's sense of identification with abuser or abused.

Helen's stifled sobs serve as an indicator to him that she has once again yielded to his wants. And yet, as with *You Know I'm No Good*, a rich layer of meaning emerges if we hear the lyrics ambiguously, as speaking for both Titcheners. For Helen, the question of her love for Rob and of his in return is precisely the source of the problematic position in which she finds herself; for Rob, the question remains as to how much Helen will allow herself to be owned by him, which is what he ultimately substitutes for love (as the logical conclusion of gaslighting). At this point, as Helen begins to crumple, there is every opportunity for Rob to ease off, but the temptation to torture Helen further is too much. He draws our attention to the background music for a second time just as the chorus of *Is This Love?* kicks in and the intertextual complexities of the simple three note question of whether or not this is love are revealed. At a primary textual level we hear Corinne Bailey Rae's song as a sombre interpretation of Bob Marley's vibrant original. Rae's cover is much more rhythmically rigid than Marley's lax reggae style, and the rigidity makes the central question undeniably prominent in the ears of audience and Titchener's alike, as well as mirroring those unyielding walls of the 'domestic prison'. We may also be aware of the touch of personal tragedy in Bailey Rae's life — of the accidental overdose which led to the death of her husband. But within the confines of Ambridge, the song pulls on an earlier time when Rob's coercive control became concretised, for *Is This Love?* was his musical accompaniment of choice to rape Helen back in August 2015.

In that scene too (27 August 2015), Rob is heard to control the music, telling Helen to wait as he chooses the romantic soundtrack to the traumatic proceedings of the evening. *Is This Love?* is heard in full, as it is on the night of the stabbing. And when, in April, Rob draws Helen's and our attention alike to the point of comparison, his sonic terrorism of Helen is clear. He doesn't ask 'Do you remember this song?'; rather, he asks about the last time she *heard* it. With this particular choice of words, he indicates his omniscience even regarding her aural faculty, since he implies he knows every time she has heard a particular song in the previous eight months. Indeed, the event of the rape also provided an opportunity for him to control Helen's emotional life via sonic means. Not only did he choose the soundtrack that evening, thereby setting the mood as he saw fit, but his behaviour the next morning underlined his gas lighting sonically. The episode of 28th August, the morning after the rape, begins with no clear sense of location; eight full seconds of bird song, followed by another eight seconds of a ringing landline phone, give the listener nothing to hold onto in this purely auditory medium, and the experience is disorienting. Such disorientation turns out to characterise the scene itself, as Helen's voice finally enters, calling for Rob to see if he's downstairs. We therefore understand her to have come down from upstairs, uncertain as to where her husband is, and presumably bewildered as to the events (and their consequences) of the previous night. But in this moment, Rob has deployed the phone as a sonic tool in his gaslighting weaponry, as Helen finds herself summoned to the scene of the trauma. And when the phone eventually rings out, she finds herself forced by the sound of the phone into the same room where she was forced by physical means to have sex the night before. The phone rings again, and Helen picks up to hear Rob asserting his upbeat interpretation of the night's events by a lightness of tone that Helen is compelled to agree with.

So, by the night of the stabbing, there is already a clear precedent for Rob's control of Helen by sonic means, including but not limited to music. But the reminder of the night of her rape (or, as it later emerges, this first-of-many rapes) is a step too far from Rob, and Helen begins to muster the confidence to resist again. The stasis of the kitchen is pierced by the melodically naive call of Henry. Helen attempts to mirror his vocal cadence but reveals both her awakening from Rob's spell-spinning and her fear for her son's safety. But Rob insists he will 'deal' with the child, and on his departure from the room, a melismatic flourish in Bailey Rae's vocals combines with a chorus of female backing singers as Helen makes her first secret call to Kirsty. The musical embellishment is opportunely timed, as if to urge Helen on to freedom from the prison. But the call is foiled by Rob's unexpected return, and he directly instructs Helen to receive the call-back from Kirsty and to feign that all is well. As she does so, late hits on the snare drum accentuate the stiltedness of the action and Helen's robotic vocal cadence, whilst more well-timed backing vocals support her desire to leave. As we listen into the phone call, we hear what Rob cannot — the layers of sonic narrative serve to code Helen as the neo-gothic Stepford Wife who got wise. Eventually, Helen announces her intention to leave, and a violent argument ensues; a tussle of power, ostensibly over an apple pie that risks burning in the oven. But the embellished repeat of the song's chorus offers a counterpoint to the rigidity of the piano, underlining Helen's determination to depart. The intensity of Rob's retort largely obscures the musical backing, and his attempt to claim ownership of Helen seems to overpower any extent to which Bailey Rae's voice speaks, as Stimpson would have it, for Helen. Not only does Rob no longer hide in plain sight but he reveals that his ownership of Helen was always his purpose. Here, he occupies much of the sonic spectrum with his rasping rage, with the odd fragment of piano, snare drum and soprano sporadically punching a way past him, such that the argument between the Titcheners is as much about the competition between Rob and Bailey Rae for sonic space as it is about the dialogue between him and Helen.

AIMEE MANN, *WISE UP*

As with the transition into *Is This Love?*, the introduction to the next song — Aimee Mann's *Wise Up* is distinctly audible in the space between the lines of dialogue as Rob thrusts a knife into Helen's hand; again, a gentle introduction brings a poignant emotional contrast to the dialogue. The lyrics of the song are incredibly telling, as the intimate singer-songwriter voice of Mann sees right into the mind of her listener, reflectively musing upon how things have changed since the relationship began, and urging Helen to *Wise Up* once and for all. There remains a struggle in this scene not just between the two Titcheners, but between Helen and this inner voice, and we hear this in the fact that so much of the music is obscured by the violence of the action, while occasional flashes of the track peek through as if to remind Helen of its emotional power, as the episode reaches its climax and she stabs Rob for the first time. If we continue to hear this instead as speaking for Rob, however, then we must hear it as also bringing his insight to the fore, asking Helen to admit the complexity of her own complicity in the abuse.

Intertextually, the song is best known for its appearance in the film *Magnolia*, in a montage sequence that uses music to stitch together several ostensibly disparate narrative threads. If we bring this intertextual reference to the table as *Archers* listeners, Mann's song echoes in this scene as the sound of the culmination of various threads, amplifying the significance of the scene in the overarching Rob/Helen storyline. It also brings with it connotations of dramatic characters identifying with the lyrics by singing along with them, and it thereby underlines the suggestion that this is in some way an inner voice of Helen. But perhaps the most striking comparison between these two texts—*The Archers* and *Magnolia*—is to be found in the similarity between Rob and the character of Frank Mackey (played by Tom Cruise). Mackey is a charismatic motivational speaker, who runs a seminar series called 'Seduce and Destroy', which promises to teach men how to pick up women using subliminal messaging and hypnotism. Although a full comparison of Mackey and Rob Titchener would surely reveal significant differences as well as similarities, the particular combination of apparent charm, insecurity regarding parental figures, and violent misogyny appears so prominent in both of them that it seems reasonable to describe one as an Ambridge-sized version of the other.

By the end of the scene, *Wise Up* speaks most clearly to the intricacies of the Titcheners' relationship. Mann's voice is fortuitously timed: 'It's not going to stop', she sings, as the knife clatters to the floor, and although the episode ultimately closes with Helen's assertion that Rob is dead, Mann's lyric suggests that all is far from over.

In conclusion, these songs do indeed speak to the listeners, partly by way of their intertextual references to an off-air musical and social world. But much like film music, they also interact with the dialogue, such that the songs seem to highlight the two parties' individual psychological machinations at various moments, again for the benefit of the listener. But in that interaction, the songs also speak within the confines of Blossom Hill Cottage between and on behalf of the Titcheners themselves. They occasionally spur Helen on to action, but not sufficiently clearly for her to leave without making a very big mess in the kitchen. Because, in the end, much of the music can ultimately be heard as one tool in Rob's battery of abusive tactics; his control of Helen is exerted sonically and musically as much as it is by any other means.

REFERENCES

Abramson, K. (2014). Turning up the lights on gaslighting. *Philosophical perspectives*, *28*, 1–30.

Barton, L. (2011, July 26). Amy Winehouse sang of a deeply feminine suffering. The Guardian. Retrieved from https://www.theguardian.com/music/2011/jul/26/amy-winehouse-lyrics

Coulthard, L. (2012). Haptic aurality: Listening to the films of Michael Haneke. *Film Philosophy*, *16*, 16–29.

Dolan, J., Hudak, J., Bienstock, R., Reiff, C., Harris, K., Doyle, P., & Greene, A. (2016, January 18). Glenn Frey: 20

essential songs. Rolling Stone. Retrieved from http://www.
rollingstone.com/music/lists/glenn-frey-20-essential-songs-
20160118/lyin-eyes-1975-20160118

Foucault, M. (1977 [1995]). *Discipline and punish: The birth
of the prison* (A. Sheridan, Trans), (2nd ed.). New York and
Toronto: Random House.

Gittins, I. (2008). The Eagles. *The Guardian*. Retrieved from
https://www.theguardian.com/music/2008/mar/24/popan-
drock.eagles

Gorbman, C. (1987). *Unheard melodies: Narrative film
music*. Bloomington and Indiana: Indiana University Press.

Groom, N. (1996). The condition of Muzak. *Popular Music
and Society*, *20*, 1–17.

Haworth, C. (2014). "Something beneath the flesh": Music,
gender, and medical discourse in the 1940s female gothic
film. *Journal for the Society for American Music*, *8*,
338–370.

Hoskyns, B. (2006). *Hotel California: singer-songwriters and
cocaine cowboys in the LA canyons 1967–1976* (2nd ed.).
London, New York, Toronto, Sydney: Harper Perennial.

Lanza, J. (2003). *Elevator music: A surreal history of
Muzak®, easy-listening, and other Moodsong®*. Ann Arbor,
MI: University of Michigan Press.

McCullough, M., Emmons, R., Kilpatrick, S., & Mooney, C.
(2003). Narcissists as 'victims': the role of narcissism in the
perception of transgressions. *Society for Personality and
Social Psychology*, *29*, 885–893.

Moi, T. (Ed.). (1986). *The Kristeva reader*. New York, NY:
Columbia University Press.

APPENDIX

0:00–2:42 No music

Helen putting Henry to bed
Helen and Kirsty talking

1:29 Rob comes home
Kirsty hides out the back
Helen lies about the pie

2:30 R suggests music

2:21 H reveals tuna bake;
awkward silence

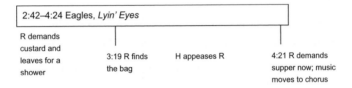

2:42–4:24 Eagles, *Lyin' Eyes*

R demands
custard and
leaves for a
shower

3:19 R finds
the bag

H appeases R

4:21 R demands
supper now; music
moves to chorus

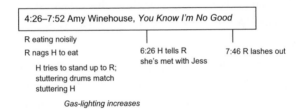

4:26–7:52 Amy Winehouse, *You Know I'm No Good*

R eating noisily
R nags H to eat
H tries to stand up to R;
stuttering drums match
stuttering H

Gas-lighting increases

6:26 H tells R
she's met with Jess

7:46 R lashes out

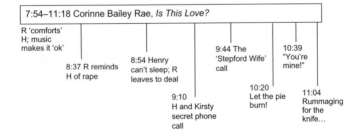

7:54–11:18 Corinne Bailey Rae, *Is This Love?*

R 'comforts'
H; music
makes it 'ok'

8:37 R reminds
H of rape

8:54 Henry
can't sleep; R
leaves to deal

9:10
H and Kirsty
secret phone
call

9:44 The
'Stepford Wife'
call

10:20
Let the pie
burn!

10:39
"You're
mine!"

11:04
Rummaging
for the
knife…

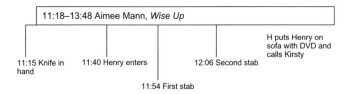

PEER REVIEW BY ALAN FRANKS, THE VICARAGE, AMBRIDGE, BORSETSHIRE.

Hindsight is a powerful thing, but I can't help but think back to those conversations I had with Rob and think I could have done better. Of course, by then we all knew how horribly he'd treated Helen. But I couldn't believe that God would create anyone beyond salvation — Rob must've learnt it from somewhere. Reading between the lines, when he told me about Christmas 2016 in the Titchener family home in Hampshire, it all sounded pretty grim. But Rob just couldn't see that *he* was the problem in his marriage and I had hoped that if I offered him a shoulder for support and relief, maybe he'd start to reflect on how he could have done things differently.

Usha says I have to let it go, that giving a shoulder for support is one thing but if the other person has an enormous chip on theirs and they refuse to acknowledge it, then there's little that can be done. But my faith tells me there's always a way; I was sure that if I could help Rob to forgive Helen's act of violence he might start to see some of the reasons why she was driven to it, and then he might even feel remorse. It's like the Gospel of St. Matthew says: 'if you forgive other people when they sin against you, your heavenly Father will also forgive you. But if you do not forgive others their sins, your Father will not forgive your sins' (6:14–15). It saddens me that Rob never did 'wise up'.

CHAPTER TWENTY-FOUR

HELEN'S DIET BEHIND BARS: NUTRITION FOR PREGNANT AND BREASTFEEDING WOMEN IN PRISON

Caroline M. Taylor

ABSTRACT

The residents of Ambridge enjoy a varied and mostly nutritious diet ranging from a ploughman's at The Bull to Jennifer Aldridge's roast venison, with the occasional tofu and quinoa paella from Kate Madikane. For Helen Titchener (née Archer) an abrupt change in circumstances will have led to changes in her diet that could have endangered her health and that of her unborn baby. Helen was imprisoned from about eight months of pregnancy to about four months postpartum, encompassing a critical period in development of her baby. This chapter focusses on the case of Helen and her baby son Jack to explore the dietary requirements for pregnancy and breastfeeding and how these relate to diet in Ambridge and in prison.

Keywords: Pregnancy; breastfeeding; diet; Helen Archer; Helen Titchener; prison

Helen would have been one of about 600 imprisoned women receiving antenatal care each year in England and Wales (Prison Reform Trust, 2012), and one of about one-hundred women delivering babies within the service in England and Wales annually (Galloway, Hayes, & Cuthbert, 2014). Pregnant women can apply to be housed in a Mother and Baby Unit (MBU) from eight months of pregnancy, enabling the option of breastfeeding, although only about 50% of applications for a place are successful (Galloway et al., 2014). Helen's application resulted in her and baby son Jack being moved to an MBU after the birth. She established breastfeeding, although with some difficulty, and was later acquitted.

DIETARY PROVISION FOR PREGNANCY AND BREASTFEEDING IN PRISON

Diet and nutrition in pregnancy and during breastfeeding are critical for the development of the baby and can have long-term consequences on health and achievement during childhood and into adulthood (Anjos et al., 2013). It seems unlikely that the budget allocated for catering in the prison service could provide the nutritious and varied diet that

Helen would require for the optimum health of herself and her baby (Jones, Conklin, Suhrcke, & Monsivais, 2014): although prisons are free to set their own allocation within their overall budgets, budgets as low as £1.87 per day per head have been reported (HM Inspectorate of Prisons, 2016). This contrasts with the NHS hospital food budget of about £10.75 per day (NHS digital, 2017).

We know little about Helen's diet whilst in prison, mirroring the vague guidance on diet for pregnant and breastfeeding women within the prison service. The service is required to provide three meals a day that are 'wholesome, nutritious, well prepared and served, reasonably varied and sufficient in quantity' (UK Government, 1999), but guidance specifically on diet for women prisoners, and particularly those who are pregnant or breastfeeding, is vague and sometimes inaccurate. For example, Prison Service Order 4800 states that 'Most women prefer and need a lower carbohydrate diet than men' (HM Prison Service, 2008), although there is no scientific basis for this (Committee on Medical Aspects of Food Policy, 1991; Scientific Advisory Committee on Nutrition, 2011). Similarly, it is stated that 'Certain groups of women will need to eat enough of or avoid certain foods — such as pregnant or lactating women' without any detail on these specific foods. There are no minimum nutrition standards for prisons, although the UK government provides detailed information on dietary requirements for pregnant and breastfeeding women (Committee on Medical Aspects of Food Policy, 1991; Scientific Advisory Committee on Nutrition, 2011, 2015, 2016). During the third trimester of pregnancy, for example, extra energy — equivalent to about two and half slices of bread — above a non-pregnant requirement is recommended (Scientific Advisory Committee on Nutrition, 2011). The requirements during breastfeeding also increase — equivalent to about an extra four slices of bread above the non-pregnancy requirement. Similarly, the requirements for some vitamins and minerals increase during breastfeeding: for example, the requirements for zinc (essential for immune function, wound healing, etc.) and calcium (essential for bone formation, blood clotting, etc.) almost double from non-pregnant requirements (Committee on Medical Aspects of Food Policy, 1991). Prisons are, however, advised to adhere to the more general guidelines of the Food Standards Agency on food in adult institutions (Ministry of Justice, 2010).

Pregnant women and those planning to become pregnant should take a supplement of folic acid to reduce the risk of neural tube defects (NHS choices, 2017b). Although we have no information on Helen taking any supplements during pregnancy, it is unlikely she received it preconceptually as her pregnancy was unplanned. Pregnant women are also advised to take vitamin D daily to help formation of the baby's bones (NHS choices, 2017b). The requirement for providing these supplements in prison is stated in the Prison Service Catering guidelines (Ministry of Justice, 2010).

There are several foods that pregnant and breastfeeding women are advised to avoid (NHS choices, 2017c): whilst still living in Ambridge, Helen would have been wise not to eat lead-shot game from the shoot, her own Borsetshire Blue cheese, and raw or undercooked eggs from Upper Class Eggs. Due to its mercury content, no more than four medium-sized tins of tuna per week are recommended (NHS choices, 2017a), so tuna casserole could have been on the menu several days a week. Indeed, fish is thought to be positively beneficial in pregnancy for the long-term health of the baby (Hibbeln et al., 2007; Taylor, Golding, & Emond, 2016). Homemade custard, with its barely cooked eggs, would not be advised, although readymade custard, either from powder or in a carton, would be safe. Avoidance of soft and blue cheeses, and soft-cooked eggs, is mentioned in the Prison

Service Catering guidelines (Ministry of Justice, 2010), but the advice on other foods given by NHS choices, such that on fish, is not.

Helen's history of anorexia meant that she was at higher risk for obstetric complications such as preterm delivery, fetal growth restriction and preeclampsia (Micali, Stemann Larsen, Strandberg-Larsen, & Nybo Andersen, 2016). Prison Service Order no. 4800 (HM Prison Service, 2008) notes that some women may enter the prison with eating disorders and urges staff to 'work together to meet [their] needs' without any further suggestion on how this might be enacted. There was no suggestion that Helen received any assessment of her eating disorder or that there was any management plan or specific treatment, in accordance with the reported poor quality of antenatal care in prison (Royal College of Midwives, 2008).

In the light of lack of information on Helen's diet in prison, we can only hope that she received a diet that was optimal for Jack's development and was able to continue with her supplemental vitamins. Whilst in the MBU, Helen worked in the prison garden, and we can speculate that she was able to supplement her diet with some fresh produce. The difficulties Helen experienced in establishing breastfeeding were largely psychological but may have been underpinned by a poor-quality diet.

CONCLUSION

There is little evidence that Helen received a nutritious diet in prison or even adequate healthcare bearing in mind her previous medical history: the long-term effects on Jack's growth and development remain to be seen. The UK prison catering service is severely underfunded and this has the potential to endanger the health of mothers and babies. The prison service guidance on diet for pregnant and lactating women needs to be evidence-based and to include clear, specific and accurate guidelines based on information that is available in government reports.

REFERENCES

Anjos, T., Altmae, S., Emmett, P., Tiemeier, H., Closa-Monasterolo, R., Luque, V., & Campoy, C. (2013). Nutrition and neurodevelopment in children: focus on NUTRIMENTHE project. *European Journal of Nutrition*, 52(8), 1825–1842. doi:10.1007/s00394-013-0560-4

Committee on Medical Aspects of Food Policy. (1991). *Dietary reference values for food energy and nutrients for the United Kingdom. Department of Health Report on Health and Social Subjects 41*. London: TSO.

Galloway, S., Hayes, A., & Cuthbert, C. (2014). *An unfair sentence. All babies count: spotlight in the criminal justice system*. Retrieved from https://www.nspcc.org.uk/globalassets/documents/research-reports/all-babies-count-unfair-sentence.pdf

Hibbeln, J. R., Davis, J. M., Steer, C., Emmett, P., Rogers, I., Williams, C., & Golding, J. (2007). Maternal seafood consumption in pregnancy and neurodevelopmental outcomes in childhood (ALSPAC study): An observational cohort study. *Lancet, 369*(9561), 578–585. doi:10.1016/S0140-6736(07)60277-3

HM Inspectorate of Prisons. (2016). *Life in Prison: Food*. Retrieved from https://www.justiceinspectorates.gov.uk/

hmiprisons/wp-content/uploads/sites/4/2016/09/Life-in-prison-Food-Web-2016.pdf

HM Prison Service. (2008). *Prison Service Order 4800. Women Prisoners*. Retrieved from https://www.justice.gov.uk/downloads/offenders/.../PSO_4800_women_prisoners.doc

Jones, N. R., Conklin, A. I., Suhrcke, M., & Monsivais, P. (2014). The growing price gap between more and less healthy foods: analysis of a novel longitudinal UK dataset. *PLoS One, 9*(10), e109343. doi:10.1371/journal.pone.0109343

Micali, N., Stemann Larsen, P., Strandberg-Larsen, K., & Nybo Andersen, A. M. (2016). Size at birth and preterm birth in women with lifetime eating disorders: A prospective population-based study. *British Journal of Obstetrics and Gynaecology, 123*, 1301−1310.

Ministry of Justice. (2010). *PSI 44/2010 Catering - meals for prisoners*. Retrieved from http://www.insidetime.org/download/rules_&_policies/pso_(prison_service_orders)/PSO_5000_prison_catering_services.pdf

NHS choices. (2017a). *Should pregnant and breastfeeding women avoid some types of fish?* Retrieved from http://www.nhs.uk/chq/Pages/should-pregnant-and-breastfeeding-women-avoid-some-types-of-fish.aspx?CategoryID=54&SubCategoryID=216

NHS choices. (2017b). *Vitamins, supplements and nutrition in pregnancy*. Retrieved from http://www.nhs.uk/conditions/pregnancy-and-baby/pages/vitamins-minerals-supplements-pregnant.aspx

NHS choices. (2017c). *Why should I avoid some foods during pregnancy?* Retrieved from http://www.nhs.uk/chq/Pages/917.aspx?CategoryID=54

NHS digital. (2017). *Hospital estate and facilities statistics*. Retrieved from http://hefs.hscic.gov.uk/

Prison Reform Trust. (2012). *Women in prison*. Retrieved from http://www.prisonreformtrust.org.uk/Portals/0/Documents/WomenbriefingAug12small.pdf

Royal College of Midwives. (2008). *Caring for childbearing prisoners*. Retrieved from https://www.rcm.org.uk/sites/default/files/POSITION%20STATEMENT%20Caring~ildbearing%20Prisoners_0.pdf

Scientific Advisory Committee on Nutrition. (2011). *Dietary reference values for energy*. Retrieved from https://www.gov.uk/government/uploads/system/uploads/attachment_data/file/339317/SACN_Dietary_Reference_Values_for_Energy.pdf

Scientific Advisory Committee on Nutrition. (2015). *Carbohydrates and health*. Retrieved from https://www.gov.uk/government/uploads/system/uploads/attachment_data/file/445503/SACN_Carbohydrates_and_Health.pdf

Scientific Advisory Committee on Nutrition. (2016). *Vitamin D and health*. Retrieved from https://www.gov.uk/government/uploads/system/uploads/attachment_data/file/537616/SACN_Vitamin_D_and_Health_report.pdf

Taylor, C. M., Golding, J., & Emond, A. M. (2016). Blood mercury levels and fish consumption in pregnancy: Risks and benefits for birth outcomes in a prospective observational birth cohort. *International Journal of Hygiene and Environmental Health*, 219(6), 513–520. doi:10.1016/j.ijheh.2016.05.004

UK Government. (1999). *The prison rules 1999*. Retrieved from http://legislation.data.gov.uk/cy/uksi/1999/728/made/data.htm?wrap=true

ABOUT THE EDITORS

Cara Courage is a Placemaking Academic and Arts Consultant, Writer/Commentator, Curator and Project Manager. She is author of *Arts in Place: The Arts, the Urban and Social Practice*, and works as an Adjunct at University of Virginia, researching and developing creative placemaking metrics, as a strategist at Futurecity, whilst running her own placemaking projects. She has been listening to *The Archers* for around fifteen years and grew up with the programme on her grandmother's farm on Exmoor. She talks about the pleasure and pain of her Archers fandom in a talk *My BDSM relationship with The Archers*.

Nicola Headlam is the Urban Transformations & Foresight Future of Cities Knowledge Exchange Research Fellow at the University of Oxford. She is an adaptable urbanist with expertise in city governance, economic development and urban policy. She is passionate about role of universities in public policy and practice, knowledge mobilisation; transfer, exchange and co-production.

ABOUT THE AUTHORS

Debi Ashenden is Professor of Cyber Security in the School of Computing at the University of Portsmouth. She is also the Programme Director for Protective Security & Risk at the Centre for Research & Evidence for Security Threats (CREST).

Debi's research interests are in the social and behavioural aspects of cyber security — particularly in finding ways of 'patching with people' rather than technology. She has worked extensively across the public and private sector and has co-authored a book for Butterworth Heinemann, *Risk Management for Computer Security: Protecting Your Network & Information Assets*.

Grant Bage taught children aged 5-13 before becoming a University Lecturer and then an educational leader and manager in the Third Sector. Having lived mostly in villages or rural market towns and specialised through his PhD in the relationships between story, history and teaching, Grant is a natural *Archers* fan, without ever becoming an aficionado. His first teacher training essay was on the issue of rural primary schools. Had it contained more about Ambridge, it might have marked higher. In 2009 he oversaw a DfE research study and guidance for practitioners on collaboration between rural primary schools, based on case studies from Cornwall, Northumberland and Norfolk. He is now a research fellow in Research Rich Teaching at the University of Hertfordshire.

Emily Baker is a third-year PhD student working on a thesis which examines the aesthetic of age in the voice in popular music. Funded by the AHRC, her work is underpinned by discourse around the voice, cultural studies perspectives on age and ageing processes as well as phenomenological, feminist and queer perspectives on identity more broadly. In other words, she spends equal amounts of time reading Barthes, Foucault, and Halberstam as she does listening to Dolly Parton, Aretha Franklin and Joni Mitchell. Most recently, her lively PhD supervisions with Freya Jarman always include a spot of Ambridge chat too.

Jennifer Brown is a chartered forensic and chartered occupational psychologist. Previously Jennifer was Head of Psychology at the University of Surrey and prior to that worked at Hampshire Constabulary as its research manager. Currently, Jennifer is co-director of the Mannheim Centre, and was also the Deputy chair of the Independent Police Commission looking into the future of policing. Jennifer researches the investigation of rape from the perspective of police decision making and the provision of behavioural investigative advice and she researches aspects of decision making in murder enquiries.

Helen M. Burrows, experienced as a Senior Lecturer in social work, is a Registered Social Worker, who works in the East Midlands both as an independent practice educator and as an Outreach domestic abuse support worker. Her professional background since the early 1990s is in Child Protection and working with adults with complex needs. She has been listening to *The Archers* since 1964.

Elizabeth R. A. Campion studied Law and Veterinary Medicine at the University of Cambridge and will be returning there for postgraduate study in October 2017. Having obtained a Postgraduate Diploma in Legal Practice, she has been employed as a paralegal and trainee solicitor since 2015. She has been an *Archers* listener since 2008.

Lizzie Coles-Kemp is Professor of Information Security at Royal Holloway University of London. She is a qualitative researcher who uses creative engagement methods to explore everyday practices of information production, protection, circulation, curation and consumption within and between communities. She took up a full-time academic post in 2008 and prior to joining Royal Holloway University of London she worked for 18 years as an information security practitioner. Lizzie's focus is the intersection between relational security practices and technological security and she specialises in public and community service design and consumption. She is currently an EPSRC research fellow with a research programme in everyday security.

Angela Connelly is a researcher at the School of Environment, Education and Development (SEED) at The University of Manchester. Her research interests lie in the assessment of technologies and tools that can help communities become more resilient to diverse environmental pressures such as climatic change and extreme weather events. She first started listening to *The Archers* 10 years ago when researching her doctoral thesis, and has been hooked ever since.

Rachel Daniels is Deputy Head, and Group Leader for Academic Liaison, at Barrington Library which supports Cranfield Defence and Security at the Defence Academy in Shrivenham, where she has spent 24 happy years. She is an unashamed fan of Jazzer. Rachel has never entered anything for a produce show but she does like parsnips.

Joanna Dobson is completing an MA English by Research at Sheffield Hallam University. Her research examines four bird narratives of the mid-twentieth century and asks what they reveal about contemporary anxieties around issues of human identity. Her interests include nature writing, ecocriticism and ecopsychology. She started listening to *The Archers* when on maternity leave and her son was born in the same week as Dan Hebden Lloyd. She hopes that the similarities with Shula end there.

Louise Gillies is a final year PhD student whose thesis has the working title *Family health history: genealogy, family communication and genetic disease* which combines the fields of genetic counselling, social science and genealogy. She uses genograms to help tease out and understand family relationships in her research, initially practising on her own family and families in *The Archers*. This is when she discovered that every villager in Ambridge can be connected to each other in one enormous genogram. Although only a listener for about 20 years, she has inducted her grandchildren into *The Archers* listening circle and is very proud that the youngest has been loudly 'dum-ti-dumming' along from the age of 15 months and the eldest requested Barwick Green to dance to at ballet class.

Fiona Gleed is a postgraduate research student at the University of Bath investigating the role of construction materials in flood resilience, with funding from BRE, the Building Research Establishment. She is a Chartered Structural Engineer with a decade of diverse design experience, from drainage to buildings, working for Arup. In 2002 she joined University of the West of England as a lecturer teaching students including trainee flood risk managers and municipal engineers. Their experiences and dedication have inspired and focused her return to study.

Ruth Heilbronn lectures and researches at the UCL Institute of Education, specialising in teacher education, linguistics and philosophy of education. She taught in London schools for many years, has held LEA advisory posts and written on practice, mentoring, practical judgement and ethical teacher education, which is her current concern. Among her latest publications are 'Freedoms and Perils: Academy Schools in England' in The Journal of Philosophy of Education, and Dewey in Our Time: Learning from Dewey for Trans-cultural Practice (UCL IoE Press).

Jonathan Hustler studied History at St Chad's College, Durham, and Theology at Wesley House, Cambridge. He is a Methodist Minister who has served in rural appointments in Buckinghamshire and Lincolnshire and who has taught a range of subjects (including Rural Ministry) to those training for ordination.

Rosalind Janssen is a Lecturer in Education at UCL's Institute of Education. She works on the Master of Teaching programme where she first met her co-author Ruth Heilbronn, and discovered their mutual love of *The Archers*. Rosalind has been an avid listener since the 1960s. An Egyptologist by profession, she was previously a Curator in UCL's Petrie Museum and then a Lecturer in Egyptology at UCL's Institute of Archaeology. She currently teaches Egyptology classes at the University of Oxford and the City Lit. She even has a course — '*The Archers* of Antiquity' — revolving around daily life at a unique New Kingdom Village.

Freya Jarman, by day, is a Senior Lecturer in Music at the University of Liverpool, with serious grown-up research interests in queer theory and voice in relation to all kinds of (western) music. In this capacity, she is the author of *Queer Voices: Technologies, Vocalities and the Musical Flaw*

(Palgrave 2011) and editor of *Oh Boy! Masculinities and Popular Music* (Routledge 2007). By night, she is co-author (with Emily Baker) of the blog Ambridge FM (http://ambridgefm.wordpress.com), casually examining the music heard in and around Borsetshire.

Madeleine Lefebvre is Chief Librarian of Ryerson University in Toronto, Canada. Born in the United Kingdom, she holds an MA from Edinburgh University as well as MA and MLS degrees from the University of Alberta. She is a Fellow of the UK Chartered Institute of Library and Information Professionals, and an Associate of the Australian Library and Information Association. Her book, *The Romance of Libraries*, was published by Scarecrow Press in 2005. In 2015 Madeleine was a appointed a trustee of the Niagara-on-the-Lake Public Library, and is passionate about the role public libraries play in the community.

Felicity Macdonald-Smith originally studied French Language and Literature at University College London; she also holds an MSc in Teaching English from Aston University, and an MA in European Language and Intercultural Studies from Anglia Ruskin University. She retired last year from Newnham College Cambridge, where she was the administrator of the undergraduate admissions office for 13 years. Her previous experience included administrative work in the French Department at UCL, English language teaching in the United Kingdom and abroad, and international youth work (Council of Europe, and World Association of Girl Guides and Girl Scouts).

Annie Maddison Warren is the Academic Lead for the Doctoral Training Centre at Cranfield Defence and Security, a school of Cranfield University, and a Lecturer in Information Systems in the Centre for Electronic Warfare,

Information and Cyber. She has worked in academia throughout her career, gaining a Masters in Corporate Management and a PhD from Cranfield University. Her research is on the management of major public sector IT projects with a particular interest in how context drives human behaviour. She won first prize for her dahlia vase at the local Produce Show in 2014.

Amber Medland attended Cambridge University for a BA (Hons) in English Literature and an MPhil in American Literature before moving to New York to spend three years at Columbia University teaching and studying for an MFA (Writing). Since then she has been living in Hackney, juggling various jobs and listening to *The Archers*.

Jessica Meyer is an Associate Professor of Modern British History at the University of Leeds. She has published extensively on popular culture and the First World War, with a particular focus on popular and detective fiction. Her monograph, *Men of War: Masculinity and the First World War in Britain* was published by Palgrave Macmillan in 2009. She is an *Archers* listener of some 15 years' standing, having started listening while researching and writing her PhD.

Christine Michael: When she is not door stepping Justin Elliott or eavesdropping in The Bull in her role as editor of her weekly blog, *The Ambridge Observer*, Christine Michael is a health journalist who specialises in the area of obesity, Type 2 diabetes and public health and has twenty years' experience of decoding scientific research for consumer audiences. In true Grundy family tradition, she is a poacher who has turned gamekeeper to research and write her paper on metabolic disorders and cake consumption in Borsetshire, a topic in which she is passionately engaged both professionally and personally.

Tom Nicholls is a Senior Lecturer in Media Theory in the School of Film and Media at the University of Lincoln. His teaching and research interests are in public broadcasting, British television drama and television crime drama. He has been an Archers listener for as long as he can remember. Born and raised in Worcestershire he feels a duty to keep listening for news from home.

Anna-Marie O'Connor graduated from the University of Greenwich in 1993 with a BSc (Hons) in Applied Chemistry. She worked as a forensic biologist at the Metropolitan Police Forensic Science Laboratory which merged with the Forensic Science Service, until it closed in 2011. Her field of expertise is the identification of body fluids and the interpretation of DNA profiles, Blood Pattern Analysis (BPA) and textile fibres analysis. She has given evidence in crown court in numerous cases.

In 2012, Anna-Marie was appointed as Senior Lecturer at the University of Portsmouth, teaching professional skills and evidence interpretation on the BSc (Hons) Forensic Biology course. In September 2014, she was appointed as Forensic Co-Ordinator at the University with responsibilities including management of collaborative research partnerships and specialist teaching on the BSc (Hons) Criminology and Forensic Studies course.

Anna-Marie is a Fellow of the Chartered Society of Forensic Sciences. She attained Fellowship of the Higher Education Academy in October 2013 and is also undertaking part-time PhD studies.

Katherine Runswick-Cole is Professor of Critical Disability Studies & Psychology at Manchester Metropolitan University. Her research interests lie in critical disability studies which seek to expose and challenge the oppressive practices associated with disablism. She believes that the lives of disabled people are sadly under-represented in *The Archers* and lives in hope that, one day, Bethany will come back to live her life in Ambridge.

Caroline M. Taylor is a Research Fellow in the Centre for Child and Adolescent Health at the University of Bristol. With an academic background in nutrition and dietetics, her current research interests are focused on the effects of events during pregnancy on child health and development: these include both diet and environmental toxins, such as lead and mercury. She is also interested in children's diets – particularly those of picky eaters, with the aim of developing advice for parents and carers to avoid or manage this difficult problem.

Jane Turner's background is in primary teaching. She is the national director of the Primary Science Quality Mark award programme, based at the University of Hertfordshire where she is a principal lecturer and researcher in the School of Education. Jane has written and contributed to several influential primary science and early years education publications and research projects. She works as an advisor to the DfE, the BBC and the learned bodies on primary science assessment and curriculum. Jane has been an ardent Archers fan since 1986, when, as a newly qualified teacher in an inner city school, she was introduced by a colleague to the delights of the Sunday morning omnibus.

Jerome Turner is a researcher at Birmingham Centre for Media and Cultural Studies, at Birmingham City University. He has specific research interests in web cultures and media audiences, being involved in a variety of projects including training citizen journalists in the Arab region, ethnography of hyperlocal community media audiences, and exploring creative citizenship practices. He has been listening to *The*

Archers all his life in one form or another, and actively tweets about *The Archers* in a number of guises.

Olivia Vandyk is a communications consultant and founder of Gingham Cloud. An Archers addict and alliteration aficionado, her specialisms include copywriting and social media marketing for SMEs. Her interests lie in the connections that can be made through social media — personal, professional and commercial. She has worked at the coalface of Web 2.0 for over a decade, hunting trolls and quoting The West Wing. Over the years she has worked with the great and the good and indeed Piers Morgan. Her social media marketing guidebook "*Share Nicely*" will be published on Amazon in 2017.

Rebecca Wood is a Research Fellow at the University of Birmingham. She is a former teacher whose research focusses on autism, education and inclusion. Rebecca is passionate about trying to create more understanding of autism through challenging current norms and exclusionary attitudes. She is a great fan of *The Archers*, and looks forward to the day when an autistic character provides a positive role model and helps Ambridge to become a more diverse community.

INDEX